# Previous works by Janis Owens

*My Brother Michael*
*Myra Sims*
*The Schooling of Claybird Catts*
*The Cracker Kitchen*

# American
# Ghost

## A Novel

❧

## Janis Owens

Scribner

New York   Toronto   London   Sydney   New Delhi

SCRIBNER

A Division of Simon & Schuster, Inc.

1230 Avenue of the Americas

New York, NY 10020

First Scribner hardcover edition October 2012

SCRIBNER and design are registered trademarks of The Gale Group, Inc., used under license by Simon & Schuster, Inc., the publisher of this work.

For information about special discounts for bulk purchases, please contact Simon & Schuster Special Sales at 1-866-506-1949 or business@simonandschuster.com.

The Simon & Schuster Speakers Bureau can bring authors to your live event. For more information or to book an event, contact the Simon & Schuster Speakers Bureau at 1-866-248-3049 or visit our website at www.simonspeakers.com.

Designed by Carla Jayne Jones

Manufactured in the United States of America

1   3   5   7   9   10   8   6   4   2

Library of Congress Control Number: 2012009163

ISBN 978-1-4516-7463-7
ISBN 978-1-4516-7467-5 (ebook)

*For Emily, Abigail, and Isabel, with love*
*And the light of the future, Lily P.*

# Part One
# The Indian Study

*An idea, like a ghost, must be spoken to a little before it will explain itself.*

—Charles Dickens

# Chapter One

Though rumors of Jolie Hoyt's star-crossed romance with Sam Lense would dog her reputation for many years to come, in truth their grand *affaire* was a little short of grand: barely three months long, and as quickly ended as it had begun.

To the casual observer, it bore all the earmarks of a swift, overheated bit of late-adolescent romance and might never have happened at all if not for the inspired manipulations of Jolie's best friend, Lena Lucas, who would later rise to minor-celebrity status as the dashing wife of an international televangelist darling. Lena would often be seen on TV, sitting in the front pew of her husband's enormous church and beaming up at him with childlike devotion.

But those days were far in the future, and back then, in the final weeks of summer '96, Lena was technically not even legal, being seven months shy of her eighteenth birthday. She'd come late to Jolie's childhood, halfway through their freshman year of high school, when Lena's father had retired from the air force and taken a part-time job managing a KOA campground in the tiny backwater of Hendrix, two hours southwest of Tallahassee, between the Apalachicola River and the coast. Their meeting was inevitable as Hendrix was hardly more than a crossroads—a scattering of bait shops and churches and listing cracker dogtrots and trailers, with nothing but the river and the National Forest to recommend it.

Lena had caused a stir the moment she set foot in town, for reasons of her personality, which was effervescent, and her looks, which were extraordinary. She was northern Italian on her mother's side and had inherited all the attendant excitability a Milanese DNA might imply, along with the copper-blond hair, olive skin, and charming, pointed-chin smile. It made for a potent package, and added to the general astonishment of her beauty was the small matter of her dress. Her father's last berth had been at Homestead Air Force Base outside Miami, where Lena had adopted a casual, seminaked personal style: bikini string tops and frayed jean shorts; pink toenails and well-worn flip-flops.

To say that it was a compelling combination would be a great understatement: when she went to work for her father at the counter of the concession stand at fifteen, she'd inadvertently caused a countywide run on live crickets and bait minnows. Jolie's brother, Carl, was among the stampede of local men wanting to make her acquaintance. Being an unrepentant skirt chaser and fine sampler of local female flesh, he made it his business to hard-sell Lena on salvation and bring her to his father's church, El Bethel Assembly. Ostensibly this was to save her soul, though Jolie surmised that he was really looking for a place to keep her in semi-virginal storage while he finished sowing his wild oats.

Jolie never delved too far into the arrangement, but she had an eye for the colorful and a taste for the eccentric, and she and Lena became quick and inseparable friends. They proved perfect foils for each other as Jolie was her near opposite: brooding and inverted, and a singularly local product—a direct descendant of the two hardy Hoyt brothers who'd sailed to Spanish West Florida from Edinburgh in the trackless days of colonial trading, half a century before General Jackson began clearing the swamps of the Indians. With true Scotch efficiency, they had adjusted to the alien culture by marrying a string of hardworking, thirteen-year-old Indian wives. Between them, they produced a virtual tribe of handsome, half-breed children who shunned outside interference and intermarried with their Scotch-Indian cousins for decades to come. Jolie was, at eighteen, a perfect example of their legacy: tall and dark-haired and fair-skinned, with a level, hazel gaze and a natural reticence made worse by the loss of her mother to breast cancer when Jolie was three. Her grief had cut deep and all but silenced her.

Lena proved outgoing enough to breach the great silence, and after Carl was foisted off to Bible school in punishment for a minor moral lapse, she'd practically moved into the parsonage with Jolie and her father; she even joined El Bethel. There, she was duly saved and baptized and Spirit-filled, though she confided to Jolie that she would never give up makeup or dancing or wearing practically invisible bikinis, not unless the angel Gabriel himself required it. This sort of good-natured defiance wouldn't have been tolerated in an earlier day, but by the midnineties, Bethel had shrunk to a few dozen faithful members, mostly old ladies (the Sisters, Lena called them, because they were called thus: Sister Noble or Sister Lynne or Sister Wright), who gave themselves fully to the Pentecostal experience, with waved hankies and shouts and many messages in tongues. Physically, it was nothing more than a simple country church of the sort that you see all over the South, white and unassuming, perched on the side of the road in the shape of a large shoebox. There were Sunday-school rooms below and a sanctuary above, small and Pentecostal-spare, with concrete floors and hard wooden pews, a faded banner from the 1925 glory days still attached to the ceiling behind the pulpit, pale lavender inscribed in Gothic script: *Without a vision the people perish.*

The Sisters called it the Tabernacle.

Lena joined Jolie as official church pet, their bond only strengthening as they finished high school and became ever more dedicated to the high calling of art (both were fledgling artists), joined in a single overweening ambition: to get out of Hendrix, as soon as they could, forever and amen. To that end, they excelled at every art class offered at Cleary High, hoping to snag scholarships at some up-and-coming art school, knowing they were at the mercy of staid admission boards, as their fathers were good men but hadn't much in the way of educational funds.

But Jolie and Lena were both bright and naturally gifted, and certain they'd win favor in some corner. After settling on design as their major (thanks in no small part to the popularity of *Designing Women*), they had set about their first official project: redecorating the living room of the parsonage, a dicey proposition as Brother Hoyt had given them a budget of precisely $25. Fortunately, both of them were natural-born junkers and they spent the better part of their senior year mixing paint and cruising garage sales and rebuilding old lamps and tables that the Sisters had donated to the project. The result was colorful and strange and apt to change by the week as new paint or plants or lumber was donated or otherwise uncovered. Some weeks, the room was calm and natural, with fern-green walls and khaki slipcovers and muted rugs. Some weeks, the walls were brilliant red, the pillows turquoise, the wood floors bare, only the slipcovers (too expensive to change) the same. Whether it was going well or falling apart, the girls kept their weekends free and spent their Friday nights in Cleary, and their Saturdays forty miles west in Panama City, where they lay on the beach and cruised the strip and ate 99-cent bean burritos at Taco Bell.

So it went, till college acceptance letters were sent out in October, when contrary to all prediction Lena had snagged a full scholarship at Savannah College of Art and Design (SCAD), while Jolie was turned down flat, her ACTs not up to par; *too weak in math,* a helpful counselor had penciled in the margin on her official letter of rejection. She'd been so set on SCAD that she hadn't applied elsewhere, and as graduation approached, her single option was a need-based grant to a community college thirty miles away, which she would commute to in the same rattling school bus she had ridden into town to Cleary High.

She pretended indifference, but as their senior year passed and graduation was upon them, Lena became increasingly convinced that if Jolie was left in Hendrix to her own devices, she would bail on college altogether and backslide into the aimless half-life she'd led before they met: hanging out with the old Sisters at church; lounging around her bedroom, listening to AM radio. Lena worried over it for months and, in the end, came up with a purely Milanese solution. What Jolie needed, Lena decided, was a man. And not just any man. Jolie needed a husband, in the strictest Roman sense of the word, one who'd stare down the Hoyts and rescue her from Hendrix and, in return for good, regular sex, serve as the springboard to the rest of her life.

Once she made up her mind, Lena was nothing if not tenacious and she spent most of the summer searching high and low for such a man, which wasn't the easiest thing in the world, in Hendrix. She had no success at all till the brink of her departure, on the third Saturday in August, when Sam Lense appeared like an answer to prayer at the high counters of the KOA commissary, checking in for a four-month stay. Lena volunteered to give him the official tour and, by supper, had extracted an encyclopedic amount of information on his past, present, and future plans.

He was South Miami–born, the youngest of three sons, and a first-semester grad student at UF, in Hendrix for a single semester, on some sort of field grant with the Department of the Interior (or maybe UF). Lena didn't pay too much attention to his academic qualifications: he was blunt, talkative, straight, and single, and the chances of his staying in Hendrix one hour longer than his degree required were absolutely nil. To Lena, that was qualification enough.

Oh, he had his shortcomings: he was too old for Jolie, and something less than tall, and talking Jolie into going on a date with a Yankee would be such a pain in the butt. But beggars couldn't be choosers. Truth be told, Jolie had more than a few caveats of her own. She had the essential attributes (that is, the breasts) to attract a man, but her religion was weird, her personal style slouchy, and her xenophobia an ongoing battle. The Hoyts' treatment of strangers was both hostile and secretly superior, as the Hoyts were shiftless, but smart, and they knew it.

Fortunately, Sam Lense looked to be a pretty sharp cookie himself, with the well-fed, horndog look of a man who'd never met a breast he didn't like. Lena was cautiously optimistic that Jolie's sulkiness would prove a minor distraction to such a man; her petulance trumped by her tits, so to speak.

With the craftiness of a master spy, Lena withheld all hint of a fix-up and waited till late in the afternoon of their final Friday-night-go-to-town supper to call Jolie at the parsonage, and in her best fake you're-going-to-kill-me voice, Lena confessed that she had invited someone to come along—a guy from the campground. No, Jolie hadn't met him. His name was Sam and he was from Miami. He'd been there only a week.

Jolie's response was quick and expected. "God help us, Lena—you're not trying to fix me up with another stray from the campground? On our last weekend? Is nothing sacred?"

Lena knew she was busted, but lied with great conviction. "It's not a fix-up. He's just some guy I met, doing some kind of study with the museum, doesn't know a soul. I told him about the shrimp special at the café and he asked to come—and what was I supposed to do? Say *no*?"

"Does he know how old you are?" Jolie inserted curiously, as Lena's being underage had made her the subject of a few local cautionary tales.

"Yes, he knows how old I am," Lena answered patiently. "I told you, it's not a date. Gosh, Jol, he's just a nice guy—not one of your local plowboys looking for someone to iron their clothes and sweep their trailer. It'll do you good to meet him—give you a taste of the Big World outside of Hendrix."

There was a prolonged silence on the phone, an almost audible rolling of the eyes, though Lena could detect a thawing. "Come and go to supper with us, and if anything good is playing, we can go to the movies—or not," she inserted, knowing she'd overstepped. "We'll eat supper and come straight home. I need to finish packing anyway."

Jolie exhaled a pained breath at the reminder of her abandonment, but in the end relented, if grudgingly. "Okay. But listen, Lena, if you get carried away and invite him to the beach, I swear I'll call Daddy and have him come and get me. I will."

Lena was never more charming than after a successful seduction. *"Deal,"* she sang, then without pause asked, what was Jolie wearing? What did her hair look like? Did she have on eyeliner?

"I thought he was just some *guy* from the campground. That it wasn't a *date*."

"It isn't," Lena assured her. "But go put on some eyeliner, Jol. You look so much better with eyeliner. Just a little brown eyeliner, and lip gloss—the melon one I got you for Easter. Be there in a jiff," she squeaked, and, before Jolie could answer, was gone.

# Chapter Two

Jolie was left standing in the hot, still hallway of the old parsonage, phone in hand, more than a little steamed at the turn in the evening's plans, thinking, Wonderful, another evening spent with one of Lena's Brilliant Blind Dates.

The last one—some guy named Greg that Lena had also met at the campground—had turned out to be a distant cousin on Jolie's mother's side.

Jolie had thought he looked strangely familiar all night, and halfway through salad, a bell went off in her head.

"My God," she breathed, "you're Aint Cynthia's nephew. You got a twin named Phil. Your daddy works at Gulf Power."

He had been good-natured enough about it, had roared with laughter in acknowledgment that marrying outside the tribe in Hendrix wasn't the easiest thing on earth, if you were a Hoyt.

He'd even tried to kiss her good-night and, at her rebuff, explained, "Hell, it's not like you're my sister or something. We wouldn't have three-headed children."

Jolie told him, not unkindly, "Son, I'll shoot myself in the head before I'd date a Hoyt."

"Your loss." He laughed and, as he climbed into his truck, had called back, with true Hoyt élan: "Gimme a call when you git off that high horse."

Jolie had put her foot down about any more fix-ups after that, but Lena was a force of nature in her sparrowlike way and wasn't to be denied. With nothing more than a grunt of exasperation, Jolie hung up the phone and went to her bedroom off the front porch (the parsonage was older than the church and had many odd structural details: bedroom door off the porch; semi-attached kitchen). She sat at the dinged and dented old vanity that had once belonged to her mother, working to add a little harlotlike color to her hazel-green eyes.

She went about it with little skill and great melancholy, astoundingly sad the summer was so quickly over: the beach and the bikinis, the lazy afternoons on the dock at the campground, the shopping junkets to the flea market in Dothan. She couldn't imagine what she'd do when Lena was gone and couldn't help but be annoyed that their last supper together had been complicated by a stray from the campground.

For young or old, date or nondate, he was no doubt already firmly under Lena's spell. He would peer at her across the table in a coma of infatuation and laugh at her goofy teenage jokes and trip over his own feet in his hurry to pick up the bill. Jolie had seen it happen too many times before—at school, at church, at Hoyt family reunions, and though she didn't begrudge her friend the attention, she did hate to squander their last weekend on a fool.

When Lena pulled up in the drive and beeped, Jolie ambled out in no great hurry and found her alone in the car.

"Where's the date?" she asked as she got in, hoping he'd no-showed, but Lena told her he was running late, that they'd have to pick him up on the way out of town.

"He had to wait in line for the shower," Lena explained as she wheeled the little Corona around and headed back to the river. "They had another flood in the bathroom; some idiot probably flushed a pad. Don't be so nasty, and don't take on that snotty Hoyt attitude till you meet him. His name's Sam," Lena reminded her, "and you don't have to worry about making small talk because he runs his mouth like ninety miles an hour, nonstop."

"Well, thank God for that," Jolie answered, with feeling, as she hated trying to make small talk with a stranger.

As they backtracked across Hendrix—a two-minute drive, if that—they discussed their beach plans for the next day: what to bring or not bring; whether to go to St. Andrews or the commercial end of the strip.

"D'you want to borrow a bathing suit?" Lena asked, meaning one of her practically nonexistent Brazilian bikinis.

Jolie was debating, weighing the guilt of deceiving her father against the undeniable joy of turning heads on a beach, when Lena added, "I'll wear the black one if you want to borrow the red. I mean, you look okay in the black, but if I looked like you do in the red one, I'd never take it off. I'd wear it to school, to church. I'd *sleep* in it. You could wear that thing on the beach in Rio de Janeiro and look just like a local—and how many people can say that, Jol?"

This was typical of Lena's generosity, as it was the single area in which Jolie could be said to outshine her, and also a great point of personal embarrassment: that wild Brazilian body on a Bible-quoting holiness girl.

"Let me think about it," Jolie said.

Lena went back to discussing the beach and the weather in her usual fast chatter, was slowing to turn in the campground when she added, as if in afterthought, "Oh—and listen, Jol—he might ask you about the Indians in the forest."

Jolie looked at her blankly. "I know absolutely nothing about Indians in the forest."

"Well, fine. No big deal. I just might have mentioned that you're part Indian, and that's what he's here to study, so he might, you know, *ask*."

Something in the way Lena said it made Jolie suspicious. "Is that all?"

Lena sent her a nervous little glance. "And—well, he might also ask about your—you know. Religion."

"*Lena!*" Jolie cried, as her faith was still very much a closet religion, one considered comically contemptible in town, a sure sign of swamp-running, green-teeth Hendrix ignorance.

"Well, I'm *sorry,*" Lena declared as she swung into the main road of the KOA. "I don't know why you're so *weird* about it. I told him I went to Bethel, and he didn't *drop dead* or anything."

Jolie was far from reassured and rubbed her face wearily, seeing the last moments of her golden summer evaporate right before her eyes. "If he asks me to speak in other tongues, I'll get up and leave. God, Lena— why did you even bring it up?"

"Well, I don't know," she said, expertly weaving around the washouts on the lime rock. "We were just talking about his study—he's writing a paper about Florida Indians—the Creek, and Yuchi—and said he'd noticed they were mostly Pentecostal—which naturally made me think of my good buddy Jolie, and how the Hoyts are part Indian, and, you know, Pentecostal—"

At Jolie's groan, Lena's voice turned pleading. "Oh, come on, Jol, quit being such a pain in the *butt.* You need to get out more. You keep hanging around the house so much, you're going to wind up like your daddy."

This was enough to silence Jolie, as her father, Raymond Hoyt, had endured a long life and a hard one, marrying late and fathering Jolie on the brink of old age. The loss of his wife to cancer had nearly undone him, and Jolie was known to be his favorite. To her, he was a massively loyal and protective presence, but even she would admit that he was a strange and unusual creature. A rare Christian son of the infamously heathen clan, he'd got saved while pulling a stint in Korea and had returned home determined to convert his brethren. His mission had not been overwhelmingly successful, but he'd kept the faith and, at seventy-three, was still a formidable spiritual leader, who stood six foot three, wore a size-fifty belt, and had a cast in one eye. From the Scots, he'd inherited his height and hazel eyes and hardheaded Calvinist sureness; from the Indians, his girth and stamina and (perhaps) the mystic leanings that had drawn him to the Pentecostal movement in the first place. Since his wife's death, he had largely withdrawn from public life, and though faithful to the needs of his shrinking congregation, his real passion lay in strange and solitary projects he worked on day and night in his workshop in the backyard (charting the end-time according to the book of Revelation, building a table-size replica of the Tabernacle as described in Deuteronomy, and just lately oil painting).

"It'll be one hour of your life," Lena concluded as she pulled into the dirt parking lot of the concession stand, where their nondate was waiting by the curb as arranged.

In an effort to appear less Hoyt and inbred and hillbilly, Jolie shook Sam's hand over the seat, not able to see much of him before he climbed in, only getting an impression of big-city restlessness and personality scarcely contained in the small seat of the old Toyota. As Lena had warned, he was indeed a talker and kept up with her machine-gun chatter word for word, not flirting with her as much as teasing her like a big brother in a fast, urban accent Jolie couldn't pinpoint. It wasn't Southern and it wasn't Midwestern; maybe it was just Miami, where he said he was born, though it was hard for Jolie to believe that such a quick-talking exotic shared her birth state.

She kept to herself, listening with a half an ear to their chatter as the long August light played across the sunburnt fields that lined the highway into Cleary, the watermelon fields long plowed-over, the peanuts planted, and the tobacco half cut, half in top flower. The fences were better, the farmhouses sturdier the farther you went, as Cleary was Hendrix's well-to-do relative, civilly speaking. It wasn't half as ancient, but had snagged the honor of county seat in a moment of hot, antebellum debate and in the past century had waxed in prosperity, even as Hendrix had sunk into obscurity. Location had much to do with it: Cleary was well inside the old Plantation Belt and had proximity to that old trifecta of transportation: railroad, river, and the Spanish Trail. The politics of the day had followed the money, and Cleary was always richer, and more typically Southern, than Hendrix, with a thriving patrician class that had produced senators, a hard-luck governor, and a row of fine old houses on Main Street, which had in a more whimsical time been christened Silk Stocking Row.

The City Café was across the street from the courthouse, tucked away in the corner of a row of brick fronts, a line of customers usually trailing down the sidewalk, though this early in the evening there wasn't a wait. Jolie got out first, and the moment she laid eyes on Sam Lense, in the long summer light, she immediately pinned him as ethnic—either Cuban or Jewish, or maybe Greek. His hair was too dark for him to be strictly white, his complexion as olive as Lena's, though his eyes were lighter, a curious, luminous gray. Light-eyed, they'd call him in Hendrix, and well fed. Not fat, but stocky and solidly built. Except for the light eyes, he could have been one of her thousand cousins.

If he noticed her close scrutiny, he didn't comment on it, all his attention on the dusty slice of downtown around them. He perused it all—the brick walls and hot asphalt and plate windows—with a sort of masculine energy strange to her; not booted and Stetsoned and overtly macho, but open and alight with curiosity, as if he'd been waiting all his life to see downtown Cleary and couldn't believe he was finally here!

He seemed particularly fascinated by the courthouse across the street—an imposing, old Victorian fortress of a building, with a domed cupola and stone pillars. It stood in a modest municipal copse of sagging, old live oak, bent of limb and dragging to the ground with beards of Spanish moss. In as classic a Southern scene as any historian could ask, a bronzed and grimed CSA soldier kept watch in the corner, peering down his musket barrel with sightless eyes. Sam seemed fixated by the common enough view and surveyed it with great interest, till Lena finally finished her primping and joined him on the sidewalk with a chipper "Ready?"

He came to himself then, as if he hadn't heard her, tipping his head to the corner oak and answering with offhanded sureness, "They once lynched a man from that oak—the big one, in the corner. They killed him in Hendrix but dragged his body back to hang at the courthouse. See? They sawed off the limb a few years ago, on orders from the City Commission. You can see the scar. Tourists were coming to gawk at it."

Lena and Jolie obediently paused to squint into the failing sun at the gnarled, graceful, old live oak that was indeed missing a lower limb, the scar plainly visible, even two blocks away. The lynching he alluded to was well-known in Hendrix where it had all begun—so common-place neither of them chimed in, but just stood there staring obedi-ently as he concluded in that mild, instructive voice, "Happened in '38—nightmare business. Historically speaking, it's the county's single claim to fame."

He seemed content to point it out and made no more of it. He just followed along, holding the door as they entered the sizzling glory of the old Formica-and-linoleum café, frequented by fans of grease and good value. Lena led them to a booth in the back, tucked away beneath an air-conditioning vent that was delightfully cold, but hummed like a nuclear reactor, Jolie sliding in on one side, with Sam across and Lena beside him.

"It looks like a dump," Lena said, raising her voice to explain, "but the shrimp is famous. They bring it up from Apalachicola, fresh every day."

Sam looked more intrigued by the grime than disgusted, taking in the beehived waitress, the rattling old jukebox, and fellow customers with that air of careful scrutiny, as if he were a developer weighing an investment. He allowed Lena to order for them, and when the waitress reappeared with tall plastic tumblers of diabetes-inducing sweet tea, he finished his inspection of the café and turned his bright eyes on Jolie, eyeing her with equal, discomfiting interest.

"So, Jolie?" he called across the table. "You're really a Hoyt? On your mother's side, or your father's?"

*"Both,"* she answered, because she was. Her parents had grown up in Hendrix and married within the faith, which meant they were distant cousins, as were their parents before them.

Such an accommodation was once standard in insular church com-munities in the South, though it was unthinkingly hilarious to Sam and Lena, who burst into laughter.

"Incest is best," Lena said, a common enough gibe around Hendrix, one Jolie had never found to be hilarious (and neither would Lena have if she had been Hendrix-born).

Jolie bore her irritation with little grace, so visibly that Sam sobered up quickly and tried to make amends with a little small talk. "So are you a mere babe in high school, too?"

He asked it as an obvious icebreaker, but Jolie was not so easily drawn out, offering nothing in answer but a slow shake of her head, so that Lena jumped in and answered aside, as if Jolie were a deaf-mute.

"Jolie graduated in May—she's going to *Chipola*."

"Never heard of it," he murmured, unwittingly putting himself back on thin ice, as Jolie's form rejection from Savannah was still a sensitive subject.

"It's the community college, in Marianna," Lena raised her voice to explain, with a wary eye at Jolie. "It's where everybody around here goes."

"Everybody *poor*," Jolie clarified, tired of Lena's obsessive smoothing and wanting him to understand immediately, unequivocally, that she might be an eighteen-year-old hillbilly half-wit, but she knew who she was; she didn't need some expert from the university to come in and tell her.

The silence that followed wasn't as insulted as it was thoughtful. Sam's expression returned to one of benign scrutiny as he met Jolie's eyes across the table, though Lena was plainly tired of Jolie's childishness and mouthed in great exasperation, "Lighten *up*."

Jolie's guilt trigger was nearly as itchy as her defensiveness, and she immediately backed off, pink-cheeked and embarrassed, thinking she was getting as bad as Carl in the game of head-butting defiance. It was the Hoyt in her. It was genetic.

The waitress returned with three heaping plates of fried shrimp before the silence could build. There were none of the usual sides—no salad or hush puppies or cheese grits, just a never-ending plate of golden shrimp and home fries and their own cocktail sauce that was spicier than store brands, infused with the heat of horseradish and red pepper.

"I hope you aren't allergic to shellfish," Lena chirped merrily, trying to reclaim their earlier ease, though Sam Lense seemed to have realized he wasn't in altogether congenial company and was, on his own side, not so easily drawn out. Lena was forced to carry the weight of conversation as best she could, till finally, in desperation, she called across the table, "Well, Jol—Sam's here to study the Indians—couldn't remember which kind," she allowed with charming honesty, "but Jolie knows because the Hoyts—they're Indian. Everybody says so. What kind?"

Jolie's father would just as soon have discussed birth control with her as his purported Indian blood, but in an effort to be agreeable she answered gamely, "Don't know—maybe Cherokee, or Blackfeet," she offered vaguely, as they were names she had heard bandied about by her cousins, who were a lot more into the ethnic variations than the old folk. She paused to let the Professional Indian Hunter jump in and instruct her, but he only plowed through his shrimp, raising an unconsciously doubting eyebrow at the mention of the mythic Cherokee, but keeping his own counsel.

Lena refused to be drawn in, forcing Jolie to range further afield, offering with even less confidence, "Though Big Mama and Uncle Ott, and Daddy—they say the Hoyts, we aren't Indian at all; we're really from Alabama. That we're—"

Before she could get it out, Sam made a noise and lifted a hand in warning, as if unable to sit silent while she offered any more homespun theories of origin. "I bet you fifty *bucks* I can tell you what your Big Mama said you were. I'll bet you a *thousand.*"

Jolie was taken aback by his outburst, equally sure he couldn't, but forbidden to gamble by reasons of faith.

"I don't have fifty dollars," she said.

He gamely flipped a fried shrimp on the table between them. "I'll bet you this *shrimp* I can tell you what your grandmother said you were."

Something in his sureness made her hesitate, though Lena was all for it. "Oh, come on, Jol. It's all-you-can-eat, who cares?"

Jolie met his eye a moment, then flipped a shrimp on the table. *"Deal,"* she said, then sat back and waited with a fair amount of certainty for him to name some obscure local tribe that would be a good educated guess. And completely wrong.

He seemed to take a lot of enjoyment in her confidence, making a great show of wiping his mouth, then leaning in and confiding in that mild, instructive voice, "Little Black *Dutch.*"

The confidence was wiped from Jolie's face in an instant, making her blink at him in wonder, while Lena asked, "Is he right, Jol? The Hoyts are *Dutch?*"

Jolie kept staring at him as she answered aside, "So they say," and to Sam, "How the *heck* did you know that?"

He looked sincerely pleased at her astonishment, picking up his winnings from the table and popping them in his mouth with great enjoyment. "Well, I *do* have a much sought-after degree in Florida history from UF—approximately worth the paper it's printed on," he allowed, "and it's a fairly common colloquial term in the South, supposedly coined by Sephardic Jews when they were kicked off the Iberian Peninsula in the 1500s. They settled in Holland and created this mythical ethnic identity to explain their lack of height and dark hair and skin. They imported it with them to colonial America, and it really caught on in the South, became a convenient little ethnic dodge—the way mulattoes, half bloods, Turkish sailors, and anyone of color could outwit soldiers and census takers and pass for white in the days of slavery and Indian removal—and the Blackfoot are Canadian, in the upper Plains. There isn't a Black*feet* tribe. It's just another variation—Black Irish, Blackfeet, Black Dutch—they're ethnic PR, indigenous to the South. They don't exist."

Jolie had never heard of such a thing in her life and just blinked at him in wonder, though Lena asked, "What d'you mean, they don't exist? What are they? *Ghosts?*"

Sam didn't laugh at the gibe, but thoughtfully deposited a shrimp tail on his plate. "The Black Dutch are. The Muskogee Creek do exist, and are the flavor of the month, as far as Florida Indians are concerned, thanks to their very flexible cousins, the Seminole. None of them are actual aborigines, but a remnant of the Hitachi and Yuchi and all the little tribes of the Southeast, who were driven south by colonial expansion to the swamps on the Choctawhatchee and the Apalachicola. The Creek are trying for federal recognition, and one of my jobs is to track down the surnames from the last Creek census in 1834. Thought it'd be easy, but when I show up at their door and so much as whisper they're not a hundred percent Scot-Irish, I get this blank, hostile look, like I'm one of Jackson's soldiers on horseback." He pointed a shrimp at Jolie. "Just like that icy stare you were giving me a while ago when I made the crack about your college. I've never met an isolate group with such an ethnic *chip* on their shoulder," he mused. "God, they make the Tutsi look *congenial.*"

The flush on Jolie's face was so comically guilty that Lena burst into laughter, though Sam didn't press the matter. He just grinned at Jolie's discomfort, then picked up his glass of tea and raised it above the table in a toast. "To the Lower Creek Nation," he intoned, "and Big Mama, one of history's great survivors. May her grandchildren haunt the swamp till the end of their days, and Old Hickory be her yard boy in the Great Hereafter."

There was no mockery in his face, just a genuine offer of something. Jolie was too inexperienced at the art of courtship to understand exactly what. But the sensation was far from unpleasant, and after a moment she lifted her glass and gamely clicked it.

Lena joined them and, once peace was declared, dominated the conversation with her usual élan, till the shrimp was gone and the tea glasses refilled so many times that the waitress began giving them the eye. Lena was flying high on caffeine and white sugar by then, and after they settled their bill and returned to the steaming sidewalk, she linked arms with Jolie on one side, Sam on the other, and announced that she simply must have one final Dilly bar before she left Florida for good.

So what began as an evening of new faces and adventure quickly took on the languor of a hundred other small-town Friday nights, even ending in the same place as they had all the Friday nights that preceded it—in the oily parking lot of the local IGA, where it was customary to park facing the highway and wave at the passing traffic. With Jolie on one side and Sam on the other, Lena sat perched on the hood of her mother's car and, between waving at honks and going out to say good-bye to well-wishers, chattered like a magpie, telling them every last detail of her future in Savannah.

Jolie was used to Lena and her mouth and loved her enough to set aside her own disappointment and let her exalt in this, her last night on the strip. Jolie just lay back on the slant of the windshield and watched the stars, listened with half an ear to Lena's increasingly far-fetched nonsense till she made one of her curious, magical proclamations, that one day she intended to build a house on the side of a mountain in Colorado and decorate it like the Kremlin, "down to the onion spires and red silk wallpaper."

Sam, who had also lain back on the windshield, didn't laugh or question it, just glanced aside at Jolie and, in a delicate move of communication, lifted one eyebrow in an unspoken acknowledgment that Lena was fun and great and entertaining and lovely—but, hey, was it his imagination, or was she a goof?

It was the first time in living memory that any man had withstood Lena's charms long enough to acknowledge this patented truth, making Jolie flash the famous Hoyt grin in reply, one she seldom showed to strangers, which answered, *Yes. But we love her anyway.*

Lena was none the wiser, just kept up her steady, stream-of-consciousness prattle till eleven o'clock finally came around and it was time to head back to Hendrix. Even then, she kept talking, Jolie not saying a word on the long ride through the woods, till they stopped at the concession stand to drop Sam off and Jolie turned to say good-bye over the seat, adding in the most natural, reasonable voice, "We're going to the beach tomorrow, to St. Andrews. Want to go?"

He said yes without pause, offered to bring towels and sunscreen, blankets and Pepsi; said he could be ready at seven, did they need him to drive or bring ice?

For the first time that night, there was silence in the car, as Lena was struck momentarily speechless, though she recovered quickly enough, stammered sure, to bring whatever he wanted, that they'd pick him up at nine.

It made for a quiet drive to the parsonage, Lena not saying a word till she halted in the drive, when she turned to Jolie with a face that was mischievously amused and chanted, "Jolie, Jolie, Jolie—who didn't want to have supper with no damn Yankee, but went and invited him to the beach for our last run of the summer."

Jolie couldn't deny or explain it, just gave a small shrug in reply. She was gathering her purse to get out when Lena added with teasing smugness, "I assume you'll want to borrow a bathing suit tomorrow. Which will it be—the red or the black?"

For a moment, Jolie paused, then answered in a small voice, "The red," making Lena burst into laughter.

"Oh, Jolie, Jolie, Jolie Hoyt, who wouldn't pierce her ears or cut her hair or go to the prom. Falling for a big-talking man from Miami. The Hoyts are gonna looove that."

# Chapter Three

S o Jolie wore the cherry-red, bandanna-print bikini to the beach the next day, and on such a trivial choice, the fate of many was sealed. Or so she would eventually think.

At the time, she was too young to be farsighted, too inexperienced with human sexuality to realize that a public outing of the Hoyt genetic ladder in the shape of her sweat-glistened, eighteen-year-old body might pack a more powerful punch than she intended, dynamite strong enough to blast her into another life. She was only concerned with the glorious present: walking in the foaming surf; feeding the dolphins off the jetties; lying out side by side on sand-covered blankets, with Sam most solicitous that she not get sunburnt, rubbing on so much Hawaiian Tropic that by the time they made it to the air-conditioned bliss of Taco Bell, she smelled like a walking piña colada.

She was already on the brink of love by then, staring over the edge of the cliff, considering a great leap. Her first such leap—not due to the strictness of her religion (where child brides were common) as much as her own reticence, and the unspoken rules of the county mating game, in which Hendrix girls were rated high in sheer animal attractiveness, but seldom considered marriage material (too dark, too poor, and too unstable, in that order). Historically, they were the girls you took to the fish camp for the weekend, who eventually grew into the women you let

live in a shack on the edge of your farm in return for certain favors, a tradition Jolie's own Big Mama had lived out, first in Hendrix, and later, in
a trailer on the Cleary end of the Cottondale Highway, where she died in
'86. Jolie had bypassed such a fate by virtue of her shyness, and because
even the horniest Cleary blue blood was wise enough to take one look
at the Reverend Hoyt—he of the lazy eye and the size-fifty belt—and
rightly conclude that there were less hazardous ways of satisfying adoles-
cent lust than trifling with such a man's daughter.

Jolie appreciated the wiggle room his protectiveness gave her against
the old thief of youth in Hendrix—sexuality—and hesitated on the
brink of love for just that reason, intrigued but not so quick to jump. She
understood there were hidden shoals and deadly currents in the waters
below and, without a mother in the house, had only Lena to guide her,
as men and sex and the whole living organism of attraction was hardly
the subject of dinner conversation at a Pentecostal preacher's table. It
was, like so many things in Hendrix, drowned in silence, so that Jolie
moved through the shock of her first true infatuation with the mute
beauty of a newly minted mermaid: curious, darting, easily startled.

Sam found her minnow flightiness as charming as anything else about
her, as he'd been smitten by her that very first night, blindsided, no one
more surprised than he. For he'd known Lena for weeks, had seen her
zipping around on her father's golf cart in her ridiculous string bikinis;
yet he had remained untouched by her schoolgirl chatter, her friendly
camaraderie. She was a beautiful, carefree child, and he'd expected her
best friend, Jolie (whom she spoke of incessantly), to be the same.

He'd offered to take them to supper as a sort of big-brother gesture
before Lena left for college and was unprepared for the brooding outsider he'd faced across the table at the café, who stared at mainstream
Anglo-Southern life with the same mix of envy and contempt that he
always had, growing up in Miami. She clearly wasn't the Indian prin-
cess of Lena's imagination, but an amazing example of yet another well-
known American archetype, one variously described as Black Dutch or
Mestee or the mysterious Melungeon.

As he'd tried to explain at supper, they weren't a documented ethnicity per se, but a recurring ethnic phenomenon—triracial Southerners of mostly Anglo and Indian descent whose ancestors had been too dark to pass for white in the rigid caste systems of the antebellum South. Pursued by the twin specters of slavery and Indian removal, they'd retreated to their swamps and hollows and intermarried for generations. They created small isolate societies that had been documented in enclaves from Appalachia to Louisiana since the mid-1600s, wherever Indian removals had left a sizable nonwhite population. West Florida certainly qualified for such status, though Sam was surprised that such a thing had endured the fluidity and blasé homogeneity of modern American life to survive this late in the century.

It was a fascinating discovery in its way, and when Sam got back to his camper that night, he stayed up till two in the morning writing the lead professor on the Creek study a long and enthusiastic letter on his new find. Running nearly twelve pages, single-spaced, it was crammed full of insight and vigor, hints to his real "find" evidenced in the emphasis he placed on one obscure theory of the Melungeons' supposed origins as the descendants of Gypsies who were kept as concubines in the Spanish royal court.

Professor Keyes might find such conjecture doubtful and unsupported, but then again, Professor Keyes had never seen Jolie running in the surf in her borrowed red bikini—an image that transcended anything as boring as hard documentation and explained so *much*.

Sam was so intrigued that he put aside caution and openly plotted romantic strategy with Lena while they drove back to the campground the next afternoon from the beach. Lena couldn't have been happier and easily fell into the role of wise younger sister, cautioning him to go slow, and easy.

"Not because of the Hoyts," she explained. "They're a pretty flexible bunch. Nutty, but flexible. It's Bethel I'm talking about. The old Sisters are sweet, but they're kind of—rigid, I guess you'd say, and they practically raised Jol. Be careful of the rules."

"What *rules*?"

"Well, they're kind of hard to explain," she said as she parked in front of the camper. "They were hard on me, at first. The main thing is, don't cuss or drink or smoke or gamble or mention that your parents do. And don't go to dances or bars or concerts or R-rated movies—or if you do, don't say a word about it; not a *peep*."

Sam looked at her a moment to see if she was serious. When he realized she was, he rubbed his chin. "*Huh*. And I was kind of hoping we could have sex tomorrow. I guess that's out, too."

He said it as a joke, though Lena faced him with unsmiling frankness. "If you're gonna talk like that—even *think* like that—you better pack up that ratty old camper and get the hell out of Hendrix tonight. These people will go medieval on you, in a heartbeat."

Sam was amazed at her intensity. "You mean her father?"

"I mean *Jolie*. Listen—me and her brother, Carl, we used to date. He was my boyfriend. Well, Jolie came home early one night and caught us on the couch in what you might call a *compromising* position, and she flipped *out*."

"How old were you?" Sam inserted in a small, prissy voice, truly that of an older brother.

Lena cast him a weary look. "I was six*teen*. I was plenty old, and we weren't in the *most* compromising position, we— Listen, I didn't have a shirt on, okay? Anyway, Jolie started throwing stuff at him, yelling who did he think he was, treating me like a *field whore*—that's exactly the word she used, I swear to God. She was livid."

"What'd you do?"

Lena shrugged. "Well, I couldn't do much—finally just grabbed my shirt and ran out, and me and Jolie didn't speak for two whole days, which was, like, an eternity. But she finally broke down and came over, asked in this weeny little voice if I could go down to the dock with her. That's where we used to sit and talk, on the fishing bench on the river, so I said okay and we went down there and talked half the night, and she told me all kinds of stuff I never knew, about her mother and how she died—"

"How *did* she die?"

Lena paused a moment. "Well, of breast cancer, I think. At least, that's what it was at first. They found it on a doctor's visit when she was pregnant with Jolie, so she was basically dying the whole time she knew her. She doesn't talk about it much—Carl does; he remembers a lot more. But she talked about her that night, and about how lonely she'd always been, how she was afraid she'd never get out of Hendrix. She said that's why she was so mad about me and Carl, because God hadn't given the Hoyt women much, just a brain and a hymen, and if they lost either one, they'd be stuck in Hendrix the rest of their lives."

When Sam made a noise of wonder, Lena assured him, "And she means it, she really does. She told me how her Big Mama, she used to run around with men in town, rich men, but when she got old and lost her looks, she had to make a living taking in ironing, sometimes from the very same men. That's how Jolie remembers her, bent over an iron-ing board, sweat running down her nose. That's her idea of hell, living in some run-down trailer around here, pressing a razor crease in some guy from the country club's dress pants."

Sam just stared at the windshield. "I think it might be mine, too."

Such was his honesty that Lena's face lightened in an instant. "See there? You two were made for each other."

Sam had taken her warning seriously. He was old enough to realize he'd better tread softly, but too intrigued to politely back out, captivated on more levels than he cared to share with anyone, especially a chatterbox such as Lena. When she left that night, he retired to the cot fitted above the cab of the camper and a battered box filled with notes and docu-ments connected to the real riddle that had brought him to Hendrix: nothing to do with the Creek at all, but a bit of sleuthing around an old Florida mystery—one he'd taken great pains to hide from both his steering committee (who would have objected on grounds of personal interest) and his father (who would have had a stroke).

Sam suffered no pains of guilt at the deception, as this project was a

strictly personal obsession, powerful enough that it had quietly steered his education since he'd arrived at UF five years before. His long-suffering parents had sent him there to major in accounting, and he'd indulged them till halfway through his junior year, when cramming for a statistics exam had proven that a life of numbers and filtering raw, quantitative data wasn't for him.

To their great teeth-grinding despair, he'd switched colleges, majors, and apartments in the same week, to history for his BA, then cultural anthropology for his master's, and all in all, it had been a happy accommodation. He was by nature curious as a cat, brilliant in the absorption of data, and so aggressive in research that he'd landed a rare first-year position at the Museum of Natural History doing grunt work. He'd been casting about for a hands-on field position that spring when he'd come upon a cheap mimeographed notice pinned to the departmental boards between offers of Overseas Study and Summers in Berlin, which included three block-lettered words that had leapt off the board and caught his attention, APALACHICOLA NATIONAL FOREST, and to seal the deal, in smaller print, HENDRIX. They were enough to make him yank the notice from the board and reread it with more interest, as he had a bit of unresolved family history with the area, and specifically the town, which was old by Florida standards, but so far off the tourist maps that you'd be hard-pressed to find anyone east of the Suwannee who'd ever heard of it.

He only knew of it himself thanks to the notoriety of the Hendrix Lynching—the one he'd mentioned to Jolie and Lena as they stood on the sidewalk of the café. The entire incident was well-known to him, and indeed, most Florida historians. In 1938 a white shop owner had been killed in a blatant daytime robbery by a black man named Henry Kite, who'd shot the shopkeeper in the face, in view of a storeful of eyewitnesses. When the town sheriff had come to arrest him, Kite shot him, too. Given the number of witnesses and the standing of the sheriff, his execution would have been a given. But the Hendrix locals hadn't put much faith in the county law enforcement and had meted out their own form of frontier justice, killing Kite's mother, brother-in-law, two uncles,

and youngest sister, who was eight months pregnant. Not content with their slaughter, they'd dragged Kite's corpse to the courthouse in Cleary, and left it for public display.

Such a thing wasn't uncommon on the Florida frontier, and the Kite lynching was mostly remarkable for the late date—1938—and the advent of modern media, which added a particularly gruesome element of public complicity to the deed. Local radio stations and newspapers posted invitations to the lynching well in advance, and when Kite himself was caught, the fever had reached such a pitch that his murder approached the level of human sacrifice, complete with mutilation, castration, torture, and public display of his body, pictures taken before and after and later sold as postcards at the drugstore.

The bestial nature of his end, combined with modern press coverage, was enough to blow this fairly routine bit of vigilante justice onto the national stage. Calls for an investigation were universal, and the weight of a few grisly eyewitness accounts (not to mention the postcards) reignited calls for a federal antilynching bill, which helped bring the greater era of lynching to a long-overdue end.

The inadvertent result was that Hendrix was entered into Florida history books as one truly creepy little hamlet, though Kite's murder was never as much of a cause célèbre as Rosewood, Florida. It was simply too messy for anyone to mold into anything approaching heroic. Kite was shamelessly guilty, but his punishment so disproportionately cruel that any close reading of the matter—especially the wanton murder of his family—ended in head-scratching wonder that human beings could turn so quickly feral. Sam himself had scratched his head the first time he'd read the small print, though his obsession with parsing the details of the lynching wasn't prurient as much as personal: the murdered shopkeeper was his great-grandfather.

His immigration papers listed him as Moshe Lensky, though on the rare occasions he appeared in the legal records after Ellis Island, he was renamed Morris Lens, whether by coercion or willingly, Sam had no idea. Even after two years searching, old Morris was to his great-grandson nothing more than a dry, lost figure in a larger family mythos; another hapless immigrant washed ashore at Ellis Island with a great American dream that had hit the shoals in a particularly deadly way. The violence of his end had produced a sort of familial PTSD, and even Sam's grandfather, who'd been an eyewitness to the murder, never spoke of it willingly, to Sam or any of his generation.

Sam's father had passed on the bare-bones details: yes, a murder; yes, it was tragic. In the end, Sam was forced to reconstruct his great-grand-father's abbreviated life by more scientific methods: ship rolls, census, Ellis Island lists. From the third floor of the UF library, he'd painstak-ingly traced Morris's journey, from his birth in Tauragé, Lithuania, to his abrupt departure at seventeen, when he'd left his family and an ancient Jewish community as many a young Jew had before him, by bribing a guard and jumping the border to Poland to escape the torment of a lifelong, mandatory conscription in the Russian army. He exited Ham-burg on a steamer in 1920 and showed up in Ellis Island later the same year, his occupation listed as tailor, his name made more palatable to the American mouth.

He lived briefly with a brother in Baltimore, then appeared randomly up and down the Eastern Seaboard for a dozen years, working as a ped-dler, and searching for an opening to start a store of his own. The primo spots of established Southern Jewry had long been filled, and Morris's search had taken him to the far edge of civilization, deep in the no-man's-land of a West Florida turpentine camp, an hour upriver from the port in Apalachicola.

He had married before he left Hamburg and was quick to send for his wife and a son, who'd been born four months after he sailed and was now, by the standards of the day, nearly grown. Two more sons—twins—were born and died in Florida, but aside from these common-place tragedies, Morris seemed to have prospered for a bare three years on his perch, there on the edge of nowhere, till the autumn of 1938, when Henry Kite showed up at the store just before closing and begged Morris to open and sell him cigarettes.

Morris had relented and been shot in the eye for his pains, and Sam's grandfather, then seventeen years old, had been offered the lead horse in the lynch party. He had refused, and the honor went to another man. Morris's son and widow had departed Hendrix by train within the hour, heading south to Tampa Bay. They'd left with nothing but the clothes on their backs and heard of the attendant savagery only through the newspaper accounts that followed.

Sam's great-grandmother had eventually remarried in Miami, and the family's only eyewitness to the murder, Sam's grandfather, had died when Sam was young. He was nothing more than a dim, benign shadow, a gregarious old man by reputation, who favored Cuban cigars and spoke often of his digestion. He never willingly discussed the details of his father's murder—the whys and the how and even where Morris's body was buried, though the old man had been known to be observant, and the proper interment would have meant something to him.

Sam gave his grandfather a survivor's pass on his silence and didn't overly judge him for it, though the utter absence of oral history made Sam's job of historical reconstruction a thin proposition. He needed solid source material to unravel the niggling details of Morris's final end, and in Jolie he caught a glimmer of hope that he might yet pierce the silence.

But first he needed hard data and began digging through the box full of federal census images he'd copied at UF, from 1860 to the last one released in 1930. They were often inaccurate and woefully incomplete, but in working out a framework of investigation, they were invaluable. He checked the enormous 1880 federal census first and found nine separate Hoyt households in District 59, a considerable local presence, as the state was only decades old. They were listed as white, which meant little to Sam, as local half bloods were ingenious in outsmarting state officials, and if they could pass for white, they would by God self-identify that way.

For a good hour, Sam scanned rows of households, working his way forward to the turn of the century, when the lumber barons began eyeing the local forests, and Hendrix became an official boomtown. By 1920, the population had ballooned to eight hundred, with a working hotel, a railroad depot, a brothel, and many independent sawmills and logging operations. They made quick work of the red cedar, and ten years later District 59 was already in decline, the loggers and mule skinners and skilled sawyers forced to take lesser jobs collecting resin and distilling turpentine. Camp Six—an enormous turpentine-distilling operation—opened in '29, and by '35, his great-grandfather was living on its boundaries in Hendrix, his occupation listed as merchant, with a wife, a son in school, and two younger males—the twins who would die before they were out of diapers.

Sam couldn't remember Jolie's father's name till he saw it in the cribbed, sixty-year-old cursive of a census worker: Ray Hoyt, District 5, seven years old in 1930, living in a rented home with a single mother who was listed as head of household, with four children—all male, all laborers; none in school. Sam held his place, then counted back to the Lens store and found a mere fourteen households separating them.

The number made him smile, as fourteen houses were nothing. Two of the Hoyt siblings were listed as millworkers, and four of their neighbors as working in "turpentine." They were still hanging on to farming—tenant or sharecropping—in '38, but lived on the cusp of Camp Six. Given the proximity to Hendrix, they would almost definitely have been customers of his great-grandfather's store.

# Chapter Four

S am waited a respectable twelve hours before he called Jolie again, prodded along by Vic Lucas, who was temporarily manning the concession stand and disclosed that Lena and Jolie had had a tough parting Sunday night, with many tears and fears on Lena's part that Jolie would pine away and die in her absence.

"Were they that close?" Sam asked.

Vic, who had the body of a longshoreman and a head the size of a dinner plate, nodded. "Oh, yeah. Really close, those two. Lena worries that Jolie—she'll get stuck. These local girls—they get pregnant, they lose focus—and Jol—you met her, right? She's too smart for that. *Maybe* too smart for that. We *hope* too smart for that."

Sam did, too, and was careful to go about contacting her with all propriety, careful not to offend the medieval father, who (rumor had it) wasn't fond of frivolous attention and was so massively proportioned that he made Vic Lucas look like a toy poodle. Sam knocked on the parsonage door the day after Labor Day—the first Tuesday in September—though the heat hadn't let up so much as a degree, the sun slanting at the old porch with a relentless glare.

The peeling white paint on the parsonage porch conveyed a general air of benign neglect, a row of wood fern and begonia withering in the furnace blast of the dog-days sun. There was no immediate answer to his knock, nor was there a car in the drive, though Jolie had mentioned her father shared a car with her uncle Ott and only used it for grocery runs and hospital visits to ailing parishioners.

Sam couldn't tell if anyone was at home or if they were dodging him—and God knows, he was used to that in Hendrix. He had gone to the great trouble of borrowing an iron and ironing his shirt and hated to have to re-iron it. After a cautious glance in the window, he caught a flutter of movement somewhere back there—a bit of steam rising from a pot perched on an old stove. He went around in search of a back door and found it on the side, a little stoop that opened to a kitchen, Cracker-style, as if it had once been detached from the house.

Jolie was there, visible through the steamed glass at the stove, carefully dropping red potatoes in a steaming pot, one at a time, frowning at the splash, careful not to be burnt. She was obviously not expecting anyone, and as Vic had warned, taking Lena's departure deeply, her expression one of profound, yet accustomed, loss, as if used to carrying such a weight. She seemed curiously diminished in the poverty of the old kitchen, which was jarringly ill-kempt to his city eyes—the screen door so torn it was almost bare, the countertop cheap, peeling linoleum, as was the floor. Student fieldworkers were warned that rural life could be primitive, and that's what it seemed to him, of the sort more easily digested when in old photos of a different generation; not someone as young and vulnerable as Jolie appeared, standing at the stove, frowning at the steam.

He hesitated a moment, then tapped on the glass. She left the stove to peer through the window, and when she recognized him, her face brightened so sharply it lifted the entire room, the air of stale despondency replaced by an all-embracing welcome.

"Hey—come in," she said. "Did you knock? I can't hear people back here."

She said it all in one welcoming burst, but he was hesitant as he stepped in the sloped-ceilinged little room, which smelled of old coffee and damp cypress and was muffled by an ancient window air-conditioning unit that roared like a jet engine. His reticence had less to do with her welcome than the zippered terry robe she was wearing, of the sort worn by old Cuban women in Miami, when they watered their hibiscus. It hit her at midthigh and was partially unzipped, revealed an intriguing inch or so of what appeared to be transparent white lace on pink, slightly sunburnt skin, making this housecoat a considerably more complex garment.

He stood there, taking it all in, till it occurred to him that, being the visitor, the onus of explanation was on him. "No—that's fine. I didn't mean to interrupt. Is your father home?"

She returned to the stove, oblivious of the robe and her casual dress, as if he were a cousin who'd dropped by for supper. "Yeah. Around back. He doesn't come in till dark, usually. Want some tea?"

Here on her own territory she talked much more quickly than she had in town; so quickly and country that he passed on the tea (because he didn't understand what she was offering) and hesitated at the door. "Well, do I need to talk to him?" he asked. "Get permission?"

"Permission for *what*?"

"To enter. Lena said he's a little strict. I believe the word she used was *medieval*."

Jolie dismissed it with a comforting ease, gesturing him to the front of the house and explaining, "She's just feeding you the Hendrix Scare. Daddy's all right. He's got a bad eye, which makes him kind of scary. But he's a teddy bear. Been a preacher for, like, fifty years."

Sam was not reassured by the assessment and followed along with his head up, through a high-ceilinged dining room to a mirror-size parlor—a sitting room, settlers used to call them—hardly bigger than the porch. It was outfitted with the same worn care as the kitchen, though there was some sense of decoration, the walls a soothing mint green, adorned with an assortment of family photos in identical flat-black frames. The mono-tone frames gave them a curious unity, as there was no rhyme or reason to their selection. Historical sepia photos hung in identical frames with a color studio shot of Jolie in her high school graduation gown, so generic it might have been taken at Palmetto High in Miami.

Sam was instantly drawn to the wall, which, Jolie explained, was a brainchild of Lena's. "The black frames—we collected them all summer and painted them. It took *forever*. She calls it the Rogues' Gallery."

"Interesting," he murmured, pausing next to a photo nearly identical to that of Jolie, only black-and-white, maybe thirty years older, of a somber, dark-haired woman, obviously closely related to Jolie, as if she were her near twin. "Your mother?" he asked, and got a quick nod.

"Her graduation picture. She died when I was three," Jolie added quickly, as if used to the order of question and adept at heading it off.

Sam raised his eyebrows at the quickness of her response, but didn't press for more details. He didn't comment at all other than for a mild "She's beautiful. Looks Apache, or Otomi. Hell, maybe they *were* Blackfoot. Was she from Hendrix?"

"Sure," Jolie answered as she dropped onto the sofa. "Her and Daddy really *are* third cousins, or something—which if you ever meet my brother will explain a *lot*."

She smiled at his laugh—a smile of uncomplicated pleasure and unexpected sweetness, which, in its way, was as fetching as the abbreviated robe and long, bare legs. She threw them out on the sofa before her with such innocence and lanky country ease that it was apparent she hadn't a clue to their power. He made an effort to ignore them, returning to the wall and her equally intriguing history, asking over his shoulder, "What was her maiden name? Ammons?" as he'd noticed a generational alliance between the two families on the census.

"Yeah. She was an Ammons. A lot of my cousins are Ammonses," she volunteered, seemingly impressed. She paused, then added after a moment, more in statement than question, "You really have dug up the county, haven't you?"

Sam was brought up short by the offhand observation, enough that he turned and met her eye and found her face interested and speculative, as if she were adding up a few internal figures of her own.

He would later regret not telling her the curious truth of his search right then—casually, no tangled loyalties, just a blunt statement of fact.

But he was too unsure of his reception to trust her with so strange an obsession and sidestepped her smoothly, with a mild admission: "That's why they pay me."

He said nothing more, just returned to the wall to inspect the other photos, many of a little boy, presumably her brother, Carl, and a cache of vintage photographs, the largest of a worn, rawboned old farmer in a slouch hat and overalls, holding a horse by the reins. *March 26, 1926* was written in labored cursive on the face of the photo, the date catching Sam's eye, as the old man was almost certainly a citizen of the 1930 census.

"So who's the old guy, with the horse?"

Jolie sat up a little to make sure they were talking about the same picture. "That ain't a horse," she murmured. "That's my great-granddaddy and his mule, Old Grey."

The blazed forehead and lanky ears looked pretty horsey to Sam, who peered closer. "How d'you tell the difference?"

Jolie's face took on a hint of amazement. "Well, try breeding them, for one thing."

The remark meant nothing to Sam, who continued down the line, occasionally asking for clarification, though the old boy with the mule was by far the most interesting find. He was itching to ask her outright if she knew the location of the old turpentine camp that had gone by the strangely generic name Camp Six, but once he finished with the Rogues' Gallery, there was nothing to interest him but her legs, which were indeed distracting.

Family history, and history in general, suddenly seemed of small consequence, and with no more talk of mules and men, he took a seat in the only chair in the room: an ancient recliner upholstered in a beaten and faded olive plaid.

"So how are you holding up?" he asked solicitously. "With Lena gone? Vic says it's been tough."

"I'm all right," she said, so stoically it seemed automatic and hardly felt, then, in a closer stab to truth: "I wish I could cry."

Sam had never met a buried neurosis he didn't like and asked, "Why can't you cry?"

She shrugged again—that small hitch of her shoulders so natural it was almost a physical characteristic, that *Who Knows?* denial of personal opinion, common among poor people in the South. "I don't know. I couldn't cry when Carl left either."

Sam just nodded, still a little distracted by her casual state of undress that was setting off a purely sexual buzz in his head that hummed like a hot wire, making a true analysis difficult. "You mean your brother, Carl? Her boyfriend?"

Jolie grunted at the word. "Well, I don't know if I'd go so far as to call him her *boyfriend*. Carl's three years older than Lena—or three years physically. Emotionally, he's about eight."

"That him?" Sam asked with a nod at the wall of photos of the dark-haired child who was obviously kin to Jolie, with the same thick block of hair and straight eyebrows.

She nodded. "Yeah, that's Carl. He doesn't have as much hair anymore. I think he's already losing it."

"Aren't we all," Sam murmured, feeling for the lever on the recliner and kicking out the footrest, making himself comfortable as he dug into the domestic history. "Yeah, she told me how you and her, you got in a fight once, when you caught them on the couch. Said you were pretty hot."

Jolie looked utterly astonished and muttered, "She *told* you that? Good *God*—what a thing to tell."

Sam found her puritanical tone disappointing (aye, heartbreaking, when coupled with her legs) and hastened to defend Lena. "Well, he *was* her boyfriend. And these things *do* happen—" He stopped short as Jolie obviously wasn't buying, her lanky hospitality literally folding up as she threw her feet on the rug and faced him with direct, gunslinger eyes.

"Yeah, it does. It happens all the time—but that don't mean it's right." Then she asked, as if giving him the benefit of the doubt, "Did she tell you how old she was?"

"Sixteen? Seventeen?" he offered, and was cut off with a snort.

"Sixteen, my *butt*. She was *four*teen. She just moved here—was barely out of a training bra. And I wasn't hot with her, I was hot with my *idiot* brother, who was raised to know better. Daddy was—he was beside himself. He put Carl's stuff on the porch—sent him away that very night."

Sam was a little shocked at the severity of the punishment for what sounded like a bit of minor philandering. "To where? You mean, like, military school?"

Jolie had the grace to look a little embarrassed at the query, sitting back and finding a sofa pillow to clutch to her chest. "Well, Bible college, if you must know. Claims to have got rededicated down there, but I don't trust him any further than I could throw him. Not where Lena's concerned."

This was more to Sam's taste, wonderfully Southern and quirky. "Oh, well, I wouldn't worry too much with Lena. Last time I saw her, she was headed out with a surfboard tied to her roof. She seems to have escaped Hendrix, hymen or not. So there goes that theory."

It was the kind of audacious remark you make to a potential girl-friend to see if she's on the same page with you, though Jolie didn't laugh.

She just met his eye levelly and commented in a dry voice, "You two must have had you a right long talk after you dropped me off from the beach."

"Not long"—he smiled—"but instructive. All about the Sisters. And the rules—which, I must say, she didn't seem too worried with breaking."

He said it in a tone of mild challenge that Jolie rose easily to answer. "Yeah, well, the thing is, with Lena, she ain't really from around here. She's got three married sisters and a rich granny in Naples and can come and go around Hendrix pretty much as she pleases. Not all of us got that luxury—you know what I mean?"

Jolie said it with those level, unblinking eyes that were daunting in their absolute certainty, the same expression that had thwarted him through many a screen door in Hendrix. But he had never minded sparring with a half-dressed woman and smiled. "No living in a trailer, putting a crease in the mayor's dress pants, for Jolie Hoyt?"

"No ironing for the rich folk. Not this Cracker."

Sam laughed aloud, as he had sprung from a long line of socialist-leaning Democrats and found her hard-nosed defiance just delightful, the stuff of birdsong and hot baths. It made him comfortable enough to lean in and kick down the footrest and ask in a tone of confidential confession, "Well, listen, Jol—can I ask you something? A favor?"

At her nod, he asked, "Could you go put on some clothes? I mean, that butt-hugging robe is just *freaking* me out—it really is. If your father comes in, I'm gonna have a heart attack and die on the spot. And he'll know what killed me."

She looked moderately peeved at the request, feeling for the zipper and working to zip it up. "Mrs. Lucas gave me this robe. She wears 'em everywhere—wears 'em to the grocery store."

"Yeah—and South Beach women wear bathing suits with the ass cut out of them, but I can't handle that either. Just go get dressed, before the Old Man comes in. Please."

She exhaled a breath but went to the bedroom and shortly returned, dressed in a respectable church-girl cotton dress that closed in the front with a long row of pearl buttons. She was still buttoning it when she walked in the room, apparently trying to allay his fears about her father.

"Don't worry about Daddy. He's not so rough once you get to know him—the nicest Hoyt around. Ask anyone. Especially a Hoyt."

She paused for a reply, but Sam had momentarily been silenced by the sight of her buttoning her dress with that intimate, casual femininity that affected him worse than the slip.

He didn't hear a word she said and blinked. "What?"

"Daddy," she repeated, her hands on her hips in a fetching kind of dominatrix pose. "He's not that bad. He's out in the shed—come on, I'll introduce you."

"What's he doing in the shed?" Sam asked, coming slowly to his feet.

"That's where he hangs out when he's not doing his preacher duties, or running his debit."

"His *what*?"

"His *debit*," she explained in a tone of great patience as she went to the kitchen, moving the bubbling pots to the back of the stove. "He just preaches part-time. He's also a policy man."

Sam's expression turned to disbelief. "Your father is a *bookie*?" he breathed.

"*No.* A *policy* man. He sells life insurance, burial policies—you know—to poor people, for a dollar or two a month, for death, dismemberment, whole life. He collects his debit twice a week, and it's huge, from Wakulla to Wewa. He knows everybody—all the beekeepers and fishermen and old farmers who never go to town. That's who you need to talk to, not the city people in Cleary. They're idiots."

Sam was taken aback by the *death* and *dismemberment* and, in a slightly lowered voice, asked, "So is he gonna be all right? That I'm Jewish?"

Jolie paused, pot holder in hand, and looked at him with great interest. "Is that what you are? Jewish?"

"Yeah. Sure. What'd you think?"

"I don't know," she said, returning to the stovetop. "Cuban, maybe Greek. Where'd you get the light eyes?"

Sam was familiar with the term—yet another echo of Melungeon folklore, where light eyes and small feet were prized. "Couldn't say. My grandfather was Lithuanian. Maybe a few Cossacks worked their way into the gene pool."

It was a common piece of smart-assery in Jewish circles, but taken as honest speculation by Jolie. "Huh," she said as she finished with the pots and tossed the pot holder on the counter. "I didn't know there were any Jews left in Miami. Mr. Lucas says the Haitians have taken over."

"Yeah, that's what everybody says. But there are a few enclaves of the Hebrews left—trust me."

Jolie smiled, hand on the doorknob, and asked, "What'd y'all do? Take to the swamp and lie to the census men?"

She said it with mischievousness so pointed it was finally, overtly seductive, as if she were offering her wit like a family secret, a sensual treat. The force of it made him stop in his tracks and stare at her with a strange foreboding, a gut certainty that this was a woman he'd love the rest of his life. The sureness of the thing was astounding, though he was an old hand at protective covering and answered lightly, without missing a beat, "Moved to Boca. Took to the condos."

"Oh, well." She laughed. "Same difference, I guess."

Sam just blinked at her and agreed: same difference, he guessed.

# Chapter Five

The shed that Jolie's father used as a workshop was tucked away in a far corner of the churchyard, in what had once been a tobacco-drying barn, the kiln still intact, though the hooks were long removed. He'd reclaimed it from the foxes and the field mice in the bad years following his wife's death when he'd needed a place to grieve in private, away from the eyes of his young children. Over the years, it had become his unofficial office and sanctuary, where he worked on his sermons, notes, and his unending, esoteric projects, which were eventually abandoned and packed away in man-high stacks of boxes that nearly filled the musty, windowless room.

Jolie negotiated the maze with the ease of a favorite child, following a dim dirt path to an army-surplus desk in the corner, where the old man sat at his books, completely engrossed till Jolie was upon him.

"Hey, Pops—supper's almost ready. This is Sam—you know, Lena's friend, from the campground?"

The Old Man's size had not been exaggerated—six-three or -four, with a girth that filled the small room, though he wore the sagging clothes and belt of a larger man. He was much older than Sam had expected, age and the stamp of poor health evident in his sagging jowls, and wheezing breath, though his preacher voice was trained to the old-school pulpit, and he fairly boomed his greeting as he struggled to come to his feet and present a plate-size hand. "Pleased to meetchu, young man."

Sam had braced himself for a distracting facial deformity, but the bad eye was nothing more than a small strabismus that made him appear to be thoughtful, whether he was looking at you or not. If anything, it made him more approachable, as flawed and welcome as his greeting, which was obviously sincere and open, but nearly impenetrable to Sam's Miami ear. Not Southern as much as gibberish, a linguistic stew of colonial Anglo, African, Appalachian, and God knew what—maybe actual Mobilian, a Muskogean-based pidgin English that had once been widely used on the Gulf coast, now thought to be extinct.

On Jolie's urging, her dad immediately returned to his seat, with an apology. "Sorry. My laig's been giving me a fit. Did Laner git off?"

The question was directed at Sam, who listened hard, but could make little of it. He instinctively turned to Jolie, who'd hopped up to sit perched on the edge of the old desk, utterly at ease in the spidery gloom.

"She's all right," she answered, "just a little homesick," then got to the matter at hand. "Well, listen, Daddy—Sam was sent here to study the Indians, but nobody'll talk to him. I was thinking you could take him on your debit and introduce him around. You know—out in the forest, and at church."

The Old Man turned an eye on Sam, and answered, not unkindly, "I didn't know there *was* such a thang as Injuns in this forest."

"Sam says there are," Jolie insisted. "He says the Hoyts aren't Black Dutch at all, but just a bunch of old Hendrix gheechies, trying to pass for white. He's working on an article for *National Geographic*. Wants to put you 'n' Uncle Ott on the cover."

She grinned slyly as she said it, as this was the way the larger Hoyt family showed affection for people they loved, by teasing them mercilessly, *trying to get their goat,* it was commonly called. As one of the patriarchs of the clan, Raymond was used to abiding by its less commodious customs and paid her no mind, though Sam could feel his blood turn to ice water in his veins.

"She's joking," Sam stammered. "I'm not a journalist, just a grad student, with the Museum of Natural History, working on an application the Creek made for state recognition. The *Muskogee* Creek," he added in a final, desperate tag, hoping it might ring a bell of recognition.

But the Old Man paid him about as much mind as he had his daughter (which is to say, none at all). He just murmured, "Well, I declare," then relented with no further conversation, as if anxious to get back to his writing. "Well, surely—you can come with me, if you want. It's a long drive, I'll warn you thet. Don't bother with a coat."

Sam caught enough of it to understand that the Old Man was extending an invitation and thanked him with great sincerity. Sam didn't speak again till he and Jolie were far out of earshot, nearly to the porch, then he turned and asked, "Why the hell did you tell him that bullshit about *National Geographic*? I can hardly find anyone who'll talk to me now," he fumed. "What'll happen after that bullshit gets passed around?"

He was so sincerely distressed that Jolie went to some lengths to reassure him, gripping the front of his shirt and telling him, "Sam, listen. You wanted Hendrix gheechie, and that's what I just gave you: the King of the Hendrix Gheechies, Raymond Hoyt."

Sam was charmed by her sudden face-off, her close, teasing face that he decided was every bit as lovely as Lena's, and even more: black hair, red lips, strange, moss-colored eyes. He lost his annoyance just like that and answered in a milder voice, "Well, I don't really need low-country gheechie. I need Yuchi, Miccosukee, maybe a touch of Chacato."

Jolie just smiled a patient smile, as if she were dealing with a half-wit. "They call 'em gheechie around here, and don't worry: the one thing they love to do is talk. You let 'em talk and they'll tell you everything."

So began a fast and fruitful ten weeks as far as Native American studies in North Florida was concerned, as Brother Hoyt was as good as his word about introducing Sam around on his debit, invariably as "a friend of Laner's, up from My-amma, attending the university."

Apparently, Lena's popularity knew no bounds, in the city nor the field, and Sam had Jolie on hand to soften the truly resistant ("Oh, he's not a *scientist*—just some poor mook, trying to pay for college, just like the rest of us") with a status-leveling nonchalance that was instinctive and, in someone so young, nothing short of brilliant. It was Sam's first, far-off inkling of her genius in people-handling—a skill absorbed in babyhood in the complicated political mechanisms of a country church, which she was generous in sharing.

On her advice, he went about unearthing local ethnicities in a more roundabout way, casually inquiring about details of their common folklore, folk remedies, and farm myths, asking if they were kin to any "granny-women"? This last was a loaded question, as it was the colloquial term for midwife, a profession half-blood women historically excelled in. Their extended families were quick to own up to such a relationship with a grandmother, or an aunt or a cousin, and with no encouragement at all would go on to describe in great detail their patented ways of treating the manifold complications of childbirth. They would recall with pride the names of the rich families in town who would send buggies out to get them in the old days because they trusted them more than any of them "high hats" in town. They had no idea how much of their cultural roots they were revealing with such stories, for granny-women were also practitioners of root medicine and a direct link to that vast subconscious ethnic heritage that these kinds of isolate communities both secretly celebrated and hotly denied.

Sam soon amassed a quantity of data, the best of it from the Hoyt Diaspora, which stretched from south Alabama to the coast. There were originally nine Hoyt brothers, but only four still anchored locally: Ray, Earl, Ott, and Obie. Earl was the oldest—a bent octogenarian who suffered greatly from emphysema and seldom left the house; Obie, a widower with four sons; and Ott, the baby of the family and runt of the litter. He was plainly Jolie's favorite, a lively little bachelor who'd survived rheumatic fever as a child and was about half the size of his older brothers, who treated her with the same delight her father did. He called her *Jo-lee,* Cajun-style, and practically ran to the door when he heard her call.

She was obviously the family pet, and as long as she was at Sam's side, he was warmly welcomed into listing, old trailers and houses so dilapidated they could truly be called shacks. Ott's bedroom walls were lined in Depression-era newspapers for insulation—a common economy practiced by tenant farmers in the South, which Sam had read about, but had never seen in real life. Jolie seemed to take great enjoyment in sharing it with him, not intimidated by either her kin's poverty or their deformities—mementos of their early years working as child labor in the area turpentine camps and sawmills. There were many cast eyes and lopped-off fingers, and an almost universal deafness that meant that Sam's interviews were held at a dull roar, Jolie shouting right in their faces, "Uncle Ott! Tell Sam about the Hart Massacre! Where the soldiers smashed the babies' heads against the STONES! Weren't they buried up at WEEK'S ASSEMBLY?"

After taking a moment to understand her, the old man would smile a dim smile and agree, "Yes'sam—up thar in Alabamer. Kilt the younguns, babies and all. Come up on 'em in the swamp, Mamer uster say . . . ," with Sam scribbling furiously at his side.

It made for much excitement in the discovery, and in only one way did Brother Hoyt continue to disappoint Sam: in his steadfast refusal to own up to his own Native American roots. These were obvious in every way: his strange pidgin English; his mystic strain of American fundamentalism; his straight hair, straighter nose, and Asian shovel teeth (all of them, including Jolie, passed the click test). Even after Sam legally traced them within the legal parameters of tribal membership to the Creek Census, Brother Hoyt was loath to acknowledge the connection and dismissed any promise of minority status.

"That's for people who need a laig up," he argued. "We git by." At breakfast one morning, he went so far as to trot out the famous old dodge, claiming that the Hoyts were Little Black Dutch.

Sam was exasperated by his denial, and close enough by then to ask him point-blank, "Well, Brother Hoyt, tell me: What *are* the Little Black Dutch? Are they *Dutch*? Are they *black*? Are they even *little*?"

The Old Man seemed not the least bit intimidated by this bald challenge; he just pointed a crooked finger across the table at Jolie and answered with calm assurance, "Thet girl right thar. Thet's one."

Sam had burst out laughing, as he'd grown fond of the Old Man, who was a strange old bird by any reckoning, connected to the modern world by the thinnest thread, and in danger of exiting it prematurely thanks to a runaway case of diabetes and a bad heart. He was a gold mine of minutiae about Old Hendrix, and from their drives on the debit Sam gathered what meager information he could of his great-grandfather, and the exact location of Camp Six, where Brother Hoyt had, along with most in Hendrix, worked on and off as a young man, when all other paychecks had failed. "Nasty, hard day it made," he said, "and I was always glad to be done."

Sam was careful to keep his cards close to his chest and went about his questioning with objective nonchalance, a full month into it before he got around to asking the Old Man about Sam's own slender stake in local lore.

"So Camp Six was basically a company town?" he asked as they threaded their way over the long bridge that spanned the river and floodplain outside town. "You bought your groceries on chits, at the store?"

"If you had the credit. They could be particular."

"Who's *they*? Who owned it?"

"Lumber company," the Old Man answered, "same as cut the swamp. Had mills here, 'n Louisiana, and Texas. Some of the folk was local. Same folk what owned the bank."

"Did they own the store? Was there local resentment? That people had to shop there?"

It was a sweltering afternoon, the windows of the Old Man's ancient, little Ford Falcon down, his elbow to the wind as he answered, of turpentine camps in general, and Camp Six in particular, "Naw—you didn't have to buy thar. It was just convenient. Used to be, the riverboats brought thangs up to the landing. But the boats quit running, so they opened the sto, same as most camps."

"When did it close?" Sam asked, feeling for his notebook and jotting notes as always, his face to the open window.

"Oh—'37, or '8. Place got robbed, then was burnt. Old boy who worked there got shot in the face, in front of his wife and childrun."

Sam kept a carefully neutral face. "Who shot him?"

The Old Man cast an inquisitive eye at him, as if surprised he hadn't heard this locally famous story, though the Old Man made little of it and explained with the same drawled candor he went at everything, "Colard feller—name of Kite. Over a pack of cigarettes, they say. Just come upon him and *pow*. Down he went."

Hearing the details of the family secret so casually recounted by a near first-source witness was affecting enough that Sam had to keep his face averted to maintain any semblance of distance, his voice dry and detached. "So, did you know him? Were you *there*?"

"*Naw.* I wouldn't have lived in camp if you'd a paid me. Usually stayed with kinfolk, working for 'em. And he wasn't from around here— German feller."

"So what happened to him, after he was shot?" Sam pressed, meaning what had become of his body, though Brother Hoyt misunderstood.

"He was graveyard dead. Dead before he hit the flo'."

"I mean, where they buried him."

"The German feller?" At Sam's nod, he shook his head. "Couldn't say. He wasn't from around here," he repeated in casual dismissal, then concluded with no trace of malice, "But old Kite swung for it. Buried *him* in Cleary. What was left of him."

He said it with a face of faint distaste that caught Sam's attention, enough that he paused in his scribbling to ask, "Were you there? Did you see it?"

The Old Man turned the full weight of his strange, unfocused eyes at him, but didn't answer. He just regarded him speculatively a moment, then returned to the steaming autumn highway. "Now tobacco—it didn't come on strong till later," he began, changing the subject with no commentary at all, other than the weight of his eyes.

Sam pressed him no further, as it was but one conversation among many. He was still confident that he could track down the exact location of the store and Morris's grave and took Jolie on many a stroll around forgotten and weed-choked cemeteries, pretending to search for the graves of the names on the Creek Census (and coming upon a couple quite by accident).

She was well into her own fall semester by then, and when they were finished with their afternoon graveyard crawls, they'd return to the parsonage for supper, where Brother Hoyt was as generous with his table as he was his memories of Old Hendrix. He seemed not unaware that Sam's interest toward her might be more than purely professional, but never made any inquiries into the matter. He just accepted Sam as part of the furniture around the parsonage, often on hand, with no threat attached. This very much annoyed the church Sisters, whose grievous loss of Lena had at least partially been compensated by Sam's appearance soon after.

He wasn't as ornamental or amusing as their golden girl, but had his own strengths. He was a man, and polite and smart and obviously in love with Jolie Hoyt—and they were all for that, the old Sisters were, as practical as Lena when it came to poor girls and dead ends and the Men Who Could Get Them Out. They gave the match their full approval and sat back and waited for the inevitable events—either engagement or pregnancy—the former preferable, though the latter not so rare as to cause an earthquake on this end of the swamp.

But as the dog days of September quietly slipped away, and the October nights grew mild and golden, they began to wonder if they'd misread the signs in this romance. For Sam never made any loverlike advances toward Jolie that they could see: never walked her to church or sent her flowers or sat with her on the porch at night. He seemed content to hang out with her father and spend his days talking to the poor folk on the

river, writing out pages and pages of any sort of nonsense those chattering gheechies came up with, something the good Sisters at Bethel (even
if they were gheechie themselves) considered a criminal waste of time.

They soon tired of the mystery, and by mid-October, whenever they
ran into Sam at the IGA or the café, they would baldly ask about his
intentions toward Jolie, though he proved oddly shy in such matters,
would blush to the tip of his forehead and stammer the most unsatisfac-
tory replies.

It made the old Sisters privately wonder if little ole Jolie, raised in a
household of men, simply hadn't learned how to court—to bat her eyes
and twitch that tail and land this particular fish before he got away. To that
end, they began inviting them to Sunday dinner as a couple; would feed
them like royalty on recipes cut from the pages of the *Progressive Farmer,*
on chuck roasts and field peas and corn bread, all the while dropping
glorious asides on the bliss of married life, trying to nudge them along.

They had a hard time gauging the effectiveness of the strategy, as Jolie
had inherited her father's inscrutability. She didn't seem to mind their
maneuverings, just ate her corn bread and smiled her Mona Lisa smile
and pretty much went her own way—which wasn't difficult as she was
on the inside of the joke and knew very well why Sam wasn't walking
her to church every week or making any loverlike moves toward her in
public. She also knew why he blushed to the tip of his hairline at the
mention of his slow courtship, because he was living a double life, old
Sam Lense was. And so was she.

They'd fallen into it easily, almost innocently, on a stifling afternoon in
early October when they dropped by Sam's camper so he could change
into his swimsuit for a quick dip in the river, and to pick up a letter
that Lena had sent to Jolie via her mother, who'd in turn given it to
Sam to pass on. It was the first time Jolie had seen the inside of his little
camper—an ancient Gulf Stream borrowed from an uncle that had seen
better days, all curled linoleum and stacked boxes.

Sam was self-conscious about the rust and the shabbiness of the place and kept apologizing about it in a way that Jolie found touching, especially given his open acceptance of the limitations of the parsonage, and Uncle Ott's old shack. Perhaps she most loved this aspect of his personality—very much akin to the appreciation she'd felt for Lena when she'd joined Bethel and started calling Jolie's father Big Daddy. Sam never went that far, never became anyone's pet, but he was genuinely respectful of the Old Man, and polite to the poor people on the river, so accepting that he couldn't understand it when she thanked him. He just wasn't raised in Hendrix, didn't realize how much crap her father took, all the time, because he was old and poor and handicapped and odd-looking, a Holy Roller who talked like a hillbilly from hell.

Carl and Jolie knew it well and reacted in their own ways, Carl with hell-raising defiance, Jolie with tacit withdrawal and steel-eyed challenge. She'd spent a good part of her youth in careful and constant patrol of her emotional borders, not realizing how exhausting it was till she sat down on the edge of his tiny bed in that camper that afternoon and read Lena's letter before they left. Even in the close quarters of the camper, he took care to be cautious and modest, changing in the truly minuscule bathroom, and came out to find Jolie sitting there on the edge of his bed with Lena's letter open on her lap, her face set and bothered.

"Sure you don't want to dive in?" he asked, as it was still miserably hot, even in October.

Jolie just shrugged, for Lena's letter read like all her other letters from Savannah, full of laughter and chatter and details of her new life, of classes and professors and projects and parties. Jolie had never once been jealous of Lena's beauty, had never even envied her lighthearted disregard for all the old Rules and Regulations of the Church, at least not till then. Sitting there in the hot little camper, reading about Lena's new life and her education and the waters of the great world she was drinking of so freely, Jolie was overwhelmed by a terrible sense of loss, hard enough to make her eyes water.

When she didn't answer, Sam asked, "Jolie? Are you all right?"

She just lifted the letter. "I'm fine. Jealous, I guess."

"Of what?" he asked with his old curiosity.

She looked at him sadly. "Of everything, everyone. Everybody on earth who gets to live, but me."

It wasn't the first he'd seen of that caged-bird frustration in her, the passive-aggressive moodiness of the good girl, restrained from life, bound by rules and culture and family bonds. He knew it was part of the bargain, part of her strength, and sat beside her and tried to console her.

"You live. You go to school. How is Lena doing any better than that?"

Jolie just shook her head, unable to articulate the frustration of being who she was.

"Well, what exactly do you want?" he pressed. "To pledge a sorority and date a Kappa Alpha and wear a mum to the Homecoming Game?"

Jolie didn't smile at his teasing, just met his eye levelly and answered in a small, honest voice, "No. I want *you*."

Sam ignored the sudden, hard pounding in his chest, told her in a friendly way, "For what? To be your boyfriend? Take you to eat at the café every Friday and pick up the tab?"

She shook her head. "No," she whispered. "Just *you*."

He lifted her face and kissed her for the first time, and it was so sweet, it was disorienting, made him forget what they were talking about. He was on to other things, easing her to her back, feeling for her buttons, though she wouldn't let him, but wiggled away and sat up, murmured, "No. Sam. You know I cain't."

He did indeed know it and didn't even argue, just lay there a moment, then rubbed his face and came to his feet. "Well, if I'm gonna jump in the water, I need to get moving."

They walked down to the pier in the waning October light, and he dove right in, though Jolie wouldn't join him, afraid of the current, and respectful of the alligators—four-foot ones, only visible by their eyes, which haunted the margin of the murky mud and hydrilla on the shallow end of the bay. Sam hadn't lived on the river long enough to have any dogs or small animals dragged off and at the end of the dock dove in the deep water that was getting cold in October, but still swimmable. The shock of cold helped him regain a small bit of his brain, enough to try to talk Jolie into joining him, but she refused, just sat there on the end of the dock and watched him swim. Mr. Lucas came by in the golf cart and asked if she'd got the letter from Lena. She told him she had, and he waved and drove away, and Sam got out and walked Jolie back to the camper, holding her hand on the way, Jolie telling him she needed to get home soon. It was almost six; her father would be wanting supper.

Sam agreed, said he needed to take a shower, that he'd hurry. When they got to the camper, he got his shower kit and a towel off the line and left her sitting there in the twilight on the edge of the bed, wondering why she was so different from the rest of humanity. Wondering how Lena could live such a carefree life, while she, Jolie Hoyt, had to carry the weight of Southern history on her back. She was still thinking it when Sam came back in his towel and cologne and sat down next to her on the bed and kissed her again, and this time she said to hell with it. Maybe it was the cologne, or that she'd worn a snap-up shirt, the kind with cowboy buttons up the front that made that first move easy, just rip, and it was open to the lace bra, and Sam was half-dressed and that made it quick, too.

Or maybe it was just youth and loneliness, Jolie starving for the feel of mouth on mouth, skin on skin, for taste and scent and smell, and she'd never had anyone kiss her like that before, much less work her out of a bra, touch her breasts, a sensation like nothing she'd ever before felt, the reality of the heat and the river and the ratty, little camper dissolving around her.

Sam was the more experienced of the two and actually not quite as lost to orbit (yet). Throughout the slow and sensual undress, the bite and the exploring kisses, the feel of her hair (silky) and her taste (of garlic, from the pizza they'd bought for lunch), he could hear the faint voice of his father, Leonard, calling him dimly, as from a great distance. It was as if Leonard were standing in his front yard in Coral Gables, his hands held to his mouth, shouting, *"Sam! This is a serious thing! This is a young girl! What the hell are you thinking?"* Sam succeeded in ignoring him till right at the point of departure, when he actually rolled off the bed, told Jolie he was going back to the shower to get dressed—thinking that he could put some distance here, but it was too late, at least for Jolie. His hands and his mouth felt too good—not rushed and impersonal, but light and loving, the kind of nurturing she'd been robbed of, fifteen years too early, when her mother died, and her father took to his shed. Just as she was regaining that magical connection of flesh on flesh, of life and intensity and warm-lipped consolation, he wanted to leave? To take a *shower*?

She didn't think she heard him right and sat up and pushed back her hair, said, *"What?"*

"A shower," he repeated, in about as much of a daze as she was, pointing toward it as if giving directions to a stranger.

*"No,"* she said, and when he still didn't move, she kicked her heels on the covers like a spoiled child. "It's too late—too late."

That was about the end of the debate. She was just too inviting, a study in contrasts, even in bed: white skin, black hair, pink-tipped perfection. The image of his father was erased as he climbed back on the bed and found her mouth, and like many a well-intentioned couple before them, they were soon over the river and through the woods, to grandmother's house they had gone.

In a manner of speaking.

When it was over and they blinked back to the reality of the ratty little camper and the river and the stillness of the late-October afternoon, they didn't have the luxury of lying there and whispering endearments, but realized with a nasty little jolt that the clock on the table showed six forty-five. Sam jumped off the bed like a jackrabbit and dug through his hamper till he found yet another couple of towels, and they jogged down to the showers (men's and women's, respectively) and scrubbed off all evidence of foul play, then dried and redressed and combed their hair and waved at Mr. Lucas when he passed them again in the golf cart. Then Sam raced her home through Hendrix, got her there at five after seven, though her father had been sidetracked by a parishioner at the church, and they found the house dark and empty.

Sam had time for one more kiss, there in the drive, then gripped Jolie's shoulders and told her that he *loved* her and would never leave her, never! Never! And *never,* under *any* circumstances, would he *ever* ask her to iron his pants.

He said it with a face that was just wildly honest and sure and intent, making Jolie—she of the long-dead mother and a world of abandonment issues—blink at him a moment in silent amazement, then, six weeks after Lena had left, press her face to his neck and finally, *finally* cry.

# Chapter Six

Whether they were tears of regret or relief, happiness or impending doom, Jolie didn't know. She just wiped her face on her shirt, then went inside and made some sort of last-minute change of supper plans that her father never commented on, never noticed. He had no reason for suspicion, as Sam was long gone by the time he came in, and Jolie was cooking in the kitchen in one of her mother's old aprons, telling him what was on for supper, that he needed to wash his hands.

So it went, through the long and unseasonably warm autumn, with all the attendant satisfaction of love and lust and lying chest to chest with someone you adore. And the guilt, too, and everything else that went with it: the "When was your last period?" and "I'll get some condoms" and "You better not buy 'em in Hendrix" and "Do I look like an idiot?" and so on and so forth.

The duplicity of it all would sometimes assault both of them at odd moments in the day, and for a brief instant it would seem reprehensible, so foreign to their natures that surely this was another couple who spent their afternoons in wide-open, naked bliss in a seedy camper on the river. Surely a straight shooter such as Sam Lense wasn't cuckolding a harmless old preacher, eating his food and discussing the Ark of the Covenant and screwing his only daughter right under his nose; and it wasn't Jolie Hoyt, either.

Not she, who hated Carl's womanizing; who went to church like clockwork and prayed every day and baked Sister Noble a birthday cake on her eighty-second birthday; who wrote her best friend, Lena, long and chatty letters about her new classes, Fine Arts (which she liked) and Algebra (which she did not). Even with Lena her afternoons with Sam were ignored; denied as a matter of emotional survival, her life falling neatly into two separate worlds: her public life and her private, two separate parts of an uneasy whole.

The public part was breakfast with her father and Sam driving her to school, stopping to do research at the courthouse or to interview one of the far-flung Creek families. The private began as soon as humanly possible, when they'd hurry back to the camper and indulge in the insane suspension of time that was good, sweet, and loving sex. Sam called them her "afternoon classes": four hours of humid-autumn languor, spent mostly in bed and mostly naked, the little camper too small to get dressed in before it was time to officially go, and too hot to dress anyway. Between lovemaking and explaining lovemaking (Sam was then, and ever, a great diffuser of information) he would prop himself up on pillows on the tiny bed and exclaim with academic enthusiasm over every aspect of her beauty. He left nothing out, but rejoiced to the heavens in her little feet, her long legs, her green eyes, the moistness of her lady parts, and the absolute Cadillac-quality of her breasts. He boldly proclaimed her the most beautiful woman in Florida.

"That would be Lena," she said, though Sam would have none of it.

"Lena, my ass. I've hugged Lena. She's a two-by-four with long hair. You should be cast in plaster of paris. You should be in a museum," he declaimed with perfect sincerity, as he was, by then, cold stone in love, and, in the tradition of all great Jewish romantics, anxious to go legit: sign lifelong vows, alert the media.

Jolie agreed to the engagement, but hesitated to go public so soon. "People will talk," she warned, with a wariness that, to Sam, defied logic.

"About *what*? You mean the Jewish thing?"

"No," she insisted. "The *us* thing. Daddy's a preacher. He has to be careful about appearances. He almost lost his church because of Carl wild-assing around. I can't do that to him."

"This isn't wild-assing," Sam said testily. "This is *love*," though Jolie was hardly convinced.

"Close enough. Just give me a little space here," she begged. "I'll talk to him, *soon*."

In the meanwhile, the old Sisters shook their heads over Jolie's lack of skill in cornering her man, and the calendar flipped to November, and the early tendrils of autumn finally began to arrive, the wild cherry and Virginia creeper turning gold, then crimson red, and the hickories, older and tougher, waiting on the first official freeze before they gave up their summer green.

Sam had been on the river almost three months and had accumulated a wealth of research; had even forwarded the first draft of his official thirty-seven-page study to the museum, along with a voluminous box of miscellaneous notes, tapes, and pedigree charts, attached to the appropriate census. He'd also culled the record for the scant details of Morris's time in the area and pinpointed the approximate location of the old store—lost to the woods, with not so much as a foundation to mark it.

He'd not made any headway on finding Morris's grave, but at least had a mental map of the area for when he returned to the search at UF. He had obviously gone as far as he could go this round and would have pulled up stakes and left immediately if not for Jolie, who told him she loved him twice a day, but continued to drag her feet about taking it to the next level.

Sam was cut to the quick by her hesitance, forced to revert to sarcasm to convince her. "Well, it's not me, Jol—it's my penis. He's calling the shots these days, refuses to leave without you. It's so *annoying*."

Jolie didn't laugh, but advised him with all seriousness, "Well, tell him to hush awhile. I'm moving as fast as I can. And who'll take care of Daddy if I leave? Carl? A nursing home?"

"Jol—you'd have already moved to Savannah if things had worked out. He doesn't want you stuck in Hendrix—and the term is almost over. I've got to get the camper back to Miami and file my great Indian study—and, shit, Jol, I don't want to leave you. Let me talk to him, in private. If he doesn't bite, I'll give it a rest and come back after Christmas and try again."

Jolie finally gave in the weekend before Thanksgiving and let him call her father and request an official appointment with the pastor, like everyone else. Brother Hoyt didn't realize the import of the request and had Sam meet with him in the same place he met anyone in need of pastoral counsel: in the sanctuary on Sunday afternoon, when it was deserted, in the first couple of pews. El Bethel was too small to have a vestibule and opened right to the pews from the front doors, and when Brother Hoyt came in that afternoon, early, after lunch, he was amazed to find Jolie there, too, sitting quietly at Sam's side.

He'd eaten dinner with her in the parsonage, and not a word of the meeting had been mentioned. Only when Raymond saw them sitting there together, looking so shifty and cornered, did he realize what was upon him. But he didn't shy away from it, just sat down on the pew in front of them, Sam not making any mention of their afternoons at the river (heaven forbid), but just asking in all humility and sincerity for his daughter's hand in marriage.

The Old Man absorbed this incredible news with his usual calm, only asking one question: "D'you love her?" which was the same thing he asked all potential grooms, hardly ever the brides. In his experience, women were moldable to marriage and could be happy in any situation if there was security and love. Men were another matter. They had to start out in love, or it'd never last.

Sam was quick to assure him that, yes, he loved her and went on to speak of his bright future in academics, even produced the letter from Professor Keyes that mentioned the teaching assistantship and handed it over the pew.

Brother Hoyt hadn't brought along his reading glasses and gave the letter the merest glance, then moved to his next question and asked if they'd set a date.

"Soon," Sam stammered, glancing aside at Jolie, who was sitting there, pale and quiet, not offering so much as a word. "By the first of the year," he added, the nearness of the date making the Old Man sit up and take notice, actually turn toward his daughter and peer at her a long moment.

"What's the rush?"

She wouldn't meet his eye, and Sam hastened to answer, "Well, I have to be back at UF by January, to start the winter term."

Brother Hoyt's eyes were still on his daughter, his expression not unkind, almost teasing. "Well, sister? Ain't you gone say a word? You want to marry dis boy?"

Jolie was more devastated by his kindness than if he'd railed at her and called her names, for she had an inkling that he knew about the camper and the river. Maybe not in detail, but he wasn't an idiot, her father. He was a Hoyt. He knew about the mysterious lure of the fast-talking outsider, and all that it entailed. She couldn't speak for a moment; finally answered in a small voice, "Yessir. But I don't want to leave you."

Brother Hoyt didn't argue, but nodded his head slowly, then reached over the pew and patted her leg. "It'll be all right, baby. It'll be fine."

And that was about it.

He braced himself on the back of the old pew and came massively to his feet, handed Sam back his letter, and told him that he'd have to pray about it—for them to keep it to themselves till then.

Sam also came to his feet and assured him they would, and since it was still barely midday, he and Jolie went out to the campground on some pretense, to be alone. They didn't head straight to the camper as they usually did, but just sat on the pier in the slant of the noonday sun, which wasn't as brutal as it'd been in August, having grown mellow and golden with the closing of the year. They were both a little overcome with the enormity of what they were doing and sat without speaking till Jolie finally commented in a mild voice, "I almost fainted when he asked us what was the *rush*. If you'd have said that idiot thing about your penis, I would have dropped dead."

Sam stared at the black water. "If I had said the word *penis* in front of your father, our troubles would be over. Because mine would have fallen off."

Jolie smiled, then laughed aloud, as his old Sam-humor was a great joy to her.

"Well, I do love you," she told him, wrapping her arms around him and burying her face in his shoulder. "When are you gonna tell your parents?"

"Oh, I don't know," he sighed, his eyes still on the water. "I was thinking next week, but hate to spoil Hanukkah."

"What's Hanukkah?" she asked, with such innocence that Sam expelled another long sigh.

"Ah. Nothing. Little winter festival my mother is fond of."

"And telling her will ruin it?" she asked, so lightly that Sam blinked back to the present.

"Not ruin," he assured her. "Complicate."

He insisted on calling them immediately, to demonstrate his good-will, though he did ask that Jolie not mention she was from Hendrix.

"Why not?"

Sam sighed. "Let's save something for New Year's."

All in all, the call went well, all polite absorption at this point ("Oh? Really? So *soon*? A pastor's daughter? How *nice*"), which Sam figured was the emotional equivalent of clinical shock, the hammer blow to the thumb that doesn't hurt for about three seconds, then, oh, yes. It hurt a lot. It *howled*.

But he was the baby of the family, the nonconformist who'd spent twenty-four years outflanking them. He rubbed his neck when he hung up, told Jolie with a wan smile, "See? I told you they'd be fine."

Once the hurdle of informing their parents had been cleared, they went about tying up the loose ends of the fall semester so they could marry as soon as the maid of honor (Lena) and groomsman (one of his brothers, though Sam was less picky) could be depended on to show up at either El Bethel or the courthouse in Cleary after Jolie's last exam in mid-December. Sam would be gone by then, or soon after; Jolie would transfer to UF for the summer semester, or maybe in January, if the right strings could be pulled. That was the plan—to be gone by January in a quick and simple flight, one complicated by the holidays, which were rigorously celebrated in Hendrix, hamstrung by all manner of tradition and family gathering.

Both Carl and Lena were coming home for the annual Thanksgiving feast Raymond traditionally hosted at the parsonage, which filled the little house to the rafters with cousins, in-laws, exes, and more than a few hunting dogs. The menfolk did the outside cooking—the turkey-smoking and the pig roast—while the women did the inside cooking and arranging and stepping and fetching. All of it came at a most inconvenient time, the week before finals, keeping Jolie in a stew of irritation and sleeplessness that made her snappy with everyone, including Sam.

He picked her up from school as usual the day before Thanksgiving, on a sterling-clear afternoon, as muggy as July, though a front was due by morning, and the first frost of the season had been forecast. Jolie was nearly done with the labyrinthine preparations of a Hoyt family feast—mountains of red potatoes peeled, corn bread crumbled, celery and yellow onion and free sage chopped. She ate a green apple as he drove her home and tried to give him a preview of what to expect of a Hoyt Thanksgiving.

"—probably thirty or forty, at least. Aunt Kibby went up to Tennessee, Daddy says, but Uncle Ott and Uncle Obie will be there, and all their wives and children and grandchildren and all their exes and stepchildren and hunting buddies, who'll only stay long enough to eat. They won't come unless it's raining or turns cold; they'll be wantin' to get back to the woods before dark."

Sam had studied the Hoyts from afar so long that he was actually looking forward to seeing them assembled, *en famille,* an overwhelmingly masculine microculture, as Jolie had, at last count, eight uncles, and twenty-three first cousins, mostly male, who ranged in age from fifteen to forty-three. Such was their devotion to hunting that they had hardly appeared since Sam had been there and weren't expected to appear till deer season ended in February. Jolie didn't seem to mourn the absence as she was more like a sister than a cousin to the larger clan, a spoiled, mouthy sister who treated her younger cousins with the same eye-rolling dismissal she did Carl, referring to them as the *Hoytlings,* and seldom missing an opportunity to comment on their unvarnished idiocy.

"They never leave the woods?" Sam asked.

"Not the first week of deer season. They've had the dogs out since September, but this is the first week they can actually shoot," she explained. "Brace yourself, because they'll be coming straight from the woods, in camo and boots, full of this overflowing machismo—*niggering*-this and *niggering*-that to try and impress you."

"Why would they think that'll impress me?"

"Because they're idiots."

She left it at that, sidetracked to discuss the supper they'd had the night before with Sister Wright, queen of the El Bethel Sisters, a spunky little woman of definite Muskogee stock who was related to the Stricklands on her mother's side and had made it to the formal tribal roll.

Like all the Sisters, she was the soul of generosity, and before dinner was through, she had given Sam many gifts: a dozen brown eggs, an angel-leaf begonia, and a big square of something she pulled out of her refrigerator, which turned out to be a huge square of processed cheese.

He hadn't opened it till he got to the camper, but now he asked Jolie, "Why did Sister Wright give me a big chunk of Velveeta last night?"

"It ain't Velveeta—it's commodity cheese. The government gives it to poor people—they pass it on to me and Daddy all the time, pay tithes in it. It's better than Velveeta; makes good grilled-cheese sandwiches. How's your begonia?"

"Alive, so far." He wondered aloud, as he often did, about how generous they were, the poor people of Hendrix. "They won't let you leave empty-handed—your father has given me four Bibles, a sewing kit, and four Independent Life fans—Sister Turner gave me a straw hat—and they hardly know me."

Jolie smiled. "They know you enough to know they like you, and around here, if you like somebody, you give them stuff. It's saying you're one of them. They're giving you a piece of them."

Sam had already described the practice (a local form of potlatch, as far as he could tell) in his just-dispatched paper, but continued to go to Jolie as the first source for all things Hoyt and Hendrix. "Why do they like me?" he asked, pleased, because he liked them, too: their eagerness to talk and their long memories, their weird and passionate convictions.

"Well, mostly because you treat them with respect," Jolie explained. "You don't look down on them because they're poor; neither did Lena. That's why they loved her—rooted for her back when she was after Carl."

"Are they rooting for Sam and Jolie?" he asked with a smile.

Jolie answered oddly, with a short bark of laughter. "Oh, yeah. They're pulling for Sam and Jolie."

An unpleasant note in her laughter made Sam glance aside. "What d'you mean by that? Are you sure they're oaky? With the Jewish thing?"

Jolie had been asked that at least one hundred times and assured him, "They're cool with the Jewish thing. They're *mighty* cool with the Jewish thing."

Again, he heard that odd undercurrent and insisted, "What d'you mean by that? What's the strange smile about?"

She suppressed the smile. "Nothing. It's an old hick thing, hard to explain. And it's kind of insulting."

But Sam was only more intrigued and pressed, "Come on, Jol. You got me curious."

By then, Jolie had come to enjoy sharing all the little strange corners of the Hendrix mind, but still hesitated on this one, glanced at him slyly, and asked, "Promise you won't get mad?" At his emphatic nod, she added, "Well, before I tell you, you got to remember that Sister Wright, and all the Sisters, they're poor old country women, never lived outside of Hendrix—"

"I told you I'm not gonna get mad," he insisted with growing impatience. *"What?"*

She shrugged, then confided in a mild, amused voice, "Well, to them, you're not just Sam Lense, nice guy. You're also"—she paused—"Sam Lense, rich Jew."

*"What?"*

"You heard me. That's why they're so happy—think I've been *very* clever, snagged me a *catch*. They really do."

This was unexpected, and indeed a little insulting to Sam, who only half believed it, arguing, "But I live in the crappiest camper in Florida. My father is a building inspector with the City of Miami. My mother works for HRS."

"That doesn't have anything to do with it. Your father could dig ditches and it wouldn't make any difference. You know Sister Noble's daughter? The one in Chicago?"

"With the white piano?" he asked, for he'd heard a good bit about that white piano every time he ate supper with Sister Noble.

"That's her. Well, she wouldn't say it around you, but that's how she got the Cadillac and the white piano."

"She married a rich Jew?"

Jolie smiled. "*Exactly*. That's why she tells you about it all the time—it's the measure of her daughter's success: not any piano, but a *white* piano."

Sam wasn't sure he was so happy with this unexpected twist and sniffed, "Well, it's nice to know that I'm loved for my own sweet self."

"You said you wouldn't get mad, and they *do* love you for your sweet self. I mean, you treat them like maybe they're human beings and step and fetch to please them, and that's all any Southerner asks. I'm saying that it's funny, all these little winks and grins I'm getting, as if I've done something *verrry* clever, landed me a *catch*."

Sam drove along in silence awhile, then finally asked, "What would they have done if you'd brought home a black man?"

Jolie quit smiling at that. "I'd never bring a black man to Hendrix," she told him flatly, with a finality that was startling.

"Why *not?*"

She'd lost her good humor and shook her head. "It'd be—" She paused, but didn't finish. "It wouldn't work."

"Why not? There are plenty of rich black men in Miami."

"It ain't about money—"

Sam cut her off. "But you said—"

*"No,"* she insisted with an abrupt, almost ill-temper. "I *never* said it was about money. I said . . ." She paused. "Oh, never mind. I can't explain Hendrix to outsiders. It's hopeless."

Sam was a little hurt that he—who'd been told how beloved he was by the locals—was now too *outside* to matter, to even comprehend the inside. He drove in silence down the wilderness highway, close to Hendrix now, almost to the church, and finally said, "Well, it's hard for me to believe that the *Sisters* are that racist. I've been here three months and haven't heard them rage on the local blacks—"

"That's because there aren't any," Jolie told him bluntly. "There haven't been, for a long time." She made one last attempt to explain. "They just grew up in a different day, Sam. I mean, Sister Noble, she's eighty-two. She remembers when they used to have Commemoration Day in Cleary, when the old vets from the Civil War used to march through town in their uniforms, the Klan marching by their side."

Jolie paused, and Sam finally said, "Yeah?"

"Well, they're all like that—Uncle Ott and Uncle Earl and Daddy. They've lived through a lot. To them, racial things—they're not far removed, some historical footnote, but close, *really* close."

"So you're excusing them for being racist because they're old? Because they saw the Klan march through town?"

Jolie was capable of a fierce protectiveness toward her father and the old folk at Bethel, and a steely edge crept into her voice. "I'm not excusing *anything.* I'm just trying to— Listen, have you ever heard of something they used to have around here called slavery?"

Sam pretended to think hard. "Oh, yeah. I think I read a line or two about it at UF. I think they had a war over it."

She ignored the sarcasm. "Yeah, they did. And they *lost* a war over it, too. Did I ever mention that my Big Mama, she lived in a slave cabin?"

"A *slave* cabin? How old *was* your Big Mama?"

He said it as a small joke, though Jolie didn't smile, but answered with a straight, set face, "She was born in 1899, as a matter of fact. But you know, Sam, it was a funny thing about the war—they didn't come in and bulldoze the slave cabins the minute it was over. They left 'em stand around here. They found 'em mighty useful, believe *me*."

"So what are you saying?" he asked as he pulled to a halt in the drive.

"I'm saying that Big Mama, she lived in this rinky-dink little slave shack on and off for *years*—a lot of people did, raised a lot of children in 'em—and it was *nasty*, makes Daddy's old shed look like a *mansion*. I mean, to them slavery isn't some far-off thing. It's real—a live, *strange* thing. It's the reason I'd never bring a black man to Hendrix."

Jolie said it with rare passion, yanking up her book bag and opening the door with a jerk, her face down, more flushed and furious than the argument warranted.

Sam called for her to stop, but she kept going, so quickly that he was barely able to catch her. "Why are you so pissed? I'm the one who should be mad. I'm the token Jew."

But she refused to be drawn out and felt for her house key with a distracted "Nothing. I'm just sick of talking about it. Listen, I got a thousand things to do—I need to get moving. I'll call you in the morning," she promised as she unlocked the door.

"You don't need me to help?"

She made a noise at the word. "No. You've *helped* enough. You've helped *plenty*."

"What the hell does that mean?"

"Nothing," she murmured, then unbent enough to add, "Just do me a favor, Sam, and don't get too moon-eyed over the Hoyts, and Hendrix, and our *glorious* past."

She said it with such bitterness that Sam repeated, "What the *hell's* got into you?"

"Nothing's got into me. I just can't believe you been here this long, and talked and talked, to everybody, and you still don't git it."

"I git that I love you," he mimicked with a chin-out belligerence.

She didn't react to it at all, only looked at him with pity. "Yeah? And since when has love done anything for anybody in Hendrix—but make more gheechies, and more shacks, and more raggedy-ass children in the free-lunch line?" She didn't wait on his answer, just hoisted her book bag to her shoulder. "Thanks for the ride." Just like that, the door shut; she was gone.

# Chapter Seven

It was their first (and only) fight, one that kept Sam tossing and turning most of the night, as a fast-moving front dipped down from the Carolinas and collided with the warm Gulf winds, producing thunder and lightning worthy of Zeus. In an hour, the blanket of humidity that tented the river was blown away, replaced with the kind of dry, brisk air he used to lie in bed and dream of back in August. Even then he couldn't sleep, but lay there in his narrow, little bunk and tried to pinpoint exactly what he'd said that had set Jolie off. He hadn't been paying that much attention, hadn't meant to insult the old Sisters, though he was disappointed that their acceptance of him was based on little more than a racial stereotype. Jolie might think it odd and charming, but he knew from experience that such generalizations were shifting sands, that it only took one wrong move by him for them to go from happy acceptance of the Rich Jew to seething contempt for the Shifty Jew, the Cheap Yid—the possibilities were endless.

The more he thought about it, the madder he got, and not until almost dawn did he finally get to sleep, only to be wakened at first light by a savage pounding on the door, and a rough, unfamiliar voice calling, "Sam? Sam Lense? Boy, *git* yo ass out here, right now!"

Some primeval part of his brain must have been expecting such a thing, as he hit the floor running, pulling on pants and searching for a weapon, wondering how close Vic Lucas would be that time of the day.

Whoever was pounding on the door—and there was more than one from the sound of it—meant business, and with no place to hide he braced himself in the flimsy doorframe, then kicked it open with one mighty blow.

There was a fast, solid thud and a yelp of pain from someone behind the door, but he didn't stop to investigate. He bounded out, taking five gazelle leaps toward the road before he saw Lena standing aside, laughing, in jeans and a fuzzy lime-green sweater, Jolie beside her, looking not nearly as amused, also in jeans, and an oversize flannel shirt she'd filched from him the week before. "It's a joke!" Lena cried, then said to someone behind the door, "Are you all right?"

The flimsy trailer door swung shut and a good-size young man stood, yelping profanity and clutching his right hand. "Damn, son, you nearly took my hand off."

"Lucky he didn't take your head off," Jolie observed drily, then introduced them offhandedly, a little distracted, "Sam, this is the Idiot Carl. Carl, Sam."

He was larger in person than he'd appeared in his high school pictures, clearly his father's son in size, six-two, well over two hundred pounds, with the Hoyt eyes, braced with good-natured laugh lines and ruler-straight brows.

He seemed to bear Sam no ill will for his injured hand, just flexed it a couple of times, then held it out for a shake. "Pleased to meet you," he said, his smile, when he finally bestowed it, as charming as his sister's.

Sam shook hands by rote, still a little shaken, then was enveloped in one of Lena's tight spider hugs, and her run of piping chatter: "I never got home at all last night—stopped at Jolie's to help her cook—like, sixty people are coming. I told Big Daddy—you need to divide and conquer next year. People'll have to eat on the porch. . . ."

She was clearly excited by Carl's return, her face high-colored, her eyes as light as a child's at Christmas. She might have stood there, with

Sam in his boxers, and talked till lunch if Jolie hadn't intervened with a glance at her watch.

"Lena—baby, you better go get the ice. Make it twenty pounds," she told them as they departed. "We'll pick you up in the truck. Ten minutes. Hurry."

Sam went inside and sat down on the unmade bed, Jolie following, closing the door behind her and apologizing for her brother. "I'm sorry I'm kin to such an imbecile. If I'd have known he was going to do that, I'd a left him home. And I'm sorry I was so grouchy yesterday. It's too much, feeding all the Hoyts at one go. It always gets me on edge." When Sam still didn't speak, she asked, "Are you all right?"

He looked at her. "That scared the *hell* out of me."

Jolie tried not to smile, but it was hard; he looked too annoyed, positively pouting. "Well, I told you I was sorry. He's a big practical joker, my brother. It's one of his annoying traits. One of *many.*"

"And I'm not a rich *Jew,*" Sam added with that same petulance. "I been thinking about it all night, and it really *pisses* me off."

Jolie tried even harder not to smile. "I never said you were. And I told you it'd make you mad."

He lay back on the bed and rubbed his eyes. "Well, how would you like it if my brothers said I was marrying you for your *tits?*"

Jolie finally smiled and lay beside him. "I'll give you fifty dollars if that ain't *exactly* what they say, the minute they lay eyes on me. Or think it, anyway."

Sam covered his face with his pillow. "Well, I'm not going to anybody else's house for supper. And I'm not taking any more *cheese.*"

She got the pillow away from him and kissed him, long and light. "That'll teach 'em to mess with old Sam Lense," she murmured.

He lost his ill-humor pretty quickly and was trying to roll her into place, but she wiggled away. "No—not now. No time. I need to go by the IGA for Jell-O—and I have to get home and check on the turkey. D'you want to meet the Hoyts smelling like sperm? And they're coming right back—"

He obeyed, albeit reluctantly, asking as he dressed, "Well, what's got into Lena? She's like a kid in a candy store."

"She and Carl are back on." Jolie perched on the edge of the bed and not looking too happy about the reunion. "She pulled in at midnight; kept me up half the night yammering about it. Claims he popped the question and she said yes."

"To marriage?" Sam felt for his shoes. "Isn't that kind of quick?"

"They've been dating since Lena was fourteen."

"That is barbaric," he muttered offhandedly.

"That is Hendrix," Jolie answered drily, as if stating an equal fact.

The house was already full when they got home. The tiny living room, dining room, kitchen, and both porches were cramped with a collection of rickety, mismatched church tables and equally ancient folding chairs, so flimsy that the buffalo-size patriarchs deemed them unfit for use. "Baby, thet thang'll fold like a pocketknife, I set my fat tail on it," her uncle James complained when Jolie tried to seat him in the dining room.

She redirected him to the living room, where her father and three of his brothers ate dinner sitting squashed on the groaning, old sofa, four abreast, using their shelflike bellies to rest their plates. In a tradition as old as the river, the men ate first, with the women serving, and the children sometimes not eating till a third or fourth seating (inspiring the old advice: take a cold potato and wait). The only modern concession to this ancient custom was that female outsiders—girlfriends and miscellaneous pickups—were allowed to eat with their dates, though this was a relatively new twist, and if any of the men needed something not in immediate view—pepper sauce or ice or extra napkins—they had no compunction in sending any available woman to the kitchen to fetch it, even if they didn't know her name (*sweetheart* and *baby girl* would suffice).

Lena was the only woman in the dining room, though squeezed between the china cabinet and table, and the role of maidservant fell to her, not just for Carl, but every other man in the room. On her fourth trip to the kitchen to refill tea glasses or fetch ice or pepper sauce, Jolie gave her the same advice she'd given her the night before when she'd announced her engagement: "Run for your life."

Lena laughed, as she was in her element, basking in the glow of Carl's renewed attention in a way that made Jolie want to strangle her. Jolie was equally annoyed at her slightly disheveled fiancé, who for all his bold socialist ways seemed to be fitting like a hand in a glove into the old Hoyt caste system, sitting at Carl and Lena's table and, from all appearances, having the time of his life, laughing his ass off at all the usual Hoytling banter.

It began the moment Carl walked in, as he was considered as spoiled as Jolie and was the target of a lot of in-family needling. After a great bear hug of greeting, his cousin Ricky bellowed, "Carl, son, look at you! Ye're gitting fat as yer daddy."

Carl was as used to the dozen as Jolie and hadn't blinked an eye, but patted his stomach with good-natured resignation, telling him, "Yeah, well, you know the Hoyts, Rick. We git old, we go fat or ugly. And we can *sho* see which way you went."

So it went, all afternoon long, this back-and-forth needling that Jolie was frequently drawn into. She was considered famously spoiled where women's work was concerned, and whenever she showed her face in the dining room, one or another of her cousins would pause in his teeth-picking to call, "Jo*lee*? Shug? Would you git me some mo' tea?"

She answered with flipped birds that they gleefully reported to her father, calling, "Uncle Ray? Yo daughter's making them obscene gestures behind yo back agin," all in a tone of teasing hilarity, nothing serious. Uncle Ray had made his bones in Hendrix years ago, and even as a stoop-shouldered, gray-haired old man, he wasn't anyone you'd care to cross, especially in the matter of his darling Jo*lee*.

Sam watched it all with great enjoyment, as the Hoyts were good for entertainment value, if nothing else, their fast, high drawls more turnip than julep, their physical presence a lively thing, full of slaps, pokes, and bellows of laughter. As Jolie had warned, they were dressed for the hunt in boots and camo, and full of macho swagger, bragging about bucks and points and tossing off racial invective so casually that it almost seemed like vaudeville. It was as if they were playing the part of the trash-talking redneck as Carl had that morning at the river, in a merry, green-eyed jest. ("You want Cracker? We'll give you *Cracker*.")

When they were done eating, they finally released the table to the womenfolk and retired to the front porch so they could sip a little dessert whiskey from quietly passed pocket flasks and smoke hand-rolled Bugler cigarettes. Sam cared for neither, but joined them there to listen to their roll of fast, semi-understandable conversation, beginning to wonder if he should relinquish the Muskogee Creek to the titled historians and do his thesis on these, their lesser known, mixed-blood cousins.

Once they had a little liquor in them, they were happy to talk race, jovially and openly, the younger men trotting out all the old myths of origin, mostly to do with the Black Irish and Black Dutch. The older men weren't so sanguine about such open disclosure, and Ray's oldest brother, the wheezing Uncle Earl, denied any aboriginal blood at all.

Sam listened impassively, arms crossed on his chest, and commented, "Pure white," in answer.

He was quoting the oral histories of the Croatan Indians, who self-described in such a way in their fight for separate schools in the early part of the century. He didn't mean to offend, but got a hard look from the old man and a hoot of laughter from the younger in response, as if he'd said something audaciously clever.

Before anyone could speak, Brother Hoyt had jumped in to explain to his brothers—all nearly as deaf as Ott—that Sam was going to school at the university, studying the Indians in the Forest.

The old men reacted with looks of blank astonishment to this odd pronouncement, one of them asking with apparent sincerity if he'd found any.

"Oh, yeah," Sam assured him. "Twenty-seven families, all legal and supported, winging their way to the museum as we speak—including the Hoyts, who are Creek through the Ammons line, which is nice, because they were matrilineal—the Creek."

They nodded in silent amazement at the strange bit of news and spoke no more of it, as the short autumn afternoon was already losing its brightness, the sun west of the old cemetery across the highway, casting the Spanish moss in long shadow. The young men soon loaded up and returned to the woods for one more run with the dogs before it got dark. The old men were too old for such nonsense and sat in their rockers and ironed out the last-minute details of their annual Thanksgiving trip to the family fish camp, four miles south of the public landing. The weatherman in Panama City was predicting frost before sunrise, but the old diehards still planned to take the boats out, gamely inviting Sam along, promising him catfish and reds, trout to die for, "cooked on a spit, just like the old days."

Sam didn't require much persuasion as the Hoyt Camp was a local legend, so far down the river that it was only accessible by boat. This was the home of all-night poker games and a particularly potent moonshine flavored with blood oranges, called Bounce (because one sip of it would bounce you on your ass). He was game for a firsthand look, thinking he might talk one of them into wading into the woods to the edge of Camp Six, so he could try to locate the exact location of old Morris's store.

When he went to the kitchen and told Jolie, she rounded on him with the same sharpness she'd rounded on her cousins. "You are *not*."

Sam might have contracted a small case of testosterone poisoning from his afternoon in the company of the Hoyts, as he snapped back, "I am *so*. I've been here three months, haven't fished yet. And I'm here to study the Creek."

Jolie's only helper was one of her uncle Earl's great-granddaughters, a spunky blond eight-year-old named Ashley, who was drying a plate with a dish towel. She looked about as thrilled as Jolie with the Hoyt division of labor and piped up in a quarrelsome voice, "Pawpaw says we're Cherokee."

"Pawpaw's an idiot," Sam murmured. Then, to Jolie: "We'll be back tomorrow, or Saturday. Ott says we need to leave—have to get there before dark."

She didn't seem to have heard him, but absently wiped her hands. "Does Deddy know?"

Sam rolled his eyes. "I'm twenty-four, Jolie. I don't have to ask *Deddy's* permission to go fishing."

She blinked at the mimic, then pinned him with a cold eye. "Well, good. Have fun. I hope you freeze your ass off."

Ashley laughed, though Sam set his jaw. "Good. I will," he said, and left Jolie to the pans, the front-porch screen slapping shut behind him after a moment with a solid thwack.

Jolie didn't go after him, just returned to the dishes with her face carefully lowered so Ashley wouldn't see her tears and run to tell Uncle Ray or her pawpaw that Jolie and Sam had a fight; that Jolie was standing in the kitchen crying. She just thanked Ashley for helping, then sent her away. Jolie was not only tired, but sadder than sad, tears of outrage beginning to run down her cheeks in quiet little rivulets.

She was careful to wipe them away before anyone saw them, the house empty when Lena wandered in an hour later and found Jolie still working on the last of the dishes, the counters piled high with all manner of plates and pans and turkey utensils. Lena knew she was in trouble the moment she saw her. "My gosh, Jol—you're still at it? Where's Sam?"

"He's going to the fish camp," Jolie answered in a small voice, making no more of it, though Lena was enough of an insider to understand the significance of this event and raised her eyebrows in surprise.

"Does your daddy know?" At Jolie's brief shake of her head, Lena asked with a mischievous grin, "Want me to run out to the shed and tell 'im?"

Jolie shook her head and concentrated on the dishes, till Lena detected the tears, which she found alarming, as Jolie never cried, never. Not when she didn't make National Honor Society (though she had the grade point), not even when her mother died (or so claimed Carl). Lena took Jolie by her shoulders and pulled her away from the sink, told her,

"Come on, Jol. What's he gonna do at the camp tonight with that old pack of geezers? Play poker? Drink beer—or, horror of horrors, find one of those ancient old titty magazines in the john?"

Jolie didn't smile at the gibe, just wiped her face on the hem of her apron. "I asked him not to go."

"Well, he can't help himself. When men get a pack like this—going fishing, going hunting, playing football—they turn into wolves, all stay together. Let him spend the night *on* the water, instead of *by* the water, and he'll get a little inkling of the price you pay to run with the Hoyt pack. He'll probably go to the altar Sunday, get saved. Just think how the Sisters will shout—a *sinner* from the fish camp comes *home*."

Jolie finally smiled at that, and Lena gave her a friendly shake. "Go to bed. I'll finish up here. You don't look so hot."

"I don't feel so hot."

"Then get some rest. We'll go to Dothan tomorrow for the big Christmas sale at Belk's; eat trout amandine with the old folk at Morrison's. '*K?*"

Jolie was too tired to argue and nodded wordlessly as she untied her apron and handed it over, then thanked Lena and went down the hall to bed, almost bumping into Sam as he came around the corner in a jog. His face was red-tipped from the cold, harassed but conciliatory. "Are you all right? We're pulling out—but I won't go if you're gonna get mad."

Jolie was relieved to tears that he'd cared enough to come back. She gripped him in a tight hug, her eyes closed at his chest. "I'm not mad. Just be careful. Be careful. It's a dangerous place," she whispered, barely audible. For a moment she stood there, holding him tight, then stepped back and wiped her eyes. "Did you bring your coat? It'll be freezing on the water."

"There's no time," he said, backing to the front door, which was open to the screen, the front yard full of brake lights and boat lights, everyone all packed and ready to pull out, apparently waiting for Sam. "I'll be all right," he assured her, though Jolie wasn't so sure.

"This camp isn't *by* the water—it's *on* the water," she tried to explain, but he wouldn't listen, just called and waved, told her he'd be fine; he'd be home in the morning.

Jolie didn't argue, just ran to the hall closet and pulled out her father's fishing coat—an olive-drab, army-issue field jacket with his Social Security number inked on the top seam that he'd been issued by the quartermaster in Germany in 1946. It was lined and waterproof, and she hastily yanked it off a hanger and took it to the porch in a run, but they were already pulling out on the highway, headed for the landing.

"You're gonna freeze!" she called. "Take Daddy's coat!"

But he either didn't hear her or didn't think he needed it, and the line of lights and boats and blinkers continued out, leaving Jolie on the porch in the raw, November twilight, the worn, old soldier's coat gripped in her hands. She stood there till their brake lights were nothing more than pinpoints of red in the gray, then went back in the empty house to the kitchen, where Lena was drying the church coffeemaker.

She looked happy and industrious in her damp apron and asked cheerfully, "Does the punch bowl go back to the church? Or in the china cabinet?"

"The church," Jolie answered dimly. "Sam went to the camp without a coat. It's already misting out there—he'll catch pneumonia."

Her leap to the catastrophic was so sincere that it struck Lena as hilarious, making her laugh as she set the old percolator on the table. "You know, Jol, in some cultures women actually enjoy being *young,* and in *love.* It actually seems to make them *happy.*"

Jolie understood Lena was trying to tease her out of her funk, but was too tired to one-up with a one-liner and answered honestly, if wearily, "In *some* cultures, the women aren't from Hendrix."

# Chapter Eight

Lena's laughter followed Jolie down the hallway to her bedroom, which was much as she had left it the day before yesterday. She wanted to take a bath and wash off the smell of turkey and gravy and hard labor, but was too tired to undress. She lay back on the spread and, after a moment, flipped up a corner of the spread to cover her; it was getting so cold so quickly. Her last thought before sleep was curiosity at how quickly the weather had changed, how swiftly it'd gone from sticky humid heat to a sharp autumn chill and now, in the space of two days, was almost down to ice.

She fell asleep quickly and slept so soundly that she was oblivious to the rest of the house: to Lena and Carl drying dishes in the kitchen, discussing their evening plans, and her father, who came inside when the cold drove him in at nine, the temperature dropping so sharply that he lit the furnace for the first time that year before going to bed. The dense, smoky smell of heating oil woke Jolie up before midnight, no longer lying on the spread, but under a blanket, her shoes on the floor at her feet. She didn't know how she got there, just felt for her bedside clock and saw the time. She thought about going to the kitchen and calling Lena to see if they'd got the coat to Sam, but she was too tired to worry with it, too warm and snug in her covers.

She turned over and went back to sleep but was awakened sometime after by a hammering on her window, and a hoarse voice, calling through the glass, "Jolie! Wake up! *Jol!*"

At first, she thought it was a dream, a mental replay of the morning, of Carl and his fake redneck roust. She sat up, blinking, and realized it wasn't a dream. She was lying on her bed in a dark bedroom, dressed and rumpled from a day's cooking, and a pale face at the window hissed, "Jolie! Come round and open the *damn* door!"

It was Carl, standing on the propane tank, calling her from her bed to unlock the front door, as he had done many a time before. She was stupid with sleep and rolled out with a curse and made her way through the dark house, annoyed and resigned, thrown back in time to their early teenage years, when Carl's life was full of small emergencies that had to be shielded from their father's eyes. He was waiting at the door, as usual, impatient and mumbling, yanking at the door before she had it unchained.

"Hold on," she fussed, fumbling with the chain, then stepping back sharply as Carl burst in, bringing a blast of freezing night air, Lena sagging at his side.

"Git her," he snapped.

Jolie jumped to catch Lena before she fell. They managed to steady her between them, a light enough weight, though hardly on her feet. "Will you *ever* grow up?" Jolie whispered to Carl as she helped him half drag, half carry Lena to her bedroom, Jolie's voice low, so as not to wake their father.

Carl didn't deign to answer. He got Lena as far as the bed, then disappeared back down the hallway, leaving Jolie to kneel in front of her and pat her cold cheek. "Lena? Are you okay? Have you been drinking? Your hands are like *ice*." Carl returned with an armful of towels that Jolie snatched from his hands. "If she's drunk, Daddy's gonna *have* your *hide*. You are *messed* up in the *head*—you know that?"

"She ain't drunk," Carl whispered as he stripped her wet sweater over her head. "She's wet as a salamander and freezing to damn death. God, it's turned cold; turned on a dime," he muttered, yanking the covers to

Lena's neck, then starting for the door. "Meet me at the truck, and git yer coat. It's cold as hell; bridge is iced." He was halfway through the doorway when he realized Jolie hadn't moved. He came back far enough to snap, "It's your *boyfriend,* okay? He's in town—come on." Then Carl was gone, his footsteps padding down the hallway to the living room, then out the door.

Jolie was too paralyzed to follow. She just knelt there, Lena's wet sweater in hand, till she heard the crack of the screen door. She came to her feet in a scramble and stumbled barefoot through the dark house to the shock of the cold porch. Carl was parked across the street at the church, intentionally trying for dimness, only his brake lights lit, his face hard in the green glow of the dash. Jolie raced across the cold asphalt and yanked open the door, shaking so hard she could barely get it shut.

"Where?" she chattered.

"In the ER, in Cleary," Carl answered as he wheeled around to the highway. "Shot in the back. Damn near dead."

He struck off the words with such stone-faced composure that Jolie didn't believe him. She sat there, staring, then burst out in unrestrained fury, "Will you *quit* with these *dumb*-ass jokes, *Carl*? He didn't go *hunting*! They didn't take *guns!*"

"It's no damn *joke,*" he snapped, his eyes locked on the thin line of highway that he sailed along at ninety. "We found him by the dock— barely got him to town—Jesus, he was bleeding," he murmured, so blunt and merciless that Jolie realized he was by God telling the truth; it wasn't a joke.

She asked for no more details, could stand no more details, her nails biting into her hands as they flew down the dark highway, tears running down her face unheeded, till they jerked to a halt in the bright tinsel light of the Cleary ER. She was half out the door before Carl stopped her, gripping her arm and telling her across the seat in a low, quick voice, "If anybody asks, it was a stray shot, Jol. A poacher or a drunk—you hear me?"

She nodded numbly, then scrambled out in her jeans and bare feet, across the cold, snagged concrete to the fluorescent glory of the sliding doors. The merciless light showed Carl to be wildly disheveled, covered head to hands in a film of gray river muck that stiffened his hair and gave his eyes a wild, minstrel whiteness. The receptionist stopped him at the counter, but Jolie would not be slowed, ignoring her to pass through the sliding doors to the inner sanctum of the hospital, as quiet and pale as a ghost. She passed row after row of examining rooms, white and stark and empty, till she came upon a gurney in a back hallway, momentarily abandoned by the nurses, the patient swathed to the neck in white blankets, and hooked to dangling transfusion and antibiotic bags.

It was Sam, obviously in the middle of transport—to surgery or another floor, or maybe the morgue. It was hard to tell which, he was so pale, so utterly bleached, his chest motionless beneath the covers, only the monitor humming with a faint, reassuring beat. She approached him slowly, halting at the edge of the bed and gripping the cold metal rails with tight, white knuckles, wondering what madness had possessed her to keep him in Hendrix so long, to open its mysteries and expose him to such risk?

Was it love or loneliness or sheer desperation that had stopped her from pulling him aside that very first night at the café and giving him the same heartfelt advice that she'd given Lena the night before: to get out while he could.

To run for his life. *Run for his life.*

# Chapter Nine

Sam Lense knew nothing of the guns or shots or the hysteria that had taken hold of his friends that night in Hendrix. His most lasting memory of the evening was the ferociousness of the swollen river, which bore little resemblance to the broad, placid friend he had been camping beside for the past three months. This was another river altogether, black and impenetrable, the current racing by as fast as a Formula One racer when they finally made it to the galvanized-tin roofs that marked the Hoyt fish camp.

As the junior member of the crew, he was the lucky bastard who got to jump out of the boat and secure them to a makeshift floating dock in a primeval wilderness so thick you couldn't see your hands in front of you. He knew that one wrong step and he'd fall headlong into the running current, would be fifty feet downstream before he could so much as lift his face and gurgle for help. On Ott's shouted advice, he tied one end of a rope to the post, then wound the other end tight around his hand for balance. With one foot on the shifting dock, one on the boat, he helped the old men onto the dock, one at a time, for which they thanked him, politely and sincerely, then quickly disappeared up the bank on a squelching mud path and left the unloading to the youngster (which was the very reason they went to the trouble every year of charming one into tagging along, to take care of such nasty chores).

As Sam wrestled with the ropes and the slippery boards and the razor cut of the freezing wind, he cursed himself for getting caught up in this macho bullshit, for being too proud to borrow a coat for a trip to the river on the coldest night of the year. Finally, after a good half hour of weaving and ducking, and several stumbles that almost landed him in the water, he got the last box unloaded and started for the camp with the fitful beam of a small AA flashlight. He could barely make out the dull metal sheen of the roof of the main cabin in the clearing ahead, the path so slick and wet and laced with cypress roots that he had to keep his face down, to keep from stumbling. He'd finally made it to the high end of the path, at the clearing that marked the actual Hoyt camp—then, with no interval, no pause at all, he was lying flat on his back in a cold, white room that somehow seemed an extension of the woods. It was as cold, maybe even colder.

Whenever he floated into consciousness, he kept wishing he'd listened to Jolie and stayed home. He berated himself for disagreeing with her, was tormented by strange, vivid dreams of the river, where he'd be huddled in the low-riding boat, whipped and tormented by the icy wind. He could see Jolie up ahead, sometimes sitting on the prow of the boat, but usually standing at the edge of the woods, her face sad and set, disappointed in him. He sometimes tried to call out, to tell her she was right, that he shouldn't have come out on the river in nothing but a sweatshirt on such a night. But in the strange and immutable laws of his dreamworld, he couldn't. She was always ahead of him somewhere, close and present, but voiceless.

He could never lay hands on her, even in his dreams.

When he finally came to himself, he was in a different room on another floor, this one warmer and darker, much better. He didn't dream here as much, but slept real sleep and woke up with a small amount of strength, enough to ask, what had happened to him? Where *was* he?

For he'd forgotten the woods by then, and the high river and his footing in the slippery mud; had forgotten about Jolie and the grimed, weed-choked cemeteries of Spanish West Florida. He was in suburban

Miami and everything around him smelled and sounded like the city: the Cuban nurse who changed his IV, the Dominican lab tech who came and took his blood, his large and extended family, who watched him with anxious eyes, told him he'd had an accident. An awful accident.

"Did I wreck a car?" he remembered asking his aunt, who gripped his hand and smiled a brittle smile.

"Save your strength, Sammy. You're fine. You're strong. You'll be home soon."

That was the tone of the conversation, saying everything and saying nothing. His father, Leonard Lense, was a hovering, grim presence, devoted to Sam's comfort, but obviously a man with a grievance, who was charming to the nurses, but otherwise incommunicado. He was formidable by nature—bald and bullet-headed and never the kind of person who suffered fools gladly, even if they were his sons.

He wouldn't speak of the Mysterious Accident at all, and Sam's usually straight-shooting brothers followed suit, filling their visits with a lightweight chitchat that was bizarre and disorienting. They offered no explanation for his excruciating chest, or the grid of stitches that itched like a son of a bitch, till one of his nephews slipped up and told him that he'd been in a hunting accident; that he had been shot.

"A *hunting* accident? When did I go *hunting*?" he muttered, unable to imagine how he, Samuel Bernard Lense, had taken up hunting in Coral Gables without even realizing it.

Only when he was moved to a regular floor at Baptist Hospital and the opiates were curtailed did he begin piecing together memories of his last days in Hendrix, of Thanksgiving at the Hoyts', of going to the river—not to hunt, but to fish. Jolie hadn't wanted him to go.

"You'll freeze your ass off," she had warned, and so he had.

When his father dropped by that night, Sam was happy to report that he hadn't been in a hunting accident because he had never gone *hunting*, though his father seemed resistant to the logic of the argument and nodded casually, and tried to change the subject. But Sam was strong enough to have begun putting pieces of the puzzle together and insisted on talking about his concern not for his own mangled chest, but Jolie: Where was she? Was she *mad* at him? Because he kinda remembered her being mad.

He asked everyone who walked in the door—nurses, dietitians, and especially his family, who seemed not the least bit troubled about the girl. There seemed to be an understanding among them that Sam was weak and not himself, and not responsible for his pleas and threats and raging insistence that, *no,* she wasn't some casual girlfriend! They were in love! They were engaged! He'd spoken to her father! He had called them from a pay phone at the campground! Didn't any of you lying, dumb-ass idiots remember *anything*?

He was so weak that for the first time in his life he was prone to tears of frustration when his family mildly shook their heads, arguing in the most reasonable fashion if he was sure he had been that serious with a young girl he hardly knew? Who never called or came to see him? Sam had no answer, but lay back, rubbed his chest, and tried to call information. But he found that his wallet and his checkbook had fallen into the same black hole as the rest of the year, with no explanations from his family, only forced smiles and sidestepped questions.

He accepted then that he was a prisoner in his own home and quit begging for information, quit appearing to think of Jolie at all. He ate whatever was set before him and steadily gained strength. He talked to his father about taking a new direction in life, thought about getting out of anthropology and maybe applying for law school. It was nonsense, of course, but enough of a red herring that his family began to believe he was moving on, showing a little common sense at last. He worked hard to keep it that way, called admissions at FAU and UM to ask about schedules and requirements, fees and financial aid. He brought up UF, as if in afterthought, said he needed to talk to Professor Keyes, see what credit he could salvage.

"At least then I won't have wasted a whole year," he told them.

His father offered to drive him to Gainesville, though Sam waved him aside, said he'd driven there plenty of times, he knew the way. He asked to borrow his father's car and his credit card bright and early one Monday morning, assured him that he'd pay him back—and once he got on the road, he stayed on I-95 all the way to Jacksonville. He turned west then on I-10 for the long trek to Hendrix, desperate to see Jolie and find out what the hell happened that night in the woods. One minute he'd been trying to find a footing on a slippery path; next minute, boom, his life was gone.

It was eating him alive, the fear, the loneliness, the not-knowing. It was all enough to keep him strong and determined, at least till he got as far as the Chattahoochee foothills, when his hands began to sweat and his head pound, signaling the beginning of a fever. He fought it for a few miles, but finally had to pull over into a rest station by the river. He took a couple of Percocet and lay down in the front seat, thinking that maybe a nap would help. When he woke up, he was flat on his back in yet another antiseptic-smelling hospital room, his mother sitting in a visitor's chair at his side.

He started apologizing immediately for lying to them, for being such a pain in the ass, but his mother would hear none of it. "Save your strength, Sammy," she told him as she set aside her magazine and took his hand. "Your father's upset. He'll get over it. He went to the hotel to sleep. A patrolman found you on the interstate, unconscious. You have a little fever, a reset rib; nothing serious."

Sam didn't argue, lay back and stared at the ceiling, didn't offer another word, till a solution suddenly came to him, so startling that he sat up and looked his mother in the eye and asked for a favor.

One small favor, and he wouldn't go sneaking off again, he wouldn't lie, he'd apologize to his father. He'd pay him back, every cent.

"What?"

Sam was energized by her acknowledgment and asked, "Could you run a line on Jolie—get her home number? I didn't have a phone up there, never got her number, but you don't understand—something must have happened to her. That's why she hasn't called, hasn't come to see me. I'm afraid that whoever did this"—he pressed his chest—"they

could have—I don't know. I don't know what happened to anything—
Jolie, or the camper, my clothes. They're still on the river, at the KOA."

She wasn't sure what had become of Jolie, but his mother could have
told him about the camper if she'd been of a mind: his father and brothers had gone up while he was still in intensive care and towed it home.
It was sitting in his uncle Dan's backyard this minute, full of Sam's
books and papers and (oh, yes) his stash of condoms he must have been
using on his good Christian girl, the preacher's daughter (and, oy, what
was he thinking? And so forth). But she was a tough cookie, was Aida
Lense—the daughter of Jewish Colombian parents, who'd started her
career as a social worker in South Brooklyn before moving to Miami in
'52, where she had worked her way high up the masthead of the Florida
HRS.

She had a reputation as a tough boss, but a fair one, who'd been married to the same man for thirty-seven years and had raised three fine sons
in the public schools: an orthodontist, a lawyer, and a dumb ass, the
dumb ass being the youngest, who was lying on the bed beside her. He
was also (possibly) her favorite, the dreamer who'd drifted around UF for
three years before he'd settled on anthropology for his master's, for what
reason, his father and she had yet to fathom.

She made no comment on the camper, just told him she'd run a line
on his friend, track her down through the state computers, if he, Sam,
promised on her eyes that he wouldn't go up there alone anymore. That
he'd take his father, his brother, his uncle—would take his mother, if
that's the best he could do.

"Not alone," she insisted. "It's enough, Sam, what's happened. You've
lied to your father, returned to that place behind his back. It's enough."

Sam respected his mother as a woman of her word and agreed, told
her where Jolie could be found, with an excitement that energized him.
He made his apologies to his father that afternoon sincere and compelling. The drive back to Miami was a much more pleasant affair, the elder
Lenses beginning to see a light at the end of this tunnel in their son's
return to normalcy.

On Monday morning, his mother took an early break and shut her office door and ran a line on the Hoyts, as promised. The daughter hadn't had much contact with the state, but her father was easy to trace, firmly entrenched in Social Security and, ah, yes—his phone number listed in Hendrix, Florida, a street address, a zip code; everything. She slipped the file in her purse, didn't mention the matter to Len, just left work early that afternoon, and found Sam sitting in his father's easy chair, watching daytime television, still thin and shallow to her eye.

She tossed the folder to his lap when she came in, along with a warning that he "keep it to himself," then went and changed into a robe and house shoes, as she did every night. When she came back to the living room, he was already on the phone, talking to someone, his face perfectly white, the color of notebook paper.

It was too much for any mother, seeing him that way, and she didn't worry with supper, went outside, and watered her hibiscus, was still there when Len came home from work at five. She kept him outside as long as she could, then went back inside, but couldn't find Sam anywhere—on the phone or in his room. She finally heard the shower in the bathroom, wondered what was up, wondered whether she was in for another long drive upstate.

Aida sent Len to the store for a roast chicken for dinner, then pounded on the door of the bathroom, called, "Sam! Open up," till he finally appeared in the door, emaciated, red-eyed, clearly in bad shape.

She was wondering if Len hadn't been right all along, if she'd been a foolish woman to reconnect her son to this nightmare, but tried to smile for his sake. "So? What's the news? Are we in for another drive upstate, or is . . . over?"

She didn't know any other way to put it, and he didn't correct her: "Over. I guess."

He tried to shut the door, but she wasn't going to let him drop it at that. Shot and left for dead? Engaged to some hillbilly, Sam dropped like a hot potato? So she asked, "She's okay? This girl? She's not hurt? You were so worried. . . ."

He looked as if he'd been hit by a truck, but took care to reassure her, "No. She's—okay. Left for college."

"College," his mother repeated, nodding sagely. "Good. Good." Then, when nothing else came to her, she asked, "UF?"

"No." He prepared to shut the door. "Design school. In Savannah."


Sam hadn't actually spoken with Jolie that afternoon, but with her father. He'd called their home number, not knowing what to expect, though the Old Man hadn't seemed at all surprised when he identified himself, asking in that booming, hillbilly voice, "Well, how's that back of yourn? Them My-amma doctors fix you up?"

The Old Man's concern seemed genuine, and Sam assured him they had.

"Well, good. Glad to hear you're up and about."

Sam had been buoyed by his welcome and had gotten quickly to the point. "Is Jolie there? I need to talk to her."

There was a pause, as if the Old Man were surprised at the question, though he offered easily enough, "Why, naw, son. She ain't here." Then, before Sam could ask: "She went up to Georger, to school."

"To Savannah?"

The Old Man agreed, "Yeah. Up on the coast."

Sam considered asking him if he possibly remembered, way in the back of his mind, a certain conversation in November, when Sam had asked for his daughter's hand in the old-fashioned way, but he couldn't bring himself to do it. He was too proud to baldly ask such a thing, just leaned his forehead against the doorframe and asked if she was living with Lena? In the dorm?

"Naw, son, Lener and Carl, they're gitting married in March—week after her birthday, right here at the house. Dress cost a pretty penny, but you know old Lener—never been one to worry too much with price."

If possible, this good-natured country chitchat struck Sam as more bizarre than his family's single-minded dismissal. It seemed hardly possible that the Hoyts were all so merrily going on with their lives without him, as if he'd actually died on the table, there at Jackson Hospital. But he couldn't say a word about it, to accuse or question. "Well, could I have Jolie's number, so I can call her?"

"Naw, son—she don't have no phone. Usually calls me; ever Sareday night."

The buzzing was beginning to return to Sam's head as he asked, "Well, can I leave her my number? Can you tell her that I need to talk to her—right away?"

"Surely. Hold on. Let me git a pen."

He was gone so long that Sam thought he'd hung up, but he finally came back to the line. Sam painstakingly gave him his number in Miami. "And tell her to call collect," he begged, "anytime," then came to a halt when he realized how pathetic he sounded, like some loser after a hot date, trying to beg some girl into seeing him again. "I was—worried about her," he added helplessly.

The Old Man was quick to reassure him, "Oh, son, don't worry 'bout Jol. Thet's what she always wanted, to go to school. Some girls don't, some do. Jolie did."

"Well, good," Sam said, but his voice sounded hollow, even to his own ears.

He hung up and turned on the shower, trying to buy a little time before his mother launched her full investigation into Jolie's mysterious disappearance. He dreaded it, dreaded having to tell her that, no, Jolie wasn't at the bottom of the Apalachicola, but going to school, just as she always wanted. In his mind's eye, he could see her that first night at the café, her sulky, green-eyed petulance when Lena had explained that Jolie was going to the local community college, where everybody around there went.

"Everybody poor," Jolie had added, and if he hadn't been such a dumb ass, such a horny, lonely idiot, he'd have backed off right then. He would have smelled the psycho bad attitude, the desperation to get out of Hendrix by any means necessary: plane, train, bus, rich Jew—who seemed like a catch, at first, but turned out to be not so rich, after all. Just another guy in need of a pair of pressed pants.

When he finally faced his mother, she knew better than to push too hard, but later that night, his father finally broke down and came to Sam's bedroom to talk to him, going about it with stoic reserve, as Leonard Lense was the product of a closemouthed generation, tough and fair and practical.

He opened his conversation with Sam with his usual abruptness, sitting on the end of the bed, arms crossed over his barrel chest, saying bluntly, "So you went back to that place," speaking of Hendrix as if it were a Land of Golem, of monsters and serpents.

Sam was in no mood to parry, even with the father he loved. He was tired, shot, and too shattered by Jolie's defection to give a shit about defending himself. "I wanted to look around. I could have found his grave. They remembered him—Brother Hoyt did. He called him 'the German.'"

Len's face didn't so much as flinch at this bit of historical update, but he made a noise of wonder. "You think, Sam, we never looked? Your grandfather saw him shot, before his eyes. It blasted his brains all over him. He was dead before he hit the floor."

Sam had been spared the part about the brain splatter and wished his father hadn't mentioned it. A month ago, it would have fascinated him. Now it added to the weight of loss, creating an awful sadness, a free fall of helplessness that made sweat break out on his forehead, as if peaking another fever.

But his father had obviously decided it was time to open up, his face distant, lost in thought as he continued, "They put my grandmother on a train—but wanted Papa to stay; offered him lead horse in the lynching party. He turned them down. He was seventeen, Sam. He never spoke of it except he said it was like his mother died that night, too. She lived to be eighty, but she never smiled again."

Sam remembered his great-grandmother in the faintest of memories, displaced from Florida and set among the concrete of suburban Chicago, where she'd moved after a late remarriage, long before he was born. She had dementia, or Alzheimer's, or some wasting mind disease—or so he'd thought. Maybe it was nothing more than the long hand of violence, the family stain of unresolved grief.

His father noticed the sweat on Sam's brow and finished with his history lesson only to discuss the hunting accident, which maybe hadn't been such an accident, at all. Len didn't think so, and neither did the surgeon.

"How could he tell?" Sam asked, as he had no memory of the day, other than the argument with Jolie.

"Because of the angle of the wound. It wasn't made by a stray shot, a nick from a couple of hundred feet. It was a deliberate single shot from a high-caliber rifle, straight in and out. It was meant to kill. And it almost did."

Sam blinked at Len in the half-light. "Who would have wanted to deliberately shoot me? One of the Hoyts? Is that what you're thinking?"

"I'm accusing no one," Len said, though he wouldn't back off, just told Sam what the official investigation had yielded: absolutely nothing.

They'd appointed a lead detective, and deputies from two counties had been put on the case, along with a man from the Fish and Wildlife Commission who investigated such matters. They knew the old men at the camp—old gator poachers for the most part, who'd fillet anything that got on a hook, but were otherwise harmless. They'd plead ignorance of so much as hearing the shot, and the officers believed them, and without much debate, they'd concluded it was indeed a stray shot by the kind of particularly stupid breed of poacher who came out the first week of the season and got so carried away in the hunt he kept chasing far after dark and sobriety would warrant.

To Sam, the ruling sounded more reasonable than otherwise. It certainly went a long way toward explaining why Jolie had begged him not to go—because it was dangerous down there at night. Too much whiskey. Too many guns. He told his father as much, but Len wasn't buying.

"Sam?" he said, leaning over and speaking to his face. "What are the chances? You go to this microscopic little town looking into a murder— and you get shot yourself? That sound like coincidence to you?"

"Nobody knew. Professor Keyes, Brother Hoyt—not even Jolie."

His father grunted. "Listen to yourself. You sound like a child. You think those people—that town—you think they have *amnesia*? They killed five people, Sam—they hunted them like rabbits, hanged them like dogs, and they *forgot*?"

Sam considered the notion of a collective guilt so consuming it would merit a bullet in his back. He could appreciate how such a ripe, paranoid delusion might keep his father up nights, but to him, it simply didn't ring true.

"It isn't some shameful, buried secret. The Hendrix Lynching—it's well researched. Historians write books about it."

"*Historians* do," his father replied with unwonted sarcasm. "In Hendrix—they never wrote a book. They never *read* a book. They did this"—he nodded at Sam's bandaged chest—"and they didn't blink an eye. You lied to them, Sam," Len said in his single moment of reproach. "You never should have gone there in a lie. No wonder this girl, she isn't returning your calls. You were a fool, Sam—I say that and I love you. Somebody has to," he concluded, fishing a handkerchief from his pocket and blowing his nose, the only sign of the great emotion that had his hands shaking, his eyes red-rimmed and swimming.

Sam hadn't the strength to argue. His absolute sureness rested heavily on his shoulders, as constricting as the maze of healing stitches, making it hard to get a deep breath. Len concluded by adding that the deputies had searched the fish camp for footprints, used casings, but the river was into the floodplain, and if there was any evidence, it was on the bottom of the Gulf of Mexico.

"And there," Len predicted portentously, "it will remain. Trust me, Sam—it is done. Finished. You're lucky you got out alive." Len came ponderously to his feet, then made his first and only comment of Jolie: that he was glad she was out of Hendrix and getting on with her life. "You follow her lead. Go back to school and finish your degree. Forget them people."

When Sam tried to argue, Len had overridden him, not by force, but hard good sense. "*Sam*. They already forgot you."

# Chapter Ten

Jolie Hoyt was neither as close nor as far away as Sam imagined, the trajectory of her life following a path molded by old dysfunction and the twin scourge of Southern daughterhood: obligation and obedience. The obligation was to her father (who deserved it); the obedience was to the Art of Secrecy and Rules of the Double Life—skills she had learned long before she met the likes of Sam Lense, in her hard and solitary childhood there in Hendrix, raised as she was between her father's rock-solid holiness and the town's famed hedonism.

It had produced a bizarre dichotomy of experience, a life of unexplained extremes. One in which she was forbidden to wear makeup or earrings or attend high school dances (all deemed sensual and worldly), yet on two separate occasions had been molested by local garden-variety pedophiles. Both men were casual acquaintances who'd ingratiated themselves to the household for just such a purpose, and since neither incident had gone on too long nor involved actual rape, these small-town, small-time demons had passed through her life undetected and unrepentant. Jolie was left holding the emotional bag with the usual fallout of such victimization: shame and confusion, and a bulwark of self-protection as high and barbed as a prison wall. As she matured into adolescence, she found it easy to take literally the Lord's command to "come out from among them." No one knew better than she that the wider world had areas of uncharted darkness, corners of the human experience where, in the words of the mariners of old, there be monsters.

Such was the emotional hall of mirrors that Sam entered when he walked into the parsonage at El Bethel, and such was the emotional whirlwind that came in his wake, in the vulnerability of first love that filled Jolie with equal parts intoxication and terror. She was petrified by the idea of going to Coral Gables and making conversation with the Rich Folk (as she persisted in thinking of them), of transferring to UF and having to pass Algebra there, and all the other butt-kicking math classes—for what if she failed? What if Sam discovered that despite her intellectual aura, her glib tongue and memory for trivia were her only academic strengths, and she was dumb as a post in math, having spent most of her mornings at Chipola huddled with a tutor in the lab, trying to figure out what the hell $x$ equaled? And worst and most horrifying of all, what if the magic of the river, which made her look so exotic and alluring, didn't stick in Gainesville, and Sam woke up one morning and realized he'd married a big, dumb country girl? And what if he quit looking at her that way, with that glowing face of love?

God, it tormented her, the doubts and raging fear, made her put him off, week after week, growing edgier as they went, culminating in the flare of ill-temper on the porch the Wednesday before Thanksgiving, which had sunk Jolie into a deep funk. When Sam left that day, she had cried for two hours, till she was finally cried out, so paralyzed that she sat on the porch far into the night, ignoring all the last-minute Thanksgiving chores, too drained to move.

She might have sat there till morning if not for Lena, who blew into town after midnight, bright, collegiate, and determined to jolt Jolie from her nonsensical despair. "You're just hormonal," Lena concluded, "need to take some Midol or something. You're not preggers, are you?" she asked in a lowered voice, eye on Brother Hoyt's cracked window.

Jolie morosely shook her head, and Lena laughed. "Well, what's the big grief about? I thought Sam was talking marriage—that you were, like, madly in love."

"I am," Jolie had answered with that air of inconsolable sorrow, as it was impossible for her to communicate the stark dichotomy of her fragmented life, which made happiness and contentment a risky business, indeed, a hundred times more threatening than mere loneliness and despair.

Lena just laughed, as she was used to Jolie's moodiness, and in high spirits, as she and Carl were once again an item, she confided gleefully. They had secretly been meeting for weekend rendezvous in St. Augustine most of the semester.

"He's really changed, Jol. He's gotten serious with the Lord."

Jolie wondered where weekends at the beach with an underage girl-friend worked into his conversion, but was hardly in a position to point a finger, and when Carl showed up the next morning, she was glad to see him. It was impossible to be otherwise. Despite their constant snipping, they'd always been close, physically similar enough to be mistaken for fraternal twins, though they were three years apart. They were both tall, with the same dark hair and hazel eyes, and the same barbed humor—but where Jolie was withdrawn, Carl was brimming with good-old-boy confidence, famous for swooping home at odd hours.

He'd come in that morning at four o'clock and, after bumming around the house awhile, had got tired of waiting for someone to wake up. He flung open Jolie's door and jumped up on her bed and bounced around like a kid on a trampoline.

"Jol-lee!" he cried. "I'm tired of waiting for you to git up! I want to hear about yer Jew boy—" The grin was wiped from his face when he realized someone was beside her, indiscernible beneath the cover. "Good God, tell me thet ain't him!" he cried as he leapt to the floor.

Jolie flipped back the cover to reveal Lena's sleeping face. "Didn't you see her car?" Jolie yawned as she got up and hugged him, not taking offense at the *Jew boy,* as it was par for the course with Carl, and not meant to belittle as much as needle the hell out of her. (In high school, she referred to Lena variously as "Lolita" or "yer child bride.")

Under less stressful circumstances, Jolie would have given it back to him in good measure, but she was too sleepy to bother with it and just yawned her way to the kitchen to check on the turkey that she and Lena had put in the oven before they'd gone to bed two hours earlier.

"How late did you two stay up?" he asked as he joined her in the kitchen. "Lena's out like a light." Then, before she could answer: "You feel all right? You look kind of peaked."

Jolie just wrestled the enormous bird from the oven. "I been busting my butt for two days, getting ready for this thing. Somebody around here has to do the work."

"Well, I made coffee." He leaned against the counter and looked around the cluttered, outdated old kitchen with a face of dry interest. "So how's the Old Man? Any more fainting?" Brother Hoyt had been having dizzy spells lately and had actually blacked out on his debit a few months before.

"He's okay." Jolie went about basting the turkey. "Moving slow, but moving. Too old to be putting up with your nonsense—so think on thet, while you're here."

Carl was used to his sister's lectures and made no reply, just stood at the window and watched the brightening dawn while he drank his coffee. "Well, speaking of nonsense—how the hell did you find yourself a Jew in Hendrix? You got your heart set on a white piano?"

Jolie straightened and stared at him levelly till he relented with a grunt and asked in a milder voice, "So what kind of fellow is he? Am I gone have to go out to the campground and break his damn neck?"

Jolie answered this with yet another flat stare, this one briefer, to show him what she thought of his redneck swagger. "He's been after me to marry him for a month. Talked to Daddy and everything."

Carl nodded with approval at the news. "Well, I'm proud to hear it. Why don't we go out there and roust him, take him to breakfast in Vernon? We got time. Hell, the sun ain't up."

Jolie had been feeling wretched all night over Sam's and her idiot fight, and for once she didn't argue, just glanced at the clock as she manhandled the turkey back in the oven. "Well, maybe. If we can get Lena stirring."

"Oh, I can get Lena stirring," Carl said with a wink, and set down his cup, though he paused to ask, "When you gone tell Deddy?"

"Already have," she told him as she shut the oven door. "He was okay. Kinda sad, but okay—about like he was when we lost Lena."

"Then what's the problem? You look like hell. You're not in the family way, are you?"

"No. I'm scared."

"Of leaving?"

"Of everything," she admitted. "Just tired. And scared. God, Carl— he gets his underwear in a wad when people say *nigger*. What's he gonna do after he meets the Hoyts?"

Carl grinned at that. "Run for his life, if he has good sense." Then, at the fall of her face, Carl offered, "Oh, hell, Jol—it'll be all right. Me and Lena'll be here, and Daddy'll keep the blowhards in line. You just go out there and try to be happy. Everything else," he promised, "it'll all fall in line."

So he'd promised, and so she had believed, against all good sense, as Hendrix wasn't a garden-variety Southern hamlet, but the heart of darkness in such matters. Henry Kite's lynching had cast a long shadow, and as late as 1965, the wooden city-limits sign had openly warned NIGGER, DON'T LET THE SUN SET ON YOUR ASS IN HENDRIX, FLORIDA—signed in happy script YOUR LOCAL KKK.

But these sorts of things were part of the Silence, unacknowledged by the likes of Jolie Hoyt. She just waffled and bided her time, sending out a variety of contradictory messages, till the moment she stood by his gurney in the hallway of the ER in teeth-chattering terror and wondered, with the cool head of clinical shock, what kind of person she was to have sucked him with such fabulous disregard into the sinking gloom of Hendrix.

She couldn't say, just stood there mute, in the numbed violence of disassociation, till an ICU nurse happened upon her and, with little fuss or bother, escorted her to the empty waiting room. Carl was inexplicably gone, and with neither shoes nor a dime to her name, she paced back and forth for hours, through the break of dawn, till midmorning, when a familiar face finally appeared at the door, a deputy sheriff named Jeb Cooke, who'd once been married to a Hendrix cousin.

He was a generation older than Carl and her, grizzled and bear-size and reassuring in his Stetson and leather jacket. He took off the hat when he saw her, not in respect for her as much as her father, who was a rare friend of the Law out in Hendrix. He motioned her to a corner of the hallway, where he presented her with a long, blue legal envelope, explaining that it was a protective notice. "A restraining order," he clarified at her face of incomprehension.

"For Carl?" she asked, so rattled she could barely speak.

"For *you*," he said, moving around to corner her, not in intimidation, but to shield her from the curious stares of the waiting patients. "Signed by the judge, hot off the press."

Jolie ripped open the envelope, but couldn't make head nor tails of the block of close-typed legalese.

"Why me, Jeb? I didn't have nothing to do with it. I was asleep—ask Daddy."

Jeb just herded her to the exit, his voice lowered as he opened the door. "All I do is serve 'em. You ain't arrested or suspected—just need to keep yer distance till your court date. Till then, no phone calls or sneaking in, or I'll have to cuff you like a regular mug. You understand?"

Such was her shock that Jolie didn't argue with this edict of the Law. She just nodded quickly and followed him into the bite of a seriously cold morning, the approaching front fully upon them, the rim of the sidewalk edged in ice. Carl's truck was waiting at the curb, the exhaust blowing in the cold. Jeb walked her to the passenger side and tapped on the glass for Carl to unlock the passenger door.

Jeb handed her in, then spoke to Carl across the seat, as if in reminder, "Just keep yer distance, old son. The young man's gone make it, but his daddy is sorely pissed."

Jeb shut the door once he had Jolie in, then went around the front of the truck and spoke in Carl's window, drily and with a close eye, feeling for a lie. "They say you found him. That it was a hunting accident."

"It was," Carl answered easily, considerably cleaned up from the night before, dressed in a coat and jeans and work boots, his eyes on the frosted window. "Probly some dumb shit on the paper-company property, taking sight-shots across the water. I told Uncle Ott they shouldn't go out the first week of deer season. Wonder somebody ain't shot every week."

Jeb's expression didn't flicker at this fast bit of persuasion, he just barely nodded, then asked plainly, "You sure you didn't see no men in hoods out there? Any flaming crosses guiding yer way?"

Carl met Jeb's eye and answered without blinking, "All I saw was one scared Cracker who was freezing his balls off. And thet would be me."

A shadow of a smile lightened Jeb's face at this bit of Hoyt hyperbole, though he wasn't sidetracked. "Did you hear the shot?"

Carl looked at Jeb in amazement. "Hell, yes, I heard a shot. I heard ten going down and twenty coming back. I'm telling you—the woods are full of idiots with guns these days. Go look at the walls at the camp—they're covered in stray shot. Looks like the walls of the embassy in Saigon."

Jeb had already been to the camp that morning, had seen the pock-marked wall and talked to the clueless old men. He seemed satisfied at the answer and didn't push for anything further, just straightened up and told Carl, "Well, do me a favor, old son, and tell yo Daddy we got it covered here in town, not to be worrying it." After a weather glance around the parking lot, he lowered his voice to observe, "Somebody on the river best be watching thet ass, is all I got to say. They'll have the feds in here before it's done."

Jolie had been sitting quietly reading her protective order, trying to make sense of it, but finally gave up and asked, "Well, when can I see him, Jeb? If Daddy brings me, will they let me?" as if Sam were an R-rated movie that she could only view with parental permission.

Jeb looked a little pained at her naïveté and rubbed his neck. "Naw, shug, thet don't matter. You need to go home and sit tight till your court date—and what*ever* you do, doan be going around Hendrix crying and showing yo ass, gitting old Ott and your daddy upset. Y'know what I mean?"

Jolie didn't and asked the only question she'd ever ask about the night: "Who shot him, Jeb? Why would anybody want to shoot him? We were leaving next week. He never would have come back."

Before Jeb could answer, Carl inserted flatly, "I'm taking her to Georgia," without so much as a glance in Jolie's direction.

Jeb made no speculation on the shooter, just nodded at Carl and affirmed, "Good plan," then tipped his hat and gave the truck a little slap on the door to send it on its way.

Carl ignored her entreaties (he was taking her *where?*) till he'd turned on Highway 90, when he answered in a fast, firm voice, "You cain't go back, Jol—got to move on. Lena ain't in the dorm anymore; has a couch you can sleep on till you git on yer feet—"

"But I cain't just run off without a word," she cried. "What about Daddy?"

"Daddy's fine. I talked to him at breakfast, told him you got that scholarship after all; had to get there tonight or you'd lose it."

"And he believed you?"

Carl snorted, "Oh, hell no. Give the Old Man some credit." He felt around in his pocket and handed over a roll of assorted bills and change. "It's a hundred bucks—all he had, tucked away in a sock drawer. You got to call him tonight, soon as we git there, and convince him this was yer idea—going off to school, just what you always wanted."

Jolie just stared at the money in her hand, then looked up. "He won't buy it, Carl. He knows—"

"Shit," Carl muttered. "He'll buy whatever you tell him—he always has. Everybody knows you and Lense had a fight—Ashley heard it. I told him you broke up—dropped him like a bad habit—*shit*, he's probably relieved."

Jolie tried to argue that, but he overrode her with simple contempt. "God, Jol—did you really think you could just do this thang, right in the sight of Hendrix—that Daddy could save you? Lense wasn't here to study the goddamn Indians—he was digging into the Hoyts and that goddamned useless old lynching. No," Carl insisted at her denial, "that's what got him shot! Hell, Jol—how many fucking Indians you ever met in Hendrix? You thank that's what he was really here for? To hear Uncle Ott's old fairy tales?"

His words had enough of a ring of truth that Jolie was struck nearly dumb, a single memory silencing her: that of Sam, that first night, when she was still freezing him out, standing on the sidewalk, his voice dry and instructive (". . . once lynched from that limb. Nightmare business").

She finally found her voice, hardly more than a whisper. "I have to talk to him."

Carl all but laughed in her face. "*Talk* to him?" He snatched the envelope from her lap and shook it in her face. "That's a restraining order, Jol, signed by a judge. They're handing them out like candy, all over Hendrix, building a case. They gone pin it on somebody, and that somebody'll be Daddy or Ott or anybody they please. Hell, Jol, didju even *know* this guy before you started running your mouth about all the Hendrix *shit*? What if he's a reporter? What if he works for the feds? Hell, they're reopening all this racial shit in Mississippi. Why d'you think they already assigned a judge?"

The surety in his voice made small tears run down her face, tears of grief at the awfulness of her betrayal. She closed her eyes, trying to stop them, but Carl was relentless.

He had no pity and advised her grimly as he wheeled onto the interstate, "And you can git that crying out on the road—'cause if Daddy hears *one* wrong note in yer voice, it's over. You hear me? Jo*lee*? You understand what I'm saying?"

Jolie did indeed understand what he was saying and waited till Lena arrived the next night to find out what really happened on the river. Lena came in late, exhausted and distracted, her little Corona packed with everything she had left the summer before, along with a suitcase of Jolie's clothes, and boxes of shoes and makeup and whatever else she could throw in her trunk. She was obviously done with Hendrix, but made little of it, hugging Jolie tightly, and tearfully, then holing up in the bedroom with Carl for most of the night, her sobbing audible through the door.

Jolie patiently waited her turn, but even after Carl left for work the next morning, Lena would hardly discuss the shooting. She'd only whisper small hints about her part in the bloody evening: how they'd literally stumbled upon Sam in the dark, how there was so much blood, "on everything," Lena told her in that low, distracted voice, "the boat, the truck. We couldn't tell where he was shot."

To Jolie's fevered questions—had Lena *seen* anything? Heard the shot? Lena just cried, "God, Jol—d'you have to ask? You know what it's like out there at night. You couldn't see your hand in front of you."

"Well, what were y'all doing down there that late anyway?" Jolie asked, but got no answer and didn't need one. They'd gone down there to use the old, abandoned bunkhouses for more than bunking, if she knew Carl.

No matter how hard Jolie pressed, that was all Lena would offer as Jolie paced and brooded and waited on her court date, which was a long time coming, the date set for December 18 on the first form, then moved to January 4, then January 26. She got the message from her father that Sam had called, but, on Lena's sobbing instance, didn't confide in him. Nor did she call Sam, on fear of arrest, or shouting, or shunning, or whatever they did these days to women who couldn't keep their mouths shut.

She was secretly glad the court had stepped in, and confident in her vindication, till a final stiff, formal envelope arrived from the sheriff's office. It wasn't a mass-produced court summons, but a crabbed, hand-written note from Jeb Cooke, informing her that the order of protection had been rescinded that morning; the shooting had officially been ruled accidental. There was no explanation, no mention of Sam at all, just a personal thanks for her cooperation, which nearly drove her crazy, as it said everything, and nothing at all.

She used all her and Lena's accumulated change to call the sheriff's office, time and again, till she finally got through to Jeb at his desk, and as far as it went, the news was good: Sam was fully recovered, back home in Miami with his folks. "His father's still on a tear, but he'll git over it—or he won't. I'm about tired of dealing with the old boy, to tell you the truth."

Jolie understood from his chip-on-the-shoulder weariness that she was treading sensitive ground, but was too desperate to worry about annoying him.

"Well, d'you have his number, Jeb? 'Cause I don't have anything, down here, and Daddy said he called and it's been two months, wait-ing, and I didn't write it down because—well, Lena said I shouldn't call."

A long, loaded pause ensued, then Jeb answered, gruff and level-headed, a fifty-four-year-old Hendrix boy offering advice to a barely legal church girl, "Well, I'm glad to hear you finally growing some sense. I expect you done all the *talking* you need to do with that young man . . . No, I *do* know him," he insisted when she indicated otherwise. "I worked the investigation, Jol—and I don't know exactly what he was up to, but it ain't what he told you, about the damn Indians, or whatever that bull was."

Jolie's heart began its furious pound, though she could only whisper, "What d'you mean? He's just in school, Jeb. Like me."

"The hell he is. He's a grown man, Jol, around here digging up dirt on that old lynching, copying records and newspaper clippings, talking to people—taping a few of 'em. He was playing you and the little blonde Carl's been going with. You girls ain't old enough to be going with grown men. You need to be more careful who you take up with."

Jolie's temper was still a hot one, enough that she answered swiftly, "I didn't *take up* with him, Jeb. We're getting married."

But Jeb was as unbelieving as Carl. "Hell, Jolie, you ain't getting *nothing*. All that love talk, it's what pimps say to runaways in bus stations—the old pimp hustle. You ever meet his parents? 'Cause they don't recall ever meeting you. And they're none too happy their golden boy got mixed up with a Hendrix girl, I can tell you that."

Jolie was too humiliated to answer. She stood there, phone in hand, till Jeb was sure his point was made. He softened then. "Baby, just mark it down to the school of life and let it go. That kinda thang—it happens every day. Be glad you got a second chance—lot of Hendrix girls don't. Hell, I gotta tell you that? Take a look around at the next reunion and tell me how many happy women you see."

Jolie was too whipped to argue, her memories of Sam's steadfastness and his sweetness poisoned by grave, stomach-churning doubts that rose and fell like the tides. Round and round she went, through Carl and Lena's wedding in March—one that made a curious turn for the righteous after the two went to the altar the week before their wedding, confessed their sins, and triumphantly returned to the faithful, flags flying.

They entreated Jolie to follow, to repent and renew her mind and find refuge in the old sanctuary of El Bethel. But she wasn't as guilt-ridden as she was perplexed and isolated, waiting on a sign and still clinging to hope. Then a small bit of damning evidence appeared unexpectedly, almost exactly where it began: in the sagging old kitchen in Hendrix, where she'd first opened the door and let him into her life.

It happened in early August, almost a year after he first appeared, when she was forced to return to Hendrix after her father had his first stroke—this one relatively minor, though his heartbeat fell so low they had to put in a pacemaker. Jolie came home as soon as she heard, on an interminable Greyhound bus ride, with stops at every little hamlet and crossroads from Savannah to Cleary. She got in at midnight, in time to see him and hold his hand and pray with him and assure him she wouldn't leave till he was home. She hitched a ride with her uncle Ott back to the parsonage and got there just after dawn on an uncharacteristically breezy morning, a hurricane somewhere off the coast well downstate, but still capable of ruffling the red cedar at the cemetery.

She let herself in with her key and found the old house strangely familiar, just stuffy, closed up for the coming storm. Her father was a creature of habit and hadn't moved so much as a doily in her absence, the place smelling of old wood and damp flooring, and, against all expectation, of home. Jolie wandered room to room, intrigued by the stopped-clock stillness of the place: high school pictures of Lena and her still jammed in the frame of her vanity mirror; the green tile in the bath as arsenic as ever; the same worn blanket on her bed, still flipped back from the last night she'd slept there, eight months before.

She hadn't eaten since she left Savannah, and while she made toast, she stood at the kitchen counter and went through a stack of junk mail that had come to her in care of her father—credit-card applications, magazine subscriptions, and glossy, useless college brochures. She was pitching them away, one piece at a time, when she came upon a small, jet-printed envelope addressed to *Ms. Jolie Hoyt, Hendrix, Florida.* The return address was Miami, and the moment she saw it, that old impatient pound returned to her heart.

She opened it with shaking hands and found a strange university letterhead, and a single, well-placed paragraph that read:

*Dear Ms. Hoyt,*

*I am writing on behalf of Dr. Arnalt, who is working on a study on the Hendrix Lynching of 1938. We have read S. Lense's excel-*

*lent work on the subject and understand you have source material
and access to firsthand testimony that would be very helpful to our
endeavor. We would very much like to interview you and possibly
your father, plus any other sources you would kindly introduce. We
will be filming in Cleary on Sept 5th and at the archives in Tallahassee till the 9th. Please call my office if either date works for
you and suggest a location (audio friendly preferred) where we can
discuss.*

It was signed Joseph Jointer, Ph.D., and below that in a flourish of
friendly postscript was *Lunch on us!*

For a long moment, it simply didn't register. She stood there, reading
and rereading it, till the cumulative effect sank in, the force of the blow
so physical that she blinked. She didn't cry out, didn't make a sound, just
sat down heavily at the old Formica table and digested this bitter confirmation that Sam was *something,* all right, but not what she thought
he was.

He was some kind of hustler—a reporter or a fed or sycophant of the
Justice Department, looking for an *in* on their dirty laundry, and wily
enough to find it, along with a few other juicy perks. Either someone got
onto him or maybe he was never shot at all. Maybe that was another con.
In any case, he'd hit the road as such men tended to do when women lost
their usefulness—turned up pregnant, got old, or put on a few pounds.
Oh, the men still had uses for you—to iron and cook and raise their
children—but they never bothered telling you they loved you anymore,
because they didn't.

They never *had.*

When the tears finally came, Jolie cried as she never had in her life.
She howled like a child at the loss and foolishness of it all—at the utter
stupidity of Hoyt women, who knew the score, *saw* the score, lived and
*breathed* the score, and yet they *never* learned.

When she finally cried herself out, she turned on a burner on the
old gas stove and touched the edge of the envelope and the note to the

blue flame. She held it till it caught, then stood there and watched it burn, filling the kitchen with the bitter smell of ash, till it burned to her fingers.

When it was gone, so was Sam. He was dead to her, and until she came upon Wes Dennis five years later at the City Café, she never willingly spoke of him again.

# Chapter Eleven

The mitochondrial DNA of the Creek was not the only trait Jolie had inherited through her matrilineal line. She'd also inherited the stoicism of the disinherited, and the passivity of a Mexican burro—one so well trained to halter that it can walk a precipice with a trunk strapped to its back never missing a step, eyes open, fast asleep. Such a skill was a cultural requirement of women in Hendrix, and so hardwired into the female brain that the idea of contacting Sam or confronting him, or shaming him for his betrayal, simply never occurred to Jolie.

She had neither the voice nor the energy to address it and just ate this insult. She digested it into the rest of the Hoyt collective rage and returned to Savannah the next week with a different paradigm of life—as a bona fide student of design. Such was her utter despondency that she didn't bother with intricate essays and chatting up alumni in the hopes of winning herself a scholarship, but just filled out her Pell grants and, when she did her face-to-face, checked the box as a minority applicant.

"Minority *how?*" the counselor asked when they called her in, with the snooty, know-it-all way of the public official, peering at Jolie over fashionably narrow eyeglasses in a pale cherry shade.

"Muskogee *Creek.*"

The unexpectedness of the answer brought the clerk up short, her face far from believing. "I assume you have legal documentation?"

Jolie met her eye and answered without blinking, "You assume *correctly.*"

She made the pronouncement with more bravado than expertise, but a flurry of correspondence with the State of Florida proved her self-identification correct—or at least failed to disprove it. Such was her moxie and obvious financial need that, come spring, she was actually living a sliver of the life she had been playacting all those months—taking basic design and riding a bike to class, adjusting her primitive lines to the rigidity of formal design.

She went at it with a singular resolve and was just hitting her stride a year later when her father had his second stroke—this one appreciably worse, leaving him with a damaged heart, a right-quadrant paralysis, and a sagging, permanent limp. Carl and Lena were the new parents of two wholly demanding baby girls, born ten months apart, and even Ott couldn't care for Ray alone, so with little fanfare Jolie took a personal leave midway through her sophomore year. With a duffel bag, a sketch portfolio, and ten grand in student loans—with the onus of repayment falling entirely on her, along with the 20 percent of her father's medical care not covered by Medicare—she returned to Hendrix to care for her father.

The good Sisters at El Bethel were generous in allowing Jolie and her father to stay at the parsonage, paying little above room and board. Jolie was left to find a job, which wasn't as easy a proposition as it had once been. She had returned under a cloud, her sterling reputation as a good church girl tarnished by scandal. The few employers in Hendrix made her feel the loss, with no takers on her job apps, even at the post office, the IGA, or the bait shop. Vic Lucas promised to hire her come spring, but in the meanwhile she cleaned condos and made tourists' beds on the beach and had pretty much given herself over to the surety of the old Hoyt curse when deliverance came from an unexpected source: her father.

Ray Hoyt had never been known for his dramatics, but he sprang it on her with a certain flare on a warm evening in late May, after she'd spent a long day scrubbing tile in Mexico Beach. Over a supper of

chicken and yellow rice, he proudly announced that he'd found her a
*good* job, right up the road in Cleary.

"Where?" she asked with some trepidation, as the phrase *good job*
could mean anything in the Hoyt vernacular, from piecework at a textile
mill to slaughtering chickens at a poultry farm.

"Working for *Mis*-tah *Alt*man," he told her smugly, as if it explained
everything.

Jolie waited on a little more detail. When it wasn't forthcoming, she
asked, "Old Mr. Altman, at the bank?"

Her father made a face. "Naw, shug—the old man's been dead twenty
years. His boy, Hugh. He owns thet florist shop, downtown. I told him
you was looking for work, and he said to come by and see him—that
he'd fix you right up. Working with art, and all, just like you like."

Ray looked extraordinarily pleased at having snagged this ambitious
lead and spent the evening recommending what she wear and how to do
her hair. He was weirdly involved in a way he had never before been, or
would ever be after. She realized then how worried he was about her and
quit complaining and dutifully dressed and drove to downtown Cleary,
around the corner from the City Café, to the City Florist—a tiny, narrow shop built of the same Georgia brick.

She was expecting minimum wage and nothing more, found the front
counter empty, stuck with all sorts of clippings of FTD bouquets and
funeral sprays, loose-leaf notebooks of teddy bears, and Mylar balloons.
She rang the counter bell three times before a harassed, well-preserved
middle-aged man finally emerged, immaculately dressed in pressed Polo
and Gucci loafers—Hughie Altman, she assumed, knowing the name
but nothing much else.

Before Jolie could so much as open her mouth, he popped up the
counter divider and waved her back. "You must be Raymond Hoyt's
daughter—d'you mind talking in the back? I'm swamped. Six weddings
tomorrow, including Cathy Kramer's, and four funerals, one in Holt, of
all places, and no one can tell me the name of the church. Do you have
anything with you but heels?"

Jolie stammered, "No sir," and explained that her father had only told her this was an interview, not an actual job. But Hugh disappeared into the depths of a long, dim back room that stretched the length of the old building and was a study in creative chaos. Refrigerators of every size and vintage lined the walls. Bolts of lace, ribbons, and every other edging known to man fought for counter space along a high, sixteen-foot table that was haphazardly scattered with baby's breath, stems, and a mountain of untrimmed long-stemmed roses, deep red and white, still in bud.

"Pity," he said as he began stripping the roses with nips of a paring knife, as quick as a sweatshop seamstress. "I could have used you. Have you ever done any arranging?"

"No sir. I'm a student—or I was, at Savannah Col—"

"Yes, your father told me," he interrupted with a wave of his hand, not rude as much as single-minded, rolling his eyes in exasperation when the bell on the counter trilled. He paused, rose in hand, and asked, "Well, would it be too much to ask you to wrap these roses while I take care of these tiresome walk-ins? At least till I get Cathy's things done? I have to finish the setup by morning so she can do a walk-through."

Jolie was, at heart, a pleaser, and with no discussion of wages or benefits, hours or conditions, she held out a hand for the knife and started peeling, with such determination that Hugh finally smiled. "That's right—just strip them and stick them in the water. Kick off those heels, honey," he ordered, "or you'll ruin your back. When they're done, stick them in the crystal vases—the red and white—use your eye. They're the reception pieces—boring, but you know Cathy. We got in a shipment of the most extraordinary delphiniums, but, no, she must have red and white roses. I told her, 'Well, stick a blue star in there and you can keep them out till Fourth of July.'" He paused before he went to answer the bell and confided, "And, d'you know, she thought I was *serious*?"

So began Jolie's long association with Hugh Altman, whose family was among the handful of insider patrician families who'd ruled the roost in Cleary for time out of mind, with the country homes, the farms, the vast acreages of an old-South fiefdom. Every county seat in West Florida had a few, the progeny of last-century planters, who'd long ago left their farming roots and become world-weary blue bloods of an archaic type, cash-poor but regal, whose preferred car was a Cadillac; favorite writer, Thomas Wolfe; and investment of choice, real estate, of which they owned a good portion.

Hugh was the oldest son of such a family, and the responsibility of managing the local holdings had fallen mainly to him, not without complaint, as he detested his sister and detested her children even more. His father had been a formidable banker in his day and, when he died, had left Hugh all manner of curious business concerns—most of which he'd wasted no time in unloading.

He'd held on to the florist shop on the advice of his accountant, as it had been a cash cow in the days before the Internet, when no prom, wedding, homecoming, or funeral was complete without a spray of white mums. Those days were long over by the time Jolie came on the scene, but Hugh persisted in thinking they would return, though good managers were impossible to find and he wound up doing much of the legwork himself. The richest man in the county was delivering corsages to prom parties in a thirty-year-old panel van.

In that and in many things, Jolie found him an enigma. When she mentioned his peculiarities to her father one night at supper, he grunted, "Baby, men like him, they make their own rules. He ain't tried to mess with you, has he?" That was the Hendrix term for sexual harassment.

Jolie was quick to assure him, "Oh, I doubt ol' Hugh has any plans for the likes of me—other than maybe working me to death."

Her father had nodded in satisfaction. "Thet's why he's paying you, shug."

He missed the note of mild regret in her voice, as Jolie had inevitably developed a crush on her boss in typical schoolgirl fashion, light-years away from the way she'd loved Sam, having few roots in reality. She was just young and lonely and Hugh an undeniably romantic figure—so rich and unattached and wonderfully hygienic, with a full-time maid who kept his pants pressed, his shirts starched, his Gucci loafers shining.

He was also a good, if sketchy, teacher, his floral arrangements, like his personality, built along classic lines, as solid and symmetrical as the famed Roman arch. Jolie had never worked with flowers in her life but was a quick study and soon began incorporating native greenery into his stiff, formal creations—curling coral vine and wisteria, and even the humble grapevine.

The results were lacy and delicate and not only garnered instant praise from their customers, but saved Hugh a few bucks in supplies, as the vine grew on the shop's back fence. She figured he was more impressed with the savings than the design, for Italian loafers to the contrary, Hugh was unimaginably cheap, truly a child of the Depression in that sense. He went on regular harangues over flower prices and overhead and practically took to his bed in March when it came time to pay his property taxes. He stood around for weeks afterward on the spacious veranda of the local country club warning his equally rich and pampered friends that America was heading *straight* for socialism, and that he, Hubert Allan Altman, had seen it coming.

But aside from his shameless penny-pinching, he was a good enough boss, hilarious in his snotty superiority, full of wisecracks and eye-rolling that he never bothered to hide from anyone, even his choicest customers (who were usually kin to him). To his credit, he recognized Jolie's talent early on and was soon introducing her around town as his brilliant new protégée in a way that Jolie thought mocking at first, but eventually realized was sincere. Hugh was of the generation that used such words as *marvelous* and *protégée* without sarcasm.

He was always casting about for new ways to make a dime and was soon setting Jolie up with small design projects for a few choice clients, whom he privately referred to as "the Garden Club set"—his mother's genteel friends who lived in the wonderful houses on Silk Stocking Row. In this, Jolie proved genius, as she was still nourishing a great mother-loss and got on like gangbusters with the Cleary old guard, who'd never met a bit of cheap labor they didn't like. She never marginalized them as Hugh did, but considered them the urban counterparts of the old Sisters at El Bethel, with their same kindness, their rigid, old ways of looking at life. While she was busy transforming their sunrooms and parlors into forest-green-and-burgundy hunt-club motifs, she kept them laughing with funny little stories of Hugh's odd ways, and the quirks of her increasingly well-known brother, the Reverend Carl Hoyt.

The latter were possibly more hilarious than the former, as Carl had gone full-bore fanatic in his return to the church, not content with being a mere Christian layman, but becoming a preacher himself, and opening a slick new church on the coast (a *ministry*, they now called them) named Higher Ground. He and Lena had struggled for a few years to establish themselves, through the birth of yet a third daughter, making for a tough little fight to keep the mortgage paid and the parishioners at bay.

Jolie pitied them enough that she signed herself up as a member and paid tithes, till a small break came Carl's way in the form of a gospel businessman who fixed him up with a late-night spot on local access cable. As soon as he hit the airwaves, his ascension was almost guaranteed, as Carl was a communicator's dream. He was big and handsome and hilarious, with a country accent he could mold like a pound cake, and a hardscrabble childhood marked with moments so tragic they might have been lifted from a Hank Williams ballad—his mother's death, his early bout with teenage alcoholism. He spoke of it all with an AA transparency that made him alive, authentic on air, and only months after his debut, he'd caught the eye of a rep from one of the huge God-channels.

Within the year, his tiny church had swelled to such a size that he rented a local theater, then a local stadium, for his Sunday services, till his own sanctuary was done, a modern monstrosity of glass and metal. Built to seat seven thousand, it was already at overcapacity the day it opened, with plans to build yet another, more elaborate church next door. Carl was a great proponent of the Prosperity Doctrine, which taught that you were blessed according to what you gave. He expected a 10 percent cut of every income of those in his church and mostly got it, his lifestyle leaping from modest to millionaire, seemingly overnight, with all the attendant perks: the McMansion and designer suits; the trips to Steamboat; and the obligatory Rolex—to Carl's father's undying amazement, after Lena told him how much it had cost. "You don't mean it" was his stunned response.

Jolie thought it little short of heretic, but her barbs and teasing were all in fun, as they were still allies, she and Carl and Lena, bound in part by the mystery of Sam's shooting, though Sam himself was never mentioned.

He was dead in Jolie's mind, gone beyond retrieval, living the high life in the academic enclaves of South Florida, or the newsrooms of Miami, or wherever the hell he had actually come from. Or so she thought, till the week of her father's birthday, when she took him to the café for a rare night out on the town.

She was sitting across from him in one of the back booths, trying to convince him that paying $5.99 for all-you-can-eat shrimp wasn't highway robbery, when a tall, faintly familiar man paused as he passed their booth, then stopped short, seeming to recognize her father.

"Brother *Hoyt?*" He smiled, then held out his hand for a shake.

"Well, Wes Dennis," her father replied, feeling for his cane and trying to struggle to his feet with his good country manners, to shake the man's hand.

Wes was an old friend of Carl's, another wild-child preacher's son who'd once been busted for selling marijuana at youth camp. He had become much more presentable in adulthood, in the kind of casual WASP-wear that Hugh favored, chambray and khaki, but not nearly as well ironed. Wes stood there and chatted awhile. Jolie told him about her job, and they discussed Carl's dazzling new house with appropriate eye-rolling all around—till the waitress was coming down the aisle with their shrimp, when Wes dropped his bombshell without warning. "Well, Jol, guess who's my new smoking buddy at work?"

She hadn't the faintest idea, and at her shrug he grinned a small, insider grin. "Sam Lense," he said, then paused, waiting for reaction.

In this, he was disappointed, as Jolie stared at him levelly, wishing her father weren't there so she could pass along an appropriate message. As it was, she accepted the plate from the waitress and busied herself with her napkin as her father smiled with genuine interest. "Well, I declare," he breathed. "I ain't seen him since he got shot. What's he up to these days? Still out and about, studying the Injuns?"

"Says he lived in Hendrix," Wes answered with a ribald lift of an eyebrow at Jolie, "that you two were once an *item.*"

She almost answered, *Yeah, and I heard you were once a drug dealer.*

But she didn't want to ruin her father's birthday, and in a stab at civil retreat, she stood suddenly and said she needed to wash her hands. She left her father to get rid of the idiot, which he did, making short work of it.

When she returned from the bathroom, Wes was gone, and her father, ever the gentleman, was waiting for her before he started his shrimp.

"Sorry," she told him as she sat down, and they held hands and prayed, then began eating. Jolie's appetite was not what it had been ten minutes before, which didn't escape her father's notice.

He plowed into his shrimp for a silent few minutes, then finally commented mildly, "So ol' Sam got him a spot at the state. Good for him. I hope he's happy."

"*I* don't," she countered quickly, without thinking, so witheringly honest that her father sat down his fork.

"What's got into you?"

Jolie refused to pursue it. She waved her father away and gave up any pretense of eating, just sat there hunched in her coat, wearily regarding the narrow little restaurant that looked and smelled much as it had that fateful night she'd first laid eyes on Sam. Six years had passed, but she could remember it so clearly: his curious gray eyes when they sat down, checking out the ceiling tile, the jukebox, missing nothing; his face when he lifted his glass and made his toast. ("To the Lower Creek Nation, and

Big Mama, one of history's great survivors. May her grandchildren haunt the swamp till the end of their days, and Old Hickory be her yard boy in the Great Hereafter.")

A great line, she thought.

A great love, briefly.

She could feel her eyes begin to water and wrestled a napkin from the dispenser. She sat there with it pressed to her eyes while her father ate in silence, not having much to offer by way of comfort. He finished his shrimp, then pushed his plate aside and, for the first and last time, addressed what he had just that moment realized was a great heartbreak in his daughter's life, a first love gone sadly wrong.

He was an old man by then and knew he was dying, so he didn't waste his breath with useless questions, just assured her, "Well, don't worry it, sister. You leave it to the Lord—He'll settle it. People think they can treat people bad and get away with it, but nobody gits away with nothing in this ol' life. Sooner or later the chickens come home to roost."

He offered this with confidence, as it was one of his favorite pulpit proclamations, a variation on the doctrine of sowing and reaping that meant that every human act, no matter how well concealed, would eventually bear consequences, as roving chickens always returned to roost at sundown.

Jolie was not overly comforted by the notion, a lack her father seemed to realize as he offered nothing more, just wiped his hands thoroughly on his napkin, then concluded with a little less Christian forbearance, "Well, I know one thang: I know I wisht I'd a never let thet trifling sum*bitch* step foot in my *house*. I know *thet*."

It was a startling reversal—the first time in her life Jolie had ever heard her father use casual profanity. He sounded like a *Saturday Night Live* sketch on Carl's pulpit style, so unexpected that she burst out laughing, even through her tears.

"Well, listen to Old Jesus Hoyt." She reached across the table and gripped his hand. "You ain't careful, St. Carl of the Beach'll quit telling them delightful little stories about you on the television every week.

People'll quit sending him money, and we'll go back to being po," she teased, as Carl had got in the habit of frequently quoting his sainted, old Pentecostal father, painting him as wise and wonderful, a sort of backcountry Jesus.

Ray was relieved to see his daughter's face clear as she stood and offered him a hand. "Come on, Old Man. I'll take you to Dairy Queen and buy you a Dilly bar. It may cost as much as a whole *dollar*, so brace yourself."

# Chapter Twelve

S am Lense had dealt with his loss of Jolie the way that you deal with any unexpected death: denial, then anger, then, finally, resolution. The denial stage pretty much ended the night he heard she had left for Savannah. The anger came and went, for months, till he finally lost hope and gained a little perspective, figured that's what Jolie had been trying to tell him with her moodiness those last few weeks, her reluctance to set a date. She couldn't face up to him, tell him it was over. She'd had a hot little fling by the river, but thought better of marriage and had taken the opportunity to opt out and follow the ancient custom of her people and take to the swamp and lie low, wait for the outsiders to take a hint and get the hell out of Dodge.

Like any grief, the sting from this brutal conclusion eventually faded, over time and with activity. The most lasting casualty was his love of anthropology. He simply lost interest, and no matter how many congratulatory letters Professor Keyes sent him, or how many inquiries he had from Native American researchers interested in discussing his work, he never went back to the committee, never answered their letters or even picked up his last paycheck. He didn't pick up a paycheck of any denomination till June, when his mother finally tired of seeing him lounging around the house all day in his underwear and hooked him up with a job with HRS in Child Protection.

She figured a good dose of cruel reality was just the ticket to launch him out of his self-absorbed apathy, and she was right. For compared to the lives of the clients on his caseload, he'd had a pretty cushy life, old Sam Lense had. He'd loved a woman who hadn't loved him, had been shot in the back and left for dead, but at least he'd been a participant in his own tragedy, had made his choices and paid the price. His young clients in social services had never had the luxury of choice and sported worse scars than his at age six, with the certainty of more to come.

In the light of their daily tragedies, he began to feel that maybe life hadn't dealt him such a bad hand after all, that maybe that thing in West Florida had worked out for the best. On his orthodontist brother's urging, he took up golf; on his lawyer brother's urging, he started offshore fishing. He met a girl at a Halloween party named Leanne Gails who was about as far removed from Jolie Hoyt as the sun from the moon. The daughter of an anatomy professor at UW, she didn't have Jolie's attractive damage, or her mischief or haunted history, but a Finnish frame, a Nordic practicality, and a raw IQ so competitive that even his orthodontist brother never challenged her at the table or made any blond-shiksa jokes behind her back.

By the anniversary of his near-death experience, he had a crappy job, but a noble one; a nurse girlfriend who thought the modest bullet hole in his back, and the web of scarring on his chest from the surgery was macho and hard-earned; and a family who were glad he was alive, who never harped at him, but beamed at his every move (even the new girlfriend, who they deemed a little too quick to be serious, but otherwise harmless). All in all, he was pretty set, and when Lea turned up pregnant that January, he wasted no time in marrying her at his brother's country club. Sam did it up right with his brothers as groomsmen, his father as best man.

Sam prepared himself for a long and sun-kissed life of South Florida bliss, cried true tears of joy when his son was born that September, and named him Brice for no good reason that Sam could think of. It was

Lea's choice and a little yuppie and wannabe to his ears, but what the hell? He was a beautiful, fat baby, the love of Sam's life the moment he laid eyes on him, a source of radiant, unending joy, which was just as well, because not long after his birth Sam's marriage began showing signs of premature strain. When they were dating, Lea had been fine with his job with HRS, but once they were married, she began a campaign to get him to change careers while he was still young enough to swing it, to go into real estate or maybe become an aluminum-siding salesman. She also wasn't crazy about his family anymore, thought they hovered a little too close and nosy over Brice, and wanted a little distance.

She talked him into applying for half a dozen different supervisor jobs, and after a few months he succeeded in getting a (slightly) better-paying job as a financial officer in Economic Services in Tallahassee. For about a week they were happy, till the same old rot set in—how he didn't make enough money and Brice got too many ear infections at the nursery, and Sam never talked to her, and on and on. Sam's answer was to talk even less and to work longer and longer hours. He was relieved when she broke down and took a supervisor's job at the state hospital at Three Rivers, which left them more time to do what they did best: love Brice and stay out of each other's way.

By then, Jolie Hoyt was but a distant memory, though when he relocated to North Florida, he occasionally ran into people with as thick an accent who volunteered they were natives of the area. Wes Dennis was such a man, a director in Protective Services who liked to brag that he had grown up in Calhoun County and lived to tell about it. Along the time that Sam's marriage began to fail, Sam took up smoking, not as sport, but as a means of emotional survival. Wes was also a smoker, and they often found themselves in the smokers' court on break and talked of the usual guy things: football and work and politics. Wes supported a handful of far-left causes with a zeal he claimed was the fruit of an overzealous fundamentalist childhood. He talked like a hillbilly when he wanted to make a point, but wore L.L. Bean and upscale field-wear, Tilley hats and Wallabees without socks.

Sam never made any connection between Wes and Hendrix at all till sometime within striking distance of his divorce, in 1999 or 2000, when a flash of afternoon rain caught them outside and pinned them under a dripping stoop. While they waited for it to pass, Wes mentioned he was going to Washington County the next day for a district meeting, was stopping in Cleary at a little place called the City Café.

"They specialize in shrimp—flash-fry it in a light batter, almost like a tempura," Wes said with that smug sureness of the educated local who managed to look down his nose at nearly everyone: his extended family for being such unenlightened hillbillies; Yankees such as Sam for lacking the soul to appreciate barbecued goat or understand jazz.

Sam was glad to top him for once and answered with a long draw on a Marlboro he'd bummed off him, "Yeah, I used to eat there, when I lived in Hendrix."

Wes's eyes widened at that, so surprised he nearly sputtered. "You lived in Hendrix? My God, *when?*"

Sam had never talked much about the Hendrix Interlude, as he sometimes remembered it, and shrugged to indicate it was a casual thing. "Not long. I was a fieldworker with the museum at UF, doing the grunt work for a grant."

"What in God's name were they studying in *Hendrix*? Syphilis? Pig futures?"

"Muskogee Creek. It was when they were trying to organize in West Florida, applying for state recognition."

Wes returned to his cigarette, a look of near awe on his face. "Well, you're a braver man than I. Hendrix—place had a bad name. When we used to go to the beach, my mother used to make us cross the bridge in Blountstown to avoid it. That forest draws a strange citizenry. There used to be a coven of witches down there, and a Klan klavern, too."

Sam made a small noise of interest, wondered if he hadn't inadvertently come in contact with charter members of both organizations, back in '96. He didn't offer anything else, though Wes would occasionally bring it up, once asking, "Well, where'd you stay when you lived on the river? One of those ratty old fish camps on the Dead Lakes? Let me tell you—if those walls could talk . . ."

Wes rolled his eyes to demonstrate that he'd had his share of romps there, with the hot girls of Hendrix, though Sam smoked and shrugged. "No. I stayed at the KOA. But I dated a girl whose family owned a camp. Jolie *Hoyt*," he added casually, as if they'd had a happy little college romance, had gone to the movies together, made out on the beach.

Wes all but choked at the name. "You're lying," he coughed, even had to beat his chest a few times to get a breath. When he finally got it, he rasped, "My father—did I ever mention what he was?" Sam shook his head and Wes grinned. "An Assemblies of God preacher."

Sam felt a small flicker of sensation in his chest at the unexpected connection, though he managed to sound bored and distant. "Really? You knew the Hoyts?"

"Oh, yeah, I knew the Hoyts. Me and Carl used to run around when we were young, when I had a car and he didn't. He was a few years younger than me—my brother Fitch's age—and one more piece of work, old Carl Hoyt. Mama told me he was back in religion in a big way—preaching down in Destin, or Navarre, one of those new megachurches. She saw him on TV, local cable."

Sam didn't spend a lot of his discretionary time watching local-access Christian programming and shrugged at the news, though Wes laughed even harder. "Now that bunch, the Hoyts." He grinned. "Now there are *stories.*"

Sam only nodded in bare agreement and didn't ask for details, too involved in his own domestic misery to care too much for any further history on the illustrious Hoyts. But it was clearly the single piece of life history Sam had ever shared with Wes that interested him.

Wes referred to them, on and off, for months to come, and in late December interrupted his moaning about the 'Noles' performance in the play-offs to snap his fingers and say, "Guess who I ran into Saturday, in Cleary? Jolie Hoyt, in the flesh," he said with that wolfish grin. "She's working for Hughie Altman—you know the Altmans? Own half the county, the bank? She's doing some kind of design thing; said Carl was getting rich as Midas, peddling salvation to the masses. I told her I worked with you."

Sam was too proud to ask what her reaction had been, and Wes was too much of a sadist to offer it freely, had to tease him. "You know what she said?"

Sam shook his head, and Wes grinned even wider. "Not a thing. Not a damn thing. She got up and went to the john, was eating with her father, old Brother Hoyt. He looks like hell, walking with a cane. She had to help him out."

Sam was forced to ask, "So they're still in Hendrix?"

"Oh, yeah. Or at least Brother Hoyt. I don't know about Jolie."

"Is she married?"

In reply, Wes (whom Sam was beginning to despise) grinned his big, redneck grin. "Not that I noticed. Though her and Altman, they must have some kind of arrangement. He's forking over plenty of money to set her up in business, must be getting more than a cut of the profits. Ol' Jol has that ripe, snotty look of a kept woman—and the attitude. *God, the attitude.*"

Sam grunted and crushed his own cigarette and vowed to give them up, if for no other reason than so he wouldn't have to hear any more of Wesley's endless news flashes on Carl and the Hoyts. And Lea hated cigarettes anyway. She was always nagging him about smoking around the baby. She didn't give a damn if he developed cancer of the face, but she did worry about the effect of secondhand smoke blowing in from the patio and choking their son. Nag number 1,059 in a marriage that had been reduced to two common goals, raising Brice and raising Brice, and came to its natural end seven months later in the most humiliating fashion, when Lea opted out of a dying relationship in the time-honored fashion by having an affair with a psychiatrist on staff at Three Rivers.

By the time Sam was served the official papers, she'd handed in her notice and packed her share of the dishes and even enrolled Brice in a

prestigious preschool in Flagstaff, all part of a well-organized plan to follow her lover to a new job in Arizona. Though Sam's marriage had never
been a walk in the park, and he'd had cause to suspect another man was
in the picture for a good many months, Sam was still shattered by the
news, not as much by her betrayal as her casual brush-off, her notifying
him after the fact. His colleagues and his brothers congratulated him on
getting out of a marriage that had never worked, but to Sam, the guilt of
the thing was unending.

For months, he wandered around their apartment in a haze of self-
accusation, until Brice came home for his first summer visit and, Sam's
gnawing fears to the contrary, seemed a bright, well-adjusted kid, excited
over his mother's pregnancy, which would give him a much-wanted
brother, whose image he'd already seen on a sonogram. Only then did
Sam admit that, well, maybe their breakup hadn't been all Lea's fault.
Maybe something was lacking in him, Sam Lense, and their debacle of
a marriage had been a two-way street. Maybe even connected in some
small way to the knowledge he'd never loved his wife one-tenth as much
as he had Jolie Hoyt. Wasn't that a joke, as he'd never made an effort to
get in touch with her, though she only lived an hour away, down a wide
stretch of interstate highway. Aside from Wes's occasional updates, Sam
never saw or heard from her, though Carl was easily traced. His glossy,
big beach church had mushroomed in three short years, and his weekly
sermons were broadcast on one of Tallahassee's cable channels.

Sam was still an anthropologist at heart, and if he happened upon
Carl while channel surfing late at night, he'd pause awhile and watch
Carl stalk around the pulpit in his $1,000 Hugo Boss suit, a Rolex on
one wrist, a thick gold chain on the other. For all his media glitz, his
doctrinal roots appeared to be sunk deep in the swamp of Holy Roller
Hendrix. In his mix of strict moral code and overflowing emotion and
bullying Calvinist sureness, Carl was nothing like his father, not at all
shy or vulnerable, but huge and forceful and dynamic, the father figure every poor bastard on earth wished he'd had, someone to set him
straight, make it plain. Carl often spoke of his poor, country upbringing

and populated his stories with a cast of colorful family characters: his saintly old papa; his comically kooky wife; his small, highly photogenic daughters, who were named odd, old-English names like Tanner or Taylor or Trent.

Sam noticed Carl never called Hendrix by name, nor did he mention his sister, who was never caught on the camera's frequent pans across the family pew. Lena was there every week, the prototype of the faithful media wife, gazing up with childlike devotion. She bore small resemblance to the carefree teenager who used to zip around the campground half-naked, but had taken on the persona of an old soul—an old Victorian soul, her dresses all lace and fluttery hem, buttoned to the chin.

As Sam sat on his couch in his boxer shorts, crunching numbers and eating leftover Chinese, he wondered what Lena had done with all those tiny bikinis now that she'd become fundamentalist Christian royalty.

He never considered calling her sister-in-law to ask, just watched them idly as he moved up the ranks to financial officer—a position that consumed his bone marrow and made for a lot of hair-pulling when the legislature was in town. He was sitting at his coffee table one night in February, surrounded by all the paraphernalia of last-minute revision— calculators and laptops and fee schedules—when he came across Carl and lingered to watch awhile. He was unloading his usual crock of money-grubbing bullshit ("seed faith," he called it) when the camera zoomed in for one of its adoring-wife shots and inadvertently captured a sliver of a woman beside her, taller and darker and eminently comfortable tucked into a pew, as if she'd been raised there. She was ignoring the sermon to whisper something aside to Lena, something so hilarious that she lost her churchy frost and slapped a hand to her mouth to muffle a laugh, her eyes as young as a schoolgirl's.

It was Jolie, albeit in profile, her hair ironed to fit a face lit with an air of pretty mischief as she undermined her brother's thundering righteousness with some little insider joke. When she detected the eye of the peering camera, she met the lens squarely, with a raised eyebrow and a dry, baiting smile that for a split second seemed illogically pointed at Sam, as if she were looking through the wire at him in his living room.

It was over in a blink, the roving camera returning to Carl, who was telling one of his hilarious down-home stories that had his congregation holding their sides with laughter. Sam waited for another glimpse of Jolie, but it didn't come, the show ending as it always did, with Carl sitting in a high-backed leather chair in one of his resplendent suits, humbly asking his blessed viewers to consider opening their lives to the great blessing that would come if they made a pledge to help support him reach souls for the Kingdom.

"Sell a suit, asshole," Sam muttered, then clicked off the television and sat there a long time, staring at the empty screen and trying to frame an explanation, a sound theory of Jolie Hoyt.

One that would not only explain the two feet of twisted scar on his chest, but her subsequent silence and the whole enchilada of his experience with her, in all its unwieldy paradox—the poverty and the richness; faith and ferocity; welcome and dismissal. Try as he might, he could find no combining thread, though the lack of cohesiveness didn't cut him off at the knees as it once had.

Mostly it just made him curious, and when Wes Dennis dutifully dropped by Sam's office later that month and reported that his mother had called and told him Ray Hoyt had died, Sam offered nothing more than a grunt in reply.

"I'm thinking about going to the funeral," Wes said, lounging in the doorway. "Wanna tag along? There'll be a big feed, and Jolie'll be there, in all her luscious corruption. May need a shoulder to cry on." He grinned.

Sam was in the heat of a final budget revision, surrounded by columns of stacked folders and working on four computers at a time. He answered over his reading glasses, "Think I'll pass. But if you talk to her, ask her if she's ironing the boss's pants yet."

Wes was a fan of overblown male rhetoric and laughed a big cowboy laugh. He was quieter on his return, making little of the funeral except to admit that he'd taken his mother; that it was nice. He was so cagey, so uncharacteristically monotone, that Sam's radar was tweaked enough to ask if Wes had had the balls to pass along Sam's message.

After all his delight in gossiping about the Hoyts, Wes seemed suddenly a little hesitant in answering, rubbing his neck and confiding, "You know, Bubba, getting in a pissing contest with *any*body in Hendrix is never a good idea. They're a tricky bunch, even the church. They take that inbred thing to a whole other level."

Wes's hesitancy only piqued Sam's interest more, and after a few days digging, Wes finally broke down and confessed, "I didn't see Jol—place was mobbed—all these people from Carl's church. I had no idea he'd come on so strong. I ran into him when I was going out to the car to pick up Mama. He's big as a house—shining suit and cuffs and gold cuff links—looks like a goddamn New Jersey mob boss in person. It's crazy. We stood there a minute talking old times, and what the hell, I jumped in and told him what you said about Jol. And, *God,* son"—Wes whistled—"he was *pissed.* Thought he was gonna pick me up and shake me like a poodle. I'm sorry, man," Wes apologized with a humility that made him seem, for the first time, approachably human. "I had no idea. If I was you, I'd keep to the highway when you're over there. A lot of dead bodies end up over there in the swamp."

Sam considered the advice a moment, then sat down his cigarette and unbuttoned the top of his dress shirt and gave a little Hendrix-scar peep show—enough that Wesley cursed, long and with feeling.

He asked the usual questions: who did it, and why; questions Sam tended to avoid, as there was no answer. He told him the bare details, which Wes found as astounding as the scar. "You mean you went hunting in the swamp with a drunken crew of Hoyts while you were shagging Jolie on the side? Shit, son, anybody ever tell you about the lynching they had down there? What they did to that ol' boy?"

"Yeah, I heard," Sam admitted as he buttoned his shirt, but it wasn't enough.

The Hendrix Lynching had become one of those historical moments that could not be discussed without the inclusion of a few more salacious details, which Wes supplied with the vigor expected of a man who shopped L.L. Bean: "It wasn't just an ordinary hanging—it was a circus; in the paper, beforehand. Invitations issued, like a goddamn baby shower. They were swamp-running savages, the Hoyts—butchered him like a hog."

"*They* did it? The Hoyts? You got proof?" Sam asked, but got nothing but a shrug.

"It wasn't a secret," Wes countered. "*Shit,* everybody was in on it. Ask Carl. He knows. Everybody does—*hell,* people kept Kite's fingers and toes for souvenirs. They sold goddamn postcards, at the drugstore."

Wes was too flustered to add more, just ran a hand through his hair and advised, "I'm sorry if I stirred anything up. If I was you, I'd just let it go, forget it. It kind of shook me up, Carl turning on a dime like that. I told Mama on the way home, and she said that was *it,* with her and Hendrix. She wasn't ever going back. If I was you, I'd do likewise."

# Chapter Thirteen

Though she was careful to hide it, Jolie was undeniably shaken when she learned that Sam was living in Tallahassee, little more than an hour down the road, and had never called, never bothered to drop by and prove he was even alive. She was perplexed enough to discuss it with Lena, who was still cagey about the shooting and offered no particular theories on either his job or his indifference, other than a hitch of a shoulder and a wry "Maybe he's afraid. Gosh, Jol, can you *blame* him?"

Most people would have bought the argument, but to Jolie, it didn't ring true. Since when had Sam Lense been afraid of *anything*?

She might have worried it more, might actually have picked up the phone and called him herself, if her father hadn't been so obviously in decline, felled by a third stroke weeks later, this one appreciably worse, paralyzing him on his left side, so he could no longer speak. He lingered another few months, till a final heart attack felled him, with no warning, in the middle of the afternoon. The hospice nurse was on hand and had him transported to the hospital in Cleary, in critical condition.

They located Carl easily enough, though Jolie was less easy to put a finger on, as she was at the moment of Ray's attack sitting on a third-story balcony of a condo she was redecorating in Destin, eating a ham sandwich and watching a school of dolphins leap by in Choctawhatchee Bay. Though by no means a rare sight on the Gulf, this particular pod caught her eye, made her forget her sandwich and pause to give them her full attention as they leapt in tandem in the glittering surf, up and down, in joyous abandon. Their unrestrained delight fascinated her, and she watched till they were nothing more than a flash of silver in the distance. She was gathering the trash from her lunch when the foreman of the construction crew came to the door with an urgent call from Hugh, who told her that her father had a heart attack. She went straight to the hospital, where the doctors were cautiously optimistic about his regaining consciousness.

Jolie didn't argue the matter, though she read the dolphins as a final message from her father that he was leaving her now, going home with abandon, leaping out with joy to a deep and mysterious sea. The image sustained her through the two-day vigil on the ICU, till Wednesday night, when even the most optimistic doctor admitted Ray was beyond retrieval. On Thursday morning, she and Carl let them unhook the respirator and held Ray's hands while he took his final breath, with Carl unexpectedly coming apart when the machine began to flatline, his sobs echoing down the hospital halls. Jolie was, as usual, the stoic and didn't shed a tear, just leaned over the bed and kissed her father good-bye, whispered to him to swim *hard,* one day she would see him again.

She left the hysteria to the Hoyt men, who never cried at anything unless one of their kinsmen died, then carried on with primal emotion, sobbing and inconsolable and most inconveniently drunk. Jolie did what she could to manage them, a thankless task not made any easier by the cattle call Carl's celebrity made of the modest funeral. The overlong, overbright service wasn't a tribute to her father as much as a tribute to Carl's ability to draw a crowd. On and on the speakers went, one more glittery than the next, by the end of it making Jolie wish she'd joined her uncles in their drink-a-thon.

The after-funeral gathering had been limited to family only, and members of El Bethel, and the difference couldn't have been starker. The service was all capped teeth and Fake Bake; the family supper was held on rickety tables in the fellowship hall, overlooked by faded, kindly lithographs of Jesus. Lena sent the girls home with a nanny so she could sit with Jolie and the last of the old Sisters, Sister Noble and Sister Wright, who'd cried like widows at the service, but regrouped in the warm light of Jolie's and Lena's attention.

They hadn't grown any more tactful with the years and wasted no time in offering a critique of the celebrity speakers, deeming their sermons canned and uninspired, and predicting Carl would soon go to fat, "just like his deddy."

They said it in Carl's full hearing as they were mighty suspicious of his new wealth, and overweening popularity, and spent the afternoon making not-so-veiled references to Carl about the perils of riches and the eye of the needle. They were scarcely less blunt with their darling Jolie. For even out in Hendrix, rumors were beginning to circulate about her and her illustrious boss man, Hubert *Altman,* of all people—and it wasn't natural, that one wasn't.

Sister Wright didn't like it a bit and asked Jolie point-blank whatever happened to thet Yankee boy she user court? Thet Sam?

Before Jolie could answer, Lena smoothly intervened, telling them that Sam was doing fine. He was married, living in Tallahassee, working for the state.

"Well, I declare," the old woman intoned with great sorrow. "He was a well-spoken young man—would have made a better husband than *some* I could name, who got more *money* than they got good *sense.*"

Their old-women meddling made for a bit of comic relief on a trying afternoon, and when Hugh came to the door at four and hesitantly knocked, Jolie almost called, *Coming, darling,* just to see Sister Wright's expression.

She didn't out of consideration for Hugh, who wasn't too comfortable in Hendrix in broad daylight and would rather be pilloried than stay after dark. He wouldn't come inside, but told Jolie that he was done, meaning that he'd finished the last chore of the florist: moving the flowers to the fresh grave, covering the gash of orange dirt so it wouldn't offend the sensitivity of visiting mourners.

Jolie was feeling a rare affection toward the old pain in the ass, for his care with her father's flowers, including a huge spray of ivory lilies he'd arranged himself, from the Altman family—an unexpected gesture that had been the talk of the after-funeral dinner. She gripped his hand and told him, "Thank you, Hugh. You've been great."

He appeared marginally pleased, told her he'd be back at the end of the week to pick up the stands and sets, a small reminder that Jolie was only supposed to take off a week from work, due back bright and early the following Monday. Punctual on such matters, Hugh showed up late on Saturday afternoon on the way home from a wedding in Vernon.

He went to the graveyard first, to gather his stands, then dropped by the parsonage, supposedly to see how Jolie was doing, though he couldn't help but make delicate inquiries about her plans to return to work on Monday, and if they were still on go. She assured him they were, for with Lena's help she'd almost finished cleaning out the parsonage. They had come upon all manner of strange objects in the task, including a bottle of merlot that some misguided accountant friend of Carl's had sent her father for Christmas.

She offered it to Hugh, who pronounced it generic, but drinkable, and asked if she would mind opening it. "I've been going like a house afire all week," he told her with a hint of reproach at her absence, "could use a glass, if you don't mind."

Jolie cared not at all, but warned, "We don't have a . . . cork opener, or whatever you call it."

"No worries." He produced a key chain that had a wine key on it.

He opened it with skill and poured himself a generous serving in an old jelly glass, the only glass containers that hadn't been packed. She refused a glass of her own and drank cold tea instead, not in the jumbled house, but on the back porch, which was lovely that time of day, the sun to the west long and golden, turning the adjoining fields a rare shade of celery green.

Even Hugh seemed touched by the charm of the place, commenting after a moment, "I can't imagine this was so bad a place to be raised.

You had the river and the woods, a green, rural childhood. Lovely vista, across the fields," he added with a wave of his jelly glass.

"It was all right, kind of lonely. And it was *Hendrix.*"

She didn't have to elaborate, as Hugh was local-born and knew all the stories. He sipped his wine and agreed, "Ah, yes, Hendrix. *Such* a reputation. You'd never think, to hear the talk, that it was this lush and green, actually quite peaceful. I must say, when I was setting up at the church, with the old pulpit, the wooden floors—I found Hendrix quite charming. Harmless, even."

Jolie smiled, as even she had been touched by a whisper of nostalgia over leaving the shade of the old swamp, which in some ways was the most beautiful spot on earth, a ruined Eden.

But she would never be as sentimental as Carl and would only shrug, saying, "Well, I don't know about harmless. The first great love of my life left here in an ambulance, shot in the back."

Like the true small-town boy he was, Hugh thrived on gossip and immediately perked up, wanting more. When nothing was forthcoming, he asked after a delicate sip of wine, "Was he a *local* boy?"

Jolie smiled at his shameless prying. "No. He was a Miami boy. A Miami *Jew.*"

"Oh, my," Hugh drawled lightly, obviously impressed. "That was very *brave,* of *someone,*" he allowed, unable to resist a gleam of delight at this fascinating revelation (oh, the joy of telling his friends in New Orleans, who knew about Jolie already, from his many colorful stories), though he tried to cover it with compassion, overlaid with his usual dry humor.

"So I assume he survived—or does El Bethel have a Jewish section I'm unaware of?"

Jolie decided maybe wine would go better with the conversation than tea and, fishing out another glass, allowed him to pour her a bare inch. She was not overly fond of the sharp, sour taste, but enjoyed the warmth and after a few sips assured him, "Oh, he still walks the earth. Has a job with the state. And a wife and a son. And a bad marriage, apparently."

She paused at that, as the part about the child was recent news, passed on to Carl by the ever-attendant Wesley Dennis, who'd come to the funeral with his mother. Jolie thought herself no longer affected by Sam at all, but hearing that he'd had a child by another woman had hit her badly, made her so bitter that she couldn't carry the light tone any longer, even with Hugh. "Women carry the Hendrix curse," she offered drily. "Men seem to get out all right."

Hugh digested it in silence, finished his wine, and offered to pour her more. When she refused, he poured himself another glass and sat back and mused, "So that's the secret of Jolie Hoyt: a broken heart. The tradesmen in Destin, and a good many local boys, have asked me about you. You seem so alone, so solitary, for someone so young. I've been telling them that you were a churchgirl, devoted to your father. Heaven knows what I'll tell them *now*. Where will you go?" he asked, as Jolie's days in the parsonage were limited, now that the parson was a citizen of the graveyard.

She shrugged. "I don't know. Carl and Lena have offered me a room in their stucco mansion, which is generous, I'm sure. But I'd have to go to his church, and that would truly drive me insane, listening to all his homey Hendrix tales, while he prances around in that idiot watch and designer *socks*."

She halted a little unsteadily as she was talking to the Gucci king. But Hugh was truly too self-absorbed to take such a jab personally and just nodded sagely, as if he certainly understood her reluctance to join forces with Carl.

"He does tend to romanticize the place," Hugh allowed, then with a mild cut of his eyes asked, "Have you ever thought of moving to Cleary? I happen to know that one of the wonderful old houses downtown will soon be on the market for the right buyer—which is to say, someone who won't immediately bulldoze it and build a Pizza Hut."

"Which one?" she asked with interest, as she had done small decorating jobs on most of the houses on Silk Stocking Row and knew their varied histories.

"The old Altman place," he told her with a small smile. "You might have heard of it. Not as stunning as the Thurmon mansion or the Jamison house, but well built and sturdy. Not air-conditioned upstairs, but always cool in the summer. Mother used to say that it was built over a cave."

Jolie was so stunned that she could only stammer, "D'you mean it, Hugh? You're really selling? How much?"

He smiled at her eagerness. "Oh, very affordable to the right buyer, as long as they promise to take care of the old girl and not rip out her claw-foot tubs or otherwise defile her—or my grandmother would haunt you and me both. Oh, and it does require membership on the city Historic and Beautification Board. They meet once a month and need new blood, as does the old house—and all of Cleary, for that matter."

"You don't mean that you'd, like, live there, too?" Jolie interjected, so bluntly that Hugh sniffed.

"No. I mean a normal legal exchange. But thank you for the compliment. It means a lot to an aging, old bachelor to know that he's considered such *desirable* company by the young people around town."

Jolie was too honest to pretend that she'd meant otherwise and asked, "But where will you go, Hugh? New Orleans?"

He gave another well-bred shrug, not of a generation who liked to divulge personal matters to the hired help, though he did offer, "Well, eventually, that's the plan. I've had an architect draw up plans for a cottage on the millpond. I think I'll be quite happy, jumping back and forth between the two. The old house is really too much for me—hasn't been cleaned out in years and years, so don't get in a hurry about all this. It'll take me forever to decide what to keep, and how to divide the family items. My sister hasn't paid a dime for upkeep since Mother died, but I've confidence that when I announce the sale, she'll fight me like a dog for every spoon and plate. I don't expect I'll have much of a summer, at that." He came wearily to his feet.

Jolie was unused to wine and a little tipsy at the turn in fortune, as the Altman house might not be an antebellum beauty, but was wonderful in its way, built at the turn of the century in the Craftsman style, with a deep front porch and a broad, single gable.

She could hardly think of the words to thank him properly and in the end resorted to humor, standing at the door of the van and telling him with the same dryness in which she used to tease her father, "And let no one in Hendrix say after this day that Hugh Altman is a heartless, old, Gucci-wearing son of a bitch."

Hugh didn't quite seem to get the joke and asked with a look of mild concern, "Who says that of me, in Hendrix?"

Jolie grinned. "Well, me, usually. But once I close the deal on the house, they are words I'll not utter never, no more, again. You have my word on it."

Hugh's patrician thin skin couldn't stand much heavy teasing. He rolled his eyes and keyed the engine, commenting with rare honesty, "You have your grandmother's irreverent humor. Has anyone ever told you that?"

"One old man did"—she smiled—"every week of my life."

Hugh followed her nod to the old cemetery, which was gray in the twilight, moss-grown and peaceful. He nodded briefly, then murmured, "Well. God grant he rest in peace," then told her he'd talk to someone at the bank the next day about the details of the house deal, see what the requirements were for the loan.

When he left, Jolie didn't go inside immediately, but stood there in the drive in the early-summer twilight, shell-shocked by the miraculous possibility that she might have somehow outwitted the Hoyt curse and might actually get out of Hendrix at last.

# Part Two
# When the Chickens Came Home to Roost

# Chapter Fourteen

The mythical chickens of Hendrix, Florida, which left in the wee hours of the morning in late October 1938, amid smoke and chaos and the gnashing of teeth, began their circular return nearly seventy years later, from a most unlikely place: an upscale, suburban household east of Memphis in Germantown, Tennessee. There a seventy-five-year-old retired businessman named Hollis Frazier was finishing up a lonely Saturday night on his computer, returning an e-mail from his daughter. Thrice-divorced, Hollis had bought the little Dell for such a purpose, so he could keep up with his children: his son, a career man in the army stationed in Turkey; his oldest daughter, an English teacher in Kansas City; his baby (at twenty-three years), a lowly grad assistant at Wellesley.

His Welleslian, Kate, had hooked up the little Dell for him and shown him how to navigate the web—slow going, as Hollis wasn't a typist and his input was painfully slow: click, click, *click*. He might have given up on it long ago if not for a double bypass the summer before that had revealed a congenital weakening of his aorta, which in his cardiologist's humble opinion could no longer stand the stress of seventy-hour workweeks. He'd been forced to give up the day-to-day grind of managing his businesses (two barbecues and a meat market in Annesdale), and for the first time in his life he was faced with the curious by-product of modern American success called leisure time. With nothing better to do, he often found himself sitting at his desk late at night, surfing here and there, checking sports scores and his competition's prices, the weather in Kansas City and Incirlik.

He eventually grew proficient enough to dabble in genealogy and run people searches on his old army buddies, even finding one or two. But on this particular night in January, his search was both more personal and more somber, launched earlier in the evening after he'd come upon a rerun of *Rosewood* on TNN. Hollis had watched it with growing restlessness, as it reawakened many old ghosts; so much that he'd gone straight to his computer when it was over and had googled three terms on a whim, to see what he'd get: *Camp Six+lynching+Frazier*.

He wasn't surprised when the search came up empty and almost left it at that, but tried one more variation, deleting the *Frazier* and tapping in only two words: *Hendrix* and *Kite*. To his amazement, he actually unearthed a hit this time, a link to a jumbled web page on the Five Civilized Tribes—or so the gaudy, orange banner proclaimed. It was actually an aggregate site, with a long list of links, and he could find no connection to Henry Kite or Hendrix at all, till he'd scrolled down to the bottom and came upon a link modestly titled *Notes on the Muskogee Creek*.

His mother had a good bit of Indian blood—Creek or Cherokee, she said—and he read along with interest, the writing clear and conversational, if a little scattered. Mostly it was a hodgepodge of loosely woven data on the Indians who'd once lived on the lower reaches of the Apalachicola River. Hollis was impressed enough to hit the print button while he was still reading, thinking he'd send a copy to his son, who didn't have access to Internet at the moment and was a great student of history.

He continued to read as it printed, through pages of all sorts of dislocated but factual-seeming anecdotes, till he stumbled across a final section, curiously titled "The Illustrious Hoyt Tribe of Hendrix." Hollis was taken aback by the name, which had made frequent appearances in his mother's and aunt's stories—an enormous local family portrayed as funny, hapless, and occasionally vicious. They weren't known to be either famous or (for that matter) hugely literate, and Hollis was impressed with the depth of the writing that outlined their history, their households, and even their location on the 1930 census.

He couldn't understand why they'd been chosen for such detailed assessment and scrolled back to the top of the page and found the author of the piece: *Samuel B. Lense, the University of Florida.* The name meant nothing to him, and he returned to his reading, searching for the connection to Henry Kite. He found it on the last page, tacked on with no explanation or warning, along with an explosive footnote.

*\*Local families such as the Hoyts still boast of owning pieces of the rope, and his fingers, which were severed as souvenirs, can still be found in Hendrix, though one native regretfully added that most of them were lost, as they'd been taken into Cleary the day of the lynching and thrown on black citizens' porches, in warning.*

Hollis had been reading so quickly that his emotional reaction was slightly delayed, so jarring that he shoved himself away from the desk and came to his feet, muttering, "My *God.*"

He stood there, agitated and unbelieving, then settled back in his chair and set himself to tracing the author, Mr. Lense of the University of Florida. The name brought up a half dozen hits, nothing connected to UF or the Creeks or Hendrix, but articles from the *Tallahassee Democrat* connected with the tragic death of a toddler who'd died while under the supervision of the state foster system in '99. Samuel B. Lense hadn't authored the articles, but was quoted in them, cited as a "supervisor at HRS," who'd come to the defense of the beleaguered caseworker.

Hollis had no concrete evidence that he was the same Samuel B. Lense who'd authored the Indian study, though his indictment of public policy quivered with the same left-wing passion ("—cannot expect a state employee carrying a ninety-three-client caseload to breach the gap of a narcissistic society that has all but abandoned these defenseless children").

Following his nose, Hollis ran a quick people-search in Tallahassee and there he was: Samuel B. Lense on the State of Florida employee contact site, with an e-mail address in a state office. Hollis bookmarked it, then went back and found the only other familiar name mentioned in the paper, a passing reference to a Jolie *Hoyt,* with no address or other information given. He typed the name into the same search and narrowed it to Hendrix. The surname popped up three dozen times, but the only Jolie Hoyt was listed as living at 115 SE First Avenue, Cleary, right around the corner from the courthouse where that luckless bastard Kite had been strung up for public amusement after they finished him off in Hendrix.

He fed the address into MapQuest and found it listed as a business, a bed-and-breakfast in the Cleary historical district, with all the usual smarmy amendments—gourmet breakfasts and shady porches. The fax and phone number were listed, but Hollis didn't consider contacting Ms. Hoyt directly, as the Hoyts were a duplicitous bunch, famous for their clannishness and chameleonlike ability to escape detection. Nailing one on the matter of Henry Kite would require finesse, bribes, and almost certainly a trip to Florida—his first since his mother put him on the train to Memphis almost seventy years before in a scene strikingly similar to the one portrayed in *Rosewood* (which had inadvertently brought the names *Hendrix* and *Kite* to his mind for the first time in many years). The notion was both exhilarating and a little terrifying, as Hendrix was no Rosewood; no celebrated injustice that had long been set to right with reparations and an official apology—or neatly tied up with a Hollywood ending.

Hendrix was another world, a dreamscape of ill rumor—complex beyond repair. Hollis wasn't even sure it still existed, though a quick Google search of the name yielded a surprising amount of information for such a small bump in the road: Population: 298. Elevation: 85 feet. Land area: 1.1 square miles. Even the racial composition was neatly broken down: White Non-Hispanic (95.6%); American Indian (3.4%); Hispanic (<0.7%); Black (<0.3%). In other words, not much had changed. It was still a backwoods Cracker paradise, white as hominy and about as tasteless, though surely it couldn't be as white as all that. Surely there had to be more than <0.3% black people in all of Hendrix?

Hollis found that <0.3% hard to believe, wondered what had happened to the thriving Camp Six, which had been populated by mostly colored folk—mule skinners and sawyers and turpentiners who'd sweated their lives away bleeding the catfacing on the yellow pine. Hollis had been so young when he left that he had little actual memory of the place. He knew of it mostly through the stories of his mother and aunt and maternal grandmother, who'd gone to their graves talking about the musically inclined Kimbralls and hardworking McRaes, and big Dave Bryant, who stood six foot six and weighed 340 pounds. "Big as Dave Bryant" was the way his mother described any big man, till the day she died.

He wondered what happened to them and their descendants, and which of them had survived to fulfill that <0.3% black population. Most of all, he wondered, would that single living survivor be willing to talk?

It was hard to say, hard to say.

If he, Hollis Frazier, had spent his last seventy years scratching out a shadowy half life in the miasma of the flat woods, he wouldn't be able to remember his name, much less a day so haunted that even his straight-talking papa never willingly spoke of it. But apparently someone was talking if the disorganized report of Samuel B. Lense was any indication.

The least Hollis could do was go down to see him, talk to his sources, and that would be that. Hollis's brother, Charley, could quit his moaning and be satisfied that they'd given it their best shot. Hollis glanced at his watch and thought about calling him, but old Chollie-Boy was six years his senior, and (in Hollis's humble opinion) not the sharpest pencil in the pack. He simply couldn't be made to understand how Hollis had happened upon this gold mine of information on the Internet—he who still shaved with a straight razor, who watched TV in black and white.

To save himself a half hour of annoying explanation, Hollis decided to wait till morning and go over the river and tell him face-to-face. Better yet, he'd take the article to him and let him read it for himself. That was the ticket, Hollis thought, and as he undressed for bed, he made a mental note to stop by Walgreens on the way and refill the old pain in the ass's prescription for nitroglycerin—because when he read that last page, he would certainly need one. Maybe two.

Hell, Hollis almost needed one himself, and when he finally got to bed, he found himself too agitated to sleep. After a half an hour of tossing and turning, he gave it up and braved the cold hallway to fetch the printed pages. He sat up in bed with a glass of Absolut and read them again, start to finish, the unemotional disclosure on the final paragraph making him whisper aloud, "Damn." Maybe Charley was right, he thought. Maybe some dumb Cracker still had them, sitting on his television, or on a shelf in his kitchen, a souvenir of a Big Night on the town.

The idea was so vividly disturbing that Hollis said to hell with it and rolled over and called Charley in West Memphis. He waited for twelve long rings till a blurred, old voice mumbled, "Hellow."

Hollis didn't bother to identify himself, just told him briskly, "*Hey. I'm coming by in the morning*—got something to show you."

"Who is this?" Charley muttered thickly. "Hollis? Whut time is it?"

"Two in the morning. I'll be there by six. Pack your bags; dress light. We're headed to Florida."

After a small beat of silence, the old man asked in a clearer voice, "To Hendrix?"

As much as he was occasionally aggravated by the old pain in the ass, Hollis found himself smiling in the dark. "Yeah," he said, satisfaction in his voice.

"*Good,*" Charley affirmed, and that was it. He hung up.

Hollis was still smiling as he maneuvered the phone back to its cradle. Charley might be old as the hills and blind as a bat, but he was by God fearless, had always been.

By the time Hollis made his way over the steaming river to Arkansas, it was after six on a blistering-cold Tennessee dawn. The view from the bridge was wreathed in a thousand pinpoints of light: passing barges, the old cotton warehouses, the commuters leaving Harbor Town, headed downtown. The Arkansas side of the river was immediately more rural, flat, mud-colored floodplain. He exited in West Memphis and made his way to Charley's apartment in a one-story assisted-living facility where he'd lived almost two years now, since he became legally blind and could no longer drive.

He could still see enough to get around and answered the door on the first knock, all dressed and waiting. Hollis didn't offer a word, just strode to the kitchen and slapped the article down on the table: "Lookit this."

Charley was literate, but his reading was limited to how fast he could move a huge magnifying glass over a page. He was painstakingly making his way across the first paragraph when Hollis tired of waiting and impatiently flipped to the bottom of the stack. "There," he snapped, "at the bottom."

Charley was often tried by his brother's boorish impatience and made a noise of annoyance, though he was curious enough to obediently apply the magnifying glass to the page in question, the room perfectly silent till he got to the end, when he whispered, "John Brown-it," a country exclamation that was the pious form of the Lord's name in vain.

"Where'd you git this thang?" he asked, flipping it back to the front and searching for a source with his magnifying glass.

"Off the computer," Hollis answered briskly, snatching back the pages, ready to get on the road. "I got a phone number and a map. You ready?"

"Yessuh," Charley answered without hesitation, as he'd been a widower for twenty-four years. His children and grandchildren were all grown, scattered from New York to Seattle.

He was collecting his walking stick and his suitcase—a handful of stuffed Walmart bags—when he paused to ask in a voice of mild disapproval, "We taking the dog?" Traveling with a dog had long been a point of contention between the brothers.

But Hollis wasn't one to be bossed about what he let ride in his own damn car and answered quickly, "Oh, yeah," making it clear that any discussion of kennels and the difficulty of traveling with a 180-pound dog would not be tolerated.

Charley made another noise at that, as he had a few rigid opinions about Hollis and his big, white wolf dogs, none of them particularly nice. But there was nothing for it. Hollis had always loved dogs, since he was a kid. He'd kept mongrels back then. More recently (that is, for the past thirty years) he'd kept a succession of huge white beasts that he named, serially, Snowflake, every one of them. Though completely unstable in his relationships with women—four wives, last count, and untold numbers of live-ins and hangers-on—he was devoted to his dogs and treated them with lavish attention and respect.

He took them everywhere he went—work, vacation, errands around town. If their massive presence wasn't welcome inside, he'd leave them to stretch out on the leather seat of his Lincoln Continental, AC running in the summer, heat in winter. The current Snowflake was unusually large, who stretched out the full length of the backseat like an albino Saint Bernard, his spade-size, six-toed feet extending between the front seats, about six inches from Charley's head.

Traveling with such a beast struck Charley as typical of Hollis's over-the-top tomfoolery, but after a few more grouses and worry over finding an accommodating hotel, Charley decided to let it go, took off his bottle-thick glasses, and went to sleep outside Montgomery. He slept so long and soundly that he missed crossing the Florida line and was still dozing when they arrived at the house on First Avenue in Cleary. That turned out to be, truly, the last place on earth Hollis would have looked for a Hoyt: the old Altman place.

# Chapter Fifteen

Hollis was so astounded that for a long moment he sat there and silently regarded the enormous old house that looked amazingly well kept for its age. The exterior was painted a soothing bone ivory, with pale pink scrollwork inside the single dormer that accented the windows like a touch of rouge on a woman's face. He was thumbing a gloved finger on the steering wheel, wondering how a *Hoyt* had come to be living in such a house, when a Honda sedan pulled up beside him and a dark-haired woman lowered her window to call, "Excuse me? *Sir?* Are you here to see the carriage house?"

Hollis hadn't the slightest idea what she was talking about, then realized she was the owner of the establishment and had mistaken him for a guest. Hollis was famously fast on his feet, and without missing a beat, he lowered his window and answered with equally good manners, "Yes, ma'am, I am."

"Well, park right there. They don't enforce the sign. I'll meet you at the front door."

Hollis had paid no attention to the rusted NO PARKING sign, so he had no problem further ignoring it. He parked at the curb and left the heater running for Snowflake and Charley, who was sleeping with his head against the high headrest, snoring quietly. Hollis took care to shut the door without waking him, then put on his coat—a big, toffee-colored overcoat with a plush fox collar he'd bought at Goldsmith's a few years before, which Kate called his "pimp-daddy coat."

His hostess, a tall, pleasant-faced, young white woman with a helmet of dark hair and a country accent thick enough to cut with a knife, opened a wide beveled-glass door. "Hope you haven't been waiting long," she apologized as she let him in. "I must have got my wires crossed—didn't know anyone was coming. Been here long?"

"Not too long," Hollis answered easily, playing along with the charade as she picked a key off a hook on the wall and led him down the central hallway.

The decor seemed almost original to the house, with the predictable fainting couches, gilt-framed oils, and velvet portieres, all very rich and shabby chic. The most impressive thing about the place was the floors, miles of polished amber planks. "What kinda wood is this," he asked, "yellow pine?"

"Actually, red cedar," she answered over her shoulder. "The Altmans deforested half the Apalachicola in their day," she confided with a wink, "but it smells like heaven when it rains. The carriage house is out back." She led him through a side door to an old-fashioned porte cochere with a gravel drive so overhung with trees that even in January it made for a green, sun-dappled tunnel.

As she warned him of the step down, she seemed to remember her manners and extended a small hand. "Well, I'm sorry, I didn't even introduce myself. I'm Jolie Hoyt. Did you find us in the paper, or online? The B-and-B site keeps going down—I never know."

Hollis smoothly lied, "Online. Is it taken?"

"Oh, no." She waved him down the drive to a carriage house tucked away at the end of the tunnel, painted the same soothing ivory as the house. "We don't get a lot of weekday business—usually only rent it on the weekends. But I'll be glad to fix it up. Will it just be you, alone?"

"Me and my brother, Chollie. He's asleep in the car."

She stopped and warned him, "There's only one bed—a king. I usually rent it on wedding packages, with the florist."

"That'll be fine. Me and Chollie shared a bed thirteen years, growing up. But I do have an inside dog."

Like the good country girl she appeared to be, Ms. Hoyt didn't flinch at the idea of housing a dog. "Oh, we're pet-friendly. The backyard's fenced, but if he gets after the cats, you'll have to put him inside."

She opened the door as she spoke, to a good-size carriage-house conversion, with the same amber floors and butter-colored walls as the house, but slightly less fusty, the bed tucked away in the alcove of the dormer, a pine table by the window, with pressed-back chairs.

"Sorry it's so arctic," she told him as she disappeared into a hall closet. "It has an oil heater, warms up fast."

With an immediate thump an oil heater came to life behind the wall, along with the wafting smell of kerosene that struck Hollis with an unexpected stab of nostalgia. He was used to odorless electric heat in Memphis and hadn't smelled an oil-burner in a long, long time.

"There's a half kitchen and a full bath, and a private garden if you smoke—not much to see this time of year, a few old japonicas—and a Jacuzzi in the bathroom."

She had started down the hall to show him, but Hollis already knew he wanted it. He felt for his wallet and asked, "Do you rent by the month?"

He got a raised eyebrow, though she was willing enough. "Well, I don't see why not. It goes for a hundred ten a night. I don't know what kind of deal we can cut for a whole month—"

"How about a hundred ten a night?" Hollis asked as he extracted his wallet.

Ms. Hoyt didn't appear to be too swift on mathematics, and after a moment she asked, "You mean thirty-three hundred dollars?"

Hollis smiled at her emphasis. "Sure. Cash." He peeled off $100 bills with a practiced hand, like a dealer in Biloxi.

He stopped at thirty-three and found his hostess staring at the money in wonder. She looked mildly discomfited by the sight and hesitantly asked, "Well, can I ask you something? You promise you won't get mad?"

At his nod, she lowered her voice. "Well, you're not wanting to . . . deal out of here, are you? 'Cause I cain't have that. I got children living across the street and right next door."

Hollis found her honesty unexpected and refreshing. "No, ma'am. I ain't a drug dealer. I own some barbecue joints, in Memphis." He felt in his coat pocket and produced a business card. "Coby's Barbecue, in Annesdale. You can call and check me out, if you want."

She glanced at the card, then pressed her hands to her flushed cheeks. "Well, I am so sorry. That is the most insulting thing I've ever asked anyone in my life. I don't know what came over me."

Hollis was not easily offended by candor and just patted the fur lapels of his coat. "It's the collar. My daughter calls it my pimp-daddy coat."

"Well, that's kind of you to say." She fanned her face with the card. "Do you still want the room? I mean, you'll be comfortable here. I'm really not as backward and swamp-running as it might now seem, but actually considered pretty cool and tolerant. You know—renovated old house, vegan menu. Very hip."

Hollis barked a laugh, as it was precisely what he'd been thinking, making for one of those pleasant little moments of connection, when you realize you're in the presence of a kindred spirit, a potentially good friend.

He assured her that he did indeed still want the room, and as she walked him back to his car, she went over the usual rental details: how many keys he got, and where he should park. "And it does include breakfast. I usually do pecan waffles for my newlyweds, but I'll come up with something. D'you and your brother like homemade sausage? I'm talking *hot*. Habanero *hot*?"

"The hotter the better."

"Then you're gonna be in heaven tomorrow because I happen to have a freezer full of my uncle Ott's private collection most people won't touch, it's too dang hot. Are either of you allergic to nuts?"

"No. No allergies."

"Well, good. I had a guy keel over on me last year, one of my newly-weds. Took one bite of pecan waffle and went into anaphylactic shock. Deadly allergic to nuts, apparently. Don't know why the *heck* he took a bite of a pecan waffle. Sure you don't want to wait inside?" she asked as they reached the sidewalk. "There's a good fire in the fireplace. You'll have it to yourself."

"Naw, I got some—errands to run," Hollis lied as he backed around the car, wanting to talk to Charley alone before he introduced him to their charming hostess. "I'll be back"—he checked his Rolex—"by seven."

"Great." She held out her hand for another shake and added in a small voice, "And, listen—I really am sorry about the drug-dealer comment. I don't know what came over me. If Hugh finds out, *he*'ll go into anaphylactic shock."

Hollis had not taken the least bit of offense, though he seized this golden opportunity to do a little digging. "Hugh Altman? I *thought* this was the Altman house." He smiled disarmingly. "How *is* old Hugh?"

"Oh, doing well, last I saw of him. He's long gone to New Orleans—gearing up for Mardi Gras. You know, he lives there part of the year now."

Hollis smiled indulgently. "Same old Hugh." He almost let it at that, but couldn't resist asking with a small twinkle of interest, impossible to wholly hide, "And you're a Hoyt? Are you from *Hendrix*?"

"Oh, yeah," she affirmed drily, with a roll of her eyes to indicate that, yes, she knew it wasn't anything to brag about.

Hollis needed no more explanation than that, understood in an instant why they were so naturally compatible, he and his green-eyed friend, though he didn't press it any further. It was enough, for the moment, to know he was in the right place, with the right people, staying in their very house.

He extended his hand for a firm shake and thanked her for her time, said he'd be back by seven. When he got in the car, he found Charley in the exact position he'd left him: faceup, slightly snoring. Hollis didn't wake him, but headed to town in search of a drugstore to pick up a few toiletries, maybe some chew toys for Snow so he wouldn't be tempted to gnaw on anyone's antique beadboard walls.

As he drove through the early-winter twilight, back to the strip-mall avenue that led into the old downtown, he pondered the enigma of a Hoyt living in an Altman house. Such a thing was not beyond the pale, and Hollis quickly constructed a probable scenario. One of the sons of the enormously rich Altman clan was sent by the family bank to do business in Hendrix, where he came across one of their famously succulent half-caste women. Before he knows it, old Hugh wakes up one morning with a green-eyed consort, thirty years his junior, which even he can't explain. Being essentially lazy, neutered, and unable to sustain even the shallowest relationship, he'd soon tire of her and move on to rob other cradles, in New Orleans or Savannah or some other bastion of Tired White Men. He'd pay her off emotionally with talk of family obligations and such nonsense and leave her in charge of his dwindling business interests around town, tolerated by his kinsmen as long as she kept a low profile on the exact details of her river-bottom birth.

It was an old story; Hollis didn't write it. To come upon such a woman and actually stay in her house struck him as the most incredible piece of luck. After he parked and let Snow out to pee, he woke Charley and told him the news: that he'd not only found their source, but had secured a room for them and the dog for a whole month.

"Where?" The old man yawned as he righted his glasses and peered around the parking lot with an owl-like blink.

"The old Altman place," Hollis told him with relish. "And you will not *believe* who is living there now."

# Chapter Sixteen

What annoyed Hollis Frazier the most about his brother was that he was a pain in the ass. He was contrary and obstinate, with no conception of the idea of team play. This was never more evident than on their first morning in Cleary, when he was alone with their charming hostess for all of ten minutes and managed to blow their cover *just like that*.

Hollis, who liked to keep his cards close to his chest, found his brother's chattiness especially galling as he'd gone to some lengths the evening before to explain the importance of Charley's keeping his mouth closed and his head up and to let Hollis do the talking. Charley had agreed without argument as they lay on their respective sides of the enormous honeymooners' bed. Hollis explained a simple plan: that he, Hollis, would go to Tallahassee the next morning to seek out Samuel B. Lense and find out the name of his other sources in Hendrix.

With that information in hand, they'd either talk to Ms. Hoyt or head out to Hendrix—it was hard to plan any further than that, Hendrix being what it was. Hollis figured that if Ms. Hoyt had been open enough to talk to a researcher from UF, she could be persuaded by the lure of the almighty dollar to share the same information with him, Hollis Frazier. He'd brought along $10,000 in cash for such a purpose, though he'd kept that small detail from Charley, who was poor as hell and might scoff at the idea of buying back what was rightfully theirs. Hollis had no such compunction. He had plenty of money, all over the damn place, and was prepared to part with it if it meant an honorable end to this nasty business, and the fulfillment of one of his father's last wishes, albeit more than thirty years too late.

That was the plan, though from the moment he woke up, it began to go awry, as the ten-hour drive had irritated his bursitis, and he'd awoken with a crick in his neck and a numb right arm. After he'd taken Snowflake to the garden to do his business, he couldn't resist a soak in the marble Jacuzzi that was equipped for honeymoon luxury with all manner of bath salts and oils. Hollis had gone about making a bath with the same expertise he created his signature Brunswick stew, with lavish handfuls of lavender and bath salt, and had barely lowered himself into the ecstasy of the hot, steaming bubbles when he heard a knock at the door and a murmur of voices as their breakfast was delivered.

Hollis could smell the coffee in the bathroom, and as he lay there in the tub, luxuriating in the steady pound of the hot jets on his sore back and shoulder, he was washed with a rare affection for the swamps and piney woods of West Florida, and their multicolored, multitalented natives. They were ignorant, lazy, and occasionally savage, but by God they were generous, if need be, with that crazy, green-eyed desire to please that you didn't find anywhere else in the South.

He was actually looking forward to going out to Hendrix. He had taken the phone book to bed with him the night before and scanned the local listings. He found Camp Six long dissolved, of course, and only a handful of familiar names listed: Johnsons and Bryants, Stallings and Hamiltons and Hitts, but no Kites. When he finally climbed out of the Jacuzzi, refreshed and relaxed and starving to death, he knew, sight unseen, that the local sausage would be a thing of beauty, homemade and country, probably the kindly remains of someone's fat-bellied hog. He was so eager to get at it that he didn't bother to dress. He wrapped a big hotel towel around his waist and headed down the hallway, which smelled deliciously of fresh coffee and fried pork. He was almost to the corner when he clearly heard Charley say, "Naw, it was on Granny's land, not the—"

"*No!*" Hollis cried without thinking, but he was too late.

He turned the corner on a chummy, domestic sight. Charley was in his old farmer clothes, sitting at the table calmly sipping coffee, the Hoyt woman sitting across from him with her own coffee, reading the pages Hollis had printed out in Memphis, her face a study in disbelief. "And it was posted online? With my name on it?"

"*No!*" Hollis insisted, clutching his towel at the waist and snatching the papers from her hands, his being undressed causing Charley to clamber to his feet and shout, "Hollis? You lost yo mind? Git some clothes on, son!"

Hollis answered in kind, then pointed a warning finger at both of them. "Hush your mouth—both of you. Not another word till I get dressed. You hear me?"

He turned on his heel and went back to the bathroom to throw on some clothes and get back and straighten it out before Charley ruined everything, but found he'd left his clothes in the bedroom. He had to open the door and shout for Charley to *bring* him his *damn* pants. He stood on the old plank floor, dancing with anger, till Charley finally appeared, unruffled and unhurried, and told him the coast was clear: Miz Hoyt had gone to work.

"Well, that's *great*," Hollis breathed, stalking naked down the hallway and ripping open his suitcase, telling Charley over his shoulder, "That was a nice move, spilling your *guts,* first chance you *got.* What the *hell* were you thanking?"

Charley was old, but unbent, and paid no mind to his brother's nagging. He just returned to his seat and poured another cup of coffee with infuriating mildness. "I never meant to creep back here like a *thief* in the *night.* I ain't got nothing to hide."

"Good for you," Hollis snapped, yanking on his pants with fast, angry hands and dressing as quickly as he could.

He didn't bother letting Charley in on his plans, but laced his shoes and hurried down the drive to his car, knowing that his window of opportunity was rapidly shrinking, and hoping to catch Sam Lense before he'd received any fair warning. He punched his dash phone to voice activation so he could drive and talk at the same time and chatted up a dozen different receptionists as he went east, till he pinpointed the office of Samuel B. Lense.

Apparently Mr. Lense was no longer connected with the archives, but was an officer in Economic Development, high enough on the masthead to have a corner office and a shared secretary who wasn't at her desk. A note taped to her computer screen said she'd be back at two. Hollis was sidetracked, but undeterred, and after a little snooping found Mr. Lense in a glassed-in room across the hall, sitting at a long conference table that was piled high with fee schedules, open manuals, and reams of computer paper. He was dressed in the uniform of the Florida bureaucrat: pressed chinos and a white button-down with sleeves rolled to his elbows. His stockiness made him look more reformer than accountant, and he had a definite hint of urban assertiveness when he saw Hollis at the door. He came briskly to his feet and extended a strong hand, shaking it solidly and asking, "Are you from District Four? You're early. Everyone's at lunch. I'm about to eat at my desk. Can I send for something for you?"

He was obviously expecting someone, and Hollis didn't forfeit the advantage. He was very understanding about the mix-up and agreeable to waiting in Lense's office, though he passed on the food. The office was as jam-packed as the conference room, with an oversize monitor full of numerical gibberish and a printer in a corner, spewing thin sheaves of pale, sickly green paper. Mr. Lense cleared off a space and, between phone calls and quick bites of an enormous club sandwich, conveyed a good bit of personal information, as if they were fellow passengers on a long layover in Atlanta, killing time in the bar. With no prodding at all, Hollis learned that Lense was Miami-born and divorced and had a kid and a brother with cancer, a widower father, and an assumed mortgage Lense was hoping to convert to a low-interest loan.

He offered the insider edition of his life as generously as he did his bag of Kettle chips, and it wasn't difficult for Hollis to maneuver the conversation in a generic direction, bringing up football, and commenting off-hand, "So, you were a Gator? What did you major in? History?"

Lense was finished with his sandwich and gathered up the trash. "Anthropology," he said, hitting the can with his wadded-up napkin in a perfect three-pointer, then turning back to Hollis and, for no reason he could surmise, suddenly seeming to smell a rat. "How the hell did you know?" Lense asked with what must have been a characteristic bluntness. "That I went to UF?"

Hollis smiled disarmingly. "I read a paper you wrote, on the Creek Indians. A very interesting paper," he added in a sincere compliment, then dropped his bomb without preamble: "Henry Kite was a neighbor of mine."

Mr. Lense's reaction was telling in its absence of guilt. He didn't so much as flinch. "Henry *who*?"

"*Kite.* The man who was lynched in '38, in Hendrix. You mentioned him, in yo paper."

"*Oh.*" Lense sat back casually and crossed his arms protectively across his chest. "What about it?"

Hollis understood that he'd shown a few cards by speaking so honestly, but Mr. Lense seemed capable of handling a little unvarnished honesty, and Hollis laid it out plainly: "Well, you mention in yo paper how they cut off Kite's fangers. Kept 'em in a gin bottle, out in Hendrix."

Mr. Lense listened closely, but his earlier gregariousness was gone, his face speculative as he repeated, "What about it?"

"Well, whoever told you it that way told it wrong. Them fangers weren't Kite's. They belonged to a neighbor of his, name of Buddy Frazier. Men from the mill come on him working his fields and cut off two of 'em trying to make him talk. Kept 'em, too—showed 'em off around town later thet night. I know that for a fact."

A local man might have argued the point, but Sam Lense was obviously not local, and obviously not connected by bone marrow or raw nerve to anything in Hendrix. He denied nothing, but unexpectedly confirmed the story. "Yeah, I heard. They terrorized the town after—set the turpentine stills on fire and killed five people, including a pregnant woman."

"Kite's sister," Hollis offered equably. "Eight months gone, and namore guilty of murder than the man in the moon. But I ain't here for the Kites. Buddy Frazier was my father." Hollis unconsciously lifted his chin. "Them fangers are mine—and I want 'em back."

Sam Lense seemed taken aback for the first time. "Want 'em for *what*?"

Hollis looked at him in wonder. "To bury with the rest of his mortal remains. Whatchu *thank*?"

Lense just blinked at the answer, then shook his head and told him plainly, "Well, I don't have 'em, if that's what you're asking."

"Didn't thank you did," Hollis rejoined quickly, touchy at the hint of big-city smart-assness when speaking of so sacred a subject. "But somebody does. I'd like to talk to your *sources*."

"In *Hendrix*? What makes you think they're even alive? I mean, I wrote that thing in '96. They were old, even then."

It was Hollis's turn to be annoyed, as he'd assumed it was recent work, a stupid assumption, now that he thought of it. In a rare show of temper, he rapped his knuckles on the desktop.

*"Damn,"* he whispered, staring out the smudged window at a depressingly urban stretch of pebbled roof and treeless parking lot. He considered it a moment, till the single obvious lead came to him. "I can talk to Jolie Hoyt. She still lives there. She might know."

At the mention of the name, Lense's face went suddenly, carefully blank. "Maybe, but Hoyt's a common name out there. Half the county is a Hoyt," he explained, though the evasion was obvious. He proved it in his next breath, when he asked with great, guarded nonchalance, "Were they really involved in the Kite murder?"

*"Hell* yes, they were involved. Everybody in Hendrix was—Cleary, too. Doan ever let 'em tell you different."

Mr. Lense didn't argue the point, but retrieved a paper clip from his desktop that he unbent absently. "Which ones?"

"Don't know no names. I'se a kid when Mama put us on the train. My brother Chollie—he remembers more. Done things to Kite I wouldn't have done to a dog. You know thet?"

Sam Lense kept his eyes on his paper clip, thoughtful, a little grim, and shrugged to indicate that, yes, he had heard rumors to that effect. "Yeah, but Hendrix was always a Red Stick town, and Florida aborigines often tortured their enemies—dismembered them ceremonially. I think Kite might have fallen into some sort of deep-seated, archetypal pattern."

"A *whut?*"

Lense refused to repeat it. "Never mind. Well, shit," he said after a glance at his watch. He came to his feet in dismissal. "Well, as much as I'd love to sit and chat about ritual mutilation, I got a quarterly meeting and budget pending."

Hollis had noticed that the empty offices had come back to life, a steady stream of clerks and secretaries and staffers drifting across the hall to the conference room. He saw it was time to be leaving and came to his feet and extended another hand to Mr. Lense, to thank him for his time.

Mr. Lense accepted with another firm shake and lowered his voice. "And I'd keep to the main roads in Hendrix, if I was you—wouldn't go down there alone unless I had to."

He said it without macho swagger, in a low-key note of caution, offered so seriously that Hollis paused in the door to ask, "It's still that way?" The comfort of the old B&B had made him think it might be otherwise.

Sam Lense met Hollis's eye a moment in answer, then took a step back into his office and yanked his shirt from his waistband with impatient hands, exposing an intricate tracery of well-healed scars, now faded to a pearl gray. Hollis was retired military and knew a rifle wound when he saw it.

"*Hendrix?*" he murmured in a small, wary voice, as if the town were a physical entity, capable of evil intent.

"A stray shot by a poacher on the river." Mr. Lense dropped his shirt and went about tucking it in. "Or that was the official verdict. If I was you, I'd go to the archives and do my legwork there. The Hoyts"—he paused—"they're a slippery bunch."

"Including Jolie?"

Mr. Lense looked pained at the question, but was grudgingly positive. "She's all right—safer than Hendrix, at least." He tucked in his shirt as he walked Hollis to the elevator. "Lives in Cleary, I hear—somewhere downtown. She's probably at work this time of day, shouldn't be too hard to find."

Hollis was glad of the tip as he'd not got around to sniffing out his landlady's day job. "She work at the bank?" he asked as he punched the down button, opening the scuffed metal doors.

"Try City Hall. The mayor's office."

Hollis raised his eyebrows. "She works for the mayor?"

For the first time, he got a ghost of a smile from the hardworking Mr. Lense, who leaned in and dropped his voice to confide, "She *is* the mayor."

"Of Cleary?" Hollis cried, more shocked at this than he'd been at the sight of Sam's chest. "A Hoyt?"

"From Hendrix." Sam grinned, then added in an even slier aside, "You ever watch televangelists—you know, the God channel, on TV?"

"Never," Hollis murmured.

"Watch it tonight, around eight. Might see a familiar face."

# Chapter Seventeen

Jolie Hoyt's meteoric rise in local politics was neither as melodramatic nor torrid as either Hollis Frazier or Sam had imagined it to be from afar. She actually walked a well-trod path blazed by the clubwomen of previous generations, who'd proved their mettle in political deal-making on beautification and temperance boards across the South. They were perfumed, be-gloved, well connected, and ruthless, and the bane of any elected official who crossed them.

Jolie emulated them as closely as she did every other mother figure in her life and took the plum job of mayor after paying her dues in the ordinary way, with a long stint on the Historic and Beautification Board, and back-to-back terms as a rare female city commissioner. Her rise had been quick, but hard-won, as she had no deep roots in Cleary proper to recommend her, other than Hugh, who alienated as many voters as he won with his smart mouth and condescending ways. Her real base was her old pals in the Garden Club set, who were her great and steadfast supporters as she transformed the faded, deserted little downtown into a well-known stop on the local antiques circuit. The oasis of cobblestoned streets and graceful Drake elms had won a Florida Main Street Award, and a bit of national attention.

After four years in office, it was still her crowning achievement, though she'd grown into the job in time and learned to satisfy the conflicting agendas of her varied constituency, which was rural enough to still be rigidly divided by race and economics. White Cleary was still numerically the majority, though they were increasingly split along the blue-state, red-state divide. The latter was working class, churchy, and pro-business in any form, be it farming, nuclear waste, or bringing in prisons. They liked homeschooling, guns, and Fox News and were generally supportive of Jolie in that she was churchy, pro-jobs, and laughed at their jokes. But she was a slightly better fit with what served as blue-state in Cleary—a vocal, politically correct handful of young lawyers and doctors and artistes who weren't locally grown, but had come to the area for the rural charm and had a great commitment to preserving a small-town aesthetic. They went practically insane at the cutting of the most rotten urban oak.

The locals called them *yuppies,* and they called the locals *rednecks,* and the white vote usually split between them, leaving the city government to be largely decided by the hitherto ignored sector of Southern politics that was black Cleary. This was a sizable base, the third generation of the slaves of a few local plantations, and the old turpentine camps, who had memories as long as the Hoyts, maybe longer. They were children of the civil rights era and had only voted for a Hoyt after Jolie had done the one thing that no white candidate had done before: she'd taken the fight to the churches.

That was her home turf, after all, and the month before her first election, she'd appeared at any church that would have her and spoken for three minutes at the end of the service. She hadn't tried to avoid the obvious, but admitted that, yes, she was a Hoyt from Hendrix, ". . . and I know that out there in your cemetery, the saints of God who have gone before are rolling in their graves this minite. Which is the reason I'm here: to tell you that I ain't a racist and I never was, and if your children went to school with me, they know that—you ask 'em, they'll tell you. Neither was my brother, Carl. He was an *idiot,* but he wasn't a racist. And if you're worried I won't give the black citizens of Cleary a fair shake, well, take a good look around the city offices next time you pay your electric bill, and tell me how many black folk you see working there now, in the cable company or water treatment, or on the commission. You ask yourself how less represented can you get than you are now. If you're ready for a change, so am I."

That was her basic message, straight and to the point, and with such a blunt appeal she had taken office and kept it two terms, running City Hall much as her father had run his church, with equal parts affection and exasperation, and a keen understanding of the imperfectability of man. There at first, she had taken pains to explain to everyone, in Hendrix and Cleary alike, that Hugh was her *business,* not her *romantic,* partner.

But as the years went by, she had mellowed in the way that all Southerners do and had pretty much embraced her reputation as a hustling country girl who'd worked her way out of poverty by dint of a good pair of legs and a nose for aligning herself to the right menfolk. That reputation, like everything else in her life, was true as far as it went (it just didn't go very far). She was never tempted to wax too nostalgic over her lost childhood, as Carl did, and aside from the occasional trip to El Bethel to attend the odd funeral or visit one of the old Sisters, she no longer concerned herself with its mysteries, till the Frazier brothers laid the matter on her doorstep.

When she left the carriage house that morning, she went straight to her office at City Hall, which, thanks to her superior skills in snagging beautification grants, was housed in a forties-era bungalow a block off Main Street. Jolie found it hopping as usual on a second Monday, as the electric bills had gone out the Friday before and such was the compactness of Cleary's citizenry (not to mention their cheapness) that the smallest infraction merited a phone call to City Hall, or in a few cases a visit to wave the offending bill in the city staff's face and demand divine justice.

Jolie didn't stop and chat as she usually did, but went straight to her office at the end of a long hall, which had once been a closed-in sun-porch and still faced a bit of original garden. She loved the view, even in the doldrums of winter, but had yet to figure out a way to properly heat the room, thanks to the bank of drafty double-paned windows. Her fabulous tiger-oak desk—a gift from Hugh on her first day in office—was cold as a block of ice, and without taking off her coat, she dropped her purse in her desk drawer and went down the hallway to the city manager's office at the far end of the house.

Tad was the junior member of the staff, a tech genius with a degree in public service, who was putting a wife through law school at FSU. He was off on Mondays, his office a study in creative chaos, though his computer was a Mac Pro, loaded with every spy, search, and storage device known to man. Jolie applied the passwords and began punching, searching the web for the irritating piece of character assassination that had fallen into her lap that morning at breakfast.

She thought she'd find it buried in some deeply encrypted file in some code-accessed database and spent the morning skimming individual files on the state archives. She uncovered much of the same old ground on the Hendrix Lynching, including the photo of Kite, tied to a tree, hanging between heaven and earth. This very image was often used as a stock photo to illustrate the practice of lynching, and Jolie paid it little mind, clicking quickly on till she came upon a poorly designed website on the Five Civilized Tribes, garishly colored, bracketed by a banner headline that flittered from ads for local real estate and cures for erectile dysfunction.

The author's name was proudly displayed: *Samuel B. Lense, the University of Florida,* the adjoining essay obviously culled from his great Indian study, with no clue from where or how the data had been drawn. It was just a disjointed pile of anecdotes, numbers, and hard history, occasionally divided by bold-faced subtitles, as if someone had scanned a file cabinet into a database. All of it was familiar—old Hendrix tales of Camp Six and the census, graveyard notes and tombstone inscriptions—until she came upon a heading provocative enough to make the hair on her neck stand up: "The Illustrious Hoyt Tribe of Hendrix."

She could feel the color rising in her cheeks as she read, this section much more casual and chatty, suggesting an immediate image of Sam lounging around the little camper in his underwear and dissecting the Hoyts with relish. There was a page or two of outlandish theory on the origin of the term *Little Black Dutch,* similar to the smart little explanation he'd given her that first night at the café. Much was made of the census and where the Hoyts appeared on it. Then the narrative broke off and was subtitled a final time: "The Hendrix Lynching."

"Son of a *bitch,*" Jolie murmured.

She expected an in-depth exposé of the Kite murder, but the section was brief and primarily dealt with odd details about the turpentine side of the Hammond Lumber Company, Camp Six. She vaguely remembered Sam's being fixated on it, back in the day, and here he did indeed wax eloquent about how awful life must have been there, his distaste seasoned with a good bit of Olde European Socialism that made Jolie roll her eyes, even as she read (liberal *and* exploitive: now there was a guy!) till the final paragraph:

> In 1938 Hendrix became a name of infamy, after a particularly gruesome lynching of a local man named Henry Kite, who was accused of murdering a shop owner in cold blood, plunging the area into four days of racial violence where five people were hanged, including the mother and sister of the accused, the latter heavily pregnant.
>
> The violence predictably fell according to racial lines, the white men all employees of the Hammond Lumber Company; the blacks, turpentiners from Camp Six, who were far down the caste system, considered dangerous and expendable.* For many years Kite's murder and the ensuing violence was shrouded in secrecy, the tree limb where he was hung neatly removed in 1975 by a city commission concerned with bad PR, though Hendrix

natives have never denied their participation in what is considered the last of the spectacle lynchings.

*Local families such as the Hoyts still boast of owning pieces of the rope, and his fingers, which were severed as souvenirs, can still be found in Hendrix, though one native regretfully added that most of them were lost, as they'd been taken into Cleary the day of the lynching and thrown on black citizens' porches, in warning.*

It ended there, on something of a cliff-hanger, with no further annotation, or explanation of why the lynching was so thoroughly attached to the Hoyts. To Jolie, none of it was new, and the most that could be said of it was that it settled, once and for all, the great mystery of why Sam was there—truly to dig into the lynching. Why, she did not know—and why he'd waited this long to post his findings, she knew even less.

What she did know was that she had surely been snookered, in a way that still rankled, making her sit back in Tad's ergonomic chair and rub her eyes, wondering who told Sam about the rope, which, as far as Jolie could tell, was pure myth. She knew that it wasn't either her uncle Ott or, God forbid, her father, if for no other reason than neither would have spoken of it with humor or spiced it with profanity. They'd certainly never discussed it with her, though she'd heard a good bit about it from Carl and her cousins, when they were young men intent on honing their reputations as Hendrix badasses. They'd heard all the details down at the fish camp on hunting weekends and took a lot of perverse, macho pleasure in rumors of the Hoyt participation, as evidence of their superior ferocity and strength. They might be dark and mixed and poor as dirt, but they didn't take any shit from anybody, they bragged, and with a wink sometimes added a smug "Ask Henry Kite."

Jolie groaned to think of it, as a good many of her loyal constituents were from families who'd been run out of Camp Six and had settled up the road in Cleary, where they'd been absorbed into the local black community. They had contributed high cheekbones and green eyes to more than a few honey-skinned homecoming queens. They knew who they were, and she them, and as long as she treated them with the same respect as she did every other man, woman, and child, they put up with her. They even swayed the vote in her favor after she took to the churches. It made for a delicate balance, and she'd be hard-pressed to talk her way out of it if Henry Kite's name resurfaced in any sort of public forum. She wished this tricky bit of political reality had occurred to her in her extreme youth, when she had been so caught up in sharing the magic of her elusive *ethnicity* with Sam Lense.

She was sitting there, tapping a nail on Tad's cluttered desktop, when the in-house line buzzed, so obnoxiously loud that she nearly jumped out of her skin. She dug around the paperwork to unearth the phone and found Faye on the line, Jolie's right hand and longtime city clerk, who was at that moment deep in the electric-bill drama, her voice harassed.

"What arre you doing, nosing around back there? We're dying up here. Can I give Farris a refund out of my purse, or do we really have to track it? I mean, Jol, we're talking four dollars."

Faye had come up the ranks in a more human, less regulated time, and with great regret Jolie told her, "You have to do it on the program. Have Tad come in early. I know it's a pain. I'll be up in a minute."

"Well, good," Faye said in the honeyed tones of a South Georgia native. "We are floundahing up heah, could use a hand—and you have a visitor most insistent to see you. A black gentleman," she said in a mildly strained voice, as if having to stretch her neck to see him over the counter. "I don't think I know him." She added, after a pause, "Neither does Tamara."

Tamara was the deputy city clerk Jolie had hired shortly after her election to—finally, forty-four years after the Civil Rights Act—integrate the city desk. If the man was black and Tamara didn't know him, he wasn't from Cleary.

A great weariness settled on Jolie's chest when she realized who it was. "Does he have a fur collar?"

"Yeah, and a hat. Looks like a *congress*man or something. Who is he?"

"New renter," Jolie said shortly, and thought about dismissing him with a time-honored dodge—telling him she was busy or at breakfast or due at a meeting. But she was known to give audience to all comers, including (and especially) Cleary's minority community. If she turned him away, Tamara and Faye would do even more eye-lifting. Between them, they were kin to everyone in the state and quick on the scent of scandal. "Send him to my office, then buzz me in five minutes for a meeting."

Faye easily agreed, as this was standard procedure with walk-ins, who regularly captured Jolie around town and unloaded their angst over a multitude of injustices—not just inaccurate electric bills, but zoning irregularities, fees for Pop Warner football, the illegitimacy of the Federal Reserve, and the like. As a rule, they didn't require action, but a compassionate ear, which she was happy to provide, as long as they could fit it into a five-minute visit; otherwise she'd never get anything else done.

She closed down the website and hurried down the hall, hoping to be seated when he came in so she'd have the psychological refuge of the enormous desk. But Faye was quick on the draw and already waiting at the door with Hollis Frazier, whom she introduced in the over-the-top Bainbridge, Georgia, drawl she reserved for VIPs. "Missus May-yah, this is Mis-tah Fra-zah, from Mem-phas, to see you."

Jolie didn't offer the old man a handshake—she was too peeved with his duplicity for that. She directed him to the leather visitor's chair, then thanked Faye and took her seat behind the football-field expanse of desk, which had once belonged to Hugh's banker father. It provided a nice psychological buffer between her and her citizens—a yard and a half of polished oak. Hollis Frazier seemed unaffected by the high-gloss barrier, taking in the well-appointed office and massive desk with great amiability, as if he found it endlessly amusing, a Hoyt ruling the roost in Cleary.

Jolie found his enjoyment more patronizing than otherwise and tried to move things along with a little honesty. "Not to be rude, Mr. Frazier, but my clerk will be buzzing me in about three minutes for a meeting. Was there something I could help you with?"

Hollis couldn't help but smile at her ill-temper, which gave her hazel eyes a truly Hendrix glint. "Oh, I think you know how you can hep me, Miss Hoyt," he answered, though Jolie really wasn't sure what he was after and held up her hands in a gesture of acquiescence, indicating that he was free to ask.

After speaking so plainly with Sam Lense, he'd given up all hope of anonymity and didn't beat around the bush. "I'm here on the matter of Henry Kite."

To her credit, the mayor didn't wince at the name, but nodded briefly, as if she was braced for the question. "How so? I mean, what are we talking here? Reparations? Access to courthouse records? Pray be frank, Mr. Frazier. I do have other city business to attend to."

Had Hollis not seen the real Ms. Hoyt the day before in all her down-home, hospitable glory, he would have been put off by her briskness, which was painfully correct and unyielding. But he knew her game, and if she wanted to play hardball, he was willing and able. "Well, according to eyewitness accounts, there are certain *souvenirs*—supposedly of Kite's—still circulating around Hendrix. Two of 'em belong to me. Or rather, me and my brother."

"Two what?"

"Fangers," he told her plainly, and held up his right hand with the middle two fingers bent to demonstrate. "Middle ones. Right hand."

After three years in public office, Jolie was used to the gonzo requests made of the mayor of a poor, black-belt town, and like her father before her, she could exhibit iron control when she wanted to. She didn't blink at the strange request, but answered impassively, "Well, what makes you think I can hep you, Mr. Frazier? I'm the mayor of Cleary. I understand Henry Kite was killed down in Hendrix, long before my time."

Hollis Frazier nearly smiled as he told her, "Mr. Lense assured me you could."

Jolie was feeling far from happy with Mr. Lense at the moment, but didn't betray it openly, just murmured, "Mr. *Lense*," in a small undertone, then smoothly came to her feet. "I'm sorry, sir, but I think you are mistaken. You need to go over to the archives, at the capitol. They have a wealth of local history—and the staff to *indulge* you."

She emphasized the word to stinging effect and, for the first time, drew something other than politeness from the manicured old man, who sighed hugely at her evasion, even as he rose to his feet. He replaced his hat on his head with great deliberation and seemed on the point of agreeable departure, but paused in the doorway. He glanced down the hall, as if making sure they were alone, then chided her in a small sing-song, "Miss Hoyt, Miss *Hoyt*—don't even try thet high-handed white-woman *shit* wid me. I know who you *are*—how you come to be sitting behind that big *desk,* 'stead of an ironing board."

Jolie had heard similar statements often enough before and didn't blink. She remained unyielding, so that Hollis unbent enough to add, "I'm a reasonable man, Miz Hoyt, and willing to pay for your time. Ten thousand, cash. It would mean a lot to my brother," he thought to offer, as it was the by-God truth.

But the ironing-board comment had possibly gone a little over the line, the mayor's face immobile as she cast a weather glance up and down the hallway, then leaned in and confided, "My grandmother was a whore, Mr. Frazier. I am not. But feel free to go on down round Hendrix and talk to anyone you meet. Ask whatever you like," she added with an edge that crossed a line of its own, making Hollis lose his good humor and all trace of a smile.

"Is that a *threat,* Miss Hoyt?"

She didn't dignify the question with a reply, but turned on her heel and went down the hall to the clerk's counter, calling, "Faye? Could you draw Mr. Frazier a map to Hendrix and give him Jimmy Tarleton's home number?" To Hollis, she added in her finest civic voice, "Mr. Tarleton is the chair of the Historical Committee. Perhaps he could assist you with your *research.*"

She was too angry to talk and would have ended it there, but he stopped her with a final question, aimed at her back, which rang out down the high hallway. "Miss Mayor? What happened to the limb?"

She turned, her eyebrows politely lifted, her face a serious hue of deep red. "Pardon *me*?"

"The *limb*, where they hung Henry Kite. The tree's still there, but the limb's gone. Me and my brother, we wondered what'd become of it."

Faye and Tamara looked up at the name like hounds on a scent, first at the stranger, then the mayor, who answered easily enough, in that smooth politician's voice, "Why, I believe the commission had all those old oaks pruned—oh, years ago. Perhaps Mr. Tarleton can help you on thet, too. He's also a member of the Beautification Board, which oversees Arbor Day, and the like. Good day, *suh*."

If he made a reply, she didn't hear it, retreating to her office and physically restraining herself from slamming the door. She got it shut without violence and for a moment stood with her back to it, obeying the golden rule of the female politician (never let them see you cry). She drew a deep breath, able to control her tear ducts, though the rest of her body wasn't so obedient, her hands shaking as if she had the plague.

She held one in front of her, small and white and boringly Pentecostal; no polish, no acrylic tips; the hand of a woman who knew how to fry a chicken and strip a floor. She looked at it as if it were an alien member, shaking independently of her reason, as she had nothing to be so terrified of, not really. The impudent son of a bitch had her by the short hairs politically, but he didn't have the power to actually harm her. She'd learned a lesson with Sam Lense and made a point of being invulnerable. She had no local lovers or ailing father or mismatched children or hungry mouths to feed. She was young and independent and well connected and secure as anyone could be in these uncertain times.

It took her hand a few minutes to accept her head's reasoned argument, and when she finally got a grip and quit shaking, she sat at her desk and buzzed Faye, asking her to put in a call to Hubert Altman in New Orleans, and another to her brother, Carl.

"Try him at the church and house, both. Tell him I need to talk to him—to call me at home, or here. Or listen, tell him I'm going down to Hendrix, to call me on my cell."

"What about the planning meeting?" Faye asked. "It's scheduled for six—and you're meeting with Glen at five thirty."

Jolie cursed under her breath. "I forgot. That idiot cell tower." She blew out her breath in exasperation. "Well, call Glen and tell him I might be late—that it's a family emergency, can't be helped." She was moving to hang up the phone when Faye lowered her voice to ask, "Well, what did the ol' gentleman want? Did he say Henry *Kite*?"

Jolie closed her eyes at the name and dissembled with little skill. "Yeah. He's a history buff, here on business. Owns some barbecue joints in Memphis, thinking of opening one here."

Faye was too old and too blunt to be drawn into such an apparent lie and had begun to say as much when she broke off their conversation to speak to someone aside in a bright, cheerful drawl, "No trouble atall. You ah certainly welcome." She came back to the phone after a few more pleasantries and resumed in a normal voice, "That was him. Nice old fellow, very polite."

Jolie straightened up. "You mean Mr. Frazier? He's still here?"

Faye answered with her earlier strain, as if again stretching her neck, this time to watch him leave. "Yeah. Needed to check his e-mail. I sent him back to Tad's."

This kind of accommodation was typical for Faye, who was a student of the old Southern School of Feminine Charm, where if a rich man asked you to saw off your leg, you'd oblige with a smile. Jolie didn't bother to curse, just slapped down the phone and ran to Tad's jumbled desk, where his computer was returned to the screen saver.

She brought up the search history, where the digital trail she'd blazed was still there: *Kite+Ott Hoyt+Hendrix*; then *Kite+Melissa Cuffey Wright+Hendrix*; and last but not least *Raymond Hoyt+Hendrix+Henry Kite*. Below were two additional searches that Frazier must had done himself, both people searches in Hendrix, one for *Ott Hoyt*; the other, *Melissa Cuffey Wright,* along with her address on Wright Circle. When

Jolie saw them, she did something that as a daughter of Raymond Hoyt she was seldom known to do: she used the Lord's name in vain, briefly and sincerely, the emphasis on the *damn*.

She deleted it all, then went back to retrieve her purse and coat, pausing at the clerk's counter long enough to tell Faye, "Ask Carl to meet me at the church."

"His church?" Faye asked, feeling for a pencil.

"No, Daddy's. Tell him it's an emergency. I have one stop first, then I'll be there—in an hour, or two at the most. Tell him I'll be in the shed."

Faye paused in her jotting. "The *what*?"

Jolie repeated herself and assured Faye: "He'll know what I mean."

# Chapter Eighteen

Sam Lense had been an officer in financial services so long that he had seldom considered the implications of the pile of raw data he had boxed up and sent to the Florida Museum of Natural History sometime at the end of his storied days in Hendrix. His father still dutifully forwarded any inquiries to Sam's old research that appeared in Len's mailbox in Coral Gables, but Sam had never bothered to open them, much less given permission for the research to be posted online.

He couldn't imagine how it had come to light, and when Hollis Frazier left, he ducked out of his afternoon meeting and, with minimum effort, found the gaudy aggregate site on the Five Civilized Tribes, where his work had been dumped with senseless abandon: copies of the census; rough drafts on the Creek application; clues to the location of Camp Six; bits of transcribed notes from his interviews with two dozen people, mostly anonymous. The Creek data was jumbled together, lost in minutiae, while the Hoyts were lavishly dissected with great testosterone-fueled delight, down to a few fanciful theories of origin, tossed out in a tone of mild self-righteousness. Their participation in the Kite lynching was offered without question, the last paragraph so smug and incendiary that he rubbed his neck when he was done and thought, No wonder they shot me.

He was spooked enough to get up and lock his office door before

he read it again, wondering how Henry Kite had come to be so promi-
nently figured. God knows he'd never gone to any pains to exonerate
the murderous bastard. He couldn't even remember who'd told him the
nasty little detail about the severed fingers—either Lena or one of Jolie's
Hoytling cousins, surely. Then he remembered. *Damn,* it was Travis
*Hoyt.*

Sam found this a *very* interesting detail and sat back in his chair
a long moment, absently tapping his pencil on his desktop in something akin to honest regret, thinking, poor Jol—she could run, but she
couldn't hide. He almost pitied her there on her hard-won perch at City
Hall in Cleary, the picture of modern woman-power in a photo that had
run in the *Democrat* when her cityscape had won some sort of national
award. They'd photographed her on the square in downtown Cleary, surrounded by an adoring band of white-haired ladies and a square-jawed
old man in a European-cut suit—the hundred-year-old boyfriend whose
itch she was apparently still scratching.

To Sam, she was a far cry from the Jolie of their youth, dressed in
a pin-striped, Julia Sugarbaker power suit, as dark-haired and milk-
skinned as ever, filled out to a handsome, formidable-looking woman.
Her fragile self-image had been cured by a high-dollar haircut, her
outsider sulkiness replaced by an insider confidence that was nearly as
Teflon-slick as her brother's, as was her personal charisma, which had
won her many friends. The legislators of the state of Florida were aging
out, and both parties were desperate for new blood and new faces to fill
the seats of the Old Capitol. Possible names were often bandied about,
and even in the cavelike honeycombs of DCF Sam had heard rumors of
a dark-horse up-and-comer from Cleary, who had the backing of both
Old Money and the Religious Right, but was somehow not a Republi-
can, but a social-justice, yellow-dog Democrat, right out of the church,
if such a thing was possible. There was talk of her running for higher
office, a state Senate seat, or maybe her appointment to the chairman-
ship of something or other; something to get her out of the backwoods
and to the national stage.

Sam never added to the discussion, even to admit that he knew her, though a few loose ends and a nagging air of irresolution remained between them—not to mention four miles of healed-over chest scar. The old man's implacable quest for justice shamed him, made him wonder if he had quit too soon in his search for his own family justice. God, when was the last time he'd thought of old Morris, moldering in an unmarked grave in some backwoods Baptist cemetery, grass-grown and unmarked? Had Sam ever even taken the time to tell Brice the sad and sordid little story? God, he was getting as bad as his father. Consciously or not, he was deep-sixing his son's history.

The thought was far from pleasant, and Sam was still sitting there, absently tapping his desk, when the phone buzzed on an outside line. He figured they were trying to shame him into joining the meeting and let it buzz a few rounds till it was so annoying he answered with a brisk "Yeah."

The line was silent a moment, then a woman asked in a small, slightly Southern accent, "May I speak to Sam Lense?"

He blinked at the accent and sat up straighter. "Jolie?"

"No," she murmured, her voice muted, as if on a speakerphone. "It's Lena. Lena Hoyt—Carl's wife," she added, as if she and Sam were slight acquaintances. "My father ran the campground—Vic Lucas."

Sam had never for a moment forgotten any of the characters of his old folktale. "Yeah. Lena. Sure. What's going on?"

His briskness seemed to intimidate her, as there was another silence, then a small, tentative question: "Did Jolie call you?"

"No, haven't talked to her. Why d'you ask?"

After a small exhalation of breath, almost a sigh, Lena made a subtle attempt to backpedal. "Oh, nothing. Just—how have you been? Are you good?"

"I'm great," he snapped, impatient with the evasion. "What's this about? The bullet in my back, or the Hendrix Lynching?" For a moment the line was open, suspended in some palpable emotion, dread or shock or fury, which only made Sam more aggressive. "They're onto it, Lena.

People are making inquiries. The cat is out of the bag." He was drawing his breath to ask to speak to her husband when she hung up on him, just like that, in a way that was just so very Hoyt and cowardly and *bullshit*.

He slammed the phone on its cradle and wiped the contents of his desk to the floor in an angry swipe of impatience—a not-uncommon gesture in the world of public finance that drew no attention at all on this end of the building. While the papers were settling, he tapped around on the computer and found a number for Cleary City Hall and, with a concerted effort at civility, sat back in his chair and asked to speak to the mayor.

He was ready to go to war, by phone, if necessary, but the clerk, who spoke in a nearly indecipherable South Georgia accent, informed him that the *may-yah* was out of the office. "Is this Brutha Caal?" she asked brightly. "Returning her call?"

Sam lied without compunction, "No, this is his assistant. He is momentarily unavailable, but needs to speak to her badly. Would you mind giving me her cell number? Carl seems to have lost it again," Sam rumbled good-naturedly.

The ruse seemed to work, as she murmured, "Well, none that would work in Hendrix. That's where she was headed. She left him a message"— she paused—"for him to meet her by the shed. Or rathah, *in* the shed."

Sam sat up. "You mean her father's shed? The old tobacco barn? Behind the church?"

Something in his curiosity must have alerted her, as she was suddenly less forthcoming, though relentlessly cordial, drawling, "And what did you say yo-wah name was?"

Sam was already standing for his coat and, in a moment of devilry, answered, "Henry Kite. You can tell her I called."

# Chapter Nineteen

Well, you sho made a mess of thet" was Charley's only comment after Hollis returned to the car and described in some heat and detail his sharp little clash with the mayor.

Enough wisdom was in the statement that Hollis didn't bother to reply; it would only lead to an argument. He wasn't proud of himself for losing his cool and wanted to follow his leads before the mayor could make any phone calls to Hendrix and warn anyone he was coming.

When the light changed, he wheeled the Lincoln around in a complete U-turn, so abruptly Charley grabbed the hand grip and asked, "Where we headed?"

"Hendrix."

*"Good,"* Charley replied, with such satisfaction that Hollis smiled despite himself.

Of all their kinsmen who'd survived the Trouble, Charley had been the least affected, due in part to his innate courage, and in part to his not having been home for most of it, but deep in the swamp, indulging in a youthful passion for fishing. He was on the far end of the swamp, seining fish and drying them on a spit, when Mr. Goss was shot and was still there two days later when the whole town exploded. He had seen not a trace of blood or gore. But he had come home that evening at dusk, exhausted and ready for bed, only to be hustled on the Camp Six train by his hysterical mother, who put a knapsack of corn bread in his lap and told him to look after Hollis, who was yet a boy in knee britches.

Charley had never run from a fight in his life and was big enough to have planned to jump the train in Cleary, with or without his crybaby brother, but a sawyer from the mill, a big Irish man, with a gimpy arm and a face of terror, read the plan in his face and begged him not to return to Hendrix, for his father's sake if not his own. "Nothing for you back thar, young man," he advised, wringing his withered hand in his good one, "and no place for a chile."

The man's fear was a terrible thing to behold, and the old train thumped and struggled along, stopping time and again to pick up stragglers along the narrow spur of railroad that serviced Camp Six, which was so far into the swamp the tracks were usually deserted. Now, they were lined by desperate faces, shouting out with beseeching voices—the voices of desperate women in nightclothes and aprons, who foisted their nursing toddlers on strangers who had a seat and begged the conductor to take more. The gimpy-armed Irishman gave up his seat to a clutch of damp-dressed, hysterical women from the Camp, who told a disjointed story of a freakish turn of evil brought to them by the hand of Henry Kite.

Charley was finally afraid when he heard the name, as Kite was a familiar character around town. Light-skinned and feckless, he had been raised by a mother and an aunt who were devoted to him and his white skin and brought him up to believe he could do no wrong. He'd taken them at their word and never worked a steady job, but drifted in and out of trouble, a gambler and provocateur, who rode about town on a fine gentleman's horse, with an air of invincibility that to black Hendrix was an invitation to trouble. Camp Six tolerated him because of his good looks and devoted mother, but white Hendrix had no use for him at all, and when the first frost fell, he'd been dogged by rumors that he was filling his mother's smokehouse with other men's hogs.

It all came to a head the afternoon Charley left to go downstream, when Kite had walked into the company store before closing to buy cigarettes from the German, who hardly spoke English and greatly depended on his son as his translator. Some said Kite had drawn. Others whispered it was the opposite—that the German had shouted at Kite, who had sworn an oath he'd never take another word from a white man and dropped him with a single shot. In any case, the German had died before he hit the floor, and Kite had lit out for his mother's house, that place of historical refuge. Such was his insolence, Kite had stayed to eat supper, or so the rumor went, and when Mr. Goss and his deputy came for him, Kite talked them into letting him go inside for his shoes to wear to jail. They had somehow agreed, and when he emerged from the bedroom, he had a gun in hand and shot Mr. Goss just as he had the shopkeeper, at point-blank range, scattering bone and brain over his shrieking mother's hearth.

Such were the rumors Charley heard that night on the packed, hysterical train, though the worse news came when he found Tempy waiting at the station in Montgomery, a neighbor's bawling child in one arm, her own baby in the other. She was hardly more than a child herself, and tears ran down her cheeks as she told him how his papa had been caught that morning, in his own fields. The men from Camp had run him down with their horses, had accused him of hiding Kite. When he denied it, they'd laid his hand on a tree stump and cut off the middle fingers with one swipe of the ax, trying to make him talk. They would likely have killed him or taken him to town and thrown him in jail with the rest, but a doe had been flushed out by his scream, a distant flash of white they'd mistaken for Kite, making a break through the brush.

They'd gone after it with a holler, and Charley's papa had made his way back to the house, his dripping hand wrapped in a handkerchief, dizzy with blood loss, though he refused to find a doctor, or to leave himself, at least till his boys came home. He sat with one bloody hand pressed to his chest, the other holding a shotgun in a vigil so taxing that Tempy later swore his hair turned white in the space of a night. The night was so evil you could feel it on your skin, taste it on the ash that began to fall at dawn after they set the gum pots on fire. The flames roared and lit up the sky, so bright that Papa's porch was as light as if in the midday sun, as the turpentiners and their families began their tramp to the train tracks, alone and in families, many wet from swimming the river.

As they paused for a drink at Papa's well, they whispered stories so savage that Papa became convinced that Charley and Hollis had been caught in town, that two of the corpses on display at the commissary were those of his sons. By midday he'd lost all hope and, in stark desperation, lit out to town to retrieve their bodies. When Tempy stumbled upon Charley in the crush at the station that morning, she nearly fainted dead away, thinking she was seeing his ghost.

She had hugged him and Hollis fiercely and hustled them off to another train—a regular one, with a porter, that she paid for with hard cash, which took them straight up the Mississippi to shelter with some of their father's Arkansas kin. The trip north was interminable, and Charley would remember it to the end of his days, sitting at the smeared window of the old coach that smelled of coal heat and cracked leather. A cousin joined them in Vicksburg, yet another shivering survivor of Camp Six. While Hollis slept on Tempy's lap, the cousin whispered details even more nightmarish than the stories told at the well. How they'd caught Kite the night before and taken him to the river to kill him; how you could hear his screams for miles around, unintelligible at first, till he'd started calling for his mother, over and over, *"Ma! Ma!"*—his voice echoing over the pungent smoke of the burning pine.

Charley was old enough to have cursed Kite himself by then, for bringing this nightmare upon them, but the story of his end was so horrifying that it made Tempy start crying again, and even got Charley to bawling, not for the murdered Kite, but for his papa. For a black man to have gone back into town that night was suicide, and the cousin claimed to know for a fact that Buddy was dead, as she'd seen his cut-off fingers with her own eyes, stoppered up in an old gin bottle. A white man was showing it off around town, souvenirs of the kill.

Charley had no reason to doubt her word, and he and Tempy and their Arkansas kin had grieved his parents as dead for nearly a month, till they unexpectedly appeared on his uncle Ned's doorstep the first day of December with nothing but a valise between them and the clothes on their back. By Christmas, all of them were there, except for Tempy's husband, Johnny, who'd insisted on staying, not wanting to give up Tempy's share of the farm. He'd survived awhile, a few months at least, till a runaway mule had overturned his wagon and broken his neck—or so they heard. Such "accidents," though, were common in Hendrix after the Trouble, and for all they knew, he'd ended up at the end of a rope like Henry Kite.

Tempy remarried eventually, and though she never returned to Florida, she and Charley's mother spoke of their lives on the river with a wistful longing till the end of their days. He could remember them rocking on the porch and recalling old family names, their faults and credits, their exact connection to the larger Hendrix clan. Over time, these stories took on mythic proportions that annoyed his papa, who had no love left for Hendrix and disapproved of such sentimental nonsense. They never farmed again. Charley took a job working on a boat on the Arkansas side of the river, where both his parents eventually died, his mother in '58, his father in '73. Only when he was dying did Charley's papa ever voice a single wish about the Trouble: that he could've got his fingers back before he left Florida so they could be buried decently with the rest of his mortal remains.

"Don't begrudge the skin I lost from my leg," he said of a shin wound he'd got in the trenches of the Argonne Forest, "but I do begrudge them fangers."

He made no more of it, as he wasn't a whiner, their papa, though the seed of a bizarre plan to retrieve the fingers took root in Charley's mind. When Hollis came home from Germany for their father's funeral, Charley tried to talk him into going back then, but Hollis wouldn't hear of it. They argued it for three straight days, till their aunt Tempy caught wind of Charley's plans and had all but taken to her bed with horror, making him promise he'd do no such thing.

She was so adamant that Charley had backed off, planning to return when she died, which was a long time coming, as Tempy was tough as a pine knot and lived to a ripe old age of ninety-three. Charley was already losing his sight by then, and though Hollis lived across the river in Overton Park, he was too wrapped up in his money and his women to take off a week to drive to Florida. Hollis told Charley that he would just as soon spend a week in hell.

But the seed was planted, and when Hollis came upon the old names on the Indian site, he knew it was time to get his ass in hand and do the right thing. Once en route now to Hendrix, Hollis put aside his bickering and described the passing scenery for his blind brother in an offhand monotone: "New roof on the courthouse; tin, looks like. Maybe aluminum. Hell of a lot of car lots, and fast-food joints. God, a scat of 'em. Fat bastards," Hollis muttered, as these same franchises were his most vicious competition back in Memphis, the $2 whores of the restaurant industry. "City Hall is where Buddy Smith used to live," he said as they made the edge of town. "The millpond's still here—a restaurant in the icehouse. 'The Catfish House,'" he read as he passed the sign, "'$4.99 Special.' *Huh.* Bet it's thet farm-raised *crap.*"

He had less to say once they were out of town and into the deeper green of the hardwood forest that had once stood in an impenetrable wall, all the way to the Gulf, peopled by tribes so fierce that even de Soto had taken a pass on confrontation and detoured south. The stretches of mobile homes and hardtop and cultivated field had thinned the forest out, but in the floodplain, the shadow of the forest returned to life, overhanging the highway, which dipped in and out of low places, offering flickering glimpses of ponds and bayous, alligators and herons posed over still, green water.

Hendrix itself was impossible to miss, built on the banks of the river in a day when water was considered more reliable transportation than bumpy earth. Hollis was sensitive to his brother's blindness, and as they drew near, he resumed his travelogue. "The river's high here, too—new bridge, goes way out. Wonder what happened to the old?" he asked, ducking to peer into the canopy as they passed.

None of it was familiar to Hollis till they were at the heart of the old downtown, two blocks of abandoned brick and asphalt, when he finally caught sight of a building he recognized. "Why there's the old commissary, surely. God, I remember going there with Papa, to get his pay. There's a new post office—redbrick. 'Hendrix, Florida,'" he read as they passed, "and an IGA—a little un, and a blinking light." Then he realized they were out of town, back on open road. "Well, that's it. Ain't nothing out here but trailers. I'll turn around, go back to the light."

A little more was in that direction, a BP station and a spanking-new Dollar General and a whole lot of trailers in between, the newer ones sitting high on concrete blocks per state floodwater regulation. The KOA was the only hint of modernity, an upbeat neon sign before the brown state sign that marked the entrance to the public launch. Hollis swung a U-turn and made a final pass, but the once-thriving downtown—that busy little brick-and-wood intersection of barbershops and moneylenders and saloons—had been reduced to the old commissary, which sat there, rotting and abandoned, on the grass-grown rails.

Hollis hadn't expected much, but couldn't hide his disappointment in finding Hendrix—that mighty figure of his family mythos—nothing more than a sagging, scattered trailer park.

He said as much to Charley, who snorted, "Whut d'you expect? Place has blood on its hands. Kite cursed it."

"Kite was a murdering son of a bitch," Hollis retorted, as he had no love for the man. "He got what he deserved."

Charley didn't argue the point, but muttered, "Nobody deserved what *he* got," then said, with a tip of his head, "Turn round and go back to the launch. I want to see the river."

Hollis obeyed, though it was damned cold on the water, the Lincoln's thermometer reading thirty-six. He let Snow out to pee and helped his brother tap his way down a gravel path to the edge of the dank, fast-moving water, which he sniffed with appreciation.

"Specks is running," he commented mildly.

His brother was quick to nip that nonsense in the bud. "We ain't here to fish," Hollis told him plainly as he felt in his pocket for the slip of paper he'd brought from City Hall. "We got people to see—'Melissa Cuffey Wright,'" he read, then looked up. "Name ring a bell?" Charley was the family's Hendrix expert now that Tempy was gone.

The old man thought a moment, then allowed, "Seem like I do remember a family of Cuffeys. Four or five girls—their daddy worked at the mill."

That was the most Charley could offer, which was regrettable, as the Lincoln's navigation system wasn't altogether accurate when it came to waterfront addresses. Hollis tapped in the address he'd snagged from the city computer, but the droning, mechanical voice kept telling him to turn left on a street that didn't exist. After circling the post office half a dozen times, Hollis admitted defeat and stopped for directions. The moon-faced clerk was most accommodating, not only sketching him a map, but asking, "Are you going out to buy eggs? Because I don't know if Miz Wright's still selling—you might want to call first."

Hollis was, as usual, fast on his feet and immediately proposed to do just that and asked to borrow the clerk's phone. He made the call right there at the counter and caught her at home. He asked if she was still selling eggs.

"Brown or regular?" the old lady asked in an ancient, wobbly voice.

"Either'll do."

"Well, come on, then. I ain't been out to collect 'em today, but if you doan mind waiting, I don't mind looking."

Hollis assured her that he didn't mind waiting in the least.

# Chapter Twenty

J olie drove straight to Sister Wright's from City Hall, hoping to inter-
cept the Fraziers. She beat them by a good ten minutes and was
immediately relieved when she pulled into the rutted, old drive as no
one appeared to be home. No smoke came from the chimney, no light
from the back bedroom. The usual riot of begonias on the porch rails
were reduced to brown thread by the frost, even the old azaleas black and
burnt at the tips.

Jolie knocked twice and was ducking to peer in the window when
she finally got an answer—a little yodel from the back of the house, the
old-timey call of visiting neighbors on a farm. Sister Wright answered in
her robe, her eyes lightening to a wide smile when she saw who it was.

"Why look a here," she cried, "my girl Jo*lee*."

She was never a giant among women and had shrunk to the size of
a child in old age, though her grip was strong as Jolie enveloped her in
a bearlike Pentecostal hug. "Well, if you ain't a sight"—Sister Wright
smiled up as they parted—"wearing them high heels, big and rich, just
like yo brother—though I *wisht* he'd quit that begging for money, week
after week. It embarrasses me to death."

Jolie's hug turned to a squeeze of laughter as no one could give it to
Carl like the old Sisters, who faithfully trooped down to sit in his front
pew and star in his sermons when invited on holidays and homecom-

ings, but were still the bane of the High and Mighty and never shy about voicing a personal opinion.

"You and me both," Jolie told her, kissing her hard head. "You and me both."

"What you doing out and about this time of the day? Everybody says you about run thangs, over there in Cleary."

"Come to see you." Jolie smiled. "Want me to build you a fire? It is turned a little chilly."

"Naw, shug, just git you a cup of coffee. I got a man coming for eggs—need to run out to the coop. Won't take but a minite. I'll turn on the stove, we'll warm up quick."

"Well, go pour us both a cup while I run gather the eggs."

Sister Wright made her usual protests as she followed Jolie to the door—about her ruining her shoes and being too dressed up for the coop. She finally gave up and stood there at the screen and called, "Well, keep an eye on thet rooster, shug. He's a cross old thang. Git you a stick and swipe him on the haid."

Jolie had gathered many an egg at the Wright place as a child and found the baskets right where they always were. She wasn't intimidated by the decrepit old rooster—an upstart Rhode Island Red, who was too cold to be overly territorial, his pinfeathers drooping. He fixed Jolie with a beady eye and let go a reedy crow when she dragged open the gate, but allowed her in the coop with nothing more than a little flapping, his chickens a fat, placid lot, feathers puffed against the chill. She gathered the eggs with both hands, murmuring the old chicken murmur ("Move over, old girl—there's a good chicka"), till she finished the line with an even two dozen. She was dragging the gate closed, warning the rooster, "Git on, old son. You spur me and I'll fry you for supper," when a gleaming town car slowed for a cautious turn in the drive.

She cursed under her breath at Hollis Frazier's efficiency and hurried back to the kitchen, which smelled heavenly from the coffee percolating on the counter. Sister Wright was already going to the door, and without a sound Jolie slipped down the hall to a tiny room that had once been a section of the back porch, now a catchall for all sorts of vintage plunder. As children she and Carl used to play hide-and-seek in a huge walnut wardrobe, man-height and filled to the brim with tulle-draped hats and yellowed hankies, old robes and gowns, and one item that used to freak them out: a long-necked, syrup-size bottle, half-full of murky liquid, wherein bobbed a few little objects that Sister Wright once explained were "fangers."

Carl had been fascinated by them. He used to take them out every time they went over, though when he asked whom they belonged to, Sister Wright wouldn't tell him. She didn't like the children messing with them and would take them away and put them out of reach on a higher shelf. "Doan know. Somebody from Camp, I expect."

"Well, why're you keeping 'em?"

"'Cause they ain't mine to throw away." The answer had seemed as nonsensical at the time as it did today.

Jolie could remember the exact shelf where Sister Wright had put them out of their reach—the only one high enough to fit a long-necked bottle. Jolie went right to it, but found nothing more than a collection of old, tissue-filled hatboxes, ancient issues of the *Progressive Farmer,* and stacks and stacks of crochet patterns. She was *positive* it was the right shelf and gave up after a moment when Hollis Frazier's voice boomed at the door, confident and country-loud. She quietly shut the wardrobe, then slipped back to the kitchen and transferred the eggs to cartons with quick hands. She took them to the living room, where Sister Wright was standing at the door talking with Mr. Frazier, apologizing over a price increase thanks to the high price of scratch.

"But they're fresh," she assured him, "right out of the chicken's butt," a line she often used with tourists from the campground, who always appreciated a little local color.

Mr. Frazier was enough of a sport to offer a polite guffaw, though the smile disappeared when Jolie appeared at the door and handed him the carton with a small bow. "Here you go, *suh*. A dozen best large."

The edge in her voice was lost on Sister Wright, who gave Jolie an appreciative peck on her cheek and told him, "Delivered by the mayor hersef." Then she asked Jolie, "You got change for a twenty?"

"No, ma'am, I don't," Jolie answered with deliberate firmness, as she needed to speak to Mr. Frazier a moment alone, and Sister Wright kept her egg change in a jar high on a kitchen shelf.

"Be back in a jiffy," she said, then disappeared down the hall, the hem of her long robe dragging behind her.

Jolie waited till she was out of earshot before she stepped outside and pulled her coat close around her. "Fast work, Mr. Frazier."

Hollis had recovered enough of his composure to answer with equal mildness, "I could say the same to you, Miss Hoyt."

Jolie acknowledged the compliment with a dip of her head and put aside the pleasantries to tell him plainly, "Leave her alone," with no particular threat in her voice, just a reasonable request among adults.

He answered with equal ease, "I ain't here to harass anybody. Just want to get *my share of mine.*" He used the old Hendrix phrase broadly, with relish.

If he was expecting an argument, he was disappointed, as Jolie just met his eye with her father's directness. "They ain't here. I just looked."

For a moment, Hollis didn't get it. When he did, he was so startled that he stammered, "Papa's fangers? They were *here?*" Until that moment, he hadn't been sure that this trip was anything but a fool's errand, a shot in the dark so dim that it was hardly explicable.

"Somebody's were."

"In a gin bottle? The middle ones? Right hand?"

She huddled deeper in her coat. "It didn't have a label—just clear glass, and a metal cap. I don't know about the gin part. Carl might know."

"Would Mr. Lense?" Hollis asked sharply, and finally hit a pocket of reaction.

"Sam Lense doesn't know *shit* about Hendrix," she said sharply. "You can deal with him, or you can deal with me. But you can't do both."

Hollis was an old hand at the game of love and raised an involuntary eyebrow at her passion, which was far more than a professional disagreement among colleagues.

"Who shot him?"

Hollis got an immediate response, snapped quickly, as if she were used to the question and had a standard response. "Couldn't tell you. Wasn't there."

Hollis tended to believe her, but felt compelled to point out an obvious truth. "Anybody shoots at me, I'll shoot back."

"I would advise it," she agreed in that brisk, no-nonsense voice. "Just keep me out of it. Keep *every*body out of it," she said, with uncommon conviction, "if you're serious about this thing and not just playing some political scam."

Hollis had rather liked the mayor till then, for her spunk and wiliness, her iron pragmatism and flat green eyes that reminded him of his beloved aunt Tempy. He liked her less at her pathetic drive to keep it quiet and asked her plainly, "Who you scared of, Miss Hoyt? The white folk, or the black ones?"

Her reply was a truly Tempy-like glare, though she answered quickly enough, "Both. And collateral damage, to people who never did *anybody* any harm—like the ole girl inside, or your papa, out minding his own business, working his own field."

"Or somebody's sweetheart, getting shot by a poacher 'cause he talked to the wrong people?"

He thought she'd argue, but she just looked at him wearily, her face pale against the black of the wool coat. "Or an idiot from the university getting shot in the back because he didn't know what the hell he was doing. And if you want to guarantee you never see your papa's fingers, just keep dropping his name. It's about as welcome around here as *Henry* damn *Kite.*"

Hollis was practical enough to see her point, and after a moment's hesitation he slipped his hat back on his head. "Then you can take it from here. But if you cross me, little girl, I'll tell everybody in Cleary more about the Hoyts than they ever wanted to know."

She didn't wither at the threat, but rolled her eyes the way his daughters did when he said something outdated and dadlike. "Can I let you in on a secret in local politics, Mr. Frazier?" she asked. "There *are* no secrets. I'm one step up from trash, and everybody knows it. And the day I quit toten their water is the day I get sent back to the farm."

Hollis laughed despite himself; it was too true to do otherwise. "Well," he said when he got the better of it, "we'll be at the house if you need us." He made his way down the rickety steps to the car.

Charley was as curious as an old hen. He'd made out snatches of the conversation on the porch, enough to know they were onto something, but wasn't close enough to make out any faces. "Was that Miz Hoyt? Did she find them?" he asked with all apparent sincerity, as if it might be as easy as that.

Hollis was used to Charley's optimism and handed him the eggs. "Not yet. But she's working on it."

"You know who she is, don't you?" Charley asked in continuation of the old Southern game they'd been playing since they left Memphis, of tracking the roots of the living back to the neighbors and families of the long-lost community of Camp Six.

Hollis, though not as good as Charley, was learning. As he backed the town car down the drive, he answered, "Probably one of Coy Ammons's great-greats. She got thet Ammons height. That sass."

Charley grunted his agreement, as he'd pegged Jolie as the offspring of a Hendrix survivor two minutes after he met her; not from her looks (which for him were too dim to decipher), but her voice, her homemade sausage, her entire air of welcome. It wasn't a matter of mechanical hospitality that Southerners, black and white, dished out to paying guests, but that strange and inexplicable connection that comes when you walk in a stranger's house and feel right at home. That's why he'd spoken so plainly to her about their quest—what was the point of deception? The Hoyts were high-flying fools, with their fish camp, their green eyes, and their big talk, but nothing more than pawns of the bosses when it came right down to it. They knew it, and everyone else did.

"Yeah, one of Coy's," Charley murmured as they pulled out of sight and he turned back in his seat, "or maybe Sincy Hoyt's—any of them girls. *Living* in town. *Stepping* for the white folk," he said, mimicking his granny, who said it of any Hendrix girl who'd abandoned the comforts of the family hearth to chase the hope of a better life in town.

Hollis made a noise of agreement, and with no pause, but as if in continuation of the thought, Charley asked, "Did you brang a pistol?"

# Chapter Twenty-one

W hen Jolie went back inside, she found Sister Wright still in the pantry, painstakingly counting out $19 in change from an enormous old Mt. Olive pickle jar. "You can put your money away," Jolie said with a wave of the twenty. "I told him your eggs were so rare and organic that twenty dollars a dozen was a steal. Old city *goof,* he believed me."

"Why the *Law,*" Sister Wright cried, and wouldn't believe her till Jolie walked her out to the porch and demonstrated that his car was gone.

"You have no idea how expensive eggs are these days," Jolie assured her. "It's the Atkins diet. Everybody's eating 'em, day and night."

Sister Wright had enough native good sense to know she was being maneuvered, but was used to Lena's and Jolie's generosity and undeniably pleased with the unexpected windfall. She pocketed the twenty, then asked Jolie if she wouldn't mind taking her to town to "pick up a few thangs," as she could no longer drive and was at the mercy of the young folk to cart her around town.

Jolie had seventy-eight new e-mails on her BlackBerry, but was glad to oblige, as it gave her an excuse to nose around downtown Hendrix, which, if possible, looked worse than it had when she was a child. It had become the kind of charmless little sprawl that should incorporate and write a comp plan, snag a few block grants before it deteriorated into an out-and-out shantytown. She didn't entertain any messiah-like hope of returning and taking on the job herself, for if she'd learned one thing in city government, it was the futility of trying to bring order to a town that had no groundswell of support, no mandate, for change. She shook her head at the overflowing Dumpsters, the stunted trees, and the general air of poverty and decay, reflecting that this was the real curse of Henry Kite. This tired and pointless disorder stood in stark contrast to the beauty of the river and the woods.

She waited till they'd returned to the house and were putting up the groceries before she broached the real reason for her visit and nonchalantly asked Sister Wright what had happened to those old fingers she used to have in that old bottle, in the wardrobe. "The ones Carl was always looking at," Jolie asked casually, making it sound innocent and intimate, something they'd laughed about at the dinner table.

"Back in thet plunder in the bedroom, I reckon," Sister Wright told her easily. "Ain't seen 'em in a long time. Never would a seen 'em, it have been up to me."

"Well, whose were they? Brother Wright's? Did he lose 'em at the mill?"

Sister Wright paid her little mind. "Naw, shug, they come with the wardrobe, when his mamer died. All that mess back there—it come then."

"Well, d'you mind if I nose around back there? See what I can find?"

Sister Wright was used to Jolie's and Lena's love of vintage plunder and told her, "Go ahead, shug. Will you stay to eat? I'm making pork and yellow rice."

She didn't have to ask twice, as the Cuffey sisters were famous cooks, and Jolie had been too rattled that morning to eat her own breakfast. "Go easy on the hot sauce" was all she asked, as she was a famous wimp where local peppers were concerned.

Sister Wright said she would, and while she heated up her iron pans and filled the little house with the savory smell of butter, saffron, and sautéed onions, Jolie went through the old wardrobe, drawer by packed drawer, uncovering a treasure trove of vintage slips and hats, yarn and crochet patterns, but no gin bottles. She was *positive* this was the right wardrobe and couldn't imagine who'd have been bold enough to swipe a set of human fingers.

She was close enough to Sister Wright to ask her that very question as she ate her pork and rice, which was a staple, there on the river. Yellow rice cooked with chunks of fresh pork, heavily seasoned with pepper and saffron, making it more Caribbean than Southern. In deference to Jolie, Sister Wright had made the mild version, which they ate on TV trays, so she wouldn't miss her *stories* (that is, her soap operas).

Jolie waited for a commercial before she brought up the fingers again. "Well, d'you think Lonnie, or any of his boys, might have got 'em?" Lonnie was Sister Wright's only son who lived locally, a contractor in Bonifay.

Sister Wright's attention was on *As the World Turns* as she answered aside: "Naw, shug. Lonnie wouldn't fool with them old thangs."

Jolie was feeling increasingly thwarted and was not even sure these were the right fingers, given that this was Hendrix. "Well, did you know any Fraziers around here, growing up? A colored family? Had a farm?"

Like all Southerners, Sister Wright was always glad to recall some old name from her youth and thoughtfully wiped her mouth on a dish towel. "Well, Dicy Hitt married a Frazier—a soldier, from Tennessee. Wadn't from around here." She returned to the television. "Didn't stay long."

She didn't specify why they left. The boastful boys and the white folk in Cleary might rehash the details of the lynching, shake their heads in mock-dismay at the mutilation, and gawk at the oak where they hanged him, but here at ground zero, where the smoke had circled, and the corpses stank, nary a word was uttered.

To Jolie it was confirmation that she was on the right track, and after making her good-byes to Sister Wright (with many assurances she'd come back Easter with Lena and go to church with her), she went out to her car and tried Carl's office again.

She spoke to one of his associate pastors, who explained that Carl was not only out of the office, but out of the country, down in Central America, and not due back till morning. The best Jolie could do was leave a message, then head into Hendrix, where she wanted to look around the only other cache of family plunder that came immediately to mind: the old shed behind the parsonage that had once been her father's refuge.

She didn't bother to call ahead to the parsonage to ask permission, as El Bethel was truly on the edge of extinction, so small it no longer employed a resident pastor, even part-time. They made do with a part-time preacher named Brother Echols, who came over from Cottondale for funerals and other assorted emergencies—leaking roofs and the like.

He was fortunately at the church that day, working on a sewer line in coveralls and leather gloves, a polite old fellow, who was obviously impressed when she introduced herself as Raymond Hoyt's daughter—not because of her father, but because of Carl, who had a huge following in local fundamentalist circles.

"Warch him on the television, ev'ry Sareday," he assured her with an enthusiasm Jolie often encountered among the pious old folk around Cleary.

He was happy to unlock the shed for her, only asked that she lock it back up when she was done, as they'd lately been targeted by local petty thieves. They'd lost a new Kubota tractor the summer before; a John Deere the year before that. "Lot of yo deddy's stuff is still out there," he told her as he wrestled the door open. "Books and pichures and sech, gitting kind of damp. You might want to thank about moving 'em."

He offered his advice mildly, though Jolie was washed with an unexpected guilt when she saw the stacks of molding boxes and assorted plunder that she'd piled on the old desk when she'd cleaned out the parsonage the week of his funeral. She'd meant to move them to town when she got settled, but had never quite got around to it. She was quick to make amends, promising the old pastor that she'd have the place cleaned out by Saturday.

He told her there was no rush, just reminded her to lock up when she was done, and to watch for snakes. "Place is full of 'em," he said as he screwed a new bulb into the overhead socket and yanked the cord, bringing the dim, high old barn to sudden shadowy light.

She worked slowly and methodically, not sure what she was looking for, but confident she'd recognize it when she saw it. It made for heart-rending work, the moldering smell of the place like a ghostly presence, evoking a familiar childhood scene, of going out to the shed after school or church and begging her father to let her go to the beach with Lena, or into town for a movie.

In her mind's eye, she could see him so clearly, sitting at the window at that ugly metal desk, a huge country man, much older than any of her classmate's fathers, and poorer, too, with a cast in one eye, and hands as a big as a dinner plate. But he'd always smile and pull out his dilapidated wallet, telling the girls with mock annoyance, "You younguns are about to dollar me to death." He never had a penny to his name, but he always gave Jolie something. He hated to see her and Carl go without, as God knows he had, his whole damn life.

The weight of it was daunting, the top boxes full of church clothes that had been too big to give away, and even more poignantly a pair of his old Sunday wingtips so polished that the leather scrolling was faded to a patina of old age. Jolie held them to the light and tried to remember if he'd ever had a new a pair—probably not. He didn't have the money and was of a generation that looked on cars and televisions and church shoes as old folks looked at marriage: till death do you part.

The other boxes were filled with the tattered remains of literally hundreds of cheap spiral notebooks, scribbled in his strange, unschooled hand. (*The Book of Danil,* one read. *Isiah,* another.) She didn't know if they were sermon notes or letters or a long-winded diary. He had been a great scribbler, her father. He was also a curious speller and had the penmanship of a trained bear.

She could make little of them in the dim light and turned to the dust-coated old desk, which was a little more organized and yielded up a few items of interest: a dozen old family photographs pressed under glass on the top—of her and Carl at their graduations, and one of their mother, taken before her wedding. The drawers were filled with more notebooks and the remains of the Great Tabernacle Project: elaborate clothes and tiny bells and tiny plastic figurines and bulls and doves for sacrifice. She closed them carefully to get to the bottom drawer, which was stuffed with a piece of stiff cloth. She wiggled it out and shook off a pound of dust and realized it was the old banner that used to hang over the pulpit in the church, faded purple letters on a lavender background, which read, *Without a vision the people perish.*

She hadn't time to do any more digging. The quick winter light was already fading, and she had yet to meet with Glen. She fished the photos from beneath the glass and gave the light pull a yank, then heard a noise outside, the crunch of footsteps on dry grass. She thought it was the old preacher, come back to check on his tractor, and was preparing to smile another round of thanks when Sam peered in the door, older and slightly stockier, though his eyes were unchanged. Even in the half-light she could see them, as light and curious as ever, taking in the dusk-covered tractor and high rafters as he stepped inside, feeling for a light switch.

Jolie was momentarily frozen in place, unprepared for the happy leap of her heart at the sight of him, so instinctive and visceral that it made her heart beat in a traitorous gallop in her chest. Hugh had for years been begging her to see a shrink, but she'd never quite got around to it. In that split second of meeting, she wished she'd done the difficult work of digging up all the roots of pathology and attachment disorder and whatever the hell made Hoyt women so vulnerable to the lure of the bad man.

As it was, she had only the old armor of indifference and detachment to protect her, and for the second time that day, she used the Lord's name in vain, quietly and vehemently, the emphasis on the *damn.*


Sam's reply was equally profane, as he was blinded by the step from light into the dark shed and couldn't see anyone. He called her name twice, which irritated her even more, as it assumed a great welcome, as if he imagined that she'd been huddled there twelve years, awaiting his glorious return.

She didn't bother with a greeting, just yanked the light chain and asked with small patience, "What the *hell* are you doing here?"

Sam raised an arm to block the shock of light and, when he saw her, didn't answer immediately, but just stood there staring with his old absorbed interest, so long that Jolie was finally flustered.

"What?" she asked, but he wouldn't be hurried.

He just lowered his arm slowly and murmured in a mild, speculative voice, "Nothing. It's just strange, actually seeing you. I was beginning to think I'd made you up. But here you are, Jolie Hoyt. In the flesh."

Jolie didn't know what to make of it, his tone not admiring as much as disbelieving, as if he truly had doubted her existence.

"Well, it's me," she assured him, trying to move things along, discomfited by his closeness, and his presence, and his old lazy curiosity, which moved from her to the wall of stacked boxes, with equal speculative interest. "And if you're on the scent of the reward, they aren't here, and they never were. I'm not even sure they're the right ones—and there was never a rope," she added with particular emphasis, as if it were a matter of long debate, as she rolled the banner under her arm in preparation for leaving. "That was some bullshit legend Carl made up at the fish camp."

She stopped abruptly and finally gave him room to answer. He offered, not unkindly, "I don't know what the hell you're talking about."

Jolie was usually not so excitable and was beginning to feel positively unhinged. "Then why the *hell* are you here?" she snapped.

He seemed unmoved by her edginess and glanced closer at the boxes, as if trying to read their labels, still on a genial hunt for clues. "Your sister-in-law called me at work—sounded a little upset."

"Lena? How'd she even find you?"

"Couldn't say," he answered mildly, moving along the walls, occasionally poking at a box for a closer look. "We didn't speak long. As a matter of fact, she hung up on me. Seems to be a lot of, ah, negative activity going on out here. A man named Hollis Frazier unearthed the old Indian study—"

"*That* was the Indian study? That rambling, incendiary bullshit about the Hoyts? *That's* what you were working on all those months?"

Her assessment was so painfully honest that Sam paused in his perusal of the boxes to point out, "Well, it was a rough draft."

"It never mentioned the *goddamn* Indians," she breathed, "just all that crazy shit about the Hoyts and the conquistadors, and Roma *Gypsies.*"

Her outrage was so matter-of-fact that Sam had the grace to look a little sheepish. "Well, that was anthropological thin ice, part of a letter I wrote Dr. Keyes pretty early on. The lynching chapter—that was an independent thing I was looking into, on the side. I forgot I even mailed it."

"Did anyone else read it?"

"Not in Hendrix. Why d'you ask?"

Jolie looked at him with her old wonder. "You might recall you got shot."

"Oh. Well, not because of that. Nobody read it but me."

*Nobody had to,* Jolie almost replied, but thought better of it, and only paused long enough to ask the real $250,000 question: "Who fed you all the insider detail on the lynching? Surely not Uncle Ott?"

"No," Sam admitted, his attention on a notebook he fished out of a box, which he gingerly held to the light. "I never talked to the old folk about the lynching. They wouldn't answer. But a few locals would talk, mostly in Cleary, and a handyman at the campground. He talked about it with pride, as if it was Hendrix's finest day. Your cousin Travis told me about the fingers."

Travis was one of Uncle Earl's bunch, an ex-Marine who'd transplanted himself to Colorado, where he spent his winters hunting elk and made a living building custom houses.

Jolie might have guessed he was the Hoyt sieve and murmured, "Idiot," with such contempt that Sam glanced up.

"Idiot because he'd discuss it? Or idiot because he was proud?"

"Both," she said, tired from the complexity of the long day: the set-to with Mr. Frazier, then the trip to Hendrix and the memories the old shed had evoked, a strange and potent grief, as if her father had just died. Even the traitorous surge of joy she'd had at first sight of Sam had burnt out quickly in the absence of touch and warmth and rekindle, leaving her tired and blunted and feeling a hundred years old.

She was ready to leave the swamp and return to the real world, get through the meeting as quickly as possible, then get home to find a more reliable source of warmth—say, in a glass of Jim Beam. But Sam didn't look at all eager to leave, his terrier-urge to dig obviously stoked by the old notebook he held to the light, still trying to read. "Is this your father's? All these boxes and notebooks—they're his old projects? They're getting water-damaged. How long have they been here?"

Jolie was already feeling enough guilt about the shoes and the banner and sidestepped him deftly with a flash of a politician's smile, calibrated for warmth, sincerity, and enough laugh lines to make it seem real. As much as I'd love to stand here and chat about old times, I really do have an appointment in town with the city attorney, who isn't too big on women mayors, or being late, either one."

"Well, great. Have fun. I'll lock it up when I'm done."

"I'm afraid I promised Brother Echols I'd make sure it was locked up. They've been having a little trouble with *theft*," she said, emphasizing the word and giving him the old mayor-stare, so he knew exactly whom she considered untrustworthy between them.

He looked mildly annoyed, but didn't argue, just asked as she was locking up, "So did you really think you'd find the old *fangers* out here with the Tabernacle and the chart on Revelation?"

Jolie was not about to fall back into the trap of being his best old girl

Friday and just set the lock, then headed for her car, with Sam strolling resolutely beside her, still yammering on about the notebooks. "You have to keep an eye on documents, Jol—especially paper. They're fragile, and irreplaceable, not to mention first-source documents. They really should be archived and kept in climate control."

Jolie found both his use of the diminutive and his professional word-dropping a little needling, a whiff of the Wise Sam of Old, who schooled her in so many wonderful things, the removal of her hymen being foremost.

"I'll take care of it," she repeated as she paused to open her trunk.

It naturally wasn't enough for an old crusader such as Sam, who confronted her squarely, as if she were abandoning a live baby. "I can't believe you're just leaving it out to rot. If you don't want to bother with it, then donate it to UF, or FSU—or give it to me. I'll come out here on the weekend and archive it."

Jolie hardly considered it. "I don't *think* so." She slammed the trunk.

"Well, why not? You and Carl don't give a *shit* about any of it, do you? You got out of Hendrix and you sucked up to money, and you put it all behind you—became these soulless sellout wonders."

Jolie didn't flinch at his reasoned appraisal, just felt for her keys. "Well, I'm sorry we disappointed you. I know you had such *high* hopes for all us poor old gheechies back in your missionary days. Same old story"—she climbed in the car—"the missionaries leave, and the natives revert."

"Missionary, my ass," he snapped, then repeated, nearly word for word, the same question Hollis Frazier had asked on the porch, not two hours before. "God, Jol—what are you so afraid of? That you'll lose your job? Or that *ridiculous,* hundred-year-old boyfriend? Tell me it's not that."

The question was absurd, but in its raw honesty, at last, endearing. He was a dumb ass, but sincere, and she tried to part in peace, pausing before she shut the door to offer a bit of hard-won advice. "Do yourself a favor, Sam. Give up on Hendrix. You *never* got it. You *never* will."

If there was such a thing as salt in a wound, this was it—so stinging that he reverted to mimic. "Believe me, Jol—nobody *gits* it better than me. What I don't *git* is why you're so damn *hostile*. You know I loved you," he said in a rising voice, as if she had argued. "And I never meant it to happen this way. I never did you any harm."

He paused at that, breathing hard, so pushing and persuasive that Jolie couldn't resist evening the score with a little hard honesty, asking him frankly, "Really? You loved me. That's what it was all about—you coming over here and talking to Daddy and combing the cemeteries and going over to Uncle Ott's? You were studying the Injuns, trying to awaken us to the glories of our lost heritage?"

His bold righteousness slipped a millimeter, but his answer was hardy. "What? You think I was lying?"

"I think you're full of shit." She reached for the latch to slam the door. "You were digging up Henry Kite and nobody was talking, and me and Lena were just stupid enough to fall for it—"

His reply was loud and profane, but Jolie wasn't interested in idling there and shouting all night. She gripped the door to slam it in his face, but he wedged himself in and held up a hand of truce, still breathing hard, but finally parting with the pivotal bit of history he'd withheld twelve years before. "Morris Lens was my great-grandfather. Henry Kite shot him in the face."

Jolie was so vigilant in adulthood that it was rare for anyone to blindside her, but he did. She just stared at him, her hand on the door latch. "The deputy?"

"The German," he answered.

"Why didn't you tell me?" she asked in a voice so mild and honest that Sam seemed too flummoxed to reply.

He released the door and straightened up and all but scratched his head, finally conceding, "I don't know, Jol. It was easier not to."

If one person on earth understood the seductive allure of silence, it was Jolie Hoyt. "Ain't that the truth?" she murmured, then added with true regret, "I'll call you in the morning."

"No," he answered immediately, no longer combatant, but spent and exhausted, as if crossing the line to truth had cost him. "I'm not waiting for any more calls. I'll come by in the morning. We need to talk."

# Chapter Twenty-two

Jolie was late to her meeting with the Cleary city attorney, Glen Malloy, an officious little pain in the ass of a man, who waited at her desk with his hands folded on his lap, the picture of judicial affront. She apologized profusely, then listened with half an ear to his usual huffing and puffing over the details of the city charter, first with her, then afterward, with the rest of the zoning board, who were equally split on the cell tower and openly contentious.

It was past eleven when she pulled in her drive, the carriage house dark, the porticoes and porches draped in winter shadow. She didn't even take off her coat, but went straight to the butler's pantry in the dining room, a relic of the days of cocktail parties and banker's soirees, a shrine to social drinking. Hugh had never got around to boxing it up when he moved, but left the mirrored, ornate shelves weighed down with all manner of snifters, tumblers, tulip, and crystal, the dusty old decanters dark with nameless spirits: old bourbons, brandies, sherries, and elixirs.

She was a purist when it came to inebriation and ignored the collectibles in favor of a tumbler of straight Jim Beam. She usually mixed it with Diet Coke, but was too tired to go back to the kitchen and just stood there in the dark, sipping whiskey on the sly like a Baptist deacon. Then the landline started ringing in the kitchen, loud and long. No one called her at that number anymore unless it was family or an emergency.

She paused, shoes in one hand, whiskey in the other, and waited for the answering machine to pick up. Her preset message droned through the empty house, then that obnoxious bleep, then a maybe four-second silence.

She thought it was a hang-up and started upstairs, shoes in one hand, whiskey in the other, when Hugh's voice suddenly sounded, light and resigned, and oddly distracted, as if starting in midsentence. "—so I guess you're not picking up the phone. I understand you had a visitor today and would like to discuss it, at your leisure, of course. When you get around to answering the phone," he droned, trying to be sarcastic and jovial, though real worry was in his voice. "I'm driving back tonight—will plan on lunch at the café."

He made no good-bye, just a quiet click of the phone. The whirl of the rewind filled Jolie with foreboding, thinking, Well, *great*. That's what you wanted to hear, right before you went to bed—that Hugh was worried enough to cancel his Mardi Gras party, which was like saying the Muslims had canceled Ramadan.

She added an Ambien to the whiskey, but still couldn't cross the border to sleep. She hovered there on the twilit shadows, trying to reorder the pieces of the Hendrix puzzle in light of the new discovery, too tired and tipsy to make any headway and terribly, terribly sad, as if the melancholia and poverty of Hendrix were a living miasma that had clung to her and followed her home. She wished she were the kind of sane human being who could cry when overwhelmed and brokenhearted, but she couldn't and just lay there, dry-eyed and desolate. On her third trip to the medicine cabinet, she saw a light flicker in the backyard and checked her clock: 3:45 a.m.

She wasn't the only resident of Casa Altman who wasn't resting easy.

She gave up the battle at six and fell into a fitful sleep, waking late and disoriented at nine thirty. She dreaded meeting Hugh, and took her time dressing. The weather channel predicted a high of thirty-six, which called for the warmest suit she owned, a Ralph Lauren, gray wool skirt-suit so stiff and insulated she never wore it more than twice a year.

She tied an apron over all of it and made a late breakfast and delivered it to the carriage house, too distracted to make small talk with the Frazier brothers. She left the tray on the kitchen table and was thinking she'd head into the office and make a dent in the work she'd missed the day before when there was a knock on the front door, so insistent it echoed through the house.

She was sure it was Hugh, that he'd driven straight through and decided to move his lecture to brunch, but when she swung open the front door, she found Sam standing there in the cold, dressed nearly identically as he'd been the day before, in khakis and a navy jacket, solemn, and a little strained. She was still feeling the effects of the pills and the booze, her first question, "What happened?"

"Mind if I come in?" he asked.

Jolie motioned him inside and realized the high, old hallway was nearly as cold as the porch, their breaths making faint vapor. She tried to lead him to the warmer kitchen, but he waved it away. "I won't be long, have a budget breathing down my neck," he murmured. "Was up half the night with my father, who has actually threatened to Baker Act me, said he was calling my brother this morning to fill out the forms. . . . Are you all right? You look a little worn."

"I feel like crap," she confessed. She took a seat on a small sofa in the parlor and gestured for him to join her, though he preferred to remain standing.

"Yeah, me, too. Didn't sleep worth a shit." He then seemed to realize he was being a less than cordial guest and nodded at the high-ceilinged, old room. "Nice house, by the way. Very plush," he commented evenly, as if trying to insert a note of civility before breaching a painful subject.

Jolie flashed a politician's smile and wished it weren't too early for a drink, as this obviously wasn't going to be good, whatever it was. Sam's eyes wandered the room even as he spoke, haltingly, as if bracing himself to confess to the most hideous crime. "I wanted to apologize for being such a duplicitous little shit when I was in Hendrix. I mean, I really was there for the Creek. You can call UF—they have the records somewhere.

But I found your pop on the census, and I did kind of grill him, discreetly. I kept it quiet because Hendrix—it was a lockdown out there. I was afraid." He paused. "I don't know what I was afraid of. I just kept my mouth shut. And I shouldn't have. Because it was chickenshit—and your pop was always generous with me about all of it. He actually knew my granddad—or he'd met him," Sam corrected, feeling in his coat pocket and handing her a two-by-two photograph of a bird-thin young man in the bulky coat and peaked cap of the Russian army, his face worn, but grimly determined, as if resigned to the hardships of life. "Your pop called him German, but he was Lithuanian, from Tauragé—right on the Polish border. It was always changing hands—maybe he preferred German. He's sometimes listed as Prussian, on the census."

Jolie went to the hall window and held it to the light. "There's a resemblance," she noted, some infinitesimal sameness about their eyes and brow.

"You think so? Nobody ever mentioned it—then again, nobody ever mentioned *him*. My great-grandmother remarried a man named Miller, but she was never the same after the murder. Never got over it, my grandfather says, and never talked about it, either. They even changed their name—added an *e*. To distance themselves, I think, from the whole thing—the lynching."

Jolie waited for the confession of their complicity in Kite's murder, their justified rage. When Sam offered nothing further, she asked, "So what really happened? What's the story?"

"There is no story. Kite robbed him—shot him in the face. They offered my granddad lead horse in the lynching party, but he turned them down. He was, like, seventeen."

Jolie waited for something further, some bit of shameful detail. When it wasn't forthcoming, she asked, "That's the great mystery? Anybody in Hendrix could have told you that."

"But nobody would." Sam took back the photo and put it away carefully. "My father has a deaf-mute approach to family history. Even my grandfather didn't know where they buried him. They hustled him and his mother off to Tampa that afternoon—left old Morris right where he fell, as far as I know. Your pops told me where the store was, but it was long gone, and I walked every graveyard in the county—public and private—but found nothing."

Jolie's expression changed to one of mild amazement. "*That's* the great mystery you came to Hendrix to unravel? What happened to his *body*? You mean, where he was *buried*?"

Sam was put off by her old tone of incredulity and answered flatly, "Yeah. He was observant. And his family in Tauragé ended up in a land-fill, courtesy of the SS. He survived being conscripted and two years in the Russian army and jumping the Polish border, only to come to America and get shot in the face over a pack of cigarettes. It was a pissy thing to happen, after all he went through."

Jolie blinked at his vehemence and murmured, "Can't argue with that."

Sam seemed slightly mollified by her agreement. "And the real kicker, the really pissy thing, is I'm as bad as my pops about deep-sixing it. My kid, Brice, he doesn't know shit about any of it, he never will. There's nothing to tell, and I could have done better. I could have asked your dad."

"Why didn't you?"

"Because I was chickenshit, tiptoeing around. I thought I could find it myself. I hiked every little cemetery west of the river."

"I thought he was Jewish."

He shrugged. "What did that matter, in Hendrix? They didn't remember his name. They thought he was German."

Jolie raised an eyebrow at the answer. "Oh, it mattered," she echoed lightly. After a moment she reached for her BlackBerry. She hit a number with no explanation to Sam other than a raised index finger, a gesture to hold on, that she was working on it.

When the connection picked up, her expression was suddenly all charm, her voice animated with political persuasion. "Hey, baby doll. . . . No, I'm still at the house, but headed your way. . . . Yeah, I know, he called. Tell him that's fine, eleven thirty. But listen, pookie, where would a Jewish man who died in Hendrix in 1938 be buried? . . . No, he was, yeah. . . . Really? Cool. . . . Lense. L-E-N-S-E."

"No *e*," Sam inserted. "Lens. Like the lens in glasses."

Jolie nodded and repeated the changed spelling into the phone. "You think? Could you check? . . . Yeah. It's kind of a big deal." Jolie smiled a white-toothed flash of Hoyt charm, as if the caller could see her through the line. "No, no worries. I'll call her back when I get in—her and Carl, too. . . . Sure. I'm on my way—putting on my coat." Jolie ended the call with another blast of affection. "Okay. Love you, angel. You're the best," she chirped.

Sam watched the performance with a face of mild displeasure. "Who was that?" he asked when she hung up. "The boyfriend? He has that kind of juice? One phone call and he can unearth a seventy-year-old corpse, just like that?"

"*That* was our beloved city clerk, Miss Faye." Jolie put away the BlackBerry and went to the closet for her coat. "Her papa was a wing-man for George Smathers, and she's a second cousin of Lurleen Wallace," she said as she searched for her coat. When she found it, she pulled it on. "If there's a record within fifty counties, she'll find it." She flipped her hair out of her coat collar. "Trust me."

She was cut off by the chirp of the BlackBerry. A glance at the call number brought a flash of her old indomitable smile. "See?" On answering, she went in search of a pen.

She found one on a side table and scribbled something in a margin of a scrap of paper that she silently passed to Sam: *Temple B'nai Israel, Albany. M. S. Lens March 1893–October 1938.*

It was Sam's turn to be flabbergasted. "They buried him in New *York*?" he whispered.

Jolie lowered the phone to mouth *Georgia*, then ended the conversation with a murmur of praise and a heartfelt "Thank you, baby. You're the best. Give yourself a raise."

When she was done, she hit the end button and held her hands wide, a magician completing her finale. Sam was dumbfounded. "How the hell did you do that? My grandfather searched sixty years."

Jolie made light of the small miracle, but her face was lit with that old pleaser satisfaction. "There aren't many temples hereabouts, and the Sisterhood in Albany—they're the queen bees."

*"Jesus,"* he breathed. "Whoever heard of a synagogue in Albany, Georgia? How can I be sure it's him?"

Jolie was used to the disbelief of mere mortal citizens when she displayed a bit of bureaucratic magic. "You can't, unless you dig him up and do a DNA—and good luck with the temple on that. And go easy on the South Florida myopia when you talk to them. They were lighting candles in Albany when Miami was a cow town."

Sam looked at his watch. "It's eleven o'clock. I might run up there right now. Want to come? It's been a long time since I walked a graveyard with a beautiful woman," he confided, happy to be back on the same team, and still, despite all good sense, unable to quit being so impressed with the power suit and long expanse of hosed leg. He was ready to forgive and forget and just be good pals again, maybe take a trip out to the old camper that night, just for old times' sake.

Jolie seemed less hostile to the prospect than she had before, almost regretful. "It's second Tuesday. The commission meets at four thirty, and we've got a little zoning war brewing."

He took it with good grace. "Ah, well, I guess enormous family mansions do not pay for themselves." He was about to try to nail a date to do something fun and nostalgic together—say, go through her father's shed looking for a pair of severed fingers, or try to talk a temple into disinterring a seventy-year-old corpse—when a phone rang in the back of the house.

Jolie held up a hand. "I need to get that. Faye only calls the house for emergencies."

She hurried to the kitchen, to the wall phone by the door, and answered without qualification, "Hey. I'm on my way."

A man responded in a thick country voice, slightly raised, as if trying to shout above the miles. "Sister Hoyt? Sister *Hoyt?*"

At the use of her old church name, Jolie knew instantly that something was amiss and pulled the cord as far as it would go, to the back door. "Yes sir, this is she."

"Well, this is Brother *Echols,*" he bellowed, "from Cottondale," the name not ringing a bell till he added in that hardy country voice, "Sorry to be calling sa early, but the sheriff got up with me. Seems like they had a little accident last night at the church. You didn't go lightin' any lanterns, or candles, or sech, when you'se poking around thet old shed, did you?"

"No, sir." She pulled the cord around the corner to the pantry for privacy. "The electricity was still on."

"Well, maybe it was faulty wiring. Fact is, the place burned to the ground last night—or early this morning. Firemen couldn't tell which."

"The *church?*" she whispered, though his voice was hardy.

"Naw, shug, just the shed. Third tractor we lost this year. Don't know what State Farm'll make of *thet.* Did you git yer Deddy's thangs?"

Jolie couldn't answer for a moment. She stood there in her big coat, her back to the door, and finally whispered, "No, sir. Not all of it," her voice so blank that the old preacher instinctively went into a professional comfort-mode and asked if he could do anything, or call anyone, as if she'd lost someone in a car accident. "I wouldn't worry it," he said. "Old place was ready to fall in. Yo brother called, too."

Jolie straightened up at the news. "Carl called? *Why?*"

The old preacher seemed surprised at the question. "Why, same as you—wantin' the keys to thet old shed. You don't thank he'd been care-less enough to strike a match out there? An old farm boy like himself?"

He said it as an insider's joke, as Carl had in his sermons taken to painting himself as something of a bumbling old farmhand, with many references to mis-sown crops and mis-milked cows and the strange ways of the lowly chicken.

It was part of Brother Echols's rural-preacher shtick and meant to be a joke, though Jolie didn't laugh, but answered in blank honesty, "I don't know, Brother Echols. Did you give 'em to him?"

"Naw, shug. I got the message on the machine. Would you tell him? I tried the number, but couldn't git through."

She told him she would, then thanked him and hung up quietly, gathering her purse and taking care to open the door without a sound and slip out onto the stoop, which was cold as an icebox. The frost had held another night, the morning hardly brighter than it had been an hour ago when she took out the breakfast tray, though the carriage house was lit and awake.

Hollis answered on her first knock, his face alight. "Didju find 'em?" he boomed.

Jolie put a finger to her mouth. "Not yet," she whispered. "I'm going out there now. Need you to do me a favor. Could you run out to Sister Wright's and take her to her son's in Bonifay? Tell her you're a state trooper, or with the EPA. Tell her the chickens polluted her well or something. I don't care what—just git her out of Hendrix."

"Whut happened?" he asked, his eyes on the strange car in the drive, Sam's state car with yellow tags, which made it look like an official vehicle of the FBI.

"No time," she told him as she headed toward her car. "Just go out and see to Sister Wright. Tell her I sent you," she whispered.

Hollis called for her to stop, but she waved him away. He went back for his keys and hot-stepped it down the gravel to his Lincoln. He popped the trunk and felt around in the tire well for a gun he kept with his spare—a good-size Glock that he took to the bank when he made his weekly deposits. He checked the clip, then flagged Jolie in the drive and offered it through her lowered window. "Safety's right there. Nine shots, automatic. Like shooting a cap gun: bam, bam, *bam*."

Jolie stared at it in horror. "I will *not*," she breathed. She kept her eyes on the house. "And keep Sam here as long as you can. Tell him I got called out on a city emergency, or the pipes burst at the treatment plant, or—I don't know. Think of *something*," she begged, "but do *not* let him go to Hendrix."

She was gone at that, whipping around and onto First Avenue, Hollis striding behind, the Glock in hand, shouting, "Take the *gun!*"

# Chapter Twenty-three

Jolie didn't pay Hollis so much as a blink of attention, but drove like the wind down the narrow country highway to Hendrix. She didn't slow till she swung into the drive of the parsonage, which was as weed-grown and deserted as it had been the afternoon before, the only sign of the night's excitement a twin set of churned ruts from the fire truck, which circled the parsonage, then exited at the road.

She followed them to the corner and stopped short at this new view of the backyard, strewn with rock and glass and blasted, splintered trees. The shed itself was simply gone, burnt to its limestone foundation, the skeleton of the tractor sitting right where she'd left it, in a waist-high pile of rubble, ghostly and blackened, sending up a dozen plumes of smoke.

She didn't get out or go any farther than the edge of the house, just felt for her BlackBerry and called Faye and (mercifully) got Tamara. She left her a message of where she was and when she'd be back—in time for the meeting, but not before, and begged her to call Hugh. "Tell him I'll see him tonight, after the meeting. Maybe I'll be back before," she hedged, though Tamara was having none of it.

"Where *are* you? Something's cooking around here—Faye all but wringing her hands."

Jolie put her off with a quick "I'll tell you when I see you. Just call Hugh—and listen, baby, call my brother, Carl—"

"Oh, he called, or his wife did. Called fifty times. You all right? Because something really is cooking around here. I don't know what, but something is *up*."

"Later," Jolie promised, then hung up and tried both Carl's and Lena's cell phones, but got no answer. She left Carl another message, and with time running out, wheeled around in the yard and headed to her uncle Ott's—his old house in town, on a side street by the post office.

She didn't bother to get out as it was clearly vacant—the curtains drawn, the chimney not blowing smoke as it would on such a cold day had Ott been home. She figured he was at the fish camp, which was damn inconvenient, as it was still famously primitive, only accessible by boat, without phone lines or indoor plumbing.

Fortunately, Vic Lucas had expanded the KOA to offer half-day boat rentals, nothing fancy, just small jon boats with kickers for tourists who were willing to sign a liability waiver for the privilege of spotting an alligator in the wild. Jolie parked at the old concession stand and nego- tiated a half-day rental with the skinny teenage clerk Vic had hired for the slow season. While he was gassing it up, she went to her car and searched through the clutter of junk in her trunk, looking for whatever stray sweatshirts or socks or gloves she might have.

She found a few mismatched socks that she stuffed in her pockets, and a thick, old Mexican blanket covered in sand that she and Lena took for the kids to sit on at the beach. She wrapped it around her shoulders like a shawl and was digging around for a pair of leather florist gloves when a car jerked to a halt in the gravel behind her. The two-tone, dove-gray Cadillac Seville, the slope-backed kind they used to make in the mideighties, was one Hugh had taken a liking to and never traded in.

He got out briskly, dressed in the loungewear he sported at his river house—a maroon wool dressing gown over a pair of broad, gray-striped pajamas. The result was almost vaudevillian, though his face was any- thing but amused.

"My gosh, you scared me," she groused, though he ignored her irritation, his still-handsome face drawn in lines of old-school, sniffling impatience.

"You're actually taking another sick day while the city braces itself for a lawsuit, and going off on some"—he paused, having a difficult time laying hands on cutting-enough words—"ghoulish, graveyard jaunt."

Jolie was running out of patience with his high-handedness and returned to her glove search. "Did you come here for a reason? Or just to nag the hell out of me?"

"I *came*," he answered sonorously, "to see if I could talk sense into you before you allowed yourself to be drawn into some pointless, political shakedown, by people who are not connected to your city or your influence, in any way."

"They're connected to Hendrix," she began, but was cut off by his noise of outrage.

"Oh? And it was the Hendrix city hall they traipsed into, with their nonsensical demands?" He moved around so he could face her, stooped low over the trunk, his voice lowered for emphasis. "They are banking on your guilt, and no more concerned with historic injustice than the man in the moon. I am frankly amazed you allowed yourself to be drawn in. Henry Kite's been dead seventy years. Let him *lie*."

Jolie was taken aback by Hugh's voicing of the dreaded name, which was anathema to the sons of the men who'd made the bulk of their fortune deforesting the swamps and maritime woodlands of Old Florida. They were educated men, the sons of planters and governors and bankers, who read books and went abroad and feared neither ghosts nor curses, sheriffs, or legal recourse. They traded in human bondage as surely as their planter fathers, but were civic-minded, building charming downtown parks, and enormous, amber-planked houses from wood plucked from the hearts of their finest groves. They were gentlemen and, among themselves, realistic about the unsavory aspects of their industry. They hired brutality if they themselves did not possess it and never thought to stand in the dock for any of it, till shortly after midcentury when the wretched big dailies in South Florida began their digging. At first, it was more annoying than anything, till the unexpected drama of Rosewood spun out, proving against all good reason that dead men could indeed rise from the grave and, in the stories of their scattered daughters, find their voice and *talk,* and walk among the living.

She blinked at Hugh in wonder. "I can't believe you even said the name."

In the silence that followed, the skinny clerk whistled from the dock, signaling the boat was ready. Jolie waved her thanks and slammed the trunk.

"I don't have a choice, Hugh. I'm in too far—"

"Of course you have a *choice,*" he snapped with rare bad manners as she headed for the dock, blanket in hand, with Hugh following close behind, still talking. ". . . you have a city to run and a lawsuit pending, and a very qualified city attorney to handle these sorts of things."

Jolie didn't answer till she was on the dock, eyeing the little boat. "So this was what it was all about? Selling me your house? Getting me in politics? To keep me *busy,* and out of Hendrix?"

Hugh looked severely peeved at the impudence of the question, but tried for prudence, lowering his voice to argue, "Jolie. The *Times* or the *Democrat* or the *Herald* has only to get *wind* of this, and it is all you'll hear of in this town, for fifty years. Forever. And is that what you want? To throw away a career and a decade of hard work and have this sordid, horrid little *melodrama* hanging over your head, the rest of your *life?*"

It was the first time Hugh had ever hinted at the burden he carried, of being the son of a man who, like Henry Kite, hadn't been overly concerned about how his freewheeling self-absorption might affect his larger family. Jolie suddenly pitied Hugh, standing there in his truly absurd dressing gown, having to pay for the sins of another day. As she untied the leads from the post, she told him with a reasonableness of her own, *"Hugh.* They'll do it anyway. And who *cares* what they say? What do we have to lose? We're nothing out here. We're *ghosts."*

Hugh had never been receptive to the charm of metaphor and didn't smile at the gibe, but only glowered at her from beneath rule-straight brows. "You'll care when the second Tuesday in October comes around and Alvin Tomlin takes back his office and turns this town into a solid concrete parking lot, a prison on one end, a pulp mill the other."

"*Good,*" she said with that chin-out defiance. "Let him *have* it. God, Hugh, it's not the last job on earth. I'll get a job in Tallahassee, or go back to design—"

"Oh, sure," he snapped. "You can open a nail salon or make fine *silk* arrangements at the drugstore. That's what we've worked for all these years—to give it up, just like that"—he snapped his fingers, his nose now beet red from the cold—"while *off* you go to the *Big City*, and to *hell* with the rest of us."

Hugh's guilt trips could take the velocity of a tropical storm, and with as much composure as she could muster, Jolie climbed in the boat and called, "I'll be back by three."

Hugh loomed above, still not letting up, but calling down in a ringing, apocalyptic voice, "It's a shakedown, Jolie, pure and simple. What're they asking? Money? *Reparations?*"

"Two *fangers,*" she answered, "and I don't think you can spare them, Hugh. Neither can *I.*"

"*Fine,*" he shouted. "But you're making a *huge* mistake, Jolene. I hope you realize that."

Jolie was about to yank the pull, but paused at his tone, as it had been a long time since anyone had played the *Jolene* card on her. His cold superiority was offset by a small tremble in his voice that made him seem suddenly very old, and wretchedly vulnerable—Noël Coward, lost in the wilderness. Loyalty was the great blessing (and curse) of the Hoyts, and she regretted her impudent needling.

She just watched him a moment, then offered in a quiet voice, "Give it up, Hugh. He was your father; he wasn't *you.* I'm going to the camp to talk to Uncle Ott. Don't worry, I won't implicate anyone else. I know how to hold my mouth right. I'm a Hoyt."

This last was a try at humor to lighten the moment, as it was reputed to be the reason that rich men were said to prefer Hendrix women to their counterparts in town: for their Indian reticence. They knew how to hold their mouths right. They were polite and assenting, never threatened to tell unsuspecting wives or make waves about niggling matters of paternity.

Hugh was schooled enough in local lore to get the jab and roll his eyes in a way that made Jolie smile as she ripped the cord once, twice, then finally hard enough to make the little engine roar to life with a cloud of white exhaust and the sharp, pungent smell of gas.

She didn't wait around for his response, but lifted a hand in farewell, then turned the nose of the little boat downstream, her last thought identical to Sam's when he had faced the same wall of cypress, twelve years earlier: *God,* it was cold on the water.

And, *God,* she'd be glad to get home.


She kept the blanket pulled high on her face, her eyes an inch above the fringe, pouring tears from the whip of the wind. Nothing marked the boundaries of the National Forest to the left or the Hoyt camp, which predated the park by a hundred years, off one of the nameless creeks on the far end of the swamp. It was closer to the beehives and tupelo trees of Wewa than Cleary, the older cabins built in the trackless days before the lumber companies had begun their deforestation—before pulpwood and turpentine, mule skinners and saloons, had become the lifeblood of the local economy. They were Spartan, even by local standards, board-and-batten shacks that had been purloined from local cotton fields and floated downstream, then perched on makeshift floating docks along the fringe of the cypress so that they became waterborne in the rainy season ("*On* the water," Jolie once explained, "not beside it").

The bunkhouse was the only permanent structure. A stooped, low-ceilinged old lodge that eventually became the infamous hideaway that Wes Dennis spoke of with such nostalgia, as the Hoyt men quickly discovered more money was to be found in cards than catfish, moonshining than turpentining. They were too isolated to be easily chivvied out by the Law, and the old fish camp hosted many a wild and freewheeling Saturday night, till the midyears of the century, when the cypress was finally cut and the feds began buying up the land—miles of it, stretching from the river to the coast, including the old lumber-company property and the farms and homesteads abandoned in the Trouble. They called it a National Forest and took their stewardship seriously, sending in conservation and forestry men and filling the books with all manner of curious regulation.

By the time Jolie came along, the camp had become nothing more than a cluster of sagging old cabins, ground zero for the men of the family, who fled there as often as they could, to fish and drink and retell stories of wilder, less fettered days. Every year the river gave the old cabins a tougher beating, so that the young men of the family (Carl among them) annually predicted that this year would be the last, that the current would finally take it and the Hoyt fish camp would end up on the bottom of the Gulf, home to the very catfish it had been built to pursue.

Jolie herself had no opinion on the matter, as she had been raised a churchgirl and was seldom allowed into the male sanctum that was the old camp. She'd only been down there a dozen times her entire life and was beginning to wonder if the river had sure enough taken it when she finally passed a small point of land that marked the edge of the Hoyt property. She cut the motor to idle and maneuvered close enough to grip the low overhang of a bent old water oak, using it to guide herself around a sharp, deep cutoff to the old dock, which was sometimes landlocked, but was now completely on the water, full of wasps and dirt-dauber nests, missing half the slats.

She shouted a halloo, but got nothing in answer except a mighty howl of dogs that rose to a deafening roar as they hurled themselves down the mud path to the dock—a motley assortment of tan and spotted hounds of curious pedigree. Ott preferred hunting hogs to deer, and these were once mostly cur dogs, but over time a few misplaced beagles and walkers had made their way across the river and added spots and yipping to the pack, which was well fed but unregulated in breeding, a few fat pups always bringing up the rear. Since Ott was the current keeper of the hounds, they were a good-natured crew, more curious than ferocious, their keening wail giving way to wags of welcome when they sniffed a Hoyt.

Jolie made her way onto the listing dock, nearly knocked off her feet by the frisking, wiggling dogs. She couldn't negotiate the slats in heels and yanked them off while she sweet-talked the alpha male in a cartoon doggy-voice: "He's a good-looking old dog, he's a tough ol' dog. Go getchure papa, tell him I'm here."

The Hoyt hounds were much like their owners—approachable by flattery—and with no more persuasion than that, the dogs followed Jolie as she climbed up the wet path, howling her arrival. Ott heard them long before he saw them and waited on the stoop of the bunkhouse in ancient work pants and a flannel shirt, blinking like a pleased old bear when he saw it was her.

She tried to call a greeting, but couldn't outshout the hounds, till Ott let go a piercing whistle that cut off the yipping in an instant.

"Well, thank God for that," she said into the sudden silence, then went up the steps and kissed his grizzled cheek. "I wish I could teach that trick to the City Commission," she shouted in his face, as Ott's hearing hadn't improved in the last twenty years and talking to him was like making conversation in a wind tunnel.

When he cared to, he was adept at lip-reading, and he grinned in reply. "Well, what's a city girl doing on the water this time of the day?"

"Come to see *you*," she answered in full shout as she followed him into the cluttered great room, which despite its reputation for iniquity was really nothing more than an ill-kept living room, a last resting place for the larger family's cast-off chairs and beat-down sofas.

"Is it safe for you to be out here alone?" she asked as she settled into a corner of an ancient Duncan Phyfe sofa that was pushed close to the room's sole source of heat—an old gas heater littered with shells from boiled peanuts Ott must have been eating for breakfast.

He fetched a dry blanket and offered her a handful of peanuts before taking a seat in the old La-Z-Boy that had once belonged to her father.

"Well, Obie's boys come out ever once in a while, and Mr. Vic, and the Fish and Game man drops by—a colard feller, named Dais. He picks me up a few thangs from the sto, if I thank to ask."

"How long you been out here?"

He considered the question a moment. "Fo'th of July. There'bouts."

Jolie made a face. "Well, good Lord, Uncle Ott. This place ain't fit for permanent habitation. What d'you do with yourself all day? It's too cold to fish, surely."

He didn't deny it, but admitted with a sheepish grin, "A whole lot of nothing, mostly. How you been, shug? How's the City treating you?"

Jolie could not hurry a family visit, nor did she want to, for the moment. She was glad of the warmth of the stove and the blanket and always happy to see the old boy, whatever the occasion. She tore open the peanuts and caught him up with City business—the cell tower and the pending lawsuit—as Ott had always been a sociable old recluse, fascinated by the insider details of city life.

"Bet a lot of skulduggery goes on with thet sort of thang," he said of the cell tower. "Lot of greased palms." That was a typical response from the old folk on the river, who thought that life in the city was full of intrigue, bribes, and big money.

"God, I wish there was," Jolie said sourly, making the old man laugh, though he believed not a word of it.

She would have liked to have sat there all day chewing the fat, but the clock was ticking. When she was done with the peanuts, she slapped the salt off her hands and jumped right in, asking him bluntly, "Well, listen, Uncle Ott, I got this idiot meeting and need to ask you something. D'you remember a family that used to live around here named Frazier? Colored? Nice people. Had a farm, couple of sons?"

"I knew a Buddy Frazier," Uncle Ott allowed after a moment. "He worked at Camp, run mules. Married a Hitt."

"That's *him*," Jolie said, trying not to sound too eager. "They left after the Trouble, went back to Arkansas. Listen, Uncle Ott, did you ever hear what might have become of his fingers?"

"His *whut?*" The old man cupped his hand behind his ear to hear her better.

"His *fingers*," she repeated a little louder, and held out her own hand, middle one bent to demonstrate, "middle ones, right hand. Men from the Camp cut 'em off, back in the Trouble, trying to make him talk. His son thinks they might still have 'em."

Her uncle looked at her blankly, as if still not sure he'd heard her correctly. "Well, I ain't ever heard of such a thang," he finally said, honestly astounded. "They cut off Buddy Frazier's fangers? On *purpose?*"

# Chapter Twenty-four

He was so genuinely amazed that Jolie knew she was on yet another blind track. She sat back and rubbed her neck.

"That's what they tell me," she said with a quick glance at her watch. Her window of opportunity was rapidly slipping away, and with no other leads before her she asked, "Well, has Carl been down here lately? You know, nosing around? Asking about Henry Kite?"

Her uncle stared in wonder at her open use of the name, though he answered easily enough, "Naw, shug. I ain't seen Carl since—oh, Christmas, I guess. Maybe the Christmas befo that. Stays gone a lot, Lener says."

That was all the confirmation Jolie needed that her uncle Ott was really not in the loop. If he were, Carl would have been by to interrogate him, just as she was doing now. She chewed her lip thoughtfully a moment, then made one final stab. "Well, is there *anything* you can think of that'd connect Deddy to Henry Kite, that might have been out in the shed, that somebody would have wanted destroyed?"

The old man blinked at the turn in the conversation and tried to put her off. "Aw, shug, thet Kite bidnis—it was a long time ago."

Jolie had never been one to bird-dog her old kinsmen when they didn't want to discuss something, but she was too pressed for time to be polite. "I *know*, Uncle Ott. And I'm not here to point any fingers or put anybody in jail. I need to know if there's *any*thing you can think of that might have ended up out there. They used to say there was a piece of the rope."

He looked even more pained, as if she'd brought up a most inappropriate subject—discussing tampons at the supper table or the like. But to his credit, he didn't evade her, just grunted. "Sister, everybody in this town uster claim they had a piece of thet rope. Why you worrying thet old mess?"

"It's just, suddenly, come to my attention, and I am having a heck of a time getting a straight answer, I'll tell you that."

"That's 'cause there wasn't nothing straight about him—ol' Kite. He was crooked as the devil's toes—kilt that German, and Mr. Goss—shot 'em like yard dogs, and they were good men. Had wives and younguns, and there wasn't such a thang as the gov'mint to feed 'em, like it is today. Back then, you lost yo deddy, you went hungry. Didn't have a *dog's* chanch."

To Jolie, it was a surprising confession, spoken with such passion by a man who'd been fatherless from conception and knew of what he spoke. It made her wonder if that hadn't been Kite's real crime, the reason they'd flayed him alive with such roaring viciousness: not for cuckolding white men, or stealing hogs, but for killing a father in a land where there *were* no fathers.

"Were you there, when they hung him? Was Daddy?"

He snorted at the very idea. "*Naw,* sister, none of us. Not for the hanging," he amended, in a bit of dissemination inaudible to anyone but Jolie. She was beginning to understand that the Great Hendrix Lynching had been a two-part affair, with a Hendrix side and a Cleary one.

Chances were, none of her kin were part of the Cleary part of the ordeal, but they sure as hell had been there for the Hendrix party. She was so sure that she asked no more questions, but just leaned in and started him in the right direction, with the bit of historical record that was agreed on, in and out of town: "Uncle Jimmie turned him in."

The old man didn't deny it. "It's a long story," he muttered, gathering a handful of damp shells and tossing them into the fire with a hiss of smoke and ash.

Jolie tapped her watch. "You got five minutes."

She was so matter-of-fact that Ott didn't bother with a lie; why should he? He had nothing to hide and spoke slowly, careful to keep his story purely his own—nothing but how it came upon him, Octavius LeRoy Hoyt, a younger son of an enormous, fragmented family, who had been twelve years old at the time and had been pulling his own wages, more or less, since he was eight. He'd quit school the year he almost died of rheumatic fever and never grew an inch further, making him a target for the local bullies, and the butt of many a cruel joke.

He wasn't physically strong enough to work at the mill, but managed to keep busy with lesser work: gathering crooks, tending the gum pots, and working for his uncle Jimmie, who owned 106 acres that he had planted in peanuts.

Old Jimmie was a well-known hard-ass, and when some of the hands hadn't shown up that morning in October 1938, he'd worked himself into a good and foul temper, which he was quick to share with the rest of the crew, shouting and threatening to take a belt to them if they didn't move it along. Ott was used to Jimmie's swagger, and as long as Ray was with them, it was an empty threat, as Ray was nearly grown and too big for anyone, even a cousin, to beat. He had let it be known that anyone who laid a hand on his brothers would have to lay a hand on him, and such was his growing reputation with a straight razor that Ott and Obie had been blissfully free of the humiliation of casual violence that had dogged their young lives.

Jimmie's bawling only slightly quickened Ott's speed, not in fear, but because big happenings were afoot in town, all of Hendrix abuzz. The evening before, Henry Kite had crossed the line from hog thief to murderer and put two men in their coffins. No one was talking of anything else, as Kite was a well-known figure around town. A gambler by profession, he spent his days lolling around his mother's kitchen, his nights shooting craps and running with women no better than himself.

The night before, hundreds of white men had been out combing the woods, with torches and rifles and dogs. They were men from the mill, mostly, and the woods riders from Camp Six, and the high sheriff from Cleary, who had nothing but contempt for the slack-jawed locals and was laying bets that Kite had got cleanly away, though Ray said the river was too high to cross.

Ott had sided with the high-hats for once and bet against his brother at the post office the night before, just to be contrary. Ott and Obie had sat up all night speculating, and Ray had promised to take them back to town that night, to hear the latest. The excitement of it all made Ott dig with uncommon vigor, till late in the afternoon, nearing six, when Obie caught him at the end of a row, breath heaving, and told him they'd caught him.

Ott didn't bother to ask who, just breathed, *"Here?"*

"Corn crib. Taking him to town. Come on."

Ott was so excited that he left his hoe in the field—a beating offense, in Hendrix—and raced to Jimmie's with a winded Obie trailing. Ray was already there, standing in the shade of a yellow-leaved fig tree, a battered straw hat on his head.

He was a grown man by local standards and conscious of his bad eye, always keeping himself a little apart. He had always been a bit of a loner and didn't comment on the hoopla, other than to grunt at his red-faced brother and remind him of their bet. "You owe me money, little man. I won't forgit, come payday."

He said it by way of teasing, poking fun at his runt younger brothers, who were filthy and winded and cow-eyed at their first glimpse of Kite, bloody, but subdued, kneeling in the back of a high peanut wagon, bound with baling cord at his wrists and ankles. Word had traveled fast, and a crowd was already forming, a dozen or more neighboring men and wives and a few children, who jockeyed with Ott and Obie for a closer look, one of the smaller boys poking Kite with a stick, as if he were a raccoon in a cage, till his father made the boy stop.

Ott was more curious than vindictive and stared at Kite through the slats, inches from Kite's sweat-streaked, coffee-colored face, which wasn't as terrorized as it was calculating, his hazel, Injun eyes darting here and there like those of a gambler trying to weigh his odds and beat a bad hand. When the bigger boys jostled Ott aside, he returned to Ray, who was older and less excitable, smoking one of the store-sold cigarettes they'd taken off Kite when they found him, possibly the very cigarettes that had cost the German his life.

Ray peered at Kite across the yard with pity. "Jimmie found him in the corn crib, sleeping like a baby. Kite let 'em take him," Ray said in wonder and contempt, then commented drily, "He'll wish diff'rent, by morning."

Ray said it with offhanded, intricate knowledge, as he had put in his time at the Camp with the bosses, who were mostly hired from out of state, veterans of the old wars, who took a bit of sport with the locals. When Ray was fourteen, one had accused him of back-sassing and, in punishment, had tied him down in the river, his nose just above water. They'd left him there all night to choke and howl and beg, to teach him a lesson, a standard punishment not infrequently fatal that Ray had never forgiven, nor forgotten.

He'd quit the next day and went to work for their uncle Jimmie, who was blood kin, but hardly better. He'd made his money early, as a moonshiner, and among the Hoyts was known to be a wife-slapper and a son-beater, and even worse, an ass-kisser. He had money enough, and sons enough, for respectability, but was always looking for a chance to impress his fellow landowners, or anyone else in town who had something he wanted—including the bosses at Camp, who had never been anyone's friend.

Kite would have been better off turning himself over to Mr. Goss and seemed to realize it belatedly, as Jimmie came out, dressed for town in his good collar, accepting the backslaps and congratulations of his neighbors with a broad, smug complacency, as if it were nothing more than his due. Ott was close enough to read the knowledge in Kite's wild eyes and suddenly pitied him, so sharply that Kite detected it among that wall of gawking, sweating faces and called out in a mild voice, "I wish one of you white gentlemen would be Christian enough to cut my throat."

He made the entreaty to all of them, but his eyes were on Ray, who was known to be a cutter and carried a razor in his hatband, and one in his shoe. If he'd have wanted to, he could have reached out and made short work of it with a single swipe.

But Kite had no truck with Ray, who'd never had any patience with trash and didn't dignify his request with a reply. He spit on the ground in answer and Jimmie mounted the wagon with a handful of his hired men and turned the mules toward town.

Ott and Obie were hot to follow, and Ray worked hard to talk them out of it, but could hardly be heard over the crush. The two outpaced and ignored him, caught up in the ragtag procession that was a considerable parade by the time they made the bridge, which was hardly wider than a single lane and unexpectedly jammed with Model T's and braying mules, and swarms of country folk, come to town for the latest on Kite. The bosses had posted deputies on all the bridges, and the deputies here, once they understood the enormity of Jimmie's catch, fired off rounds in celebration, and to clear room for the wagon to pass. Obie was caught in the crush, while Ott was lithe and quick enough to hop back aboard, out of reach of Ray, who shouted for him to let go, to come back!

But Ott was carried away by the excitement of the shouting and milling crowd and clung like a monkey to the slats, ignoring the receding figure of his brother, who paced the far end of the bridge like a pinned Frankenstein monster, his shouted rebuke swallowed up in the roar of victory that went before them. The crowd parted like the Red Sea, opening up the road to the commissary, a high-raftered, old hall—once a mule stable, then used to grade tobacco—behind the Masonic lodge.

The smell of mules and manure and unwashed bodies was strong in the heat of the old barn, which was packed from door to ceiling with a chattering, smoking mob of mostly men—not just locals, but city men, too. Ott was shorter and smaller than most and got swept along in the press till midway through the hall, when Kite jerked to a halt, as if yanked on a rope, and began flailing and shouting in earnest, his cries those of a madman. Ott ducked and bobbed to stay clear of the flailing and was practically lifted off his feet by the buckling crowd, then nearly dropped and trampled. When he looked up, he saw what had driven Kite mad: a row of bodies that were strung up from the high center rafters from a single, looped rope, as lifeless as slaughtered hogs, five of them, straight across.

They must have been hanging all day. Their faces were piteously uncovered and hideously swollen, the color of old pumpkins. So distended and abused, the faces were hard to recognize, even to Ott, who'd grown up in Hendrix and knew everyone in Camp, at least by sight. Standing there beneath them, buffeted by Kite's flailing, he made out Willie and Hiram Kite—both so bloated they were hardly human—and a girl, surely, in a long skirt. Dear Jesus, Polly Kite, who was big with her first child.

Ott was dumbfounded by the sight, as Polly was a churchgirl, quiet as a mouse—her brother's near-opposite. He couldn't see how she'd been drawn into his mess and was shoving back against the jostling crowd when he recognized the body next to hers. Not nearly as swollen, it was without a doubt her husband, George Washington, a skinny, sixteen-year-old turpentiner who'd worked the gum pot with Ott. He was too skinny to have been rendered unrecognizable in death, but hung there on a broken neck, with a missing eye and a protruding tongue.

Ott was close enough to childhood to burst into tears at the merciless prank death had played on his friend, his twisted neck and battered face dangling uncovered before the jeering mob of men. Ott refused to see more and kicked and clawed the wall of bodies around him, trying to escape the heat and slaughterhouse stink and get back to the door. But he'd allowed himself to be jammed like a cork in his hot little corner of hell. He fought as desperately as Kite, punching and kicking and crawling over the backs of fallen men till he finally found a free spot, narrow and unsought, at the front, where they'd managed to pin Kite. Ott found his feet and was casting about for a door to escape when he realized he was standing barefoot in a shallow, namelessly foul puddle that had formed under the dripping bodies in their decomposition—wider under Polly, the waters from her baby. He leapt back in horror and, above him, not five feet away, recognized the last of the dangling forms, the one that had sent Henry Kite flailing around on his chain and shouting like a madman: his mother, old Miz Kite—a fat, hardworking, old colored woman who like Ott's own mother did laundry for a living. She was so heavy that her neck had become grotesquely stretched, like a fat old turkey's. Ott's heart was clutched with terror and pity as they all knew Miz Kite around Camp—a good enough woman, who gossiped like a magpie, but kept a clean house. She had sacrificed Polly to her pretty Henry, always putting him first, but by God she didn't deserve this, her bare, calloused feet hanging lifeless, covered in waste and alighting flies. The hellishness of the night—the roar and stink and bits of scattered laughter—was encapsulated in her image. Ott pitched forward and vomited a stream of yellow bile on the backs and legs of the men around him, adding the stench of his own foul waste to the rising reek.

It earned him slaps and booted kicks and curses as he stumbled down the wall, crawling over stalls and through mildewed hay and weathered dung, still retching like a dog, till he was at the side door, where Ray stood, a head taller than the crowd, searching for him. Ray let out a shout when he saw Ott, and waded in, sweating and furious, swatting people away like flies. He was big enough to physically grip Ott by the neck and muscle him outside like a puppy, through the mobbed sidewalks and side streets to Obie, who waited at the bridge, red-faced and prancing, angry at having missed the fun.

Obie was full of a shouting curiosity that was lost on Ott, who had a weak stomach on a good day and, between the stink on his hands and the stink on his feet, couldn't quit heaving. Ray finally hoisted him on his back and carried him home like a sack of corn, a hike of a mile or more, on a pitch-dark and moonless night, which made for falls, stumbles, and a steady stream of fraternal curses at Ott for not minding Ray! For nearly gitting himself killed!

Ott was beyond caring, spitting blood by the time they made it home, to the two-room, pine-plank cabin where they lived when they worked for Jimmie. It had neither heat nor electricity nor running water, but Ott stank so bad that Ray insisted he bathe. The tedious chore that time of night took a dozen or more stumbling trips to the well at the bottom of the yard to fill the old tub.

Ott was too sick to help, and Obie was made to do the stepping, though he refused to go back alone after two trips. Something was out there, he said, the woods full of ghostly life, faceless shadows that skittered down the pig trails, alone and in families, heads down, not speaking. Ray went out on the porch and watched awhile, said they were headed for the tracks.

"No train this time of night," Obie had answered, his face pale with fear of the shadows, though Ray was only speculative.

"There must be tonight."

Ray was curious enough to wade into the woods and returned after a while with a set face and reported the ghosts were nothing more than their fleeing neighbors—black folk from Camp Six. "They torched the quarters—said you could hear Kite all over town, calling for his ma."

Ott felt like doing likewise as the sharp, hot smell of burning resin began to fill the air as the night deepened, a familiar enough scent in the woods, but too close and hot now for normality, one which would forever in his mind carry with it the copper taste of terror. Obie was equally frantic, afraid the woods would catch fire and they'd be caught, like rats in a trap, but Ray refused to run, saying Ott wasn't fit to travel.

Ray paced the yard till dawn, then loaded the family shotgun and took a seat on the front steps and grimly promised that if anyone showed up unannounced, he'd do to them what Henry Kite had done to Mr. Goss. "And thet includes Wayland Dorris and *Mister* Mitchell and Hubert *Altman* himsef," he added in uncharacteristic defiance, as they were the names of the big bosses at Camp. The latter was their mother's longtime employer, whose pants she was probably pressing in town, even as Ray spoke.

Jolie was pierced by an unexpected pity at Ott's story, which was a world away from the braggadocio of the young bloods around town, but an accurate assessment of a truly evil day in the long history of the Hoyts, when in their passion to ascend they'd sold their birthright like Esau of old, had lost not only their honor, but their very identity, their history. They'd snuffed it out so efficiently that even now, seventy years later, secrecy and silence were their legacy. Maybe that was the curse of Henry Kite, she thought, the voiceless ruin of her father's shed returning to her, forever lost.

She had one question, which she put to Ott in a voice hardly more than a whisper. "The storekeeper—did you know him?"

The old man seemed relieved she hadn't taken him to task on any of it and answered quickly, "Not but to trade with him. He didn't speak good English. His boy did most of his talking."

Jolie nodded and thought that so he must have continued, till he passed down the story to his own son, and his son after that. Who came back to hear the details firsthand and nearly exited the town feetfirst himself.

"A bullet in his eye, over a pack of cigarettes," Ott continued, with a wry shake of his head that was interrupted by a fresh outbreak of howling outside, so loud even Ott heard it and smiled dimly. "Why, thet'll be Mr. Dais, right thar. You kin meet him."

Jolie was feeling spooked about all these coincidental meetings and insisted on answering it herself, gingerly opening the door on a grim and unsmiling face: Sam Lense, hands in his pockets, jacket zipped to his chin. He was obviously in the grip of a mighty offense and ignored her completely in favor of her uncle.

*"Ott?"* he shouted in full-voice shout. "Could you call off your hounds? We're about to have the *mother* of all dogfights out here!"

Ott was quick to oblige him, hot-stepping it to the porch and piercing the rising growl with a sharp little whistle that didn't quite work its earlier magic. The pack was too agitated, the curs standing with stiff legs and bared teeth, the whole yard humming with a cacophony of musical growls as Hollis Frazier appeared on the mud path, taking long country strides. He was dressed in all his fur-coat glory, with Snowflake padding along at his side, making for such a strange and extraordinary sight that the hounds didn't seem to know what to make of it. The white bear-dog was outside their range of experience—neither bear, nor hog, nor human, but some different creature altogether.

For a moment, the dogs held their ground, hackles raised and growls rising, then, being essentially track dogs, they seemed to think better of a hasty confrontation and turned tail and ran in abject retreat: bitches, puppies, and alpha males, straight under the porch in a businesslike rout, as if a drain had been pulled.

"I'll be *damned,*" Sam said into the sudden silence.

Ott hadn't seen him in twelve years, but didn't greet him, all his attention on Snowflake, whom he regarded with a countryman's reverence, going down the porch steps and asking Hollis in his usual muted shout, "Now what sorter dog is thet? An albino shepherd?"

"A Great Pyrenees." Hollis held out his hand for a shake. "Hollis Frazier."

"Louder," Jolie called from the steps. "He's deaf."

Hollis nodded and repeated his greeting, and this time Ott shook his hand and asked, "You kin to Mr. *Dais?*" Black people were so rare on this end of the river, surely two of them, showing up in the same decade, must be kin.

"He's a *Frazier,*" Jolie shouted from the porch. "Buddy Frazier's *son,* I was telling you about." Then to Hollis: "This is my uncle Ott! He knew your papa, back in the day."

Hollis's face broadened into a magnificent smile. "Well, how 'bout thet?" He took off his hat in a country sign of respect, clearly pleased to make the acquaintance of a living, breathing character from his mother's memories: Ott Hoyt.

The runt of the Hoyt boys.

The kindest of them, Tempy used to say.

# Chapter Twenty-five

Jolie's job as all-around interpreter was sidetracked by Sam, who was more than a little annoyed by her abrupt departure, which had resurrected painful memories of her Great Abandonment of '96. He pinned her on the steps and asked, "Why'd you go running out like that? What am I—the village *idiot*?"

Jolie was none too comfortable with his presence at ground zero, not fifty feet from where he had once been shot, and made a small effort at appeasement. "We might want to discuss this in private."

But he was a man with a grievance and snapped, "Private my *ass*. What's with all the sneaking around? What are you running from?" he demanded, so insistent that Jolie was forced to do the unthinkable: tell him the truth.

"Somebody torched the shed," she told him in a low voice, a weather eye on the old men, who were bent down, petting the dog.

Sam's irritation was gone in an instant, replaced by a flash of that old galloping interest. "Your father's shed? Who would have done that? Who would have even *known*?" Then in a reflective murmur: "God, it's like there's a secret police out here, dogging your every step."

"Yeah, and I know the name of this particular *Nazi*—the same devious son of a bitch who foisted me off to Savannah twelve years ago."

"*Ott?*" Sam offered blankly.

"Good God."

Sam couldn't resist one more try. "The *Klan*?"

Jolie held up a hand for him to stop with the guessing and told him plainly, "Carl Hoyt." She glanced at her watch. "Whose plane should be touching down right about now."

"No, it's not. He's here."

Jolie looked up. "Here, *where*?"

Sam nodded at the river. "The dock by now. We passed him, not five minutes ago, on Vic's pontoon, headed here. Looking for you."

Jolie started backing to the path. "Keep an eye on the old boys. No," she said when Sam tried to argue. "I'll be right back." She turned and bounded down the steep, slick path, through the fir smell of the old cedars to the sagging dock, where Carl was securing Vic Lucas's old party barge to a rail.

Jolie was so mad she called ahead as she went down the path, "Why, there he is—Hendrix's newest pyromaniac, the Reverend Carl Hoyt!"

He straightened up when he saw her, but didn't dignify the gibe with an answer, just finished tying off the boat as Jolie mounted the shifting and sinking old boards and faced him. "I saw what you done this morning, and it is beneath contempt. It is despicable. Burning Daddy's stuff like it was trash. What are you afraid of, Carl? That your precious flock'll find out what your old Mayberry hometown is really about? Or that your old kinfolk killed a pregnant woman?"

"Neither," he told her mildly. "And quit hollering in my face. I ain't deaf."

"Don't even try to deny it," she insisted, moving when he tried to sidestep. "That's your real calling, ain't it, Carl? To clean this family up with your little stories, your sermons, your fancy damn suits. Did you even look at Daddy's stuff before you torched it? It didn't mean *shit* to you, did it?"

Like all the Hoyts, Carl could only take so much abuse before he reacted, his eyes glinting, "Well, listen, Jol—if you were so into Daddy's stuff, why'd you keep it stashed out here in thet old shed all these years?

Why'n you move it into that fine big house in town, with Hughie and the rest of the Altmans?"

It was similar to the accusation Sam had made at the church the night before, and it hit a little too close to the bone for comfort, making Jolie back up a step and snap, "You're no brother of mine."

She turned on her heel and would have left, but Carl stopped her with a quiet voice.

"It was Lena," he said, so unemotionally that Jolie turned.

"What?"

"Lena. She burnt the shed."

Jolie stood there, apparently unbelieving, till Carl added, "My plane didn't touch ground till eight thirty this morning. When did I have time to git to Hendrix, much less torch the shed?"

He was believable in his immobility, and after a moment Jolie stammered, "*Why?* There was nothing out there but Daddy's old shoes, and sermons. I looked yesterday. I was just there."

"I know. Your clerk called the church. Said you'd run out like a bat out of hell, heading to Hendrix, and Lena—it freaked her out. She called and called but couldn't get up with you—thought you'd get yourself killed down here. She always thought you're the one they wanted to shoot, back when they nailed Lense—that bullet was meant for you."

Jolie gaped at him. "Why? Because of the Kite lynching—the fingers?"

"What fingers?" Carl asked with a look of great foreboding.

"The ones at Sister Wright's—you know, in the back room."

"In the gin bottle?" He had that face of wild disgust, not at the fingers as much as Jolie's incessant digging into the darkest corners of their shared past. He looked to be about at the end of his pastoral rope, and in a voice nearly pleading, he asked, "Why you wanna keep digging all this shit up? Don't we have enough real-life crap to deal with, without plowing up all the family crap? It's ancient history. It's dead."

"Not to me," she answered with a directness that only made him madder.

"And that's all that matters, ain't it? What the baby girl wants, she gets. Hell, Jol, you ever thought of the rest of us? You got one man shot, and Lena out torching houses, and the moment any of this shit hits the papers, you'll be out on the sidewalk—and for nothing. A pack of fish-camp tall tales—and it's over, Jol. It doesn't matter, and it *never* mattered."

Jolie just held up her hands as she had with Hollis at her desk and answered quietly, "It matters to me. Where's Lena? At the house? Is she answering her phone?"

"At her pop's, waiting for us," Carl answered, harassed and red-faced as he followed Jolie to the boat. "She won't come on the river no more—and she won't talk about it," he warned.

But Jolie had made up her mind to settle this once and for all. She kicked off her muddy heels, tired of dealing with the damn things, just tossed them in the jon boat, then shimmied in after. Carl called from the dock, "Well, go easy on her, Jol—and don't be running your mouth about that ratty old shed. She didn't know Daddy's stuff was there."

Jolie ignored him, yanking the pull till the motor finally fired. Carl followed her as far as the listing dock would allow, shouting even more unheard advice and instruction as she concentrated her energies on turning the boat and nosing it upstream, tougher going with the current against her. The little motor whined with effort, coughing and catching. She finally caught a glint of an RV in the woods and spotted a small, familiar figure perched on the far end of the private dock.

From the back, Lena looked hardly aged, but as straight-shouldered and waiflike as she'd been at fourteen, brightly dressed in a red knit cap and scarf and a down vest of some sort of upscale outdoor-wear—Orvis or L.L. Bean or the like—her hair darkened with the birth of her children, but still gold enough to glint in the sun.

When she heard the boat, she came to her feet by rote and helped

Jolie tie off, her face more aged than her silhouette, her nose and cheeks chapped from the wind, little raccoon circles of mascara below her eyes.

"Did you see Carl?" she asked when the motor was cut, her face apprehensive. "He was looking for you. Your clerk called yesterday. She said you needed to talk to him, that it was an emergency. Did you see him?"

"I did." Jolie tossed up her shoes and blanket, then accepted a hand to the dock.

Confronting Lena was a different proposition from confronting Carl, and Jolie was casting about for a delicate inquiry when Lena burst out in unexpected confession, in one fast rush, "I burned down the shed at Bethel last night. I thought it was empty, didn't know there was a trac- tor in there—a John Deere." She teared up at the name, as if it were the unpardonable sin to burn a name brand. "Carl is so mad."

"He'll survive." Jolie took Lena's cold hand and squeezed it. "Can we sit a minute? I have to go to work." Jolie glanced at her watch. "Crap, I got fifteen minutes. Just sit a minute," she begged. "Carl and Sam won't be long—"

"Sam Lense?" Lena asked in a voice little short of incredulous. "You brought him back to Hendrix?" She was so upset she began crying again, angry little tears that she brushed away with an impatient hand that made it hard for her to speak.

Jolie was moved by her fear, which was so deep and grounded that Lena trembled like a frightened dog. Jolie gripped Lena's hand tighter and found them a seat on the old fishing bench, gray and weathered by a century of summer sun.

Lena sat down obediently, but was agitated and clearly annoyed, chiding Jolie as if she were one of her children. "What d'you think you're doing, Jol? Your office called—they called *three* times. Faye is so worried, said you were out digging around the shed for something about that old lynching—and there was nothing out there, Jol. The place was falling down."

Jolie began to see the picture now: Faye, in all her wheedling curiosity, unwittingly lighting a fuse. Jolie saw no reason to lie and crossed her arms for warmth, her teeth beginning to chatter, not in fear, but cold. "Then why'd you torch it, Lena?"

"Because you wouldn't leave it alone!" she cried, more frustrated than fearful, as if confounded by Jolie's stubbornness. Lena dug out another wisp of Kleenex and angrily wiped her nose. "Isn't it enough Sam got shot? Who's next? Carl? One of the girls? When does it end, Jol?"

It was the first time Lena had ever hinted that Sam's shooting might be something other than accidental, her tone so matter-of-fact that Jolie could feel a slight movement of gears in her chest, as the conversation slowly moved into uncharted water. She was careful not to spook Lena and asked, "You mean it was intentional?"

Lena waved her away impatiently, as if the question was beside the point. "Who knows? Intentional, accidental—all I know is it happened. He was nosing around, asking too many questions. He was too close."

"Close to *what*?" Jolie asked, her heart beginning to beat heavily in her chest as if she was closing in on a momentous revelation. "You mean the lynching?"

"Yes, the lynching, that's why he was here," Lena said, returning to the old argument, "not for the Indians. That's why Travis shot him," she added, with no inkling of the effect it had on Jolie, making her literally lose her breath, as if she'd been kicked in the stomach.

"*Travis Hoyt?*" she managed, as he'd never occurred to her as the shooter—never, not once. He was one of Uncle Earl's grandsons, and too young, maybe seventeen that year, so young his father had to sign for him when he joined the Marines—not long after, now that she thought of it. Not long at all.

Her surprise was so evident that Lena dropped her Kleenex and asked her plainly, "You didn't know?" Then said, even more shockingly, "*Sam* knows."

# Chapter Twenty-six

If Jolie was stunned before, she was now speechless, as Lena volunteered with that casual, matter-of-fact assurance, "Carl told him—he had to, before the statute of whatever ran out."

"*Travis?*" Jolie whispered. "You're *sure?*" as they were speaking of the same Travis Hoyt who'd sat at the Thanksgiving table with them at dinner that day, one of the redneck Hoytlings who'd ragged her about bringing him tea.

"Sure, I'm sure. I was sitting right there—and it happened so quick. And you know how it was that day, at dinner—all that teasing and poking fun, all of 'em, going at each other. Me and Carl, we took Daddy's boat to go down to the camp. But, God, it was cold that night, ten times colder than today, like, fifteen degrees. Felt like fifteen below, and all around you could hear gunshot—deer hunters, zinging around. We were thinking about turning back when we came on Travis and Bill Goin, and Bill's little brother. You know, the short one . . ."

"Chuckie?" Jolie offered.

Lena nodded. "Yeah. Chuck Goin. They were finishing hunting for the day, out spotting deer and drunk as the seven earls, shining the spotter on us and catcalling, till Carl threatened to come up out of that boat and beat their butts. But it was still okay, they were just messing around, giving us a hard time." Lena paused and gave Jolie a cagey look. "You sure you wanta hear this?"

At Jolie's nod, Lena shrugged. "Then they started in on you—about how high-and-mighty you thought you were—going to college, giving it up to the first man who threw his hat in the ring. And, God, it made Carl mad. He was about to come out of that boat. But it was still just a goof, really, Travis and him calling back and forth, ragging each other like they always did. Then one of them, the little one, with the spotter, he must have saw something downstream because he shined it down there, said, 'Now, what do we got *here?*'"

Lena paused, her nose beet red from the cold, though her small face was still blank with disbelief, her voice slightly lower as she dug deeper in the memory. "And it was so crazy, Jol—it happened so quick. I mean, one minute I was sitting there telling Carl to let it go, that they were just drunk, and then Travis—he put his rifle to his shoulder and *boom*—he took a shot. I didn't know what was going on, about jumped out of my skin, and Carl—he jumped out of the boat, right into the river, after Travis. He was only maybe three feet from the bank, but the water was so high, so fast, it was like jumping into white water. Travis took off like a rabbit, but Bill helped me drag Carl out—close to the dock, about froze to death. That's where we found Sam, just up the path—never would have seen him, but he'd dropped his flashlight and it was still on."

Lena lowered her voice even further, to a bare whisper. "And even then, we didn't think it was that bad, thought he'd nicked him on purpose, as a goof. But the bleeding—it wouldn't stop. It got on everything—our coats, the boat. We couldn't tell where he was shot."

Even as she spoke, the pontoon appeared at the bend, the sound of the motor displaced by some trick of the wind so that they could see it before they heard it. Carl was steering, Sam aside, talking to him, their faces averted. Lena's face registered relief, and she came immediately to her feet. "Thank God," she breathed, though Jolie wasn't half as sanguine.

She came to her feet, too, but paid no attention to the pontoon, gripping Lena's lapels and asking to her face, "Why wouldn't you tell, Lena? You lied to me."

Lena seemed emboldened by the return of the menfolk and pulled away with scarce patience. "Tell *who*? My dad, who had to live out here? Or that judge? Or that *idiot* deputy? They were already trying to pin it on Carl or your daddy or poor old Ott—the crazy old Hoyt brothers, out on another killing. And he was okay. The doctors—they got him in time," Lena insisted. "He was fine."

"He almost *died*," Jolie cried, shock giving way to a cold rage that made her voice tremble.

Lena wouldn't budge. "So did *Carl*—and so did *I*, trying to get him in the boat—and we didn't have nothing to do with it, Jol! It wasn't *our* fault he came out here lying and digging up all that nasty crap and got everybody so *pissed*."

"Then why didn't you tell me, Lena? Why didn't you and Carl just come in that night and say, 'Hey, Jol, your boyfriend got shot, take care of it'?"

"Because we *loved* you," Lena answered with equal passion, "and you're too *Hoyt*," she said, spitting out the name like an expletive. "You can't let anything go. You still can't, till this day. Look at us," Lena cried. "Here we are, still talking about it! Twelve years and we're still talking!"

Jolie was conscious of the fast approach of the pontoon and determined to leave before Sam arrived. She yanked up her shoes and told Lena, "That's because it's not over."

Lena yelled at her back, as did Carl, and Sam, who were yards away from docking. Jolie had no intention of waiting around for yet another round of denial and explanation. She felt equally defeated by all of them and went to her car as quickly as her idiot heels would permit, wishing she had hurled them in the river when she had the chance.

She was tired, freezing, flat-haired, and furious and would have made a clean getaway if she'd been barefoot. Sam caught her at the car, wind-blown and pink-cheeked, but relatively warm in his coat. He didn't bother to try to stand and argue, but slammed himself in the passenger seat.

"That's why I came over," he said, "to make sure you know about Travis. Carl was supposed to tell you, God, six years ago. *Shit,* I knew you'd be *pissed.*"

Jolie was too livid to answer and too tired to get into another round with anyone. She felt as if she'd gone ten rounds with Joe Louis and just concentrated on getting to town, so glacially silent that Sam had no choice but to continue his defense in that querulous voice, as if she had argued.

"And I wouldn't be too quick to point a finger about keeping secrets from the rest of the class if I was you. You were MIA, missing in god-damn action. All those weeks I was hooked to an IV in Miami—did you ever think about doing something really modern and *outré* like actually *picking* up the phone and calling?"

She was finally provoked enough to answer, without turning, her eyes on the flying ribbon of highway. "*No.* I never did."

The reply was insulting in its brevity, its shameless honesty; so much that Sam didn't speak for a moment, but watched her across the seat with less fury than his old curiosity as they hurled along the highway.

He had long ago lost his fascination with the Hoyts, and their contradictions, but was, finally, curious enough to ask, "Why not?"

He asked it honestly, without rancor, and inadvertently resurrected the Jolie of the Campground, the Queen of the Paradox: pale and dark, devout and savage, headstrong but pliable as a child. She offered him a mere glance as she confessed, "Because I *loved* you. And I did *everything* I could, to protect you, and I *couldn't.*"

The candor in her voice was inarguable, so much that Sam's jaw softened. "From *what?*"

She offered nothing but an angry shake of the head and a sharp tap of her knuckles on the side window, indicating the passing woods that grew close to the highway, flat with a tropic excess in the palmetto and vine-wrapped palms.

"From Hendrix"—he pressed—"or your idiot cousin? Because that little shit'll never step a foot in Florida again."

He said it with great confidence, but Jolie was hardly convinced, provoked enough to snap, "You don't know that. You took a pass. You're as bad as Lena. You're worse than Lena."

"I took *nothing*. Shit, Jol, I work for DCF. D'you think I don't know how to prosecute a felony? When you get to town, call the lead detective—the old guy from Hendrix, who used to be married to someone."

"Jeb Cooke?" she asked, incredulous, as she still occasionally saw Jeb around town and never a word had he spoken of the matter.

"Yeah, Cooke. He works for the highway patrol. Was happy to hear it, but it was too late. The statute of limitations had expired. Carl thought it was six years. It was three, for assault with a deadly weapon. Shelton concurred."

"*Shelton?* Who's Shelton?"

"My brother," Sam said as the exurbs of Cleary began to pass. "He's a lawyer, in Coral Springs, does real estate—closings, shit like that."

The mildness of the answer brought a truly crazy cast to Jolie's eyes. "You went to a *real estate* lawyer? With attempted *murder?*"

Sam's expression was equally crazy, not least because she hadn't slowed for city traffic, but continued to sail along, darting between cars. "Will you slow down? You're gonna kill us both. And who am I? J. Paul *Getty?* You think I have a fleet of lawyers on speed dial, waiting on my calls? Shelton wanted to send me to a civil rights lawyer, but, *shit,* Jol—it wasn't racial. It was *tribal,*" he proclaimed with his old anthropologist confidence. "It was more about me poaching one of their women than some racial *shit.* It was a lot of things," he corrected at her noise of disbelief as she slowed for downtown. "I shouldn't have walked into such a thing in a lie—should have come clean that first night I saw you. And I shouldn't have fucked you—you were too young and your father trusted me and it was exploitive," he continued, on a fast, soul-bearing little roll that Jolie brought to a halt.

"Yeah, well, that's bullshit," she said as she braked in front of her house to let him out. "Minimalizing and rationalizing—we know it well, in old Hendrix town." She pinned him with a final, deadly question: "Does your father know? That you let Travis walk?"

Sam was finally squashed at that and told her plainly, "If you tell my father, I'll hang myself. So will Shelton."

"*Good.* I'll buy the rope," she said, so sincerely that Sam looked at her in amazement.

"Well, God, Jol, I don't know why *you're* so pissed. I'm the one who got shot in the back and left for dead."

"Oh, no, you weren't. It was *my* back, too, Sam, and your father's, and he's right—you can't just let them *walk.* You let them walk, and they'll just do it again, to someone else. You got to keep your *thumb* on their *head,* your *boot* on their *neck,* or they'll take over the god*damn* world."

She was so furious her chest was heaving, though Sam seemed untouched by her fury, more curious than defensive. He watched her a moment, brow furrowed, then unfastened his seat belt and offered a final bit of Sam Wisdom. "Beware of collective guilt. It's a seductive notion. But it is a lie."

He got out and shut the door with no kick, no complaint, just a resignation that struck Jolie as a sort of abandonment. She drove to City Hall with a spate of tears rolling down her cheeks—not for Henry Kite or Sam or the brothers Frazier and their doomed search, but for herself, Jolie Hoyt. Because she was tired and cold and lonely as hell, and her father's scribbled old notebooks were gone and she *had* forgotten about them, living the high life in town, planting trees and peeling paint and working so hard to preserve a history that was not even her own. What was she so scared of, anyway? That she'd lose her job? End up like her Big Mama, ironing for the rich folk? How would that be any worse than what she was doing now, wrestling that miserable commission into shape every day of her life?

*Hell,* she *was* ironing for the rich folk, she thought as she turned into the packed parking lot, where the line of political demarcation was clearly drawn, the cars of the members of the Historical Committee parked in one direction—ancient Mercedeses, Volvos, and a Seville or two—and those of the Chamber of Commerce members in the other— Lexus, Lexus, Lexus, all brand-new. She went in the back door through the kitchen to the long, raftered hall that smelled of charred oak and oil heat, and decades of public smoking, long outlawed, but once so furiously practiced that the pine floors seemed to have absorbed a layer of Lucky Strike.

The commission members were already seated on a raised dais at the front of the room, so physically similar as to appear to be members of the same well-fed tribe. Their ages varied by forty years, but they were all dressed in pressed khaki and Van Heusen dress shirts, monotone ties, and Red Wing boots—a workingman's uniform designed to designate them as local, prosperous, and up-and-coming.

Tad was at the sound board, testing the equipment, Faye at his side, the MAYOR folder clutched in her hand, checking her watch. "Thank God," she said when she saw Jolie. "Juddy was about to start without you."

Juddy Hewitt was a bulked-up, crew-cut former 'Nole linebacker. The youngest commissioner on the bench, and lately pro tem, he was only slightly less impatient than Jolie and always wanting to get the show on the road. When he saw her pause to speak with Faye, he had the temerity to emit a sharp whistle in her direction, as if she were an errant cow who'd gone through the wrong gate.

Jolie was not in the mood to be whistled at and murmured darkly as she took her folder, "Will somebody tell that Cracker I'm not one of his hunting dogs?"

Faye was used to Jolie's moods and just sent her up to her seat. She was conscious of her stringy hair and soggy suit. Jolie apologized for her ragged appearance as she took her place in the middle of the long wooden bar that served as the commissioners' desk and, with no more discussion, called the meeting to order. As predicted, a lion's share of the night's agenda was concerned with the cell tower. Only Jolie and a handful of beautification committee members were at all concerned with the possibility of their quaint little downtown's being afflicted with a tall and blinking red monster of a tower. The cell company had obviously been doing their homework with the commissioners, who would likely have pressed the matter to a premature vote if Hugh hadn't appeared at seven thirty, just in the nick of time.

He came in quietly, with Georgia Anderson on his arm, one of the county's grande dames, whose father had actually built the Cleary Hotel, back in '22. The place had changed hands many times since, but the Andersons still had a few holdings around town and still had enough of a sniff of prosperity and power that the hustlers on the commission paid heed when she took the podium and pleaded for caution before her father's masterpiece was desecrated. When she left the microphone, Jolie immediately suggested a workshop before the matter was voted on, which was quickly seconded and carried, which was all she wanted—a little more time for the old Historic and Beautification Board to regroup to battle the forces of modern evil and urban blight.

She appreciated Hugh's coming to her rescue and met his eye a moment before he left—or would have, if he would have consented. But he was obviously still furious and only there to squash the cell tower, and left as unexpectedly as he had appeared.

Jolie went about refereeing the rest of the meeting, which was relatively uneventful, as the cell-tower controversy was plainly their new municipal pain in the ass and would be for many months to come, the cell-phone people threatening them mightily with all manner of drawn-out lawsuits and legal challenges. Jolie took it all in stride, and by seven o'clock they were on to New Business, with Tad briefly taking the podium to put in a word about a coming change in cable regulations that didn't require a vote. There were no discussions or questions on the matter, the meeting plainly at an end, aside from the small matter of public comments, at the end of the agenda, when citizens could stand and air grievances.

A few people lined up, for or against the tower, mostly friends of Jolie's from the old Garden Club set. Their comments were tart, precise, and quickly done, and the room was relaxing with the relief that comes toward the end of any fractious meeting when the double doors at the back opened, and two latecomers unexpectedly appeared. Everyone, even Faye and Tad, turned to give them a second glance, as they were an odd mix: a snappily dressed black man in a fancy coat, and another black man, with a cane and a look of squinting interest. There was a small fear that they were there to weigh in on the cell tower and would pin everyone in for another round of questions, but they seemed to have nothing to do with the business at hand and took seats quietly in the back row.

After a little more eyeballing and neck-stretching, the audience returned their attention to the mayor, who should have been bringing them down the home stretch, but seemed distracted by the newcomers. She let the final speaker yammer on far too long about the high cost of his new cell phone, which had nothing to do with anything.

The mayor just sat there, slumped in her wilted suit, her face pale and thoughtful, till he finished yammering. She finally bestirred herself and made the call for unfinished business, which this time of night shouldn't have been much. It was late and everyone was ready to leave, an obvious fact that only the mayor didn't seem to grasp. While the rest of the commission buttoned coats and shuffled paper, she went to the great trouble of explaining what everyone already knew: that this was a free forum, that *any*one could make a citizen's comment and have it entered into public record—*any* single thing concerning the city of Cleary, no matter how forgotten or *historical*.

She ignored the air of disgruntlement from the commission at what sounded like a clear invitation to the wing nuts to take the floor. Juddy, who sat to her immediate left, was bold (and desperate) enough to lean out of the range of the mike and whisper, "What is this, Jol? A *goddamn* altar call? I have to be at work at five tomorrow morning."

Jolie withered him with a glance, then sat there, gavel in hand, sweating them out, till to the room's great, groaning horror, one of the latecomers came quietly to his feet: the pimp in the flashy coat. He made his way to the microphone with great presence, his race and fur collar having an almost visible effect on the older commissioners, who hated being held captive by the kooks and the pimps and the goddamned minorities, who had by God taken over city politics and were always yammering for their share of the pie.

These commissioners sent many dark looks down the table at the mayor, whose full attention was on the podium, where the pimp had to stoop a little to speak. "Well, I'm not a citizen of Cleary, but I do have a little city bidnis to take care of while I'm here. I'm Hollis Frazier from Memphis, Tennessee," he began, introducing himself as he had to Sam and Jolie. He even introduced the other old man—his brother, he said, who made no gesture, just sat there, his cane between his knees, listening. The impatience in the room was increasingly palpable, the commissioners at the far ends of the table leaning forward to see what the hell the mayor was thinking, drawing out an out-of-town crank when God knew they had plenty enough to deal with right in their backyard.

There was a world of grimacing, grunting, and many exhalations of breath till Hollis got to the heart of his request about the return of his father's fingers with the same simplicity he'd used before, holding up his own hand to demonstrate which fingers ("middle 'ens, right hand").

The bizarre leap from cell tower to severed fingers made everyone, aside from the outright dozers (there were always one or two), spring to life with new interest, if politely concealed. All along the rows, everyone—black, white, cell reps, and city activists—muttered, murmured, and mouthed among themselves. They gaped at Hollis Frazier with expressions that varied from incredulous surprise to blank astonishment when he offered the reward: $10,000, cash.

Jolie grimaced at the public offer in a rare display of emotion (if the wing nuts weren't out by now, they would be shortly). But it was too late to argue, and when he was done, she opened the floor for question and discussion. This was usually not such a bother at this time of night, everyone ready to be done with it and get home. The citizenry uttered not so much as a peep, their faces curious but undecided, as if they were not quite decided if this was an April Fools' prank, or the ghost of Henry

Kite raising his head at last. They were prepared to go home and sleep on it and call a few dozen relatives and talk about it in the morning—all but Commissioner Wynn. A local auto-parts salesman, he had a keen ear for local nuance and recognized a political windfall when he saw one.

He had long coveted Jolie's good office and made a point of sitting on the far end of the long table so he could swivel in his seat and face her in debate with ponderous gravity, in a voice that was actually born in Cincinnati, but could go Kentucky colonel in moments of political expediency.

"Well, Miss May-yah," he drawled, "I can appreciate the gentleman's request, but ah don't quite see how it comes under the province of the City of Cleary. Didn't the Hendrix Lynching happen in, well, Hendrix?" he asked with a rumble of amusement at his small jest. He left the unspoken portion of the question unspoken (*by yo people*) and sat there like a confused old owl, as if sincerely trying to wrap his mind around a puzzling mystery.

He was famous for such old-school manipulations, and Jolie equally famous for outflanking him. She swiveled around and answered him to his face, with scant patience, "Well, I believe you're right, Commissioner Wynn. But from what I understand, Mr. Kite was actually hung in Cleary, from a live oak on our own award-winning town square. The limb's gone, but I'll be happy to show you where it used to be, before the City had it pruned."

The admission was so open and odious, and so polar opposite to what the Garden Club and Historic and Beautification Board had sought to achieve with their time and money and fabulous renovation, that it would have drawn an audible groan if the ladies of both organizations hadn't been too well-mannered to make such a public utterance. They blinked and sniffed and put their purses in their laps and stared straight ahead with such unbending efficiency that JW conceded the point with nothing but a small smile that said it all (*Miss Mayor, you are headed back to the farm*). Jolie accepted the stab and let it pass, then called a second time for discussion, this time with the gavel in hand.

She was met with stark silence, even the garrulous old courthouse sitters too shocked to comment. They were blindsided by the fingers and the reward, but possibly even more stunned that a canny politician such as the mayor would make such an absurd misstep this far along in the game. She offered up another moment or two, then adjourned the meeting with a swift crack of the gavel, precisely six minutes too late to salvage her budding career.

Four of the commissioners were smokers and could not have cared less if Jolie had publicly impaled herself; they just needed a smoke. They scuttled out like cockroaches, leaving Juddy to glower with wounded indignity, clearly having not absorbed a word of the proceedings after Jolie so bitchily refused to recognize him from the bench, his ass so high on his shoulder it was almost apparent to the naked eye. Being the eternal pragmatist she was, Faye paid no attention to the larger questions, but met Jolie at the bottom of the stairs with a terse "You go find Juddy. You hurt his feelings, and if he tells his mama, she'll be on your neck for twenty years."

It was sound advice as far as it went, as Juddy was the golden boy of a large faction of landowning Crackers, whose matriarch was possibly the only woman in the county more territorial than Jolie herself.

Jolie handed Faye the lapel mike and the folder and said, "I know." She found Juddy among the smokers and pulled him aside and apologized, profusely and sincerely. When he failed to unfold out of his crossed-arm knot, she actually laid a little truth on him, lowering her voice to confess, "I'm having a tough little go of it this week. Got called out to Hendrix on a family emergency."

Juddy was local enough to understand this was not a good thing and, curious, asked, "Who's the pimp? Who asked about the fingers? God, do we have more kooks around here than any little town on earth, or is it me?"

"We got kooks," Jolie admitted, then backed out and got away before the other smokers could circle and ask about the pimp and the fingers. She didn't have the strength and left her car for morning and beat a fast, quiet retreat along the hedged sidewalks and across the newly treed, beautifully manicured courthouse square.

She passed the old oak that had once bent under the weight of Henry Kite, pausing to look at the backlit silhouette for the first time in many years. The landmarks around it were unchanged since '38. In the darkness she could imagine it precisely: the tree and the dust, the press of the crowd and the shouting. If she closed her eyes, she could almost smell the stink of the slaughterhouse—the blood and skin and rot of decomposition that Kite must have foreseen himself, being raised on a farm. A snippet of his last request returned to her: "I wish one of you white gentlemen would be Christian enough to cut my throat."

Most versions of the story omitted this small, telling detail, which to Jolie's ears sounded perfectly authentic. Cagey and pathetic, it was the last request of a man who was a skilled gambler and knew the ways of his captors. Who, in his utter desperation and terror, had appealed to their most prized possession: their very whiteness—for all the good it had done him.

She shook her head at the futility of it all and started home in the early twilight, her head down, her arms crossed on her chest. The motion detectors at her gate flickered on as she passed, lighting the walkway with its usual panoramic effect, like the Spirit of the Lord on the face of the deep. She let herself in the front door and turned the bolt lock behind her. She was unbuttoning her limp, wet jacket when she realized Sam was lying on the parlor sofa, a bottle of whiskey on the table beside him, a row of Ritz crackers in hand.

"So how did it go?" he asked.

# Chapter Twenty-seven

He spoke so casually that Jolie was more startled than frightened, pressing her hand to her heart and murmuring, "My God. You scared the hell out of me. How'd you get in?"

"Kitchen window," he said without shame, pouring himself another shot of whiskey, obviously neither his first nor his second, his face flushed and relaxed. If he was not drunk, then he was comfortably oiled.

He had two tumblers on the table and offered her one. She took it and killed it in a single throw—not in it for the taste but for the nice little sunburst of heat. Sam raised an eyebrow at the gesture. "So, I take it, not so well."

She was glad of the warmth of the spirits and extended her glass for a refill, holding this one close to her chest as she sank into a shabby club chair. Eyes closed, she offered a brief outline of the meeting, including the ending.

If she expected praise, she was disappointed, as Sam just grunted, "*Huh*. I was afraid self-sabotage was in the works—almost went back and warned you."

Between the whiskey and the club chair, she was feeling warmer and less hemmed in. She worked her way out of the damp, wretched jacket and tossed it aside. "It wasn't self-sabotage, it was self-serving. I wanted to be *seen*," she confessed. "I'm tired of being a ghost."

Sam regarded her a long moment, then lifted his glass in toast, just as he had that first night at the café: "To resurrection."

Jolie had always liked his toasts and raised her glass in answer. "To resurrection," she echoed with a smile that was tired and pale-lipped, but affecting to Sam. It was his first glimpse of the Jolie of their youth, wry and watchful, but not so very tough.

"God, I'm glad to see that smile. I haven't seen it since Thanksgiving night, when I left for the fish camp. You were so pissed," he said in wonder, as if it still didn't quite add up, her anger of a decade past.

"I didn't want you to go." She finished the second shot of whiskey and held the tumbler to her chest, eyes closed, feeling the warmth.

The details of that Thanksgiving evening were still vague to Sam, who asked, "Why were you so adamant? Was there talk"—he tapped his chest—"of what was coming?"

She was drinking on an empty stomach and answered honestly, if a little vaguely, "There didn't have to be talk. I knew I was losing you the minute you walked out the door. It broke my heart."

"How did you know?" he asked, setting down his empty tumbler and leaning forward as he did when engaged.

She answered frankly, with her eyes closed, "Because women in Hendrix lose everything, eventually—friends, money, mothers. It's a losing kind of place. You tremble every minute for your love."

It was the first time she'd said the word in twelve years and meant it, her face drowsy in repose, but peculiarly wounded, in a way that moved Sam to a bit of honesty of his own. "Well, God, Jol, you talk like we're a hundred years old. It's not too late—it's never too late."

She bestirred herself enough to argue the point. "You're married. Wes told us."

"Yeah—and divorced about as quick. All I got out of it was a kid, my son, Brice. He's ten, he's a sweetheart—does good in school," he said offhandedly, as if genetically unable to mention his son without throwing out a bit of praise. "Don't worry about me, I'm free, I'm good. And you're just as well as free—just need to unlatch yourself from the millionaire dipshit and get the hell out of this mausoleum. Yeah, it's beautiful, but God, Jol, what would your father think? Is it worth your soul?"

His voice had dropped to the level of an altar call, so compelling that Jolie blinked out of her drowsiness and sat up a little straighter. "You know, Sam, I don't know what nonsense you've been hearing about me, but I own this house"—she yawned—"or co-own it, with the Bank of America. If it didn't have historic exemption, I wouldn't be able to pay the taxes."

Sam was more charmed than offended by her denial and answered patiently, his elbows on his knees, as if truly leading her to the Lord, "You don't have to lie to me, Jol. I'm not gonna go tell on you to the Baptists. This"—he waved his empty tumbler—"is not the house of a public servant—and trust me, I know. I crunch numbers for the State. Somebody around here has money. Old, capital-gaining, accrued-interest money, and, baby, I've been to Hendrix. And I know what city governments pay. And that someone ain't you."

If Jolie was used to one myth, it was that she was Hugh's kept woman. Even Faye half believed it, though Jolie worked hard to dispel it. It was almost impossible to talk anyone out of it; the more she denied it, the more ridiculous she sounded. She was too tired to get into it, but made a stab at explanation. "You might recall that I was once a struggling young student of design. The only things that are Hugh's are the rugs and curtains and sideboards. He's been promising to move them for years, but he's too cheap to hire a mover and he's lazy as hell."

Sam wasn't buying but was feeling chummy enough to indulge her. "Well, good. Tell him to move his shit tonight. I'm serious, Jol. Nobody'll ever take you seriously till you break it off with the sugar daddy. One phone call," he assured her, and even demonstrated, holding his thumb and pinkie to his ear, saying, "'Hey, Hugh. It's Jolie. It's over.' Then, *click*." He hung up the imaginary phone. "All done. Free as a bird."

Jolie watched the performance with slightly raised eyebrows, then put him out of his misery, leaning in and confiding, "He's my *uncle*, Sam."

She expected surprise, but not the look of mild disgust that wrinkled his face. "You're sleeping with your *uncle?*" he murmured. "Well, that's *nasty,* even for Hendrix."

Jolie stared at him a moment, then answered in the purest honesty, "You know, baby, if you ever get tired of the bureaucracy at the State, you might consider running for Cleary City Commission. I think you'd fit *right* in, like a hand in a glove."

Sam hadn't grown much in the way of humility over the years and swallowed this insult with poor grace. He didn't argue, but sat, grievously insulted, but beginning to come around, taking in the high ceiling, the ornate old woodwork, till it finally began to dawn on him, what she'd just told him.

Such was his pride that he didn't venture any more questions, but concluded in a light, bemused voice, "His father was one of your Big Mama's men friends—the ones she ran around with when she was young; ended up ironing for when she was old."

Jolie raised her empty tumbler in a gesture of assent. "Bingo. And I'd appreciate it if you'd give him a little slack. He's an anachronistic, controlling old pain in the ass, but he makes a stab at humanity from time to time. And I owe him."

Sam was less confident by then and offered hesitantly, "For the house?"

"No." She yawned. "The house was bribery, to run his city for him. But he once did a purer favor, for Daddy, a long time ago—after his second stroke, when we were broke, and I was looking for a job. Nobody in Hendrix would touch me with a ten-foot pole, and I was about to start cleaning toilets for a living when Daddy came home one night with big news: that he'd found me a *good* job, in Cleary, working for Mis-*tah Alt*man," she said, mimicking her father with a smile.

"And I don't know how it went down. Daddy must have swallowed his pride and put on his good suit and went hobbling into town that morning to find me a job. Knowing Daddy, he didn't call ahead—just appeared out of nowhere. Hugh's old Holy Roller half brother from the woods, with a gimp eye and gimp leg, there to beg a job for his girl, Jolie. Hugh could have pretended he didn't know him or brushed him off, but he told him to send me on, and he must have been sweet about it, because Daddy was so happy that night. He was over the moon." She smiled. "And I'm sure it was just guilt on Hugh's part, or noblesse oblige. But you know, Sam, I really don't care *what* it was. It was having mercy on the poor and the powerless, and it won't be forgotten. Not in this life, or the one to come. Not if I have anything to do with it."

She said it with her old level-eyed flatness, no longer a very young woman, and never as beautiful as she was powerful, with that implacable idea of right and wrong she'd inherited from her father. The sheer force of it made her striking in an ageless, mythic way that eclipsed modernity completely, made her seem like an old, forgotten goddess, a displaced Circe, capable of mischief and capricious devilry. But also capable of metamorphosis, of turning men to their true nature.

Sam was sober enough to respond with a smile of his own, one of capitulation. "Well, I like your style, Jolie Hoyt." He came heavily to his feet. "Give me a call sometime when you have an opening on your dance card. I'll take you down to the City Café. Buy you a shrimp special."

"You're leaving?" she asked, taken aback by his unexpected capitulation, in the awkward position of being too drunk to rise steadily, but not drunk enough to beg. "You can't drive, you're half-lit. You can sleep on the sofa."

Sam wasn't buying and answered, not unkindly, "Jol. I'm not sleeping on a hundred-year-old, four-foot couch while the woman I love sleeps one floor above, alone, in a billionaire's bed. It's demeaning. It's emasculating. I'll sleep in my car. Then I'll wake at dawn and drive to work and drag my unfucked carcass through another day of crunching numbers for the State, which is my miserable lot in life. I'll be fine," he said, with such resignation that Jolie was thrown into a great quandary, gripping his sleeve and wishing she hadn't drunk on an empty stomach.

"Hold up a minute. Let me think," she whispered, so unsteadily that she embraced him, first for balance, then pleasure, her face pressed to his warm neck, which smelled of the same drugstore cologne (British Sterling?) that he used to wear in their camper days, that evoked just the warmest memories.

He circled her waist with his arms as he used to do at the camper, though before he would have felt under her shirt and got a handful of a breast. As it was, he just gripped her waist and whispered to her hair, "You need to go to sleep, Jol. You're drunk."

"I don't want you to go," she confessed to his neck, then added in a small, petulant voice, "You just don't know what it's like, growing up in this little church world, where everything is prescribed and in order and it's black-and-white and good and evil, and right and wrong. And then you leave that little world and *nothing* is black-and-white, and at every turn in the road, you have to stop and decide, is this right or wrong?" She drew back. "It's so confusing."

He combed back her bangs with his thumb. "It's called adulthood, and it's your call. Do I stay or do I go?"

Jolie just blinked at him, pale and exhausted, then returned to his embrace. "Just promise you'll never leave me again, with a sink full of dishes, to go fishing with my cousins. It really did break my heart."

She was so sincere that he smiled finally and parted enough to assure her to her face, "I won't break your heart."

He kissed her, long enough, and deep enough, but she had a hard time tasting him under all the bourbon. She wasn't sobered up enough to get a real sense of him till halfway up the stairs, with the dim hallway looming above, the transoms to four different passageways gleaming. He paused and breathed, "Which one of these bedrooms is yours?"

She smiled at him in the darkness. "Bubba, *all* these bedrooms are mine. Take your pick."

# Chapter Twenty-eight

Jolie appeared at City Hall the next morning at nine sharp, with her game face on, braced for whatever the day might bring. She found Faye and Tamara long at their desks, fielding call after call from curious constituents who wanted to get the official lowdown on exactly what the mayor had said at the commission meeting about Henry Kite and the oak tree. Was she sure it was the one in the corner? Their daddy had always said it was the big one, in the back?

Between calls, they wandered into Jolie's office with their coffee and offered all manner of doomsday scenarios about race riots and lost elections, till Tad came in at eleven and put them to work on less mundane matters: cable bills and the like.

It left Jolie to sit alone at her desk on pins and needles, waiting for the citizenry to show up and add their voice to the discussion. But she seemed to have stunned them to momentary silence, the lobby and hallway empty till just before lunch when Jim Nichols, editor of the *Ledger*, dropped by with a vanilla envelope that he laid on her desk with a terse "Lookit this."

Jolie opened it gingerly, expecting the worst, but only found a sepia-tinted photograph of the lynching that had been widely distributed over the years, in historical journals and even posted on an Internet lynching site. She was about to tell Jim as much when he slid it aside and revealed another photo, completely different, taken at a different time.

"Bet you never saw this."

She hadn't. It wasn't the usual Hendrix Lynching shot, of Kite dangling from the courthouse square, but a different photo altogether, of a line of men standing shoulder to shoulder, a jumble of corpses at their feet, grotesquely stiffened in rigor mortis, ropes still knotting their hands. It was a startling photo, not randomly snapped, but posed and defiant, the men dressed as for a wedding, in black suits and straw boaters and knotted ties over striped vests, cigars and shot glasses in hand. Their faces were caught with the crystal clarity of old-fashioned photography, handsome men in any day, a few boys among them in knee britches. The boys had the grace to look involuntarily stunned, though the men appeared untouched by the massacre before them, which included at least one woman. She was young and bound like the others, her heart-shaped face piteously uncovered in the sprawl.

"Polly Washington," Jolie murmured, "Henry Kite's sister. His mother was there, too—somewhere. My God," she whispered, "I didn't know such a picture existed."

"Neither did I." Jim took a seat on the edge of her desk. "It's not the file copy, but out of somebody's private stash. They must have slipped it in the mail drawer this morning. No note; unsigned. You wouldn't happen to recognize any of them smiling faces, would you, Ms. Mayor?"

Jolie didn't answer immediately, but turned it over to the back, saw that it was an original, not a postcard or reproduction. She flipped it back and held it to the light, told him after a moment, "Well, I don't know for sure, but it was probably taken at the commissary, in Hendrix. That's a Hoyt there," she said of one of the men who stood proudly beside the city men, though he was perceptibly more country, his collar open, his grizzled cheeks unshaven. "Jimmie Hoyt."

"Are you kidding me?" Jim asked, feeling in his pocket for a notebook. "Someone from Hendrix is actually naming names?"

"James Lea Hoyt," she repeated without relish. "Standing over the corpse of a pregnant woman and looking mighty pleased with himself. A lot more pleased than he is now, burning in hell as he is."

Jim scribbled the name. "Any more?"

Jolie had an idea but wasn't certain enough to accuse. "Maybe. The ole boy in the middle—he has a banker-y look about him, does he not?"

Jim made a noise of mild hooting and scribbled down another name. "Girl, you're meddling now." He laughed, then admitted, "I already had him ID'd this morning, at the café. Easiest of the bunch—his picture hangs in the lobby of the bank. Got anything else you'd like to add? Somebody told me it was as bad as *Rosewood*."

"Somebody told you right." She didn't jump at his offer, but recommended he search out firsthand witnesses. "There are a few, here and around. I have a couple of guests in the carriage house from Hendrix. They might talk to you."

He scribbled down their names, then added as he slipped the photo back in its envelope, "Well, take care of yourself, Miss Mayor. This thang's rattled a few cages, I can tell you that." He shot a glance at the door to make sure they were alone. "This morning at the café, I had one upstanding citizen—and not a crank, either, but a pretty intelligent guy—tell me straight up that the reason you're making such a *deal* out of it is the Jewish influence. In *Cleary*," Jim said in a voice of utter disbelief. "I pointed out that your father was a preacher, your brother, Carl *Hoyt*— but he was set on it. Seemed to think it was the reason you'd folded to this liberal shit—that Jewish *stain*. And when you get to that point, you're in *koo-koo* land—might get a swastika scrawled on your gate or a cross burned on your yard. Kind of shook me up."

"I'll be all right," she said, a little more bravely than she felt, dreading the inevitable call from Hugh, which came soon enough.

Faye buzzed her on the inside line. "It's Hugh, and he sounds mighty cold. I can tell him you're at lunch if you want."

Jolie rubbed her eyes. "Put him through." She sat back, eyes closed, till he came on the line.

He had none of the comic-tragedy he had the day before and spoke without preamble, his voice dry and matter-of-fact, and very, very distant. "Jim Nichols says you verified a mob photograph some well-wisher put in his mail drawer."

He said it as a statement, not a question, and Jolie answered honestly, face down, eyes closed, "I did."

"I see." He added without breaking stride, "Well, I'm off in a bit. I wanted to give you a heads-up, that Dottie Lowe will be by next week sometime, for a key to the shop, to do an informal inspection."

Dottie was a Realtor, the news an absolute surprise, so much that Jolie opened her eyes. "You're selling the shop?" The florist shop had long been turned over to the hands of a manager, but was still Hugh's baby.

"Yes. I'm putting it on the market. The river house, too. The drive is so long, and really, Florida investments—they're tricky these days, and gas so high. It's hardly worth the effort." The delicacy of the backhand was such that Jolie was caught off guard, momentarily returned to muteness, as he rolled ahead, "I'm more than willing to sell back my share of the B and B, if it comes to that."

Jolie had no polite answer to the offer as both of them knew her capital was nonexistent and bank loans on hundred-year-old money pits had long vanished. He was basically telling her she was history, though with enough silky finesse that she had no room for reproach unless she wanted to grovel.

"I see," she finally managed in pale mimic. "Well. I don't know what to say. It was fun while it lasted."

She said it in a try at levity, but Hugh was truly beyond stabs at resolution or charm. "It was a waste of time," he corrected, and without even a good-bye, the line was dead in her hand.

Jolie hung up slowly, stunned by the completeness of his withdrawal, and frankly unused to avuncular rejection. She felt suddenly, terminally wretched. Her abandonment was not made any less affecting by the view from her desk. The bank of old windows offered an idyllic snapshot of the old house's backyard: bare, drooping chinaberry trees, climbing ivy. The greened and grimed marble birdbath was original to the house, too heavy to move. It had been there since the midtwenties, shabby, solid, and elegant.

No one could deny it wasn't beautiful. No one could deny it was as fragile as a hothouse orchid and, just like that, *gone.*


Jim Nichols was as good as his word about penning a story on Henry Kite, though when the piece finally ran in the *Ledger,* it had been hugely edited and gutted of controversy. His publisher was a media company already on the ropes, and the new mob shot was quickly deemed incendiary and squashed for fear of lawsuits and lost advertising.

He was made to substitute it with a cropped version from the archives in Tallahassee, which was well within public domain, of Henry Kite's battered corpse hanging from a limb at first light. The photograph was preferable in that it was taken at a side angle, so that the genital mutilation wasn't obvious. Kite's battered corpse was illuminated by the ghostly flash of an old camera, dust-covered, broken-necked, but isolated from all community, with no smiling faces circling him. No hint was given of the partylike atmosphere of the sturdy citizenry who'd posed around him to celebrate the collective murder of his kin.

To compensate, Jim ran a sidebar on the Frazier brothers and their peculiar search for their father's fingers, with the mayor quoted as giving them her full support, commenting with Hoyt dryness, "I wish I knew where they were. I'm about to be unemployed, I could use the money."

In Hendrix, her dry humor was repeated with great appreciation, though not so much in proud Cleary, where her reopening of this long-forgotten epoch in local history was seen as tasteless and over-the-top, a sign that the essential instability of her Hoyt nature was rearing its ugly head at last. The rumor of the Jewish boyfriend didn't help, and his frequent sightings, at dawn and at dusk, and picking up takeout at the café, were noted and disapproved of, if for no other reason than no one quite knew his name.

The talk ran hot and high for nine or ten days, but when no takers of the reward and no sign of the fingers appeared, the whole matter was written off as dramatic, pointless, and uselessly divisive. Now, as then, Henry Kite was too corrupt a figure to garner much sympathy on either side of the tracks. By the following commission meeting in February, the whole matter was firmly back under the rug, the commissioners looking to October for their revenge at the polls, their best energies returned to the pitched battle over the cell tower.

At breakfast every morning at the B&B, the Frazier brothers woke early so they could discuss their search with Sam, who had to leave by seven to beat the traffic on I-10. He was never optimistic of the chances of recovering seventy-year-old relics, but the brothers continued to entertain a small hope that their public call for the return of their papa's fingers would be answered. Black Cleary was still a close community, and as the weeks passed, they were often buttonholed at the barbershop or grocery store and offered other leads: names, kinfolk; distant aunts and cousins the brothers had lost touch with who still lived in West Florida.

They followed up on all of the leads with the tenacity of a private eye and, in time, unearthed a tiny remnant of Hitts, Bankses, and Kendalls, sprayed out in a crescent-shaped diaspora from Tallahassee to the Alabama line. Among them was a long-lost niece of their uncle John, even older than Charley, who'd spent her retirement pecking out genealogy records from the local courthouse and generously donated copies of her voluminous Hitt files, which went back to Adam. They spent a pleasant few evenings with her at her house on Lake Talquin. They even waded, *en famille,* into the National Forest on the east side of the river with Mr. Dais as their guide and found the limestone foundation of the original Hitt homestead. Hollis had no memory of it at all, but Charley was much moved by the visit to the old limestone foundation of the house and tobacco barn, including the old brick kiln where their papa had cured his homegrown tobacco.

Charley was too blind to identify many other markers, but was sure of the kiln and stood there, his hands on the arch of brick, and talked about his good father, who hadn't as much faith in King Cotton as he had in night-shade tobacco and had spent many afternoons at the old store trying to convince his neighbors likewise.

Charley took one of the loose bricks when he left, figured it was as close to a memento of his papa as he'd find. Hollis was too stubborn to admit defeat and was implacable in his search for the fingers themselves. He left the house shortly after Sam every morning and talked to people in Cleary and Hendrix and all the way to the coast. In the afternoon, when the cold was gone, he drove Charley down to the KOA to fish from the bank with a cane pole. The local fishermen who daily launched and returned at sunset could not resist stopping by to comment on Snowflake's breed, size, and likeness to a polar bear. They'd read Jim Nichols's article in the *Ledger,* and once they connected Hollis to the Great Finger Search, they were quick to volunteer their own family histories of the Trouble, with none of the Chamber of Commerce squeamishness of the townsmen in Cleary, nor any doubt that such relics still remained. Pieces of the rope were the most common report, but few of the current generation had seen any actual *fingers.*

Even Hollis began to understand the uselessness of the task and, with the end of their month's lease rapidly approaching, was making noises of resignation and acceptance. Then on the morning of the eleventh, as Jolie was driving to work, she was interrupted by Vic's teenage clerk, who was calling on Vic's orders and was hopping with excitement. He wouldn't divulge any details except to say it was *big,* it was *incredible,* it was *crazy.* Jolie and the old men should come *straight* out, as soon as they could, they wouldn't believe it.

Jolie turned around in the intersection and rounded up the Frazier brothers and drove them straight to the KOA, to the worn oak counter of the concession stand. Vic and his clerk and a storeful of tourists waited there, Vic red-faced and practically hopping, he was so excited. His sense of military ceremony called for a moment of gravity as they gathered at the counter, his face darting around the room.

"Is Sam coming?" he asked. "No? Well, then I'll show you. Out of the blue, you will not believe. Left on the steps, no note, just there. I don't know if they're the right ones, but, God, they're somebody's." He reached under the counter and triumphantly slapped a small, fluted bottle on the counter, clear and flask-shaped.

Hollis murmured immediately, "It's gin. That's a gin bottle."

Jolie had no interest in looking at anyone's severed fingers, then or ever, and it took a bit of persuasion to get her to brave a peek. "Maybe," she offered helplessly. She passed it to Charley, who couldn't see well enough to make a call, leaving Hollis to act as resident expert, holding up the bottle and trying for a better look in the dim light. He turned it this way and that and finally jumped up on the counter and held it to the fluorescent light for a better look. He stood there, peering closely at the dusty old bottle, then bent and hopped off the counter with the vigor of a younger man. He told his brother, "They got calluses, and dirt under the nails."

Charley took the bottle back and turned it over in his hands, feeling the scrolled, raised lettering on the face of the cloudy glass. "Whut does it say?" he asked Hollis. "There's something on the bottle."

The glass was too cloudy to read, and an Ohio Yankee, who'd wandered in to buy the *Times* for the crossword, provided his pencil for a quick rubbing of lead on an old receipt on the countertop. The image emerged on the back of the thin paper, written aslant, in curvy, sideways lettering: *H & A Gilbey LTD* and to the side, in that same flowing lettering, *Gin.*

When Hollis read it aloud, Charley finally smiled, brilliantly and without reserve. "Thet's it. Thet's what they told me," he murmured, feeling around for his brother and gripping his fur lapel. "Hollis. It's them. It must be."

Vic and the bystanders clapped and yammered and pressed for a closer look, though Hollis was momentarily too moved to speak. He lifted the cold glass to his lips and kissed it, whispered, "Papa, you're coming home."

# Chapter Twenty-nine

The Frazier brothers left the next morning, anxious to reunite their papa's fingers with the rest of his mortal remains at the Veterans Cemetery in North Little Rock. Jolie brought them their breakfast early and chatted with them while they finished the last of the hellishly hot sausages, then presented them with a parting gift—small, flat, and tissue-wrapped. She thought they "might like a copy of it, to take back to Tennessee."

Charley thanked her even as he was tearing off the tissue on a silver-framed sepia photograph of an upright old farmer standing in a cutover cotton field the first day of seeding. He was holding a brace of mules by their traces in a standard photograph of the day. Charley couldn't make much of it, even with his magnifying glass, though Hollis smiled when he got on his reading glasses, told him, "Well, it's Sip—out standing in a field, with his mules. He's mama's oldest brother—died of malaria. I declare. Where'd you find it?"

"Sam dug it out of the State archives. He's a Hitt, on the 1842 Creek Census. You'll be pleased to hear you two gentlemen are now eligible for minority status in the gret state of Florida."

Jolie walked them down the cold drive to their car and helped Charley put away his Walmart luggage, while Hollis settled Snowflake in the back. Hollis was anxious to get on the road, though he hesitated before he got in himself, a little awkward now that their parting was upon them as he'd grown fond of their landlady. She was a true swamp-running smart-ass of a Hoyt, but by-God faithful, in her way. Neither she nor Vic Lucas, or even his skinny teenage clerk, would take any of the ten-grand reward, which didn't please Hollis as much as it made him feel uncomfortable, as if he hadn't carried his weight here among the homefolk.

He offered it again, there in the drive, but Jolie just shook her head. "You know, Mr. Frazier, you ain't the only one around here whose Papa didn't get such a fair shake. Finding them fangers was the only good luck anybody's ever had in Hendrix. I was proud to be a part."

Hollis could hardly argue with such a stand and let it go at that. He just glanced around the deep lawn and ivory-colored house and allowed after a moment, "Well, you got a nice place here, Miss Hoyt. You done well for yourself." That was about as high an accolade as they gave, down in Hendrix. He climbed in his car and lowered his window. "I need to brang my girls down here sometime. They'd like your house. They like old stuff, both of 'em."

"I'd like that." Jolie smiled, then asked with a glimmer of Hoyt needling, "You gone take 'em out to Hendrix?"

Hollis lost his smile in an instant. "Shit," he said, so shortly and succinctly that Jolie burst out laughing.

"Well, you take care of yoursef, old man," she told him, then bent to the window and told Charley the same. She told him to come back and go fishing when it was warm. "Not cane fishing—fishing down in the swamp. They still got fish down there, catfish the size of footballs."

Charley assured her he would, and with a few more waves and promises to keep in touch, the brothers backed out. They exited the county much as they'd entered it: up Highway 231 and upcountry to Montgomery and Birmingham and crosswise through Tupelo, crossing the Tennessee line just past dark. It was a long drive, but pleasant, their talk still focused on Hendrix and Camp Six and the long-scattered families who'd once lived there. They reminisced about their good papa and their hardworking mother; about the musical Kimbralls and Big

Dave Bryant. But mostly they talked about the Hoyts, whom their aunt Tempy had often recalled in her exile. Her stories were of a tall and unruly clan of half bloods, with white pretensions and quick-tempered ways, who owned the rowdiest camp on the river and lost their daughters to rich men.

Tempy wasn't too forgiving of either their pale skin or their heathen ways and would usually conclude, "Never had no sense, not one of 'em." She would sometimes allow with a faint twitch of her cheek, "But they were funny. They could by God make you laugh."


It was a tradition the latest generation of Hoyts continued for many years to come, Carl's humor his chief device in converting the masses to the Gospel via his sermons, which are still broadcast practically round the clock on the different Christian broadcasting networks, squeezed in between the likes of Creflo Dollar and Kenneth Copeland. (Carl is the fattest of the three and talks like the King of the Hillbillies. He often speaks of his father.) Lena is still often caught on tape, sitting there in the front pew in her elaborate Spencer Alexis creations, watching Carl with a childlike devotion that isn't mere posturing, but wholly (and weirdly) sincere. Her sister-in-law is occasionally at her side, listening to her brother's sermons with a look of mild, dry curiosity.

The camera seldom lingers long on her as she has the unsettling habit of rolling her eyes at his more outlandish doctrinal claims. This seditious gesture has once or twice been caught on tape and broadcast around the globe. Next to her are her children: her stepson, Brice, now well into his teens, and a set of perfectly matched little girls, identical twins. The boy is light-eyed; the girls are dark enough that members of their uncle's flock sometimes ask them what they *are,* as their accent is straight out of Br'er Rabbit stories, though they are obviously not your typical Southern belles.

They are friendly children and don't mind the question, but grin and tell them they are Jewish Crackers, which is what their paternal grandfather calls them, with affection. ("They talk slow, but they talk a lot," he explains to his neighbors in Coral Springs.) Their mother sometimes describes them, with equal affection, as Little Black Dutch, and she should know, as she is the unofficial state expert on the breed, working on her third grant with the Department of the Interior when she's not busy with small design projects around Cleary, or serving as the chair of the local Historic and Preservation Committee. Their father works in Tallahassee for the State; probably will till he retires.

If you run into him at the Super China Buffet or the 4th Quarter on North Monroe, don't be afraid to approach, as he is still a talker, this Sam Lense, and he never eats alone if he can help it. He'll be glad to discuss the Muskogee Creek or Miami football or the dismantling of the DCF at the hands of the nefarious Republicans, or even the scar on his chest, faded in middle age to a pale silver-gray. He's never been the kind of man ashamed of his own myth, or his personal scars—even the ones that almost killed him.

# Acknowledgments

This story has deep roots in the past, and I must first thank four great professors from my undergrad days at UF: James Haskins, Smith Kirkpatrick, Richard Scher, and Harry Crews. They set me on this journey many years ago, and I couldn't have told it without them, nor without the firsthand testimonies of a handful of truth-tellers who had the courage to meet my eye and give me a straight answer when I brought up the barbaric custom of spectacle lynching. It would have been easy to take a pass and pretend ignorance, but they didn't, and for that I am grateful. My agents, Marly Rusoff and Mihai Radulescu, have held my hand a very long time with this book, and my editor, Whitney Frick, was heroic in helping forge it into the novel it is today. Writing is a mostly solitary pursuit, but I am blessed to be surrounded by a magical circle—my husband, Wendel, daughters Emily, Abigail, and Isabel, and their husbands, Evan, Johnny, and Christopher, and the darling Lily P. If that weren't good fortune enough, I have fallen heir to friendships with some of the finest storytellers of the age: my poppa and mama, Pat and Cassandra Conroy, the late Doug Marlette, and the often imitated but inimitable Bernie Schein, who provided the final key. I tell all of you I love you so much that it almost seems trivial to say it, but you are my heart. Love, again.